Rise of the Dragon Lord

Volume 1

By Edward Grimsley

Copyright ©2025
All rights reserved. Written permission must be secured from the author to reproduce any part of the book.

Printed in the United States of America

ISBN: 979-8-3493-6321-4

10 9 8 7 6 5 4 3 2 1

EMPIRE PUBLISHING
www.empirebookpublishing.com

Acknowledgement

I am grateful for the help I received from my friend Fletcher who read the book and offered valuable criticisms and suggestions

Disclaimers

This novel is a work of fiction. Names, characters, places and incidents are either the product of the authors' imagination or references to historical persons, places or events. Any resemblance to actual living persons is entirely coincidental.

Warning: some readers may be offended at the contents.
Puritans and Feminists may find it particularly offensive.
Read on at your own discretion.

Photos and Drawings by Author (EAG)

Some Artwork by Matthew Clark of Maeca Art (MC)

FORWARD

Welcome to my tale. This is a chronicle the day-to-day adventures of a fairly ordinary soldier who finds himself thrown into a most extraordinary situation.

Unlike most Isekai stories the protagonist does not have flashy, over-powered attacks or fantastic abilities. He does have some advantages but he also suffers from common human failings; he makes mistakes – some of them painful.

The story cuts across several genres and touches on different themes – military, supernatural, technology, slice-of-life, science fiction and harem.

There are a few references to historical events, places and persons. If you are not familiar with them, or are curious, they can be looked up on Wikipedia or Google – I checked!

Note there are a lot of extra lines in the text. These show that the point of view of the narrative has changed. Typically it means the location of the scene is different or that some time has passed. It can also show that the speaker is focused on inner thoughts or a flashback during a conversation.

The story is intended to be entertaining and has a fair amount of humor – to offset some of the more dramatic situations. Be warned, the protagonist is from 1936 – his attitudes and behavior may not sit well with a 21st century audience but I don't think there is anything truly offensive.

-EAG

Table of Contents

Chapter 1
    How the hell did I get myself into this mess? 1

Chapter 2
    Where the hell did I end up now? 40

Chapter 3
    Hiking to Karnet Village 57

Chapter 4
    What did those messengers say about me? 79

Chapter 5
    Why is a nice Trade City so verdamnt intense? 106

Chapter 6
    Why am I babysitting a beautiful Nun? 132

Chapter 7
    Why are we running into orcs? 154

Chapter 8
    What is up with all the Bunnies? 183

Chapter 9
    My first history lesson 204

Chapter 10
    What is going on here in the Capitol? 217

Chapter 11
    How the hell do I beat The Devil himself? 246

Chapter 12

  And now the Demon Slayer is a bookworm. 275

Chapter 13

  Just how much can I do for these people? 308

Chapter 14

  I've settled in – and now I'm moving? 327

Appendix – Pronunciation Guide 342

Map of the Local World

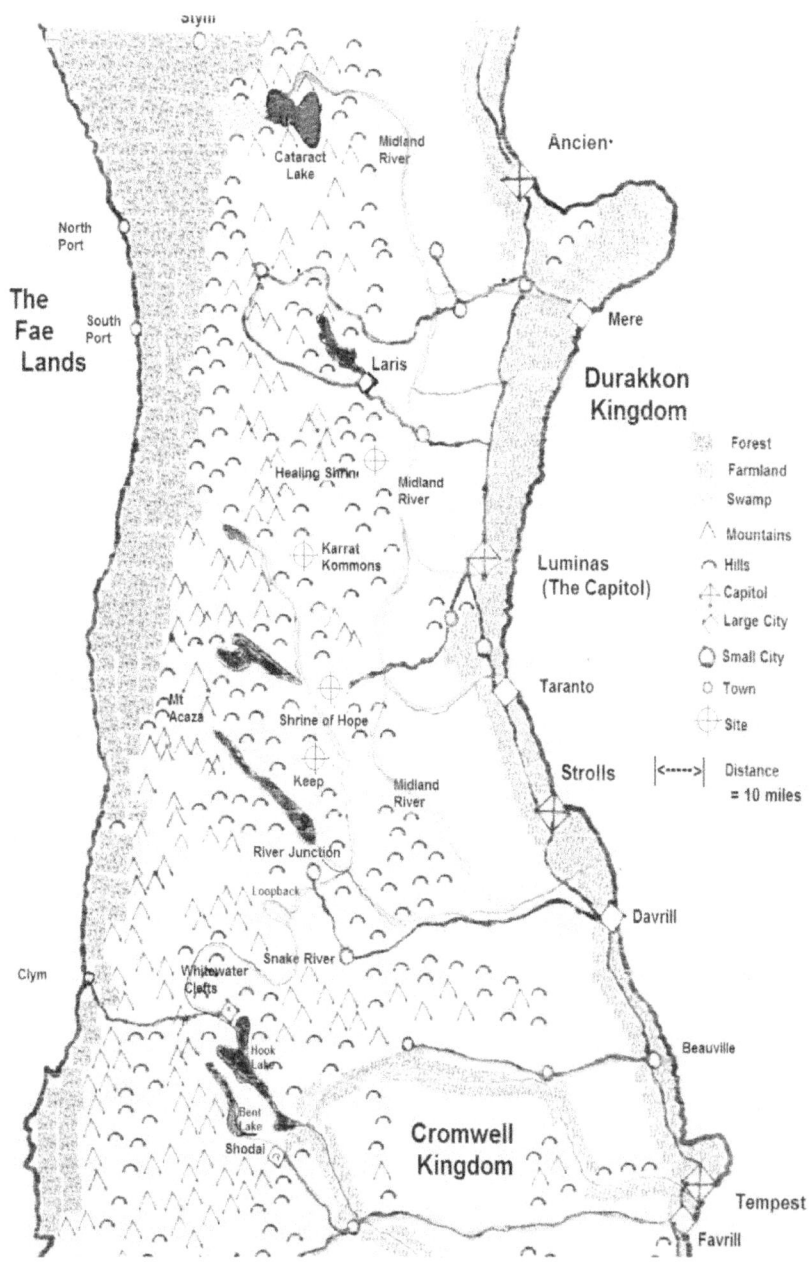

Chapter 1

How the hell did I get myself into this mess?

Jakob Roy Drachus felt he was a successful man. He wasn't rich or famous but after 16 years as a professional soldier he was still alive and in one piece. However, right now he was falling into total darkness with absolutely no idea of what lay below. It had started out as such a simple joke of a job – how the hell did it all go so very wrong?

The sturdy 32 year-old Swede woke at his usual time, about 5 am. He wasn't sure how but he always managed to wake up on time. Due to some social unrest, one month ago he'd been hired by the Mayor of Bilbao to whip some of the less-than-capable city militia into shape.

Unfortunately, Drachus hadn't heard the cause of the unrest: Spain was about to have a civil war. Even worse his employer was on the losing side and exited quite early; the mercenary had barely escaped with his hide intact. He was now broke and seeking any legitimate employment he could find on this cold week before Christmas of 1936.

Cormack, a young Scottish mercenary he'd worked with several times, had a good job working as a bodyguard (?) for a local rich guy named Arevalo. Drachus had come this way hoping his old pal could at least get him hired on temporarily. Instead, Cormack told him the local officials were trying to organize a rescue operation in the local area on very short notice.

Arevalo had already said that the Scottish lad and his co-workers would be involved. The young Scot had remembered Drachus having a good head for tactics and organizing so he thought he should talk to the Mayor about taking the job of setting it all up for them.

As he quietly dressed his hand hit the bottom of the hanging lantern. It was a small room at a small inn on a quiet night so the rattling loose glass chimney seemed unnaturally loud in the still morning air. There were drawbacks to being 6' 6" tall but it was thanks to his stature he'd been accepted for militia training at only 13 years old. After all, with most of the adult men called up for the national army due to the Great War, the militia commanders were taking just about anyone taller than a rifle!

The noise made the auburn-haired lady who'd helped him make it thru the cold night gave a whimper of protest. Checking the time on his pocket watch he saw it was 5:06. He patted her trim bottom as she rolled over and pulled up in the blanket.

"Sorry Salana but they'll be here soon; they will want coffee" he said apologetically.

The gypsy beauty whimpered as he handed her the woolen waitress dress she'd worn for a while last night. Climbing from under the covers she muttered "Callarse la Boca" and began to dress. Drachus recognized the mildly rude phrase but chose to interpret it as "Good Morning to you too, pal."

She saw his watch as he put it away; from her expression she found it odd for a man to carry one these days.

His grandmother had given it to him when he'd left Gotland Island at 16 years old to work security at a Swedish company's mine in Brazil.

"Take this, for luck" she'd said. "Your grandfather carried it when he fought for the Prussians way back then; he came home without a scratch."

Grandpa had annoyed her for going off to fight in a foreign war but always bragged about how he'd come home safe to her. She put up with it because the Drachus men were always drawn to military service at a young age.

"Your father carried through the Great War and made it back unharmed; he didn't even have to replace the crystal!" she added. With the rigors of trench warfare, that was something to brag about. "If you keep it with you, you'll come home, take a lovely bride and give me many great-grandchildren." Given his luck so far, old Nana just might have been right.

Moments later the tavern owner knocked on the door. "Mister Mercenary – the elders are here."

"On my way" Drachus said.

The old innkeeper was a bit gruff and couldn't be called friendly but he'd agreed when Drachus asked to be awakened when the elders arrived. The old guy was helpful even if he wasn't sociable; he hadn't even raised an eyebrow when Salana followed Drachus upstairs the night before.

He stopped to check his self in the cracked dressing table mirror. He needed a shave but his clothes were clean. Other than height, his appearance was average; he kept his light brown hair short and had no (visible) scars. The appearance of the man in the mirror was unlikely to offend ordinary townsfolk.

When he arrived downstairs Drachus saw the only ones in the main hall was a group of six unhappy men at the table near the warmth of the crackling fireplace.

From the medal of office hanging around his neck he recognized the grey-haired man just taking his seat as the Mayor. The badge, sidearm and ceremonial saber on his belt marked the hawk-faced fellow as the Head Constable. The muscular one with the shaved head wearing the polished cuirass was certainly the head of the local militia. The other three looked like ordinary folk in clothes that ranged from well-dressed to quite fancy.

At his approach the Mayor stood and smiled. "Thank you for responding to our request, Captain Drachus."

As he took the extended hand the tall Swede smiled.

"Just Drachus – the rank went away along with my previous employer – as it always does" he said.

Sitting down Drachus could see that no one was happy to see him – the face of Mr. Cuirass had an especially sour expression. He wasn't terribly concerned about that; mercenaries rarely received a genuine warm welcome, especially from the typically underpaid local forces.

As he got a better look at the clothes of the three citizens, he realized that one of them was quite wealthy; his attitude showed great self-confidence, almost arrogance. His clothes were a bit heavy with lace trim and the aroma of perfume was obvious. Drachus often heard men who dressed like this called 'Spanish Peacocks' - now he understood why.

The one sitting next to him was in clothes just as nice but his long black hair was lank and unkempt; he couldn't be more than 15 but his youth starkly contrasted the haggard air of one who hadn't slept in days.

The third man, with the deliberately bland expression and shaved pate, wore plain but expensive clothes. Though aloof he'd watched Drachus closely as he approached. Even without a cassock the mercenary pegged him as a church official; from the traces of grey in the stubble flanking his skullcap Drachus knew he was older, maybe even a Bishop.

"Let's not waste time on time on pleasantries," Drachus began. "What kind of work do you folks need done?" The locals looked back and forth trying to decide who was to start. After a moment Mr. Cuirass spoke.

"We need you to organize the rescue of five kidnapped girls being held in the old fortress."

"Well, that certainly seems straightforward enough" Drachus said with a wide smile. "So it obviously isn't" he continued as his smile vanished. "What's the catch?"

Hearing that, the Mayor smiled. "We'd heard you were very intelligent; that should prove to be most helpful. The fortress was occupied 10 weeks ago by a group who claimed to be theological scholars." The maybe church official scowled on hearing that. The Mayor seemed a bit embarrassed when he saw that. "You could not have known the truth Your Grace" the Mayor said, obviously trying to not appear offensive.

So he was a Bishop - Drachus figured this job might be more profitable than he'd first thought.

"They're actually a radical cult that may have discovered how to use magic ..." The Mayor broke off as Drachus rolled his eyes and groaned.

"You have issues with doing good works, dealing with dangerous heretics?" the Bishop interjected. Something about the man's eyes told Drachus he might have trouble getting paid for this; since the Bishop was in ordinary clothes, this wasn't likely an official church-sanctioned job.

"I don't have issue with anyone's religion; I heard that the Devil once said he has enough room in Hell for all of us. The problem is that religious fanatics are an unholy pain-in-the-ass, quite literally!

They're unpredictable, won't surrender and to stop them you have to kill them; all of them. They'll fight to the death; they have already been convinced that if they die here they are going to some-place better than ..."

At that the ragged youth jumped up shouting. "He's right - they're crazy - they'll never stop. The sacrifice is tonight and we'll all die!"

Drachus noticed two things about this kid he couldn't see before. Fresh bruises, cuts and broken fingernails showed he'd done some desperate bare-handed digging recently. Plus, there was a new tattoo around each wrist, a chain of flaming links surrounding a large red eye with a slotted pupil. Drachus suddenly understood all too well.

"You were one of them" he stated flatly. The young man paled and might have fled if the Spanish Peacock hadn't firmly pulled the boy back down to the seat.

"You are correct. Young Diego was lured to their ranks but the wisdom of the Lord did prevail and he came to his senses" the Bishop explained in a patronizing voice.

Drachus didn't buy that for a moment. "Why did you really leave?" he asked the boy directly.

Before the young man could answer the older one sitting next to him responded. "My son realized these people are dangerous. They have taken my daughter, his older sister, as one of their sacrifices. I've heard that you have a reputation for aiding girls in jeopardy. If you are successful, I assure you the reward for this will be far more than you expect."

"Ok, how did they get control of the fortress in the first place?" Drachus asked after a bit of thought.

"Before our scholars departed for the winter, their representatives approached my office about utilizing the facility for their own so-called research. Apparently they wished to exploit its rumored 'Ley Lines' for their magic potential" the Bishop answered.

"Why did your people leave?" Drachus asked.

"Our scribes work with ancient church texts. Winter weather is too harsh; heating the old facility to protect the delicate manuscripts would be nearly impossible. The facility is vacated during that time; they left due to the early snows. The sum these – scholars - offered was reasonable; with nothing of value there I saw no reason to deny them" the Bishop said.

'And you pocketed their fee, of course' Drachus thought; no wonder this was an unofficial mission.

"For the first two weeks, everything seemed fine. Then we began to notice a series of unusual events in the vicinity. A woodcutter was reported missing. Even after a search we found no trace of him. Over the next few weeks, five young girls who were tending sheep and goats went missing one after another. The remains of one did turn up later, apparently killed by wolves" the Constable said.

"We initially assumed there was a larger that average pack of wolves in the area, so hunting parties were assembled from the constabulary and the militia to assist several professional hunters" the Mayor elaborated.

"They only found dead wolves. That's when my men started patrolling the region" Mr. Cuirass added.

"Shortly after that these 'scholars' would come to town to recruit 'helpers'. They offered generous wages and promised to teach their new helpers how to read Latin and other foreign languages" the Mayor said.

"Is that how they got the boy?" Drachus asked.

"Yes. My son always had more interest in art than business" Señor Arevalo said. "When told he could sketch the statues and murals in the keep, he couldn't resist."

"Why did you join them?" Drachus asked him directly.

"They are so persuasive – they said if I joined them I could become a prince in the new world" the boy answered.

"Ruthless ones such as they wielding generous promises can have quite an influence on those weak of will" the Bishop added with a sneer.

"Why did you run?" Drachus asked him directly.

As the boy's lower lip quivered, Arevalo replied. "My daughter Katarina was to return from school last week; she never arrived." At that the boy's face went white.

"They took her - I saw her being carried into the forbidden tower. There were other sleeping girls in there too. I breathed in this weird smoke and my vision began to blur. When I went to the old garden to get fresh air I saw It. IT…! They told me if I left, it would hunt me. Then they told me 'The Solstice.' That's tonight - the darkest night of the year - the darkest night ever – that's when they are going to do it - on the Solstice!" he cried.

Drachus realized that the boy was only barely holding his self together; whatever he'd been through, the kid was nearly incoherent. The Swede knew tonight was going to be the Winter Solstice, the longest, and therefore the darkest, night of the year.

"They said if I stayed I'd be one of the few who ruled. The next night I went back for Trina but saw it again … and I ran!" the boy finished before his voice finally broke.

After a few moments thought, Drachus decided he'd take the job. He didn't like being held to such a short timetable but there really wasn't a lot of choice here.

"How many men do I have to work with?" he asked.

After an awkward silence Mr. Cuirass responded.

"5 men of the Constabulary and 14 of the Militia are available for this mission."

"Are you serious? A town this big should be able to field a full company! Where the hell are the rest of them?" Drachus asked in surprise.

The Constable seemed annoyed as he answered. "The Toscana Road was buried by an avalanche last week. Many from the town and Constabulary were dispatched to clear it. A messenger was sent when we learned of this but with the distance and snow it is unlikely they'll return in time."

When Drachus cast a look at Mr. Cuirass, he responded "Many of the militia was called to Radova to augment security against a rumored bandit strike at the silver min. It supplies the government mint at Oviedo; I had no choice. It would take days to recall them even if I could."

Then Señor Arevalo spoke up with a wide smile. "I have 9 men in my employ who are familiar with firearms and close combat. They will assist as well."

"28 total, not too bad." Drachus mused. 'And since Cormack is one of Arevalo's men, the rest are likely adequate as well' he thought to himself.

"I assume they are all armed with at least militia-grade rifles and big-bore cartridge revolvers – no old percussion weapons I hope?" he asked.

Both officers nodded in the affirmative as Señor Arevalo spoke. "My men are armed with more modern firearms. I assume you are familiar with the 'Chicago typewriter' from America? "My men are in possession of three" Arevalo said with a smile.

The surprised Drachus was indeed familiar with it; he'd heard them called a Tommy-gun more often. They were even more effective than shotguns for close combat assaults like the one they were contemplating here.

Feeling a bit more optimistic, Drachus said "Excellent. Do we know how many fanatics we're facing and the current layout of the fortress?"

Mr. Cuirass pulled drawings from a nearby box and arranged them on the table. As Drachus looked over the plans his enthusiasm began to fade. The complex sprawled over several acres up, down and across the mountain. Like many old mountain-top fortresses it was centuries old; its history was noted along the margins of the plans.

Originally built during the Reconquista, it had been used as a justice palace – an inquisition torture center - in the 15th century. In the 16th it was expanded into a monastery, in the 17th it was used as a prison and in the 18th it was abandoned. In the early 1800's it became a palace for an exiled Arabian prince. In the Great War it was an ammunition depot for coastal artillery. The central keep was now used by the church to work on old manuscripts but only during warmer weather.

"How secure are the gates and doors" he asked.

"While it was being used as a workplace to restore valuable books, its security was of some importance. The doors and gates are solid; the main keep is well-maintained with good windows with shutters" the Bishop said.

The plans showed that left more than a full acre of reinforced gates, doors and solid stone walls to deal with. "How many cultists - are they armed and if so with what?" was his next question.

"They have no firearms, just ceremonial daggers and crossbows." At Drachus' surprise Mr. Cuirass continued "Those are props made for a motion picture; they do work - the cultists have killed several wolves with them. Since they are not firearms, they required no license for approval."

Even without guns, the close walls of the keep would force the rescuers to take hours to fight their way in. Drachus noted a lack of a complete response to his question.

"How many are there?" Drachus repeated.

With some reluctance Mr. Cuirass handed him a list of cultists. After a moment he realized it was likely dictated by young Arevalo. As he read Drachus' heart dropped; other than a six servants, there was one High Priest, 11 acolytes, a choir of 16 chanting monks and 42 armed guards!

"You're kidding; even with only crossbows they could hold you off for days. There is no way a frontal assault will succeed in time" he said.

"It was implied you were an expert tactician who had never lost a battle. Is this situation too much for your skills, sir?" the Bishop asked rather snidely.

"Even Caesar lost every so often. Against these odds, in a secure fortress and with your available men it could take all night just to get in. This fight will be in the dark with only lanterns and moonlight; any fighting, even with rifles, will be at hand-to-hand range. These fanatics have lived in this antique stone mausoleum for months; they know it's every nook and cranny by now. These plans don't show a lot of the interior details. How many of your men have ever even been inside of it?" Drachus asked.

In the face of his grim, realistic appraisal the local officials went silent. Drachus took the time to study the plans and maps of the local area carefully. As much as he hated to admit it, he did want to save these girls.

On one of his earliest jobs he'd been part of a team going to clear out a bunch of similar fanatics in South America. He's seen what had happened to the village workers who'd been taken hostage and used for bizarre rituals; the young girls had been treated most brutally of all.

Drachus had three younger sisters. He loved them dearly and had always worked to protect them. Imagining those terrible things being done to them had made him sick. Over the years he had gone out of his way to rescue endangered girls. When Arevalo mentioned it, he'd been surprised that reputation had spread - until he realized Cormack had likely told him.

During the awkward silence Salana served them coffee and freshly baked rolls. Young Arevalo was in a bad state. His hands shook so much he slopped some of his coffee on the fortress plans. As the Bishop scolded him, Drachus noted the spot of one of the coffee stains and it triggered a memory.

"You have an idea sir?" Mr. Cuirass asked as he noticed the sudden smile on the mercenary's face. His question silenced the querulous cleric and grabbed everyone's attention.

Drachus began asking rapid fire questions. "Exactly when did the boy escape? Can you locate a dozen or so big non-combatant volunteers? Do you have any explosives; dynamite or such to breach the gates? Do the cultists do roll calls? Do you have any stick flares, like for night skiing? Does anyone here have a pair of snowshoes?"

As they struggled to respond to his queries Drachus began to feel hope rise and he outlined his plan to the officials. He would leave midafternoon and travel alone to the fortress rear by old game trails on snowshoes; you could see the towers of the huge thing from anywhere nearby so it was almost impossible to get lost along the way.

An hour before sundown the 28 combatants bolstered by as many big volunteers as the Mayor could recruit would head out to the fortress. The road was passable in good weather but now it was choked with snow so it wasn't clear enough for trucks; they'd have to march up.

Some of the men could ride; they would use their horses to help clear the way through the snow for the men. The non-combatants would carry torches, hot soup and warm clothes for the girls; the fighting men would carry weapons. Wielding so many torches, the cultists will obviously see them coming.

The fact that they were coming at night meant the authorities likely knew what the cult was up to; the large number of approaching rescuers would ensure that all of their guards would be deployed to the front to stop them. The soldiers would challenge the defenders, be denied entry and exchange fire with the guards.

During this Drachus would enter from the rear by the same route young Arevalo had used to escape; once he located the girls he'd rescue them during the confusion being caused by the battle out front.

Afterwards, the officials left to gather supplies and personnel. The plan seemed to be a bit too simple; the Bishop was doubtful and pressed Drachus for more details.

"If you are to accomplish the rescue from the rear, why must the others attack the front? And why go in alone?" was his main complaint.

"The timing is the important part of the plan" the mercenary began. "Unless something disastrous happens, the forces should arrive out front about two hours before midnight. I'll enter from the rear at the same time to reconnoiter and locate the girls. The gunfire out front should start about the same time as they are preparing for the ritual. That smoke the kid mentioned is likely from hashish, opium or something similar. They are drugged now but for the cult to prepare them, they'll have to be moved. The girls should wake soon after and once the shooting starts I'll get them free during the confusion."

"Yeah, the Priests are going to wake them up to bathe and oil them before the sacrifice" young Arevalo added.

"As for going in alone, I don't know how good any of your men are; in a close-combat night operation like this I find it's safer to work alone than with uncertain troops. Plus Arevalo's experienced men will be needed at the gates."

After a pause for a sip of hot coffee, Drachus continued. "During the rescue I'll certainly have to shoot a few cultists inside. Gunfire from in there would immediately alert all of the defenders to the rescue unless there was even more shooting at the front of the keep."

The look on the cleric's face showed the Bishop at least understood why the men were needed at the front.

"When the shooting starts everyone but the guards will hide; clearing the way out the back for the girls. I'll exit with them and light the flares. Illuminated by them the girl's position should be easy to find for the non-combatants; they collect and dress the girls so they won't freeze. I lag behind to deal with any pursuing cultists" the mercenary finished.

The Bishop still seemed to be unconvinced. "Can you guarantee you can get there in time? How will you find the passage that young Arevalo used to escape in the dark of night? If they have noticed he is gone, won't they have searched and found it? Are you certain the cultists haven't blocked off that escape route?" he asked.

"The moon will be up a few hours after sundown; that should make it easy to move around after I leave the roads. I grew up in Sweden; I'm accustomed to snow. The kid was scared to death by that 'guardian' whatever; since they don't do roll calls they will likely think he is just hiding from it" Drachus said.

Then he reached over pointing to young Arevalo's scratched hands. "How did you get out, the old ammo warehouse?" he asked.

As the boy nodded the Bishop asked "How did you know that?"

"He was one of them; he would know they certainly watch the front road" Drachus explained as the young man nodded again. "His only chance to get out was the rear. The only part of the fortress in use that doesn't face the road is the warehouse."

A glance at the plans confirmed that for the Bishop.

"He likely dug through the ventilation ducts. In munitions storage facilities these are high on the walls to prevent water from leaking in and not easily bricked over. When this was closed the shafts were likely covered with wood. As this rotted, blown seeds would sprout into plants. Their roots attract nesting birds that will clog them. I've had to clean out more than a few when old warehouses were reactivated" Drachus grinned and replied.

Young Arevalo's head was bouncing up and down. "Yeah, I had to rip away a lot of roots and old bird's nests to get out. Then I jumped down into the snow and I ran!"

After a few seconds of silence the Bishop asked "This is a large complex. How will you find the air shaft he used?"

"He escaped three days ago; last night the innkeeper told me it hasn't snowed around here in a week. The old snow will still have his footprints in it" Drachus said.

At this point the Bishop decided not to raise any further objections. It certainly appeared Drachus was familiar with this sort of endeavor. Also, the Constable and Mr. Cuirass had returned; if this mercenary was successful any further objections might make the clerist look foolish afterwards. The Bishop would bide his time and if the wretched sell-sword failed he could claim the arrogant miscreant had fallen to God's will after all.

Shortly after Salana served breakfast the Mayor returned saying he had 20 volunteers. If they only had to carry torches and clothes for the rescued girls, it would be easy to get more.

Drachus wrote a list of instructions for the non-combatants and a second list for Mr. Cuirass and the fighting men for their part in the job. Then he left with Señor Arevalo and his son to see the new weapons.

Arriving at the Arevalo estate Drachus was shown to a building near the stables. Inside the well-equipped workshop was a tiny older man assembling a Tommy-gun; it was a new, imported weapon, not a local copy.

Then Drachus saw a rack of older American pistols, a large caliber double action revolver. He'd used an export version of it in England last year. These seemed to be in very good condition. As he examined one he noticed what looked like a box of brass cylinders nearby that were loaded with exposed rounds.

 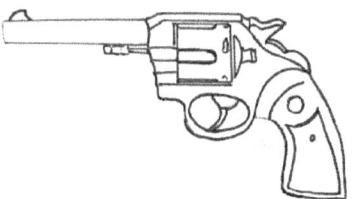

"What's up with these?" he asked.

"Ah, yes; those are Prideaux Load Devices. They were designed to quick-load an English Webley. The dimensions are close enough so if you are careful they work just as well with the American weapons. I like those big Yankee cartridges; the 45 Colt was originally designed for a heavy charge of black powder - they can hold more of the new smokeless bulk varieties than the Webley brass" the old armorer answered with a wide grin.

Considering a change in his original plan Drachus tried the loaders; they did work fine. After a few tries he found they easily loaded six new cartridges to the revolvers' swing-out cylinder.

The old armorer turned to Arevalo with a grin. "This one knows what he's doing" the older man said.

"Aye, he should, he taught me all about those things" a voice from the side called out in a heavy Scottish brogue. A slender young man with bright red hair had come in.

"Halo, Cormack!" Drachus said with a smile

"Side by side, eh; just like Dublin" Cormack said.

"Sorry, but no, not this time" Drachus said. "I'm going in through the garden."

"Like when you 'rescued' that overbearing old Tuscan Count's pretty young daughter?" Cormack said.

"Ah, yes; I recall she was grateful I got her out of that arranged marriage mess. Her father wasn't so happy when the priest insisted she had to get married a few weeks later. I guess helping her hide out with that shopkeeper boyfriend of hers wasn't such a good idea" Drachus said slyly.

"Yeah, that old Italian tyrant is still calling you seven kinds of a 'Self-serving Shanghai Swede" roared the laughing Cormack.

"I'd like to test fire the pistols" Drachus told Arevalo.

"We have a small range out back" the Spaniard said.

Rather than take time to set up a target, Drachus took aim at an old wooden crate about 10 paces away; it was nearly the same size as a man's chest. He fired six rounds from each pistol noting they were quite accurate.

He was pleasantly surprised to see the armorer had added oversized grips; that made the recoil easier to handle – military revolvers tended to have small grips which annoyed men with large hands like Drachus.

After going back inside he spoke with Arevalo. "I'll take two of the pistols, along with some loaders."

"Not a machinegun?" the Spaniard asked in surprise.

"No; my work inside will be close; pistols are best close in and the more noise out front the easier getting out back will be" Drachus explained.

Arevalo nodded and told his armorer Kropatsche to get him the two best from the last shipment. After fetching them, the older man an ammo locker.

"Will you want the expensive ones?" he asked.

Seeing Drachus' confusion, Arevalo explained. "Last month we learned that the cultists were using silver tipped crossbow bolts; we found several wolves killed with them."

Drachus had read enough of Lovecraft's odd stories to know silver was supposed to have some power over supernatural creatures. As he checked out the Prideaux Loaders he could see some were filled with hollow-point bullets that shined much brighter than lead would.

"Why would they go to that expense?" he asked.

After a short pause Arevalo's face showed a wry grin. "My son says the cultists already summoned two lesser demons. Tonight, they'll summon one powerful enough for the 'Cult of the Great Dragons' to conquer the world."

After a pause Drachus said "You're kidding, right?"

"I know; on top of his earlier demeanor it implies my boy has lost his mind but there is evidence" Arevalo added.

"May I see it?" Drachus asked. Arevalo nodded to Cormack who went outside. The older man walked over to unlock and open a tall cabinet to pull out a long rolled sheet of paper as the younger mercenary returned with a canvas-wrapped bundle the size of a backpack.

The bundle was the frozen front half of a wolf carcass; it had been torn apart. In its jaws was a piece of what looked like a lizard's scaly hide.

On the paper Drachus saw drawings of a creature with the body like a gorilla covered in snake-like scales with claws like a hawk and the jaws of an alligator. Noting the disbelief on Drachus' face Arevalo explained.

"My son has no head for business but he's a good artist. Two months ago the cultists summoned this. It went wild, killing several and escaping into the woods. They tracked it and found it dying from wounds suffered while fighting a pack of wolves; it had killed an entire pack of seven with just its claws and teeth."

At the mercenary's shocked expression Arevalo continued. "I agree it's a lot to believe. For the next several weeks the cultists prepared. On the new moon two weeks ago they summoned another. This time they had silver-tipped crossbow bolts and a lot of raw meat ready for it. While it was eating, their High Priest conducted a magic ritual and placed a gold collar around its neck. After that, it obeyed the priest's orders" he said.

As Drachus shook his head Arevalo added "I had Kropatsche make silver bullets, just in case. If you don't believe..."

Before he could say more the Swede cut him off. "It doesn't matter if I believe it or not; the cultists believe and they are going to sacrifice five girls regardless. My job is to rescue them, whether from cultists or demons it's all the same to me. However, just in case, I think I'll try those silver bullets, just to see if they work" he said with a wry grin.

Drachus loaded each pistol with two of the expensive silver-tipped cartridges he might be using tonight. Then he went back outside and test fired them. From the recoil and muzzle blast he realized that Kropatsche had loaded these rounds a lot hotter than the factory ammo; they might be as powerful as Elmer Keith's new .357 Magnum he'd read about – no wonder the old man had enlarged the grips!

Back inside Cormack carried over a tray with two pistols, a gun belt with two heavy-duty military flap holsters and eight Prideaux Loaders in leather belt pouches. There were also two boxes of cartridges marked 'Argent'. Drachus smiled at that.

"I think I'll go ahead and play Lone Ranger with the silver bullets" he told Arevalo.

"It's only money after all" Arevalo said with a smile.

"Speaking of that, what's my pay if I make it alive out with those girls?" Drachus asked.

"$50,000 in American or a similar amount in another currency if you wish" Arevalo replied quietly. That was a lot more than he'd expected. After a questioning glance the Spaniard reluctantly elaborated.

"My son is devoted to his older sister but he himself has shown little interest in ... fatherhood. My daughter is my best ... and likely my last ... opportunity for a successor to carry on my family line. I really have no choice; she must be rescued, regardless of the cost!" After watching the worried Spaniard's face for a few moments the mercenary smiled.

"I think I shall retire after this" he said. As Drachus loaded the silver bullets into the pistols and Prideaux devices he asked Cormack "How do they perform?"

"Fine close in but after 10 yards they start to stray. They are sized and beeswax-lubricated but you can't swage cast silver as well as lead with the presses we have here; there are likely voids inside unbalancing them, causing wobble. After 25 yards, its pot luck" the younger man said.

"Well, tonight's work will be close in; that should be fine. With luck I won't need to shoot anyone at all" he said.

Drachus returned to the inn to check on preparations. He asked Mr. Cuirass for a good rifle he could take along.

"I thought you would be working inside, at short range only" the militiaman asked.

"Some of the cultists may pursue us out the back. I'd like something with a much longer range to cover the girl's retreat if needed" Drachus said.

"I have just the thing" Mr. Cuirass said with a smile.

He came back a few minutes later with a new German Heer rifle; it had an extended magazine that was definitely not regular army issue.

"I didn't know Mauser 98's came with longer magazines" Drachus said.

"Yes" Mr. Cuirass said. "That is a 'trench magazine' from a rifle I acquired after the Great War.; it gave a soldier 20 shots without reloading – very useful when charging into a trench. That original rifle was rather worn and prone to jamming – I didn't feel like trusting it – so I had Kropatsche move the magazine to this newer one; I tested it and it works just fine."

After checking out the rifle a thought occurred to Drachus. "Can you get me a cuirass to wear? It won't stop bullets but the bad guys do have daggers; some of tonight's work will be up very close" Drachus said.

After a glance at the mercenary's torso Mr. Cuirass replied "Yes, I'm certain we have one that will fit you."

As he went upstairs to nap Drachus saw Salana at the bar. "Make certain I'm up right after lunch." The pretty auburn-haired lady smiled, making him a rather pleasant alternative to a nap.

Attractive as the offer was he turned her down – he needed rest today. Tomorrow – maybe even the next few days - would be a different story.

After one last check with Mr. Cuirass, Drachus left that afternoon. While slogging through the powdery snow Drachus realized he hadn't used snow shoes in years. He needed to make good time in the snow on the back trails to arrive behind the fortress before the men out front.

He was glad the locals didn't see him re-learning how to use them. It might have damaged their morale to see their highly paid professional soldier falling flat on his face into the snow as the front tips dug deep into the powder and tripped him; using snowshoes was tricky!

At sundown he stood next to a ruined gatehouse that once controlled the access road. He could just make out a group of 60 or so men headed towards the fortress. He could easily see that more than half of them carried torches while the rest had rifles slung over their shoulders; after watching for a bit Drachus saw their pace in the snow made it likely they would arrive on time.

Two hours later he arrived near the old munitions warehouse. He doffed the snowshoes and placed them atop a pair of low tree branches. Using this as a makeshift shelf, he stacked the skiing flares on top of them. He hid the rifle in a crook in the trunk at the base of the tree then hung the ammunition belt from a lower branch. This would help him quickly locate the right tree after their escape.

Following young Arevalo's foot prints in the snow he approached the building. A few yards away he saw a set of small footprints coming from the forest and heading to the building.

Whoever made them had walked up an old game trail then exited the woods heading towards the building.

Drachus stopped to consider the possibilities.

The footprints were very fresh; there wasn't even any wind-blown snow in them yet. It was likely no one from town had come up to execute a rescue; they would have seen all of the preparations and known better. With so little to go on, he decided to press on and hope for the best.

Making his way in through the ventilation shaft was easy; the footprint maker had cleared the debris and attached a rope. He scouted the dark space inside for several yards before hearing men laughing in a lighted area to his left. As Drachus peered around a stone pillar he saw two big men had a young woman pinned up against the wall.

Young Arevalo had described the guards' gaudy and rather improbable outfits. On top they wore brown duster coats with a pair colorful dragons embroidered on the cape. They had knee-high dark brown riding boots, grey trousers, white silk shirts and maroon leather vests. Their slouch hats and crossbows were scattered about on the floor.

'Whoever put these outfits together did a lot of traveling' Drachus thought. He'd seen American cowboys wearing these kinds of coats but the wingless dragons on the cape were Chinese –  he'd seen lots of these embroidered on dresses in Hong Kong. The slouch hats were Australian – he recalled ANZAC veterans wearing them but the enameled badge on the flip side was altered: it said something like 'Dragons Bring Victory' in Latin.

The cavalry boots were French or Italian; English and German boots didn't have that many silver accessories – those kind of excessive details were considered effeminate!

Their captive was not even 5' tall, with long blonde braids. She wore an ankle-length, hooded white military winter camouflage cloak; her very slender body was clad in tight-fitted black woolen coveralls.

The men spoke German but thanks to lots of work with a Prussian fencing instructor Drachus understood a bit; he heard what sounded like them trying to decide who was going to go and who would stay. Eventually one of the guards said "All right; you take her inside. After I load mine I'll reload yours."

Drachus waited behind the pillar. He could see the door the guard was headed to and hoped he had time; the girl's struggles were slowing him down a lot.

The crossbows had most likely fired when the guards originally captured her. Weapons had a habit of going off when you dropped them to the floor. That or these guards were just very bad shots; she hadn't been hit!

As the guard loaded the second weapon, Drachus quietly walked to the loaded one leaning against the wall. He took cover behind a pillar so the guards couldn't see him; then he aimed at the one manhandling the girl.

He had used crossbows before - to shoot grappling hooks over the wall of an Irish castle on a job with Cormack. They had to get in without making a lot of noise so their Scottish armorer had refurbished a few of them. This one even had modern rifle sights.

As the loading guard grunted while pulling the strong bow Drachus used those sounds to cover the 'klang' noise as he shot the other guard in the head; the man died without uttering a sound. The girl let out a yell as the body fell on top of her. The loading guard looked over at the noise and laughed.

"No time for that now Ulrich; later ..." his comment ended as Drachus came up behind him and clubbed the man to the ground with the butt of the crossbow.

The slender girl had crawled out from under the dead guard and was running towards the exit. Drachus cut her off and grabbed her around her waist. As he tried to clamp his other hand over her mouth to keep her from screaming she kicked him on the leg unbalancing him and they fell to the ground; she wasn't going to be captured easily, not again!

As they hit the floor she struggled while squealing to be released. The mercenary was surprised to hear her speaking French. He rolled her over, clamped a hand over her mouth and signaled for her to be silent. He couldn't let her go; she had information he needed to know.

Distracted by her pretty face, bright blue eyes and long blonde hair that had come unbraided during her struggles Drachus hesitated until she signaled with her hands for him to uncover her mouth. After he did she wriggled her jaw a bit then said "Who the hell are you?"

Fortunately thanks to a long stint with a Foreign Legion Company in Algeria Drachus was fluent in French. "I am the one who's here to tell them they are dead; they should just lie down like good little boys so they can all be buried in their silly little costumes" he whispered back.

She giggled quietly at his joke.

"Why are you here?" Drachus asked.

Averting her eyes she said "Looking for the souvenir shop?" Then Drachus noticed she reeked of cheap perfume.

"You're a thief?" he quietly asked helping her up.

"What of it?" she whispered indifferently.

Drachus needed to know a few things so they chatted for a while. As they talked she admitted she'd been hired to steal a rare silvered triptych that was supposed to be stored here; she knew nothing about the cult.

Once he told her she wanted to run away but he needed to know how they'd caught her. After a bit she told him they had said they were waiting here to see if a runaway boy decided to come back or bring the authorities.

That threw a huge monkey wrench into Drachus' plans. If they knew about Diego Arevalo's defection and this entry he couldn't use it; there were likely guards further in where it was warmer – so they could rotate out to avoid fatigue due to the cold. His only other option on this side of the complex was the garden, where he had intended to exit.

However, that was easy to see from many places in the castle. With the distraction of the gun battle up front it wouldn't have been an issue during the escape but using it to make the initial entry was very risky, especially if they were aware of activity at this side of the complex.

After watching him think, her face sported a sly smile. "You have to get in there without being seen, don't you?" After he nodded she added "You let me steal what I can and I'll get you in without alerting the guards."

"How?" he asked suspiciously.

"Through the greenhouse; it was my second choice – I really wish I'd taken it in the first place" she said sweetly.

'Greenhouse?' Drachus mused; there wasn't one on the plans he'd seen. He wasn't sure if he could trust her but didn't have any choice; they shook hands on the deal.

"I am Twerle le Moineau; you should put on one of the dead goons' silly outfits in case we run into others. We can pretend I am a prisoner, get close and finish them off quietly with their own silver daggers" she said with a smile.

It was a ruthlessly good idea; this was obviously not the young lady's first foray into such activities. The guard unit was small, so they'd likely know one another by sight but he could hide his face with the hat as they closed.

Fortunately, one guard was close enough to Drachus' size for it to work. In fact, the man had been a bit bigger than Drachus; his vest was loose enough the mercenary could still wear the steel cuirass beneath it. However his hat was a bit floppy.

As he examined the outfit he found there were two rigid leather cases that had been recently mounted on the front near the sides of the leather vest. Each had six crossbow bolts, five were quite thick and one was much longer and thinner; those two had silver points.

As he changed the girl peeked a few times - she was French after all - and offered the occasional complementary appraisal about his ... height. After strapping on his gun belt he placed two loaders and his watch into the vest pockets.

They left the warehouse and walked to the other side of the keep where there was a big glass greenhouse attached to the side of the main structure. This had been marked as a kitchen garden on the old plans; at some point it was glazed over without the plans being altered. He worried what other changes hadn't been annotated!

As they approached it, Drachus pointed to the light coming from the kitchen windows. "How are you going to do this without being spotted?" he whispered. The kitchen was close; he could hear the cooks.

"Watch and learn dragon-boy" Twerle said with a smile. They continued around to the far side of the greenhouse, reasonably far enough away from the kitchen.

Around her waist she wore an old belt of leather magazine pouches. After sliding it around her waist she pulled two items from its pockets. One was a small rubber suction cup on a string which she attached near the corner of a large glass pane in a ventilation window at ground level.

The second was a bar of soap. She used that to draw a damp soapy circle around the suction cup. After replacing it in her belt, she pulled out a small ring box with a diamond solitaire ring.

"You are a lovely young lady but do you think this is the time for the two of us to be getting engaged?" he whispered.

Now a bit miffed, the thief muttered in something other than French as she used the ring's diamond to etch a line in the glass under the soap ring.

Knowing how loud a screech from scratching glass can be Drachus panicked a bit until he realized the soap deadened the noise perfectly. Once she had a complete circle she cleaned the ring, put it away and pulled out what looked like a toy-sized brass hammer and steel chisel.

Then she waited, listening carefully. After a bit Drachus was about to ask what was wrong when a stiff breeze blew and rattled loose glass panes of the old greenhouse. Then Twerle tapped the etched line with the toy hammer and chisel cracking the glass underneath; the rattling glass panes masked the tapping noise perfectly. As the wind slowed, she paused.

While waiting, Drachus smelled the perfume again. "What's with the cheap perfume?" he whispered.

"Dogs" Twerle replied. At his confused look, she continued. "If they try to track me with dogs I pour on a new, stronger scent to confuse them. The dogs lose track of me and I get away." Drachus pantomimed applause and Twerle smiled sweetly as a breeze let her tap some more.

Then she bit on the suction cup string and waited. With the next breeze she finished tapping and the round piece of glass fell inside the greenhouse. The string stopped it from hitting the floor and Twerle slowly lowered it silently to the ground. "Finis" she said with a pretty smile.

Comparing the size of the 6" diameter hole and her admittedly trim derriere Drachus whispered "No way is *that* going to fit through *there!*"

Wrinkling her nose she muttered something obviously insulting in a language that Drachus now recognized as Darija, a Moroccan version of Arabic; he'd heard it – and similar words - rather often in Algeria. That explained her dusky complexion, blonde hair and blue eyes; many French colonials had fathered half-bloods with their prettier Algerian maids.

She pulled a towel from her cloak, fed it through the hole then reached in. With her arm protected by the towel, she undid the window's lock and opened it. As she tried to recover the towel it caught on the frame. "Merde" she sneered and abandoned it.

Drachus pulled it free as he walked in shaking his head. "Careless" he whispered as he sniffed the strong perfume on the towel before stuffing it into his pocket. "Even if they won't be able to track you, you shouldn't leave evidence behind" he said.

Twerle stuck out her tongue and grinned as they moved in through the old moldy planters towards the tiled veranda adjacent to the keep.

Just then a cloud bank passed over the moon cutting down on their light; they had to move even slower to be quiet. Being careful not to kick over clay pots, they crept to the veranda. Several times along the way Drachus thought he heard something odd but couldn't make out what it was.

He knew from the fortress plans that the veranda had four portals; the one he was interested in was on the far left. It led the main hall, south tower and living quarters at the keep's center. According to young Arevalo, the captive girls were being held in an isolated room in the south tower.

As Drachus turned to speak to Twerle there was a break in the heavy cloud cover. His eyes were adjusted to the dim light of moonlit clouds by now. Even through the dirty glass panes the bright moonlight let him catch a glint of a golden collar worn by a large shape moving towards them. Suddenly recalling the 'It' that had frightened young Arevalo so badly he grabbed Twerle and dove off to the side behind a pile of old furniture. He covered her mouth in case she screamed when she saw the demon.

It was shuffling its way towards them slowly, sliding its feet along the floor as if it couldn't lift its feet. With a shock Drachus realized it had no eyes, just a wide bony ridge where they should be; its ears and nose were larger than young Arevalo's drawing had shown.

When he saw its nostrils flare he realized what that odd noise he'd been hearing was – it was sniffing them out and Twerle was soaked in perfume!

He turned to whisper to her but she was barely conscious; he'd landed on top of Twerle when they fell and knocked the wind out of her. He outweighed the tiny woman by 120 pounds. After a few seconds, her eyes fluttered, going wide when she saw the demon. Replacing his hand over her mouth to muffle her scream, he leaned in and quietly whispered "perfume" in her ear.

Glancing back at the demon she realized it was tracking by scent; the clever thief grimaced as she realized that her evasion strategy was leading it straight to them.

Drachus felt her hands working around her pouch belt and moments later she pushed a small bottle into his hand. As she had been retrieving it he'd concentrated and was certain he felt a draft from ahead. He pushed the bottle back into her hand and motioned for her to throw it that way. As she drew her arm back he held his hand up for her to wait a bit.

By now the demon was only a few steps away. Drachus quietly and carefully stood up and drew two crossbow bolts, one of the slender and one of the thicker; he didn't know what they did differently so having one of each was likely his best option.

As the bolts came into view both he and Twerle were surprised to see the silver tip emanating a pale glow. She looked at him with a questioning glance. He shrugged and she rolled her eyes - annoyed with his ignorance.

Grinning, he motioned for her to throw the perfume. They were startled to hear how loud the sound of that cork being pulled seemed to echo through the room. The demon let out a snort and both of them froze. Drachus looked back to see if the demon really heard it.

He saw the noise likely wasn't what startled it; the gold collar was glowing like the crossbow bolt tip! The demon seemed confused; the cultists had created the bolts and collar to keep the demon from running amok so Drachus guessed their magic must be connected; maybe it was telling the demon not to attack them?

Whatever was causing it didn't matter; he motioned for Twerle to throw the bottle and she tossed it. When it hit the wall the demon spun and began shuffling that way.

A few moments later the smell of the perfume reached him; Drachus was shocked at how pungent it was. He turned to face

Twerle and the 'Whew' look on his face must have been obvious. She stuck out her tongue again and turned her smiling face away from him. He remembered that this was supposed to get dogs off her scent, not attract a man. Well, it smelled strong enough to put off dogs.

Flipping the bolts around so he now held one in each hand like stabbing daggers, Drachus took several steps toward the demon, jumped up to reach the 9' tall things head and stabbed the bolts into both big ears. In most animals and people, this was a direct route to its brain.

As he leaped he perversely found himself making a silent prayer 'I hope those demon-worshipping cultists who made this magic stuff did their jobs well.'

Drachus felt the bolts hit home. So did the demon; it immediately arched its back and flung its arms wide – in total silence! Off his feet and hanging on its back Drachus took the full force of the jolt and was thrown back several yards; this damn thing was strong.

He hit the wall head first and saw stars. As he felt himself start to fall down the stairs to the dungeons Drachus realized his left foot wasn't touching the floor. Momentarily dazed he tried unsuccessfully to catch himself then suddenly felt something soft press him into the wall, stopping his fall. Twerle had caught him just in time.

"Clumsy oaf" she whispered. As he smiled they heard a crashing sound of the demon smashing through an old wooden planter as it charged straight at them. It hit them before he could shout a warning.

The collision hurled all three down the steep stone stairs. As they fell his head hit hard stone again; Drachus saw more stars and then darkness as he blacked out.

When the mercenary regained consciousness he realized several things at once – all of them bad.

His head was pounding; he probably had at least a concussion. On top of that he was having trouble moving his legs; at first he feared his back may have been broken in the fall but realized there was just something heavy lying across his legs. Then there was the overwhelming smell of fresh blood and the stink of burning flesh.

Opening his eyes Drachus saw the landing was dimly lit by a torch further down the stair. One of the demon's legs was lying across his knees; its head was literally blown apart. Apparently, the gold collar had an explosive charge. Another torch was lying at the demon's side sputtering as it burned away some of the monster's scaly skin. Looking to the left he saw Twerle lying unconscious on the bottom stair.

Sliding his legs out from under the demon he stood up and found that wasn't a problem. "OK, no nausea or dizziness, so no concussion. Just a big lump and a pounding headache" he muttered quietly to himself.

Moving to Twerle's side he touched her cheeks until he saw her bright blue almond-shaped eyes flutter open. "You still in one piece?" he whispered.

She gingerly moved body parts before saying "Bien."

"Good; now I don't have to carry your fat butt back to town" he quipped.

Feigning offense she shot back "Who has a fat butt, you clumsy clod!" As he stood, Twerle plopped the slouch hat on his head. "Now you look ridiculous again" she said.

As Drachus laughed the pain in his head flared. "Ow! My head hurts so bad I'm surprised you can't hear it pounding" he muttered. Twerle gave him a startled look.

"That is one hell of a headache – I can hear it!" she said. Drachus laughed again then got serious.

"Wait, that's not my headache, its gunfire - from the front gate" he said checking his pocket watch. It was still intact; grandmother was right – this thing seemed to be virtually indestructible. It was 11:51. "Ah, crap; we're late - da verdamnt planen isst bruten!" he shouted.

As they ran out onto the veranda he checked up the stairs to the main hall. Drachus saw it was illuminated with an eerie yellowish-green light flickering in time with the sounds of chanting. Praying he wasn't too late he heard movement from behind; Twerle was following him.

"What's up? Those verdamnt cultists are dangerous! You're not getting paid for this." he said.

"Hey, little girls have to stick together, especially when big mean men are pushing us around" Twerle said.

"Hey, I don't push girls around" Drachus said.

Looking askance at him as they reached the second flight of stairs, Twerle suddenly sported a wry grin. "No, you look like the type who uses shiny trinkets and sweet words; and then you're gone in the morning!" she said.

He grinned as he realized the little lady really had a good heart. "Well, with my job and looks that's sort of …" His comment cut short as they entered the main hall.

Both stared in amazement at the weird tableau before them. They were on a balcony circling the hall with four staircases evenly-spaced leading down to the floor. In the far end of the ballroom the marble floor was marked with concentric circles of red and black symbols.

Centered in the circles was a shimmering column of greenish light reaching to the ceiling. In the column was an atrocity, a thing right out of a biblical nightmare from hell!

It stood at least 20′ tall. Extending about that much from it to either side were bat-like wings of the same creepy shade of dark red as its skin. Huge horns like elephant tusks came from its head and there were claws like cavalry sabers on its fingers.

It threw its head back with a roar like a freight train exposing rows of sharp teeth. It wore a belted loincloth and had bright red glowing sigils on its chest that pulsed in time with the light as though reacting to the summoning spell.

Movement in front of it caught his eye. Standing on a dais at the edge of the glowing column was a dark figure in decorated robes. From its arm and head movements the High Priest of the dragon cult was chanting.

Flanking him to both sides were three priests in elaborate robes, their hands and eyes glowing. Behind them were choirs of monks with glowing eyes. Drachus assumed they were chanting because he could see their mouths moving but he couldn't hear over the roar of the demon.

More important to Drachus was the red pentagram-shaped table on the floor between him and the demon. Chained down on the table were five half-naked girls struggling in terror; their heads at the apex of each corner and their arms manacled along the edges of the tabletop.

Standing at each corner was another robed priest holding a serpentine dagger; the dagger blade, their hands and eyes were all glowing. Drachus knew time was short and they had to act fast.

He was about to yell at Twerle when something flashed past his head, hitting the wall behind him. Running along the balcony from the right were two guards. Drachus fired several rounds from one pistol to drop them.

He turned to tell Twerle to move but she was already heading to the girls. Drachus smiled as he followed. 'I wonder if she'll retire with me after this is over' he thought.

The pretty lady had guts, a good heart and her legs seemed to be long – topped by a trim little derriere it made quite the attractive package; he wondered what the dusky French-Algerian beauty looked like in a negligee.

Movement on the balcony to his left drew his attention away from her and Drachus dropped two more charging guards. When he looked back he saw one of the sacrificial priests fall over, the hilt of a dagger protruding from his back. Twerle had kept one from the guards who'd caught her; apparently she'd found a use for it.

He moved to cover her from attack by the others but they'd not even noticed; they were too focused on the ritual! Drachus emptied his pistols killing them as he approached.

Twerle was already freeing the girls when Drachus arrived. "No keys - just simple bolts" she shouted.

"Good" he called back. Just after he'd reloaded he saw two guards shooting at them from the stair on the left. He fired, killing one; the other fell back to reload.

"I'll keep them busy while you get the girls outside" he shouted. Twerle seemed shocked at that. Glancing up from gathering up the silver chains – she was a thief after all – she looked at the half-naked cuties. "In the snow outside they'll freeze their nipples off!" she cried.

Drachus smiled as he shook his head and called back. "That's covered; we have friends with warm clothes waiting outside. Forget the silver; just get them out!"

Drachus reloaded his pistol again; he hadn't emptied it yet but the second rule of a successful soldier was to keep full loads in your weapons whenever you can; you might not live long enough to regret it if you didn't.

He pocketed the shells and the empties from the partial load and headed to the stair. Passing the first guard he'd killed, he pulled a thin and thick crossbow bolt from his vest to replace the ones he'd used to kill the first demon. If he ran out of ammo they'd come in handy; he could use their own crossbows against them.

As he climbed the stair he spotted two guards topping the stair behind the glowing column. Glancing back he saw Twerle and the last of the girls heading down the stairway to the veranda. Drachus prayed the torch bearers were out there waiting or those girls were going to freeze more than just their nipples off – it must be bitterly cold outside at midnight!

Now all he had to worry about was getting his self out while covering them. Moving along the balcony he saw the guards at the far end drop to one knee army-style and point crossbows at him. Ducking behind a column to spoil their aim he saw one of the bolts get caught in a wall tapestry; these guys *were* bad shots!

As he darted around the column to shoot the villains at the far end while they reloaded Drachus saw the thick bolt stuck in the tapestry seemed to have a trail of smoke and sparks coming from its nock.

He also saw the guards had charged instead of reloading. As he brought his pistols up to shoot them he heard a loud gunshot from behind. Not wanting to be flanked from front and rear, he spun to his left.

Behind he saw a man in a militia cuirass running towards them as he cycled the bolt from his huge rifle; apparently some of the rescue force had already managed to get inside. Turning back to the guards in the front he saw one was down; it had been hit by the shot from the militiaman.

He brought one pistol up to block the other guard's dagger. These men were strong; as both weapons into the darkness the smoking bolt caught in the tapestry exploded!

The force of the blast knocked all three of them off the balcony and down to the dais below, *with the demon*! Once they were all inside the glowing column the demon let out another deafening roar and swept a kick at them with a cloven hoof that looked big enough to crush a horse.

Drachus rolled away and escaped but the cult guard was slow. The kick was so powerful blood sprayed from all of his orifices as the screaming wretch was hurled from the glowing column into the darkness; this demon was strong.

The thing was slow but too big to kill with a pistol ... so Drachus shot the priest casting the summoning spell instead. As the silver bullet struck a look of shock played over the old fiend's face as he fell over dead.

Drachus jumped to his feet to escape from the demon but before it could kick again the light around them turned to a swirling purple and then darkness. He felt the floor beneath his feet disappear and the man began to fall.

And this is where our tale began. Jakob Roy Drachus, a successful, not-so famous but still-alive professional soldier, felt his self falling into total darkness with no idea of what lay below. It had started as such a simple joke of a job – how the hell did it all go so very wrong?

Chapter 2

Where the hell did I end up now?

Drachus felt chills and almost electric hot flashes running up and down his body as he fell. During all of this he heard a woman's soft voice in his head.

"Many people of this world wallow in despair. Death is often their only escape. My sisters and I failed them. Unfair though it may be I ask you to take up the challenge. Your knowledge can give this world hope; your skills can help it survive. In exchange I save your life and grant what aid I can. I regret that I must foist this burden upon you."

After what felt like an eternity, the sensation of falling stopped. Drachus found himself standing on a platform lit by the brilliant noon sun. As his eyes adjusted he crouched to reload his pistol. That's when he realized his right arm was numb; he'd hit the floor awkwardly falling on the dais.

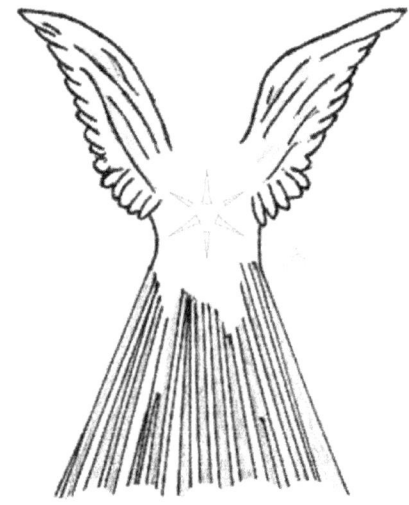

Drachus suddenly saw movement. Bringing his pistol up, he froze after seeing the ghostly image of an angel floating in front of him.

Then he heard that same voice in his head again. "Cultists of two worlds joined their powers to release a great evil. I wish good fortune for you and those who join their lives with yours to face the challenges ahead."

The angel's image shrank until it was just a small bright sparkle which darted towards him. Still a bit stunned, Drachus could only stare as he felt it sting his chest, but not hard enough to hurt. Feeling no injury there, he dismissed it as his imagination.

After loading his pistol he shook his right arm to eliminate the numbness. He felt most of the muscles in his body complaining loudly. As his vision began to clear Drachus saw he was on a circular marble pavilion surrounded by white marble columns.

Outside the columns were triangular fountains, one to his left and another to the right. Atop a 6' pedestal in the center of each stood a 10' marble statue of an angel.

As he holstered his pistol and stepped towards a fountain, Drachus felt something soft wrap around his right foot. Looking down he noticed his slouch hat. He put it on to shade his eyes from the sunlight.

Looking about he found himself near the center of a magic circle like the one from before - but this one was filled with a hundred men in dark cultists' robes lying motionless. Drawing the pistol he rolled the nearest over to see if he was alive. No he was not; the robe was occupied by a skeleton!

As his sight cleared he saw many of the robed figures were skeletons. A clattering sound drew his attention as a long, silvered dagger slid from between the ribs of the skeleton he'd turned over and fell to the marble surface below.

As he walked out of the circles Drachus checked robes at random. Each held a skeleton stabbed through the heart with a silvered dagger. Even though he was accustomed to battlefield casualties Drachus found this all to be quite creepy.

As he exited the circle, he saw this – temple? - was deep within a green forest. There were three large triangular fountains just outside the circle of columns. Between each was a smaller triangular planter of tiny yellow flowers. If viewed from above, the place would probably appear as a six-pointed starburst.

At the center of each fountain were triangular pedestals topped with larger-than-life angel statues facing towards the circle of columns. Water flowed from their outstretched palms filling the basin.

It had been midnight late December in Spain but it felt like high-noon summer here - and this flatland forest definitely wasn't the mountainous north west of Galicia on the Iberian Peninsula. While trying to figure out what to do next, he heard a rustling sound from behind.

Spinning into a crouch as he drew his pistol to see what was coming at him now. He saw a young girl, probably no more than 10 or so. She had stumbled from the forest and seemed startled to see him. The skinny girl with short black hair was covered with scratches. Her dirty grey dress appeared to have been patched many times and was torn in new places as well. She was filthy, sweating and panting as if she'd been running for some time.

After a second of surprise she called out in a frightened voice. "You have to run; it's coming!" Before he could ask what was coming, he heard a roar from above. Looking up he saw the same demon he had just left behind moments ago landing on the pavilion.

"You are here again, lizard worshipper? I will show you what happens to those who stand against the Demon Warlord Kreeger!" it called out in a very rough voice.

Drachus realized it remembered him from his old world - and wasn't happy to see the man here as well. It roared as it charged. Lacking any real alternatives, Drachus fired. It was three times the size of a man so he went for head shots hoping to blind it by hitting its eyes.

As it closed he saw that the glowing sigils from before were gone. There was also what appeared to be a dimly glowing red gem or horn in its forehead; the bright summoning light must have kept him from seeing it before.

Two steps before it got to within claw range, one of Drachus' bullets must have hit the red glowing thing; it shattered with flash of bright red light. The demon staggered, wailed in agony, fell to its knees and began to glow with a red aura.

Pretty certain red glows were a bad thing Drachus dashed to the nearest cover he could see - the ledge of the fountain. On the way he ran by the exhausted girl; wrapping her up in his arms he carried her along for some protection.

Luckily, the event was mostly fire with little concussion; there was no significant physical force from the blast. Once it was quiet he stood up checking the scorched clearing; the demon was gone, there wasn't even a body!

Drachus felt the girl trembling; she was just as scared of him as she'd been of the demon. He couldn't blame her; she didn't know who he was and the kid must still be terrified. The tall Swede sat her down on the fountain's ledge where she silently watched as he scanned the area for further dangers. Seeing none, he did the practical things; he reloaded his empty pistol, holstered it and then washed up in the fountain.

When finished with all that, he went to look at the kid's injuries. After a cursory examination it seemed most of them were minor scrapes and scratches. It was obvious from the smell that she needed a bath really bad. "You should clean-up. That old dress of yours could use a washing while you're at it" he said. He wasn't certain she could understand him. "What's your name little quiet girl?" he asked.

"Chia" she said in a soft, pretty voice.

"You should clean up whenever you have the chance" he repeated "you never know when your next bath might be." As the girl glanced up and hesitantly plucked at her dress Drachus realized he was being insensitive.

"Wait" he said then went over to scavenge among a large pile of discarded equipment under the nearby trees. Tying several poles together he made a frame; after shaking out the bones, he hung a cultists' robe on it.

"You can use this for privacy" he grinned. "I promise I won't peep." The girl seemed more surprised by this than anything. She walked slowly behind the shelter, a few seconds later she peered out from one side checking to see if he really wasn't going to peep.

Drachus found that adorable; she reminded him of his young sisters. He wondered how they were doing. He hadn't seen them in years and had planned to visit this summer – he'd heard they were married with kids now.

He heard rustling and tearing noises from behind the makeshift lean-to; it sounded obvious her tattered dress wasn't salvageable. Drachus searched through the cultists' remains to find her something else to wear. Rummaging through bodies was never pleasant but these must have been gone a long time - there wasn't any 'goo' left in them.

Some of their robes and clothes were a bit scorched but otherwise intact. It was strange that there were no bloodstains or decayed flesh. Even if undisturbed for years there was usually a bit of soft stuff left behind.

As he searched through the robed skeletons he found the body of the militia man he'd seen before. Apparently he had been too close to the explosion that knocked them all off the balcony; the poor fellow was dead.

Searching through the man's gear he found a standard infantry harness with two ammo pouches for his big rifle and a gun belt just like the one Drachus got from Arevalo. His pistol and all eight Prideaux loaders were untouched. His rifle ammo was down by about half.

The rifle itself had not landed well – the stock was broken, the bolt handle sheared off and the barrel was obviously bent. Drachus pulled the pistol and loaders from the belt to refill the empty spots in his own belt – the extra loaders went into his coat pockets.

After a moment's thought, he consolidated the remaining 32 rifle rounds into one ammo pouch and pocketed that as well. The rifle might not be salvageable but the ammo might come in handy later.

Nearby were shoulder bags and small crates that likely belonged to the dead cultists. Among these he found a shaving kit with hard soap, a straight razor and a leather razor strop. "Hey, Chia; I've got soap and a towel out here for you" he said pulling Twerle's towel from his pocket.

"Really?" she called out in surprise.

Drachus smiled as he slid them under the hanging robe. "I'll keep looking through all this stuff to see if I can find something sturdier than that old dress for you to change into. I'm not going far so just yell if anything scary shows up, OK?" he said.

Chia's quiet "OK" was barely audible.

'Such a quiet kid; I wonder if she can scream' he thought.

By the time he was done searching Chia had finished her bath. When she heard Drachus coming back she ducked behind the lean-to unsure of what to do. He understood some concern was justified. She was a helpless, naked girl with no idea of who he was and what he would do.

Realizing she wouldn't be very happy in a dead cultists' shirt, Drachus shucked his white silk shirt and tossed it over the side of the lean-to.

"I saw a comb in that shaving kit; take care of that mop of yours while you're at it" he called out.

He carried a dirty grey shirt he'd taken from a skeleton to the other fountain and began to wash it.

After a few minutes Chia knelt nearby saying "I'll do that." He saw her hair was quite long and worked into two braids dangling over her back. "I guess that's why it looked short before" he muttered.

As Drachus handed over the shirt he saw that her hair was dark brown, not black. 'It must have been really dirty' he thought to himself. As he stood to check his gear he heard her stomach growl loudly; she blushed.

He hadn't found any food with the cultists' gear but had seen fruit and nut trees in the forest around the temple pavilion. "I'll get us something to eat" he said.

Chia smiled and said "Thanks." Drachus realized that with a clean face she had a very pretty smile; the girl was innocence incarnate. In a few years she'd break a lot of hearts until she picked the guy she wanted to keep.

To avoid sunburn Drachus donned the red vest and duster. Without a shirt it was a bit scratchy but better than a burn. He didn't think he'd need to wear the cuirass to gather food. He spent an hour gathering striped apples, pears, peaches, walnuts and almonds.

Though the ground was overgrown the mature trees were planted in straight lines; this had obviously been orchards in the past so he figured they weren't poisonous. Oddly, there were no buildings here, not even a gardener's shed.

After they'd eaten, Chia washed up in the fountain. As she walked back the girl stumbled and fell. When Drachus helped her up he saw she had a badly bruised knee; she'd been so dirty he hadn't seen that up to now. 'She probably got hurt while the demon was chasing her; that's why she moves so slowly' he thought. He also saw that she had two different colored eyes.

Until now Chia had kept her bangs covering one eye so he never noticed one was green, the other a brown so light it might as well be called gold. A camp follower who'd been with him once had had the same thing. She said a priest once told her it was called heterochromia iridum.

When Chia realized he'd seen her eyes she began to cry. "I wasn't trying to hide it" she sniffled. "I was going to tell you I was demon-touched" as she slid further away. He sat down next to her and put his arm around her shoulders. As she tried to pull away saying "No, you'll get dirty" he pulled her in close and held her tightly.

Drachus had worked in a lot of backwards regions and knew that some cultures were rather hard on those who were born 'different'. As he recalled the untouchable caste (Dalits) in India, Drachus remembered they were considered low-born and often discriminated against.

Several of the government officials he'd dealt with on that job considered them trash. He guessed little Chia here belonged to a similar segment of this world's population.

After a few seconds she stopped trying to pull away. "You had no say in how you were born so I have no reason to hold that against you. You've had a bath, you're nice and clean now; you even smell like sweet soap. I see nothing dirty about you at all" he said.

She did smell nicer. Drachus recognized the scent as Twerle's 'dog repellent'. Apparently there was enough of it left in the towel to give little Chia a somewhat better scent; diluted as it was, it was now rather pleasant.

After a bit of quiet sniffling she collapsed against him and began crying like a baby. They sat like that for a while before he realized she was asleep; she must have been exhausted. He laid her on his duster in the shade of a tree and set about checking his gear he had left.

The 48 pistol rounds in the Prideaux loaders from the dead militiaman's belt were normal lead and he still had 24 silver rounds from his own original ammo load. He retrieved the Prideaux Loader and empty cases from where he'd dropped them; they might come in handy later.

The eight loaders with lead rounds went into his belt pouches, two with silver tips went into his vest pockets and the last loaded one and the empty went into coat pockets. One pistol was loaded with lead rounds, the other with silver tips.

This way he could keep track of which he was using. The silver ones would be reserved for demons while ordinary humans and such would get the lead ones. As Drachus realized he was already getting accustomed to dealing with demons he laughed; 'Yesterday I didn't even believe they were real – now I'm getting ready in case I have to fight them again!' he thought.

All of the empty cases went into a leather pouch he salvaged from the cultists' equipment; it was unlikely but he might be able to have them reloaded later.

He saw the bolt cases still held 10 of the wide-body bolts and two of the long, thin ones; he didn't have a crossbow but decided to keep them just in case. While checking out the crossbow bolts he saw a small silver ornament above the left breast of the vest that he was certain wasn't there before; it was in the same place he'd felt the hit when the angel's sparkly silver thing had flown at him.

Examining it closer he saw it was shaped like a small set of wings. Other than small inscriptions along its surface that might be magic symbols like the ones on the summoning circle, there was nothing else he could see. It was imbedded into the leather; he couldn't remove it but his fingers tingled when he touched it. He'd need to have a long talk with Chia tomorrow about magic.

The sun was still well above the horizon so he figured he had some time before he needed to sack out. The first thing he did was bury the dead militiaman. Using tools he found with the cultists' gear he dug a grave under one of the larger trees. He marked the grave with the man's cuirass after he carefully scratched "E. Garcia' on it. That name had been inked to the inside some of the soldier's gear – Drachus hoped it was his.

Then he decided to check out the crossbow bolts to see if any of them were like the one that exploded. He did this on the other side of the pavilion just in case; if he screwed up, Chia wouldn't be hurt in the blast.

The slender bolts were just high-quality ones made in a machine-shop; the thicker ones with steel tips were the boomers. Both the point and the brass nock screwed into the thin-walled steel tube of the body. Inside was a small block of cast explosive with two fuses. Behind the point was a simple impact trigger; the one in front of the nock was a short-burn fuse.

From what he could see, if you fired it from a crossbow the force of the bowstring would actuate a plunger starting the short-burn fuse. If it hit something solid, the impact trigger would set it off immediately. Otherwise, a few seconds after firing the timer would detonate it.

'A genius little package' Drachus thought to himself. While he wasn't an explosives expert, he was familiar enough with the stuff and guessed the cast explosive block was just about as strong as a hand grenade.

The sun was touching the horizon by now and he was beginning to feel the need for sleep. The grey shirt had dried so he put it on, then the vest. He decided not to sleep in the cuirass – that would hurt!

Drachus rolled his gun belt into a makeshift pillow – seventh rule of a successful soldier; in unknown territory keep your guns and ammo close. He took off his boots and lay down next to the tree where Chia was sleeping. The weather was warm; he probably wouldn't need a blanket.

Movement nearby woke him later. It was dark but the half-moon high in the sky let Drachus see what had disturbed him. Chia was curled up beside him, wrapped in his duster – she was using it like a sleeping bag. As he looked down he could see her cute face flanked by the embroidered dragons on his duster as she closed her eyes to go back to sleep.

She had apparently woken up and decided to sleep near him. The poor kid had been through a lot today; she was probably afraid to sleep alone – it reminded him of a night when he was just five years old.

During a thunderstorm his three-year old sister had run to his room crying. She'd never heard one before; the flashes and loud noises scared her. Their mother was down in the nursery feeding their newborn sister and their father was away on business; her big brother was the only one she could run to for protection from whatever was going on.

As the girl cried on his shoulder he kept telling her it would be all right, that he would keep her safe. Eventually she fell asleep there. This started a tradition; whenever Lisle was frightened she'd run to 'big brother'. Wrapped up in his strong arms she felt safe, like nothing could hurt her.

Drachus himself developed a protective nature; whenever one of his little sisters – or any other small girl nearby – seemed to be in danger he would move to protect her. He quickly earned a reputation for it – as well as growing into a strong fighter from brawling with bullies!

Drachus saw her trembling hand clinging to his shirt sleeve as he lay down to sleep. Looking up through the tree limbs he saw there was a smaller moon one right next to it to the real one! He tapped on Chia's shoulder then pointed up. "How long have there been two moons?" he asked.

She looked up and smiled saying "They've always been up there" before curling into a ball to sleep.

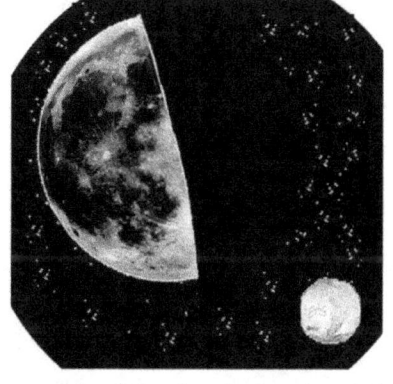

'We are definitely not in Kansas anymore, Toto' he thought to himself.

When he woke the next morning he and Chia breakfasted on fruits and nuts. Afterwards they washed in the fountain; this time Drachus also shaved. While she washed her hair again, he'd told her his name. With the insanity that went on yesterday on top of the beating he'd taken during the rescue the night before he'd completely forgotten to introduce himself.

Chia was surprised by it. He had a rather strong foreign accent and she may have had water in her ears making it hard to understand 'Drachus, Jakob Roy Drachus'. "I've never met anyone important enough to have four names! Can I just call you Dragon Lord?" she asked with a grin. That seemed odd until he saw her staring at the dragons on his duster's cape. Drachus thought the way she said it was cute.

"That'll be fine" said with a wide grin.

As it dried he saw Chia's hair was an even lighter brown than before, almost the same color as his. Apparently, she hadn't been able to wash it in a *very* long time; now she really looked like one of his little sisters.

They spent the day talking about this world. As they chatted he learned that the demon he killed yesterday had been sealed away 200 years ago, here in the Shrine of Hope. It must have escaped because two nights ago arrived at Chia's village at the end of the Summer Solstice Festival and demanded a sacrifice to not burn the village to the ground.

She was cast out; as a demon-touched slave the villagers thought she'd be a small loss. The demon chased her all night, toying with her like a cat terrorizing a mouse.

'No wonder she was exhausted' Drachus mused. He also thought the timing was odd. The summoning he had interfered with on his world had been on the Winter Solstice but it was now the Summer Solstice? Why did it take him six months to get here? That fall he endured before arriving had seemed to last forever but before he shaved he'd only had a few days of stubble.

He chatted with Chia to learn basic information about this land. Most of what she knew was legends and rumors; as a demon-touched slave, she'd never been educated though she'd learned to read a little on her own.

This was the cursed lands in the west of the Durakkon Kingdom. The kingdom wasn't ruled by a King; that bloodline died out in plagues a century ago. The 'kingdom' was run by nobles and officials of the church.

There is no Pope but there are 5 powerful Cardinals and three respected High Priestesses. The priestesses had titles based on the names of the Angelus; Tierri, Solus and Lunai were angels who'd descended from the heavens 250 years ago to save the world from a demon invasion.

'I guess that explains the shrine design' he thought.

Before the demon was sealed it cursed the west lands. They were poisonous, barely able to grow anything. Even the water in most wells was tainted. Chia's old village had a well that was a usable, so they could farm a little but if you drank too much from it all at once you'd get sick.

When the Angelus created the Shrine of Hope, some of the land near it recovered from the curse. Hunger is common; only the east coast had fertile lands; most of it controlled by nobles, the church and wealthy merchants.

When he asked about any military Chia told him that there was a Royal Army. She had heard they wore metal armor like his cuirass and swung swords – some used bows. She had never seen any herself but the people in her old village talked about them, so she guessed they were real.

The church had Holy Knights and cities have a City Guard; towns and villages have a militia. There was an Adventurers' Guild that took quests to protect people, find things or kill monsters. Drachus figured they were hunters rather than mercenaries; they didn't often fight other people.

It sounded like the Early Middle Ages on his Earth; poverty, oppression and concentrated wealth made life heaven for the rich, hell if you're not. 'If it weren't for magic I could make a good living as a mercenary' Drachus thought. However, he wasn't certain how to deal with magic; it was a completely unknown factor - that made it worrisome and dangerous.

Drachus thought 'Durakkon' sounded a lot like 'Dragon'. "Are there dragons here?" he asked jokingly.

"Oh yes," Chia said. "They live in mountains to the west. That's where dwarves, orcs, dark elves, demons and other monsters live too."

He took that with a grain of salt. Unexplored regions were often said to hold dangers. Drachus had seen old maps with 'Beyond Here Be Dragons!' scribed outside the known realms. However, there was magic and he'd killed one demon, so he wasn't ready to dismiss it as fantasy just yet.

He asked about nearby towns as they gathered food.

"I've heard visiting traders talk. Karnet trade village is north of here; farther north is Laris city. The capitol is east on the coast" Chia said.

Drachus thought it over for a while. He needed to learn a lot more about this world than Chia could tell him but he didn't want to go into a large town or city before he had some idea of the lay of the land. This Karnet village sounded like the best place to start checking on things.

"I'll be leaving for Karnet in the morning. Would you like to come with me?" he said.

Chia seemed surprised when he asked. "I was so afraid you would abandon me here" she whispered.

"Why would I do something like that?" he asked.

"I'm demon-touched, disposable. All my kind is useful for is slave labor. That's why I was cast out" she said while holding back tears.

"You are not disposable! You are valuable and I will not abandon you" Drachus told her. He wasn't kidding. Even if they didn't realize it, children knew more about the locale that most thought.

On many jobs his best source of information came from chatting with the local kids.

Chia had already given him some useful information; he owed her for that. Besides, there wasn't even a shed here; if he left the kid behind she'd be living in the woods like an animal. If Karnet really was a 'village', there might be a family willing to take her in.

When she realized he was serious she began to cry. It took several minutes for her to calm down.

"I hope all this crying is just a phase; if you run out of tears, I'll have to find some way to refill them" he joked. For the first time since they'd met, Chia laughed out loud.

That afternoon Drachus went through the cultists' abandoned gear carefully. He found several clean and durable sacks, a blanket and a large silver flask. Before washing the sacks and blanket he hung them in campfire smoke to rid them of bugs.

The flask was a mystery. When he found it was full of clear liquid. Uncertain of what it was he poured it out. As he did a small glowing gem fell out; when he picked the gem up it bit his fingers like a bee-sting! He quickly dropped it.

"Have you seen anything like this?" he asked Chia.

"No, never" she said. As they spoke a small puddle of water formed around the gem. After rinsing and filling the flask at the fountain he'd seen the puddle had become much larger.

"Maybe the gem is making the water?" Chia said.

On a hunch Drachus emptied the flask and scooped the gem back into it. A few minutes later the flask was again full of cool, clean water. No matter how many times they emptied it, it always refilled in a few minutes.

They stayed at the shrine again that night; it had good food and clean water. Tomorrow they would start for Karnet. Chia was still too afraid to sleep alone; she spent the night curled inside his duster, clinging to his shirt sleeve once again.

Chapter 3

Hiking to Karnet Village

After breakfast they walked along an old road leading north. As they passed through the forest they filled the sacks with fresh fruits and nuts. The forest around the shrine was only a few miles deep; once outside of it their trail had merged with a wider but not-so-well-traveled road.

After a few hours walking through fairly desolate flat lands they encountered a tall earthen ridge. Rather than go through the pass the road led to Drachus climbed on top of it to get a good view of the surrounding area.

To the west he could easily see the mountains Chia had mentioned yesterday. They were currently walking through low foothills. The area alternated between small valleys separated by earthen ridges like the one he was currently atop. The valleys held regular patterns of ditches and elevated walkways between large flat areas that showed it had once been farmland. Every so often they would see a ruined manor house or farmer's cottage.

There were springs but they stank of sulfur; there were lizards and snakes crawling around them. Drachus didn't think they were safe to drink from. Fortunately, his silver flask was always full whenever they checked.

As they walked, Drachus carried Chia on his shoulders. Her injured knee made walking painfully slow for her; he washed and bandaged it often but without any real medical supplies that was all he could do.

Drachus was concerned about weight. He was carrying Chia and his gear – it all had to be over a hundred pounds. He'd once hauled an 85-lb 50-cal machinegun up a mountain trail; that had nearly done him in.

He could handle the cold (he was raised in Sweden) but heat could be an issue. Wearing a cuirass, his vest and the duster he worried about overheating but carrying Chia with his coat open he wasn't suffering. It was a bit warmer here than Sweden; he wondered how cold winter got. As they ate lunch he asked Chia "How hot does it get here?"

After a few moments thought, she said "After the new moon it'll be hotter but right now is just about right."

Not a professional meteorological assessment but if this was normal he wouldn't have any problems.

As they walked he insisted she wear his big slouch hat. "Look, you'll burn and I don't have any skin cream, so you'll have to wear the silly hat until we find one suitable for your little head" he said. As big as it was on him, on her head it was like a beach parasol!

"Why are you so pale anyway?" he asked.

"No one in the village wanted to even look at me; so they made me do all of my work at night" Chia said quietly. A few minutes later he noticed tears.

"What's wrong?" he asked. "Does your knee hurt?"

"Oh it's not that!" she replied. After a bit she added "No one ever cared about me before; you are so very sweet!"

They saw no one else all day as they walked. Drachus thought that was rather odd until Chia explained "This is a dangerous area. Merchants travel with guards due to bandits. It is summer now so they have to carry water to so the caravans only travel once a week or so."

'That does make sense' Drachus thought to himself.

Near sundown they stopped at an abandoned hut to spend the night. Chia once again wrapped up in his duster to sleep while he lay down on his fumigated blanket.

She would sometimes wake him at night with sudden movements. The first time he came awake with a pistol in hand, thinking some danger was near. Looking down he saw Chia twitch in her sleep as though she were having a nightmare. He heard her whimpering "please, no, it hurts."

'Poor girl must have been through hell even before that demon' he thought to himself. He patted her head saying "Don't worry kid; I'll keep you safe from now on." After he lay back down she tugged at his sleeve, as if to make certain he was still nearby.

This wasn't the last time she woke him due to nightmares; she always had tears in her eyes when it happened. He always made certain she could hold onto his sleeve, so she could tell he was nearby when it happened.

After three days he was getting worried about food; their supply of fruit and nuts was getting a bit low. On the morning of the fourth day the desolation seemed to fade and the condition of the land began to improve. Near midday they saw what looked like a large farm. There were fields for several miles and then a compound with wooden buildings surrounded by a low stone wall.

As they got closer he saw the compound held four medium-sized and one large building. The first building on his right was a barn with an attached corral with several horses. Next was a small two-story residence, probably for workers or traveling merchants staying overnight.

The first one on the left was a three-sided semi-outdoor workshop. There were several tables holding unidentified objects. A brick furnace that seemed to serve as both a kiln and blacksmith's forge stood towards the rear. There were fire pits with roasting meats on spits to the side.

The next building in appeared to be another inn but with armored men lounging in the shade out front Drachus assumed it was a barracks. The central building was the largest; obviously the trading-post itself.

He saw numerous folks working the fields – some of them rather short. 'I guess there are families here – some of the older kids are working the fields like normal. Maybe I can get a family to look after Chia. That will be a lot better for her than having me drag her around on the road' he thought to his self.

As they got closer Drachus saw a large sign over the main gate that read 'Karnet Trading'. Two men wearing leather armor with metal studs and swords were on guard at the front gate. Drachus had seen armor like theirs in museums – brigandine he thought it was called. The studs were actually rivets holding small metal plates on the inside; it was a bit heavy but good protection.

Their clothes weren't fancy but were in good repair. The men were tanned and muscular as expected of medieval warriors. He saw that they were sweating more than he was. 'I guess the locals call this hot' Drachus thought.

At the front gate one of the guards spoke up. "What's your business?" he asked. The man wasn't aggressive but he wasn't relaxed either. They had obviously seen him coming; it was a clear view of the road for several miles.

"Trade" Drachus responded simply.

At that, the guard glanced up at Chia saying "You know ... we're a freehold." After a few seconds with no answer the guard added "No slave trading." Obviously the guard had thought he was here to sell Chia; she was all he appeared to be carrying.

"Good; I don't like slave traders" Drachus said. Though it was illegal on his old world, he'd had to deal with their evil ilk on several occasions while raiding underground auctions. Some local 'recruiters' were not all that picky about how they got their workers.

With a grin the guard pointed to the big building. "The merchants are in there. Good Luck."

Drachus saw it was a three-story building at the center with one story annexes angling away from either side. On the left was a tavern along with a kitchen and bar. From the variety of merchandise he could see through its open doors and windows the one on the right was a general store of some sort.

There was a coach and four saddled horses in front of the tavern; a tween boy was watering the horses. Inside were four well-dressed men seated at an indoor table; four stocky men in polished brass armor sat at an outdoor table.

'Merchants and guards' Drachus thought.

There was a cargo wagon with two large water barrels and a pair of scruffy men in front of the trading post. 'Driver and groom' Drachus figured. It all looked like an old painting he had seen in a museum outside of Rome.

In the main building a small group of men were looking over a pile of crates and bundles in a central floor space between two counters. An older man in dusty clothes was receiving coins being counted out by a thin-faced man at the left counter. At the right counter two heavy-set men were poring over several sheets of brown paper and occasionally pointing to various bundles on the floor before making notes in a ledger. Further inside Drachus could see doors leading to offices and a stair leading up.

Drachus was surprised to see paper and ledgers; he thought those came after the medieval era. Recalling the two moons, he thought 'I guess there are more differences than I first thought; I'll have to be careful'.

When he entered, all the activity there stopped; they must have thought that a giant had just walked in. With Chia on his shoulders wearing his big hat they were so tall he'd had to duck down to clear the doorway.

The men's reactions went from momentary panic to amusement. As they returned to their work he set Chia down in a chair near the front wall.

"Wait here, I have business to do" he said quietly. Chia smiled with a nod, then took the hat and began to brush away smudges of dust.

As he walked up to the counter Drachus saw several small houses through an open door at the rear of the trading post. These were behind the main building so he hadn't seen them as he approached. Several women were working nearby doing laundry and watching small children.

'Good, there are families here' he thought. Chia would almost certainly be better off living here than traveling with him on the road. After all, he did attract rather violent people; it was an occupational hazard.

Drachus realized he didn't have much to trade; they needed most of what they had. The dead cultists' had no coins or other supplies; apparently they'd been dropped off expecting to die. The water flask, the bags, shaving kit and several of the daggers were all he'd kept.

The daggers were a foot and a half long and heavy but silver was worth money. Thirteenth rule for a successful mercenary; don't load up with unnecessary loot - it slows you down and that can be lethal.

A short man with a florid complexion came to the counter. He seemed to be in the early days of middle-age but his eyes were sharp and bright as a hunting hawk's. He reminded Drachus of Arevalo's armorer Kropatsche; he even looked a bit like him!

After seeing how tall Drachus was, Mr. Florid stepped up onto a small stool so their faces were closer together. In a pleasant voice he spoke. "Welcome to Karnet, good sir. Are you buying or selling today?"

Then it occurred to Drachus that everyone he'd seen here was short! Chia was a child so her small stature wasn't a surprise. The guards at the gate were strong, well-built men but they were a foot shorter than he was. The men in here were even shorter; the two at the counters were only inches over 5' tall. Drachus was taller than average but no one yet came close to his 6' 6" in height.

Realizing Mr. Florid was waiting for an answer Drachus reached into the pocket of his duster and pulled out a silvered dagger. "I'm selling today" he said.

The clerk was startled when his customer pulled out a weapon and glanced to his right. Following his gaze Drachus saw an armed guard behind a curtain chatting with a cute maid; for a moment the man was more alert. Both of the surprised men relaxed when Drachus placed the dagger on the counter and slid it to the clerk hilt first.

"Ah, a long dagger; there's always a market for these. And I see that it is silvered as well" Mr. Florid commented. The man's smile vanished from his face when the dagger cleared its sheath; the engravings on the blade must have identified its origins.

In less than a second Mr. Florid's eyes flicked up to Drachus, over to Chia and finally back to the dagger as if he were trying to guess what was going on here. This cult was obviously well-known - and feared.

"I'm sorry; my expertise doesn't extend to this ... Item. Have you something else ..." the clerk said nervously.

"Is there anyone here with the expertise? I don't like to be pushy but time does mean money" Drachus interrupted quietly.

Mr. Florid was sweating even though the breeze from the open doors made it comfortably cool in here. Drachus didn't want to force the issue but they needed local currency. After a pause Mr. Florid said "I do believe our senior merchant has experience with this ... *Item*."

Drachus realized 'Item' must be some sort of code word to call for the boss to come deal with a possible problem. Sure enough, looking around he saw the maid from before pointing him and Mr. Florid out to an older, well-dressed man who'd approached from off to his left.

After a quiet exchange with Mr. Florid the merchant took his place and examined the dagger. He sniffed the blade and then the scabbard, 'checking for poison' Drachus guessed. Then he ran a finger along the edge slowly and carefully checking for nicks.

The merchant started to ask "The previous owner ..."

"I burned what was left of him" Drachus interjected. Though not entirely true it wasn't a lie either; Drachus had destroyed the demon and the resulting firestorm had scorched some of the cultists' bodies. A quick smile flashed on the man's face; while feared this cult was not well-liked.

Placing the dagger on the counter he motioned for a reluctant Mr. Florid to come back and whispered something as he returned to the rear office.

After a few deep breaths Mr. Florid forced a smile. "Now Dear Sir, how much do you wish to obtain for this ... merchandise?" he asked.

"A fair price" Drachus responded.

Mr. Florid gulped yet again as he pulled a small steel box from below the counter and pulled out small silver coins. He placed a stack of six next to the dagger.

Drachus had no idea what the local coinage or dagger were worth but he'd bartered in primitive marketplaces often enough to hold his own. His lack of response to the initial offer brought 4 more coins to the table.

His raised eyebrow at that brought out 16 copper coins, 8 each in two sizes. Drachus didn't want to push too hard so he ended his barter by silent intimidation after a single, larger silver coin was added to the pile.

"That looks about right" he finally said.

"Thank you for your patronage good sir!" Mr. Florid practically sang as he put the coins in a small leather pouch and slid it across the counter to Drachus. As the mercenary pocketed that the clerk noted their transaction in his ledger.

Drachus was about to ask for directions to Laris when he saw a large map on the wall. Laris was well-marked as was the Midland River. It appeared that the road he and Chia had been walking along would run into the river and a road that ran parallel to it further ahead. They could follow that road all the way to Laris; if the map was fairly accurate they wouldn't get lost.

After studying it he saw the map was hand drawn; the large sheet was actually made up of a dozen smaller sheets glued together. Even if they had paper it wasn't from a factory; it was likely made by cottage industry.

Glancing at Chia another issue suddenly came to mind. "Excuse me, but does the store over there sell clothes?" he asked as he pointed to the other building.

"Yes, they do; though they don't have a very large selection" Mr. Florid said with a weak smile.

As Drachus picked up Chia and headed over to the store, he thought he heard a collective sigh of relief from those in the office as they exited. Once outside Chia asked "Did everything go well?"

"Great. Let's see if we can get you something prettier to wear than my second-hand shirt" said Drachus. He wasn't sure but he thought for a moment her expression looked a bit sad.

At the store they were greeted by a pleasant young woman in a clean dress. Her long dark brown hair was braided on both sides like Chia's – apparently that was the local custom. Chia's had hung down her back when he first saw her - that's why he had first thought her hair was short.

The clerk's braids popped in front as she curtseyed. "How can I help you sir?" she asked with a wide smile.

"I'm looking to get the young lady something practical to wear. It needs to be durable. She'll also need proper shoes" Drachus said as he pointed to Chia's ragged, badly worn sandals. If he dressed her in new clothes, it might be easier to convince someone to adopt her. If needed, he could also provide a bit of the coin he'd just received to improve the chances.

However, the girl frowned as she looked Chia over closely. "We don't carry a lot of clothes to begin with and even less in children's sizes. But if you have some time I can take her measurements and see if we can alter something down to fit her?"

"We're not in a really big rush but just how much time are we talking about?" he asked.

"Two or three hours; our seamstresses aren't very busy today. The measurements will take only a few minutes." she said.

"That's fine; in that case we'll have lunch across the way as you do the sewing" Drachus said.

The smiling clerk and Chia chatted as they went to the back. While he waited, Drachus asked a young stock boy working in the shop to collect traveling supplies for them; a week's worth of food, and a large water skin.

After Chia returned they went to the tavern for a real meal. If her tummy wasn't growling a new family might be more likely to accept her.

Even though half of the tavern was open air, it still had the typical array of aromas – burnt wood, cooked meat, stale beer and strange spices. After they sat down a young woman came over. She looked like a farm girl; sturdy and solid with plenty of youthful energy. So far, this seemed like it would be a fairly nice, safe place to leave Chia.

"What's your pleasure?" the waitress asked.

Seeing no menu Drachus asked "What's good?"

"Marrying a wealthy noble's son and getting out of here would be great" she quipped with a smile.

"How about for lunch?" he asked with a laugh.

"The kettles stew hasn't killed anyone … this week" she shot back with an even wider smile.

"Ok, we'll have two" Drachus replied with a grin. Suddenly he recalled he hadn't asked the shop clerk how much the clothes were going to be; he really needed to find out how much his coins were worth. He stopped the girl as she turned to go to the kitchen.

"What's that going to cost us?" he asked.

"Three coppers … and a few hours of heartburn" she said with a grin.

Drachus and the waitress shared another laugh as she walked away. He pulled out the leather pouch Mr. Florid had given him and showed it to Chia under the table.

"Which one's a copper?" he whispered.

She smiled pointing to the smaller of the two copper-colored coins. Before he could ask about the other coins the young waitress returned with their food. Seeing how hungry they were Drachus decided the other names could wait until after they ate their overly spiced lunch.

After the meal, they ate slices from one of the striped apples he'd picked in the shrine forest to kill a bit more time. Drachus saw Chia watching children playing out back. She probably never got to play much in her old village.

"Want to go out for some exercise?" he asked. As she glanced back over at the children he remembered. "Oh, your knee is probably ..."

"No it's fine. Miss Gillian used some nice medicine on it after she took my measurements; it doesn't hurt so much now" Chia said happily.

"Go ahead then; we've got time" he said with a grin.

Chia smiled and kissed his cheek as she left. He hoped the medicine was real and she wasn't so happy to play she was ignoring the pain. Drachus should have known better than to allow her to go running off but in his defense, he had forgotten how to deal with young children.

Over the next two hours the waitress chided the kids several times when their play got too noisy. During that time Drachus noticed an argument going on in front of the store across the compound. He recognized Miss Gillian, the young clerk, Mr. Florid and the senior merchant.

An older woman he hadn't seen before was berating Miss Gillian. The girl tried to appeal to the merchant several times but the old woman angrily cut her off each time. After several exchanges the merchant said something that made the old woman angry. That made the merchant angry and he gave her an order with a pointed finger.

The older woman grabbed the Miss Gillian by the hand and dragged her back to the store. Both men looked over to the tavern before returning to the trading post. Drachus felt this needed looking into but as he stood up a well-dressed young man approached his table; he recalled seeing the guy sitting with some older well-dressed men at another table.

"May I have a bit of your time, good sir?" he asked.

Drachus nodded and pointed to the empty seat, not wanting to raise suspicions by seeming to be in a rush. The Dragon Lord saw that the man's eyes paid particular attention to the embroidered dragons on his duster's cape as he sat down. His visitor seemed to be working up courage to say something so Drachus broke the ice.

"Was there something you want to know?" he asked.

The fellow seemed to welcome the opening. "Since you ask, I'll come straight to the point sir. Are you the Dragon Lord who recently destroyed the Demon Warlord Kreeger that had escaped from the Shrine of Hope?" As Drachus practically choked on his ale the young man continued.

"Your delightful companion has been fascinating my employer's nephew with the details of your exploits!"

Buying time to think by finishing a long draw from his ale Drachus frantically considered what to say. He knew some facts about religious places were too sensitive to blurt out. On a job in Peru a casual remark about a ruin he and his men had walked through had nearly gotten them all killed – the locals considered it a taboo place of evil! Ever since then, an alarm would go off in the back of his mind if he was going to talk about these sorts of places – like it was now.

He finally decided to bluff through the inquiry by mixing a little truth with some fiction. "Oh dear" he said "is little Ki making up stories again? I'm sorry but you know what kids can be like on long trips. My name is ... Drago Lors. After an old friend gave me that coat my niece has taken to calling me 'Dragon Lord' as a joke. I don't know where the rest of that story came from." It wasn't a great bluff but Drachus hoped that would cover it.

"Oh yes. I am Maras by the way and you are so right. I have three younger siblings and you would not believe the fantastic tales that explode from their fertile imaginations when they get bored!" the fellow added with a grin.

Before Drachus could relax, Maras' eyes narrowed. "By the way, wasn't the fruit you and the young lady enjoyed a stripple; the striped apple that can only be found growing in the forest at the Shrine of Hope?" he added.

'Verdamnt; I have to end this quick' thought Drachus.

"Is that what it's called? We passed through the forest and collected a few. There was a scorch mark by the fountain; I thought it may have been a lightning strike but Ki jumped to the conclusion the demon must have ..." he started. Drachus' voice trailed off as he realized that Maras wasn't buying this, not at all.

Storytelling on the fly had never been his forte; he decided to use intimidation to end the issue. Before he could speak, he heard a disturbance out front. With a glance he saw a big man dragging Chia by her hair; behind them were two shorter men and the bunch of kids from out back.

In front of the store the older woman and the young clerk watched the whole thing. The older woman was gloating while Miss Gillian seemed upset and about to cry.

"Verdamnt" he muttered. Standing and donning his duster Drachus said "I apologize but that is an issue I must deal with immediately."

Maras followed his gaze outside and exclaimed "Oh Dear" as he went back to his table.

The tavern waitress was at the doorway with an unhappy grimace twisting her young face. As Drachus passed her she cried "Hey you haven't paid!"

He pulled a small coin from his pouch without slowing down and tossed it back to her. He'd planned on telling her he'd pay the rest later.

"This is silver!" she called out in surprise.

"Keep the change" he growled instead.

As he approached the children spotted him and started chanting "It's the Dragon Lord! It's the Dragon Lord!" Laughing, the big guy with the nose that had been broken more than once tossed Chia down into the dirt.

Turning to his friends he gloated. "Look, the demon-touched's Draagooon Looord is gonna save her." The men laughed and the kids crouched in the dirt.

As Drachus approached he thought 'Demon-touched really are treated like dirt on this world. There is no way I'm gonna leave her here!'

He ignored the laughing trio and looked down at Chia. While shaking his head he spoke to the crying girl. "Idiots can't handle the truth. It's best to ignore them, to let them go about their way molesting sheep, little boys or pigs, whichever they prefer. However they choose to pass their sweaty nights is no concern of ours."

These men weren't the brightest but did realize they had just been royally insulted. From their scruffy appearance, foul odor and missing teeth Drachus assumed they were brawlers - farm workers not soldiers; they'd go for punches before weapons.

He expected that after a few insults the big one would strike; if he fell fast, the rest would run. That's usually how it worked with bullies. As if on cue the big one drew his fist back. Drachus quickly stepped in close and delivered an uppercut to the underside of the bully's jaw.

The Dragon Lord had learned this strike at a dojo, a martial arts training hall, in the Japanese port city of Osaka. He'd seen several foreign sailors accosting two local girls; the older sister had used it to great effect on one of the drunken attackers.

After he helped deal with the rest of the jerks, the girls invited him back to meet their uncle who ran the training hall. In gratitude for helping the girls, he had taught Drachus a few simple martial arts moves. This blow is delivered like an uppercut but not with a fist; you use the heels of both palms. That way, you can hit much harder without breaking your delicate little finger bones on the targets thicker and harder jaw bone.

Delivered properly, the blow slams the jawbone up often causing damage to the teeth, tongue and cheeks; it may even bounce the brain off the inside of the skull causing a concussion. It almost always results in a knockout. This blow can break the neck of a small opponent but Drachus wasn't worried; this bully was the tallest man he'd seen since arriving here, only a few inches shorter than himself.

The blow was delivered perfectly, so well the thug was lifted off his feet and flung back a full yard. He landed flat on his back raising a small cloud of dust. Drachus knew he'd hit properly but was surprised at how far the guy flew. The thugs' friends were laughing and telling him to get back up and fight but he remained motionless.

While the dust settled several guards walked over from the barracks and the kids ran back to the tavern; the funny show they'd expected to see had just turned into something that might be very dangerous for anyone nearby.

Drachus stood waiting with his arms down at his sides. The approaching men were all clean, muscular fellows wearing the same emblem on their brigandine as the gate sign. They were soldiers, not just brawlers; Drachus would have to handle them very differently.

"I suggest you get him to a healer" he began calmly. "The fellow may die anyway but you will at least have tried" he said as they drew their swords; they seemed to be quite surprised that Drachus was so calm.

Before their fight could start a woman screamed and there was a sudden shout of "Wolf!" From behind the tavern a small, sandy-colored wolf bolted into view headed to the outer wall with a lamb in its jaws.

Drachus had been standing with arms at his sides because he knew this might turn into a real fight; once he dropped the first thug it could involve weapons. He'd drawn his pistols as they laughed at the downed man and kept them hidden under the flaps of his open duster. Now he pulled one up, aimed and squeezed off a shot.

The report of the gunshot startled those in the compound even more than the yelp from the wounded wolf. It stumbled at the bullet impact and dropped the dead lamb. Then it watched, growling as Drachus slowly walked towards it. As the wolf seemed about to pounce he aimed and squeezed off a second shot. It hit the wolf in the head and it dropped dead with a loud yip.

Drachus holstered his pistols as he went back to pick up Chia. "If you will excuse us, the young lady and I have to finish shopping. I wasn't kidding about a healer" he said, calmly looking at the unconscious man; the brawler now had trickles of blood coming from his ears!

'I hit him hard' Drachus thought. "You should be quick unless you want him to die" he said turning towards the store. From their expressions he knew that between the Shuto and gunshots the men were intimidated enough not to stab him in the back.

As he approached he saw the shocked older woman run back into the store; Miss Gillian was waiting, all smiles.

Drachus glanced at Chia; the girl was smiling and crying simultaneously. "You need to not talk so much, starting right now" he chided her quietly, nodding to the waiting clerk.

"Oh she said she wouldn't tell on me" Chia said.

Of course the clerk would notice the girl's multi-colored eyes; she couldn't have missed them while taking measurements. The informant had been the older woman, despite the order from her boss not to cause trouble.

Apparently, not everyone on this world treated the demon-touched badly. Drachus decided he would have to give the girl a tip. Maybe that might convince others to be a bit nicer as well in the future but he still wasn't going to leave Chia here; it was too likely she might be abused again.

After Chia had gone to the back with Miss Gillian Drachus looked outside and saw the compound was empty but for a slowly settling cloud of dust. The wagon, the coach and all four riders had suddenly departed.

The brawlers were nowhere to be seen but two of the regular guards stood in front of the barracks watching the store. The third guard was in the trading post speaking with the senior merchant and Mr. Florid.

Stepping to the side where he was hidden from their view Drachus checked and reloaded with loose lead rounds; since a wolf wasn't a demon, he'd used the pistol with the normal lead ammo. Then he watched the guards and waited to see what would come next.

After a few minutes Chia and Miss Gillian returned. The sleeveless dress could never be called high fashion but it was sturdy and clean.

Drachus grinned when he realized they had taken an old army dress uniform tunic and adjusted it to fit her like a jumper – using the original sleeves as legs. The red tunic still had the stiff black leather collar and gold shoulder braid; she almost looked like a toy soldier!

Having seen him carrying Chia on his shoulders when they arrived, the clever clerk had told the seamstresses to fashion a skirt split like trousers. Her new sandals had a thick sole but were two sizes too big; their straps had freshly-punched holes so they could be tightened enough. Even with that, she had to wear several pairs of socks to make them fit her tiny feet!

The smudges from being dropped in the dirt had been cleaned; they'd brushed her hair and even given her a pretty hair ribbon. Her light brown locks now flowed down her back unbraided.

Behind them came the same young boy from before, now even more nervous. He carried a bag with the supplies he'd ordered; dried meat, cheese and a large water bag.

As he collected the sack with their supplies he saw Chia was holding his hat which someone had retrieved from the tavern; inside was his folded white shirt. Smiling, he pulled it out and put it into the shoulder bag. Seeing another pale bundle he pulled that out as well; this was a set of new underwear for the now-blushing girl. With a quiet growl Drachus put those in the bag too. Then he pulled out his coin pouch.

"How much do we owe?" he asked the young clerk.

Before she could respond Mr. Florid called from the doorway. "Thank You for Your Business Kind Sir - There Is No Charge for Today's Transactions!" then ducked back and ran to the office.

Smiling even wider Drachus realized the merchants were a bit scared but he was still outnumbered; he might still have to kill a bunch of guards to get out alive. He decided to execute a grand gesture as he exited, to ensure that didn't happen. Since these were merchants, he knew it should be related to money. With a sudden inspiration he tossed the entire coin purse to Miss Gillian.

"You are as kind as you are lovely. I am grateful for your help here today" he said. He never had been good at holding on to money and planned on tipping her anyway.

She was quite surprised but caught it with a smile even brighter than the waitress and curtsied as they turned to leave. After they stepped from the store Drachus hoisted Chia onto his shoulders, she put on his silly hat and they headed out the gate.

After about 20 minutes, Drachus spotted movement to his right. He saw two men with water bags jogging to the northeast. Remembering the capitol was that way he figured they were on their way to tell the authorities what had happened at Karnet today.

"I wonder just how much truth will be in their report about the dangerous, evil 'Dragon Lord'" he muttered.

"Oh you're not evil or dangerous; you're nice" Chia chimed in with a wide grin and a few new tears. Then she added "You really are wonderful you know; no one has ever bought me new clothes before!"

Drachus hoped they could travel far enough and fast enough that medieval communications wouldn't have people lying in wait for them somewhere down the road.

By The Way – What became of the rescue mission?

After Twerle and the girls made their escape out back they did safely meet up with the men carrying the soup and warm clothes. Though he hadn't lit the flares one of the men was a hunter who had spotted Drachus' tracks in the snow; as he followed those they met up with the fleeing girls. The girls were dressed quickly enough to avoid any injuries from the cold and were safely escorted back to town.

As Mr. Cuirass penetrated the front gates with a charge of blasting powder supplied by Kropatsche, a huge fire started by the failed summoning spell began gutting the main keep. No cultists' survived; as Drachus had predicted many fought to the death; those who didn't died in the fire.

Katarina Arevalo refused to leave home ever again, so she didn't return to school. After she identified Twerle le Moineau as one of her rescuers, Señor Arevalo hired her as a tutor (babysitter) for his distraught daughter.

With a lot of encouragement from Señor Arevalo, Twerle spent much of her time with young Arevalo helping him recover too. She didn't have much luck interesting him in fatherhood but his many paintings of the petite beauty (most of them nude) did sell quite well. After each failed seduction, the passionate lady would salve her frustration with a 'riding lesson' from a big, strong stable hand.

Despite her later marriage the traumatized and perpetually fearful Katarina had a lot of difficulty, often falling into fits of crying melancholy. Trina never did fully recover from the ordeal, though she did have three sons to ensure the family line would continue.

The townsfolk worried the girls had been touched by evil; they were not welcomed back with open arms. Instead, they became Arevalo servants. Eventually marrying some of his retainers, they led relatively happy lives.

Even after a thorough search, the only traces of Jakob Roy Drachus they found were empty shell cases and Prideaux loaders in the ashes. They found his clothes, neatly folded in the old ammunition warehouse. What became of him is still a mystery to his former employers.

They were rather pleased that they didn't have to pay him; such is the common epitaph of a mercenary.

CHAPTER 4

WHAT DID THOSE MESSENGERS SAY ABOUT ME?

After leaving Karnet, Drachus walked towards Laris carrying Chia on his shoulders. Over the next three days, they saw few travelers. On the second day they were passed by a caravan but it was going the wrong way; neither felt like returning to Karnet.

On the third day 12 men in blue armor on armored horses passed them moving quickly; they held their lances up with pennants flying. Drachus thought 'That must be tiring' until he saw the lances' butts were in heavy leather cups hanging from their saddles; like a flag carrier harness worn during parades. The men just had to keep them upright. They appeared to be more of an honor guard than actual protection.

These men were escorting a coach. Drachus thought the crest on it was similar to the one he'd seen on the gate at Karnet. However they were also going to wrong way. The polished blue armor and barding trimmed in yellow (under a thin coat of road dust) matched the color scheme of their lances and pennants. Drachus thought they might be Holy Knights; the colors seemed too decorative for army issue.

"I've never seen a Holy Knight so I can't say. I did see a noble's coach pass through my old village once. There were men in dark armor riding behind it" Chia told him.

As they passed Drachus saw the saddles had no stirrups. 'That explains the squires in the wagon. Without stirrups, it must be a bitch to fight from horseback in heavy armor' he thought.

On the plus side Drachus' water flask always refilled. In addition to the foods in the shoulder bag, there was a small ceramic jar with a dark yellow cream inside.

"That's Rosen Salve; Miss Gillian gave me some. You use it to treat boo boos!" Chia told him.

Drachus used it on her knee each morning before they began walking and again each night before they went to sleep. Not only did Chia say it reduced the pain, the injury seemed to heal quicker than he'd expected. It also didn't get infected – that was a big concern; infections could be lethal – especially in a medieval world!

Late each day they would stop at an abandoned farmhouse or barn for shelter. As always, Chia would wrap up in Drachus' duster to sleep curled up in a ball next to him while holding his shirt sleeve. It seemed less often but she would still jerk in her sleep; she had tears in her eyes each time so he assumed she was still having nightmares.

On the fourth morning they were walking through a tight pass in a ridgeline when Drachus heard a high-pitched screech loud enough to echo; he thought it was the cry of a bird of prey. Moments later men appeared from behind dirt ridges. Since they were arrayed to his front and rear, Drachus saw they were trapped. Since most of the two dozen carried poor quality weapons and wore more rags than armor he realized they were just low level bandits.

'They are better organized than most; that screech must have been their signal' he thought.

This could be a problem, even with pistols. There was Chia to consider; he decided to try and talk their way out with no bloodshed. While he looked over the bandits he sat Chia on the ground between roadside boulders for cover.

Finding the leader wasn't hard; moments after he left Chia an ugly guy rode up on a horse. Drachus looked him in the eye. "I know the answer is pretty obvious but what do you boys want?" he said in a low, bored tone of voice.

The tall thug with rotten teeth and a white scar on his cheek smiled. "Impressive! How could you tell I was the biggest bad-ass here?"

"A thug leader is always going to keep the best loot for his self" Drachus said. Without mentioning the horse he pointed to the man's weapon adding "That sword on your back is a bit better than the crap the others have, so that makes you their boss."

He hoped to goad the leader into combat and take him out quickly; that would usually kill the morale of thugs. If he could make them break ranks there wouldn't be much fighting; if they fled it would keep Chia safe. While he was thinking of another insult to use on the bandit leader, Drachus saw shadows on the ground; two men were sneaking up behind him.

When they were close enough he took a step backwards, spun and knocked one out with a Shuto just like in Karnet the other day. Drachus managed to impress himself as he grabbed the thug's dropped club in midair and with two swings beat the other bandit senseless with it.

The bandit leader smiled; he seemed impressed too. "Kraal, why don't you and your brothers have a go at him? You can't do any worse than those two" he said with a grin.

As three better armed thugs moved to surround Drachus he threw the club at the biggest one who was closing in on him first. As he ducked the thrown weapon Dragon Lord stepped forward, kicked him in the groin, took the sword from the cringing man's grasp and used it to kill one of the others. When he turned to deal with the last one he heard a shout from above.

Looking up Drachus saw falling stars dropping down on top of the bandits to his rear like a bunch of mortar rounds! As they hit, the bandits started shouting, running away and dying.

'More weird magic' he thought. After a demon summoning, being transported to a whole new world by an angel and a demon disappearing in flames Drachus had become almost accustomed to bizarre happenings like these. Magic mortar rounds almost seemed routine by comparison.

Looking to where the voice that had come from, above to his right Drachus saw a girl with long blonde hair. She stood at the ravine's ledge wearing a lavishly-decorated outfit; the many layers of brightly-colored cloth fluttered in the midday breeze. "She must be sweating her butt off" Drachus muttered.

Smiling at the chaos, she waved a glowing scepter. "Pierce their filthy hearts - Divine Starlight!" she shouted and another round of falling stars began killing bandits.

Seeing Chia was at the edge of this beaten zone, Drachus dashed over to cover her. He felt something hit his back but didn't feel like he'd been hurt. Laughing like she was having a grand old time the crazy little blonde dropped a third salvo, oblivious that Chia was in the middle of it.

Furious about her careless attack Drachus yelled up at her. "Cut it out; there's an innocent girl down here!"

The blonde seemed to be surprised that he was still alive. After a moment she pointed the scepter directly at him. "Slay the evil before me - Holy Lance of Divine Light!" she shouted. Something like a long spear made of sparkling light shot from the golden wand straight at him.

Though it was fast he could have dodged it but then it would hit Chia. The other lights hadn't hurt so he took it straight on. Like before, when it hit he felt a sting but was unharmed. That seemed to shock the little blonde.

Hearing Chia crying behind him, Drachus snapped. Furious as he was, the man wasn't about to shoot a little girl, even if she was slinging lethal lightning. Picking up a softball-sized dirt clod he hurled it at the crazy spell caster instead. "Cut that out!" he shouted.

Dodging the dirt-rock caused the little blonde to slip; she slid down the wall of the ravine landing on her butt in a most undignified manner - just a few feet away from Drachus. He stomped over to her to take her shiny stick away – it seemed to be shooting the deadly lights.

Grabbing the thing he felt a shock in his fingers, as though he had touched a live electrical wire. Startled he tossed the stick away then glared at the girl. Frightened by the tall, angry man looming over her, she grabbed a small silver whistle on a chain around her neck and blew a loud, shrill note.

Hearing an answering whistle from his left Drachus turned to see a twin column of men in silver armor on silver-armored horses galloping around the bend.

They wore gear like the armored men who had passed them yesterday; just silver instead of blue. Figuring her 'Holy" this and that meant the little blonde was a priestess, he assumed these were Holy Knights.

The lead knights lowered their lances and with loud shouts they charged. Seeing he still had a few seconds before they would get to him Drachus drew his lead-loaded pistol. "This is either going to very good or very bad" he muttered as he slowly fired four shots into the air. Since he'd seen no firearms here, he hoped the horses would not be acclimated to gunfire like modern cavalry horses.

At the sound of the 'thunder' echoing in the ravine they began to buck and jump. As the knights fought to control their mounts, they fell one after the other, stunned and unable to get up quickly in their heavy armor. Seeing her knights neutralized the frightened little blonde scooted along the ground, backing-away as fast as she could.

Still furious Drachus holstered his pistol as he followed her. Once close he saw she was younger than he'd first assumed; she wasn't even much bigger than Chia! Angry as he was he couldn't hurt a little girl.

Since she didn't have her stick, and her knights were crawling around on the ground, she likely wasn't dangerous anymore. As he stood wondering what to do next the fear left her pretty face leaving her now just confused. Suddenly her brown eyes went wide as she let out a very un-ladylike scream and rolled to her hands and knees.

"Ow; that hurts!" the girl cried. As she crawled away Drachus saw dark red things swarming her backside; she had sat on an ant's nest! Fearing the big biting bugs might be poisonous and she couldn't brush them off herself, he grabbed for the girl.

"Ow! Don't touch me! Ow!" she cried as she twisted to avoid him. She was also trying to shake off the ants at the same time; her struggles were just making things worse. Drachus grabbed the skirt of the overly-decorated dress and used it to hoist her up from the ground.

Pulling her over to the road away from the ants, he heard a loud tearing sound. Now he understood how she could wear this outfit in the heat without sweating half to death; the thin material was gauze-like – and weak.

Suddenly he was holding halves of what had been her dress; she was standing there in only a gilded cowl, lacy lingerie and short boots! His first thought was 'What kind of church lets a priestess dress like a Parisian Tart?"

Seeing ants crawling in the dress, Drachus threw it to the road side and shook the remaining critters off his hands.

The little blonde seemed to be in shock; he could see her legs involuntarily twitching so he assumed she was still being bitten. Drachus turned her around, knelt down and pulled out his handkerchief.

He had to be careful; he really was trying to help, not just get a quick grope! After a few seconds of him brushing ants away the priestess issued a scream of rage, incredibly loud for such a small girl. It panicked some of the horses that had only just settled down from the gun-shot thunder.

"Molester! Pedophile! Pervert!" she shouted at the top of her lungs after jumping away from him. Seeing her scepter nearby, she ran over. After grabbing it, she pointed it at him shouting "Spay the weevil .... Slay the dilvi.... Slay the evil before me, Holy Lance of Divine Light!"

She was so upset it took her three tries to get it right. As before, the spear had no effect on Drachus. So many ants were crawling in the pieces of what had been her dress it appeared to shift in the roadside dirt. As that movement caught her eye, her anger was redirected and intensified.

"I-I-I call upon the fires of perdition - Flame Storm!" she shouted. A tiny tornado of flames appeared at the tip of her scepter and grew to the size of a tree as it flew towards the ants. She kept it spinning on top, burning the ants for some time before allowing it to dissipate. When she was done, the dress and the ants were nothing but ashes.

As she stood catching her breath she calmed down a little. Finally realizing she was standing there in nothing but her underwear and ankle boots, the girl saw her nearly-naked self was exposed to the view of Drachus and several of her men. With another shrill scream she turned and ran to a coach which had followed her knights along the road.

She must have been running with her eyes closed; she ran face first into the door. It closed as she fell to her knees. Glaring at the coachman she shouted "Open the door right; you useless fool!" When he did she clambered in and slammed it shut.

Checking out her rear quarter as she ran, Drachus saw the ants were gone but some of the bites were already swelling.

"Before you sit down you should treat those bites; those ants may have been poisono..." he shouted.

Her sudden, painful scream of "Ow!" was only lightly muffled by the coach as was her following shout of "You Beast!"

As he shook his head Chia limped over to tug his sleeve. "Is she going to be all right?" the worried girl asked.

Drachus turned to reply and saw several Holy Knights nearby, staring, totally amazed at what had just transpired right before their very eyes. They didn't seem to be about to attack, so he spoke to the nearest one.

"Hey; she is a priestess, right? Can she do healing on herself?" he asked. At his questions two nodded yes. He turned back to Chia.

"Yes, she'll be fine; a bit embarrassed but otherwise fine" he said to reassure the little kid.

Chia smiled, relieved saying "That's good."

Three nearby knights pointed at the coach and whispered among themselves for a bit before the shortest walked to the door with a scowl.

"Do you need any help, milady?" he asked.

"Go away! Ow! It hurts!" she screamed.

Grinning in relief the knight walked over to help with gathering up the spooked horses - apparently she wasn't a popular boss so her men didn't seem to be in any hurry to help. "Is she always this way?" Drachus asked the two who hadn't gone to talk to her. They looked around, as if to make sure no officer was listening.

"To be honest, she's usually worse" one of them said. Feeling sorry for the men – he'd drawn escort duty for nasty bosses more than once his self - Drachus shook his head as he went to make certain the ants were dead.

As he checked he saw something shiny in the ashes. He found several gold, silver and copper coins; her purse had been in the dress. Knowing they'd need cash, he pocketed the coins. As he did Chia looked on with a disapproving glance.

"She tried to kill us; I saved her from the poisonous ants; giving us a little traveling money is the least she can do" he said. Chia didn't look convinced but said nothing.

Drachus decided there wasn't any reason to hang around here. As he looked about, he saw the horse the bandit leader had been riding was still tied to some scrub brush. It hadn't even tried to get away from the 'thunder'.

He had never been in the cavalry but he did know how to ride. Once he got close enough he realized it was an old, sway-back nag. It was impressive for a bandit but it would have been long-since retired at most riding schools on his old world.

'Well, better than nothing' he thought. Untangling the reins he led it to a young knight who was giving orders. "I'm claiming this" he said.

It appeared the knight was going to argue but an older one nearby cleared his throat and tilted his head to the half-dozen injured men on the ground waiting to be treated. The young officer thought better of arguing about it.

"Well, it's not one of ours; that will be fine" he said.

Drachus led the horse to a large rock. He climbed on the rock and slid onto the saddle. Muttering "idiot saddles with no stirrups," he motioned for Chia to climb on the rock and he lifted her into the saddle behind him.

They slowly made their way through the battlefield debris of dead bandit bodies – including the ugly bandit leader. Reaching him Drachus stopped the horse for a moment as he stared at the sword on the thug's back. It had several spots where the gold gilding had worn off. "I doubt it's even worth the effort" he muttered and left it there as they headed down the road towards Laris.

Far from where this battle was fought there was a small circular cavern. Its walls were lined by amethyst gems, some in light, pale violet and others in shades of purple so dark they almost seemed to be black. At the center there stood three tall columns of pure, clear crystal. Floating within were the glowing images of three beautiful angels.

Two of the images smiled as the center spoke. "Sister, I was unsure at first but I now concur. He may be exactly what this world needs." The one on the left nodded.

"Dear sisters, he's only just begun!" the one on the right said with an amused laugh.

"I was surprised you could move your scrying from the shrine to that little silver trinket" the one on the left said. After an even larger sly smile appeared on her pretty face the other two looked concerned.

"Well, we should be vigilant. He is wandering in an unfamiliar world; he may yet need further assistance from us. We must be prepared to do all we can to assist him with his efforts – for his mission of course."

Their quiet groans made it clear they weren't certain of her motives; apparently not all angels are well-behaved.

As they rode along, Drachus loaded with lead rounds. He put the empty cases back into the Prideaux loader and the loader back into his pouch. After that, he began to quietly think. He was so quiet it worried Chia.

"Is there something wrong?" she asked.

After a moment Drachus smiled and replied "No, just thinking. Do you know anything about this Laris place?" he asked. Not really listening he mulled over the things that were bothering him.

Firstly, these 'Holy Knights' didn't behave in a very 'knightly' manner; there was absolutely no chivalry. Drachus thought that might just be a reflection of their unpleasant boss so he decided to let that go for now.

Thinking about the results of the last few fights, he was pleasantly surprised. Drachus knew he was better trained and more experienced than those he'd fought so far but he'd done a bit too well. Killing the demon was luck and taking out the Karnet bully was too quick to be sure.

This fight had gone on for a bit and he'd had multiple opponents. He was sure his reactions were faster than before; back on his old world he could never have taken out so many that quick without gunfire, not even thug bandits!

He had been carrying Chia without issues and after that last dust-up, he wasn't even winded; he obviously had more stamina now. The angel who brought him here said she would 'grant what aid I can'.

Remembering the hot and cold flashes he'd felt while 'falling' to get here and the stiff muscles he'd had for days after, he wondered what else she had done to him besides putting that little silver trinket on his vest.

After slowly riding for a few hours they turned onto the riverside road. As they rode along it they encountered more foot traffic. Most of those they encountered were small groups; these well-armed and often heavily armored individuals had a variety of gear that rarely ever matched.

Chia said they were likely adventurers on quests. They eyed the odd pair with some suspicion but no hostility. There were some very fearful individuals who avoided them whenever possible and several small groups of well-guarded merchant wagons. No one seemed to think the two of them were worth investigating so they had no difficulties.

After the horse began to limp Drachus had walked alongside with Chia sitting atop it. They stopped late that day at a crossroads inn and he had the stable master look at the beast. "A stone bruise; it'll take several days for that to heal up" the grizzled old man told him.

The innkeeper inside added more bad news. "I'm full. Two coppers a night for the stable; plus one for meals."

Even a stable was cleaner than the abandoned houses they'd been using, so Drachus was OK with that.

He didn't want to stay until the horse healed though. "How about one night plus meals for the two of us and you keep the horse" he said.

The innkeeper quickly agreed; it was a sway-back nag but the saddle was worth more than three coppers.

The meal was stew and rye bread. As before, Chia curled up next to him as she slept. Drachus was certain now that she had fewer nightmares that night. He hoped so; it would be nice if the little kid could start getting over all the previous drama in her young life. He hated drama!

They left on foot the next morning and arrived at Laris late mid-afternoon two days later. They made quite a stir as they walked through the outskirts approaching the city proper. Drachus heard several people gasp as they wondered if the 'really tall guy' was 'The Dragon Lord'.

"How'd they hear about me so fast?" he muttered as they stopped at a guard post. "Is there a hotel nearby?" he asked the armored young man on duty. It took a bit to get an answer; the fellow was staring at the strange sight of grinning Chia on his shoulders under that silly floppy hat.

The guard eventually just pointed straight ahead and muttered "Main Square." Drachus was glad she was there – her legs hid the embroidered dragons on his duster; otherwise they'd be obvious.

"Thanks" Drachus replied as he headed off. As they approached the center of town, it became clear Chia had never been to a big city before; she looked about gasping "Oohs!" and "Aahs!" every few seconds.

After Drachus felt her tummy rumble he realized he was hungry too. Locating a food cart by the aroma of roasting meat and some sort of spicy sauce, he bought them what looked like small meatball sandwiches. It was pretty tasty and Chia "Yum'd!" a lot before she'd finished hers.

"That was so good!" she said with a wide smile. He couldn't be certain but he thought her teeth were a bit less yellow than before.

When he first met Chia, he had noticed her teeth weren't the best. She was missing several molars, one front tooth was cracked and the rest were all yellowed. With medieval dental hygiene, that wasn't odd.

Drachus recalled the striped fruits from the shrine forest caused a nice tingling sensation as they ate them; it reminded him of using high grade tooth powder. He thought the fruit might have some sort of cleansing effect on the teeth while you ate it. Maras had said they only grew at the shrine but they were known, so maybe he could buy some; they only had two left.

'I'll save the seeds of these last two; maybe we can plant some wherever we end up. Medieval dentistry will be very painful!' he thought.

The city seemed odd as they walked in. Unlike most medieval cities this one had no outer walls. There was no central castle or fortress; the guard post had been nothing more than a small stone building next to the road. The buildings looked fairly new and were built in the same architectural style. The main road was well-paved but had a lot of wear and tear from heavily-laden wagon traffic.

Apparently Laris was a relatively new city constructed for the purpose of trade.

He noted the prevalence of large glass windows in the shops along the way. The panes were 2-3' on a side and had few swirling distortions caused by medieval glass blowing. Plate glass shouldn't be common here.

Drachus had seen in some of the more backwards areas he'd worked that a craftsman would blow a large cylinder of glass then cut it open and flatten it while it was still hot enough to be malleable. Given the size, number and quality of the plates he knew this city of 10,000 or so must be pretty wealthy to buy so many that were this big.

About two miles in from the gate at the main square, Drachus spotted and entered the tallest hotel there; it was fittingly named 'The Apex'.

There were placards at the main entrance that Chia said showed it was a hotel. The upper had a well-painted image of a fancy plate flanked by a spoon and fork. Below it was a second placard with an image of a bed. Illiteracy here was common, even among the wealthy!

Setting Chia on the floor he walked to the reception desk. There was a balding man standing there who was far too old to be just a clerk; Drachus figured he was a manager. The man's face adopted a typical customer service smile as he approached.

"Welcome, sir. Shall it be a room for yourself and the young lady?" the manager asked politely.

"Yes, that's why I'm here" Drachus said casually.

At that response Chia spoke up with some surprise. "I get a room too? Dragon Lord, you really are so sweet!" Wondering where demon-touched usually slept Drachus saw the manager react after hearing her say 'Dragon Lord'; as the man glanced at the dragons on the duster's cape, his suddenly sweaty face went pale.

"Don't worry. My name is ... Drago Lors. Ever since I was stuck with this silly coat my niece has been calling me the 'Dragon Lord'. It's sort of a joke" Drachus said with a laugh. The manager wasn't convinced but some of the color did return to his face.

"I'd like a suite with a bath on the highest floor available" Drachus said. As an experienced traveler he knew that mice, burglars, bugs and other common irritations of backward city life tended to stay close to the lower floors; higher up there was a lot less of these to deal with.

Glancing at Chia's odd dress and Drachus' dusty coat the manager flashed a snide smile. "Well Sir, Our Imperial Suite on the very top floor is available at one Solar per night. We do have less expensive rooms on lower floors."

As Drachus laid out the coins from the crazy blonde's dress he heard a gasp of surprise from the manager. Assuming they had more money than he'd first guessed he smiled. "We'll take it. How soon can you have a nice, clean hot bath ready?" he asked as the manager slid a small gold coin from the pile into his sweaty palm.

"I'll have one prepared immediately, sir!" he said.

Drachus pocketed the remaining coins and followed the manager up the nearby stair, both matching little Chia's slower pace. The ceiling of the stairway was too low for her to ride on his shoulders, even without the hat.

At a second floor landing the manager opened an unmarked door. "Hot Bath, Imperial Suite, NOW!" he hissed to a maid inside. She scampered to stairs on the other side of the room grabbing what looked like a fancy silver dipper hanging on the wall as she left.

The manager closed the door and they continued slowly up to the fifth floor as he prattled with the blah-blah of services the hotel staff would be happy to provide. As he had expected, the higher up they went, the cleaner the air smelled. This suite obviously didn't get rented often. Even with windows open, it was stuffy - though it was clean.

The manager gave them a tour; the suite had a balcony, sitting room, large bedroom, small bedroom, tiny servant's bedroom, lavatory and a bath. The clean, hot water in the overly-decorated claw foot tub had steam rising from it. Then the manager took his leave.

Drachus realized the fancy dipper must have been some magic device; slow as they had walked there was no way the maid could have filled a big tub with just that!

"You should have a bath first. It has been two weeks since we left the Shrine" he told Chia. She seemed reluctant so he added "Don't give me a hard time about who goes first. And quit calling me Dragon Lord; it scares people! Just call me Drachus."

"Yes, Dragon Lord Drachus" Chia giggled as she limped to the bath. Drachus just groaned and sat down to think. A minute later he recalled the hotel did laundry.

"Hey, give me your dress and I'll take it down and have it washed." As Chia started to protest he said "It would be a waste of time to put on dirty clothes right after you just had a bath, wouldn't it?" She couldn't argue that and tossed out her dress. A few seconds later her new underwear flew out too.

"I've never worn these before; I always wondered what it would be like. They are really soft" she called out.

After rolling her undies in the dress, Drachus went downstairs. The manager assured him a maid could have them clean within the hour.

Almost exactly one hour later, with Chia freshly bathed, knee re-bandaged and in clean clothes, they came down the stairs. The manager stood at the desk talking with two maids, the bath filler and a younger one. As they approached the manager smiled from ear-to-ear.

"How can we can be of any further service to you this day, good sir?" he asked.

"Is there a nice clothing store nearby where I can get the young lady attired more appropriately?" he asked.

"Cottlewinds is an excellent store. Go east for 10 minutes. You can't miss it; I'm certain you'll be satisfied with the results from that establishment" the manager said. Behind him Drachus saw both ladies shaking their heads.

"Thank you" he said turning to leave.

"Excuse me, sir" called the younger maid. "You have some dust; Let me take care of it for you."

As the older maid talked with the manager to distract him the younger brushed at the imaginary dirt to whisper "Tofferd's is just past there; they make better children's clothes quicker and won't cheat you."

Out of the manager's view Drachus pulled out a small gold coin – which he'd just learned was called a Solar – and dropped it into her apron pocket. "Thank you dear" he said as she gave a wide-eyed smile. Recalling the reactions the staff had been giving, he worried if he was throwing too much money around.

"I hope it doesn't cause any trouble" he muttered.

Drachus easily found a big shop with large glass windows and a fancy sign that said 'Cottlewinds'. Two doors down was smaller shop with small windows and a plain sign labeled 'Tofferd's'. As he ducked under the door jamb and stepped into the smaller sweet-smelling atelier he was greeted by a pretty young tween in a green dress; she bore a strong resemblance to the ladies back at the hotel.

'Nepotism is alive and well in Laris' he thought. "I'd like to get the little lady fitted for clothes better suited for walking in the city." Drachus said as he set Chia down.

"Well yes; sturdy as play-clothes are a lovely young lady should have finer attire for city life" the girl said.

After a moment the mercenary recalled that dressing little kids up to 'play soldier' was a practice he'd seen in many wealthy households. Chia's dress had been an old military tunic altered into a makeshift dress by the Karnet seamstresses; that's likely what the clerk was referring to.

"What sort of budget do we have to work with, sir?" the girl asked after smiling at Chia.

Drachus fished the coins from his pocket and looked to see just how much of what he had left. He had one small gold coin (a Solar), one large silver and a dozen coppers.

Thanks to a shopping trip to buy clothes for a lady-friend in Paris, Drachus knew women's clothes could be very expensive. He was going to use the Solar when he noticed that this silver was different from the other ones.

They had been smaller, had a castle on one side and a woman's face on the other. This one had another building, likely a cathedral as it looked more religious than militant. The other side was embossed with a six-pointed starburst, like the shrine fountains.

It was too heavy to be tin or zinc and he was sure it was larger than the other big silver he'd seen so it was probably worth more. However, since it was silver it wouldn't be worth as much as the gold coin. "This should do, I think" he said as he handed it to the girl. Her face blanched and he thought she was going to faint.

In a rather shaky voice the young clerk said "Just-just one moment sir, and I'll fetch Master Tofferd - immediately!" and darted behind a curtain. Less than a minute later she returned following a slender over-dressed man with slicked-back hair, a neatly trimmed goatee and a long mustache. Seeing Drachus he immediately broke into a wide smile.

"Good sir, you intend to spend an *entire* Holy Star on clothes for the young lady?" he practically giggled.

'Not knowing how much these coins are worth is really becoming an issue' Drachus thought to himself. With a forced smile he replied. "Why yes, that should do it."

From the way he was grinning, Drachus figured Tofferd thought he had just won a lottery. "Marla dear, please take the lady to the back for measurements. Let us see what we have ... what we can do for her that might be suitable!" The smiling Marla took Chia's hand and headed towards the rear of the shop. Immediately seeing the girl limping, Marla altered her steps so her dear new - and apparently very wealthy - little customer wouldn't be inconvenienced.

Tofferd himself was being a pest, hovering about offering wine, snacks and anything else he thought his *very* valued customer might like. Drachus had other ideas.

That Paris shopping trip had shown him that buying women's clothes was not only expensive it could take a REALLY LONG TIME! Rather than wait here, he had better things to do.

"Pardon me, Master Tofferd" he interrupted. "Can you recommend a ... discrete and reliable dealer in artistic collectibles? I passed several along the way but I'm new in town and didn't recognize any of the names. I have some business to transact and rather than rush things here I thought to take care of that while you dress my niece."

"Why of course sir!" Tofferd said. "Nolemande is the most discrete and reliable dealer I know of in the entire kingdom. His shop is but a few moments from here." Drachus remembered seeing a shop by that name.

"Is that the one with the mermaid?" he asked.

"Oh yes" Tofferd responded. "I adore that sculpture; I might even be able to convince him to sell it to me now ..."

Drachus stopped his ramble with another question. "How long will it take for a single outfit, one suitable for dining at a nice restaurant? Again, not that I wish to rush you but I'd like to see we leave in time to enjoy a nice dinner. We have been traveling all day."

"I understand completely! One lovely dinner ensemble should require an hour, perhaps less. With her measurements and a proper fitting ..." Tofferd started to ramble until Drachus stopped him again.

"Fine, I'll be back in an hour or so." He left amid a bunch of flowery salutations and headed for Nolemande's.

Drachus found the shop in just a few minutes. He wished he'd remembered it due to superior reconnaissance skills - but in reality it was the mermaid sculpture in the front window that had stood out. It was large, nearly as big as Chia and quite detailed, especially her ample bosom. A clever twist of her lower body meant that from outside the store you could not see if the sculpt of her nether region was equally accurate but her trim derriere certainly was.

Drachus wasn't here for amorous aquatic indulgences; he had spent most of the coins he'd salvaged from the little blonde's purse and they needed funds. Though he hadn't been paid for the rescue he did have some paper currency in his two wallets. Of course he had *two* wallets; pickpockets in some cities are very skillful.

Paper currency might be small but it is incredibly detailed. The idea had occurred to him as he and Chia had walked to Tofferd's. He'd seen several shops with small paintings displayed in expensive-looking frames hanging in their windows. He was willing to bet rich collectors would pay well for the high-quality art produced by 20th century currency engravers of his world. Besides, he had an angle...

Drachus entered the shop and looked about. Sure enough there were several pieces of art hanging on the wall that were easily detailed enough to grace the halls of the rich. Despite the serious nature of his mission he couldn't resist checking out the mermaid sculpture from inside the store. Moments later he grumbled "I don't like goldfish."

The sculptor had a sense of humor; several had been placed as part of the sculpture in a manner that would please any old dowager obsessed with putting fig leaves on the ancient marble statues of naked Greek heroes.

As he glanced at the mermaid, an older man with grey hair came from behind a curtain. He gave Drachus a curious smile. "How may I help you young man? I hope it's not my little lady you've your heart set on. I sculpted her myself. I'm afraid she's not for sale."

"Where did you find such a model?" Drachus asked.

"Would you believe I awoke one morning to find her lying right next to me in bed?!" the old man said with a big grin. Drachus' eyes went wide as he played along.

"Where could this bed have been that such a beauty was found there so easily?" he asked.

Both laughed before the old man replied "I jest sir; the model was none other than my lovely young wife."

"You have led a very fortunate life!" Drachus noted.

With another laugh Nolemande ended their pleasant opening banter by asking "What is your pleasure this day sir? Buying or selling?" he asked.

"Selling" Drachus said as he approached the polished mahogany counter and pulled three bills from one of his wallets. He'd acquired these while working in Siam and Hong Kong years before and kept them as souvenirs. An older mercenary had once told him such souvenirs could save your butt if you suddenly found yourself broke.

Nolemande's eyes went wide when he saw them. "From where did these originate sir? In my youth I was well-traveled but I do not recognize these scripts!"

Drachus froze; he only just realized that he could read the local writing and spoke the language just fine but he could still read just as little of these scripts as before; they were definitely not the local alphabet. 'More magic' he thought. Recovering, he chose to play it mysterious and replied with a sly smile.

"Master Nolemande, I too am well-traveled. So much so that I can't even remember how many lands I've visited."

Once the antiquarian examined the bills they began to dicker in earnest. It was a friendly exchange, so much so that Drachus suddenly realized they'd been at it for over an hour. Since he needed to leave soon he decided to deliver the coups-de-grace.

"These artisans have a unique skill; they not only can paint on the front and rear but *within* the vellum" he said.

When Nolemande scoffed, Drachus picked up one and pointed to a small blank area. "Look here with the light behind it" he said. The old merchant's jaw dropped.

Drachus hadn't seen any and since they didn't use paper currency, he was sure their paper-makers had never conceived of the watermark. With their ghostly appearance, these would seem almost supernatural to the locals.

That sealed the deal; Nolemande paid Drachus six Gold Crowns for the three bills. These largest of the gold coins were paid out with a selection of coins at his request.

As Nolemande counted them, Drachus learned their names and values. In ascending order, the large copper-colored coin was a bronze penny, the smaller copper penny he already knew, the small silver was a Lunar, the larger silver a Sovereign, the smaller gold Solar he knew and the larger gold was a Crown.

Unlike medieval societies on his old world, the coins' worth here was set evenly, at 10 times the smaller. So a copper penny was worth 10 bronze pennies and it took 10 coppers to make a Lunar.

"Are you familiar with a Holy Star?" Drachus asked. Nolemande seemed surprised at that.

"Why, yes though I have only rarely seen one. Unlike most coin, it's not minted by the kingdom. Those platinum coins are minted by the church." Drachus suddenly had a sick feeling he'd screwed up by giving it to Tofferd.

"Generally, it's not used for routine trade, only for very large transactions. The church sets the value at 10 Gold Crowns but if connected to very famous clergy they have been known to fetch as much as 50 in private transactions."

No wonder the manager and dressmakers were stunned when they saw it – and that he was willing to spend it! Drachus felt a bit better now; he just thought to his self 'Chia is going to have one hell of a huge dress collection before too long.'

At his return to the clothing store Drachus was greeted like a prince. Tofferd was practically gushing. "Your lovely little princess is almost ready, good sir!"

As if on cue the curtain to the rear opened and Marla slowly escorted a nervous Chia out onto the main shop floor. Drachus was a bit surprised. She wore a light violet silk dress with a darker violet embroidered waist belt, hem, cuffs and collar. In addition to white stockings she wore a pair of polished Mary Jane's - packed with several pairs of short socks to make them fit her tiny feet. They had even arranged her hair into a side ponytail with a red hair clip.

"Lovely" was all he could say. "Master Tofferd, you have exceeded all my expectations." Several ladies who had been watching nervously through the curtain – wondering if he would be happy with the outfit - came out to fuss over the blushing Chia.

When they did Drachus saw through the curtains the walls of the work room behind them were covered with not only bolts of cloth and strands of lace there were half-finished garments of many types, all quite small.

He suddenly recalled the hotel maid had said Tofferd's was faster for *children's* clothes than Cottlewinds.

While seamstresses made the shy girl even more nervous, Drachus realized this outfit was likely originally made for the daughter of some noble to attend a really important party. He recalled that purple was considered a noble color since the dyes were so expensive.

On his Paris shopping trip, that atelier had also kept a lot of half-finished garments in her shop. A client in a hurry could pick out something pretty about the right size that was mostly finished. She'd make adjustments, add a few garnishes and have the happy customer on their way in an hour or two instead of the two or three days a custom dress normally takes to finish.

Of course, Drachus' lady friend wasn't easy to please; he'd demolished the dress she had been wearing – a skirmish with a drunk had included dragging her to the ground - so he was paying the bill. Still, even with mostly prêt-a-porter stuff available, it had still taken half a day to get a dress that *she* was satisfied with!

Seeing Tofferd might be able to provide more than just a single dress, Drachus turned and spoke. "Master Tofferd, this will do nicely for tonight but lovely as this is I think something a bit less decorated will be best for walking around town, traveling and other such activities. Do you think you could help us?"

"Oh absolutely sir" The tailor said. "We have her measurements and a lady so ... slender ... fits quite easily."

'Slender; that's a nice way to say she's skinny' Drachus thought to himself.

"We're accustomed to making lovely clothes for sweet little ladies like Miss Chia. I'm certain we can finish several and have them delivered by evening, a dozen or more by tomorrow midday!" Tofferd added.

"Fine; we are at The Apex, Imperial Suite" he said.

Tofferd's eyes went wide as he giggled even louder. "I'm certain we can have the lady's new wardrobe delivered quite shortly" he practically sang with a huge grin.

Remembering how much a Holy Star was worth and how expensive The Apex was Drachus knew that Tofferd would keep the seamstresses working at it all night long; he might even call in more relatives!

'He must think I'm really rich' Drachus mused. 'Chia will have a lot of clothes to try on over the next few days.' As they turned to leave, something else occurred to him. "Could you recommend a good restaurant? We've never been here and I'd like to sample the cuisine" he asked.

"Oh, my yes; the Timberland has the finest food in the city; I'm sure you'll be satisfied!" Tofferd said with more giggling. Drachus wondered how many relatives he had working there but it sounded good.

As they walked back to the hotel Drachus he could see Chia was struggling to keep pace with him. He realized Chia couldn't sit on his shoulders like before - his head would be up her skirt!

After a few yards The Dragon Lord picked the girl up and sat her on his left shoulder. Tiny Chia was still a bit off-center so he wrapped his arm around her legs to be sure she didn't fall. Then he noticed her squint in the afternoon sun. "Look, we still don't have skin cream so ..." he said. With a giggle Chia grabbed his big hat and put in on her own head.

Once back at the hotel lobby Drachus asked the manager to have a maid sent up to take his clothes to be laundered. While they took care of that Drachus took a bath.

When he touched the tub his fingers tingled. It must be like his little Angel Wings – a magic thing; that's how it was filled and heated so quickly. As he bathed he wondered how common magic stuff was here on this world. After a bit he realized the hot water had cooled, so he got out.

He asked the same maid he'd tipped so well earlier if they could summon a coach to take them to the Timberland. When she heard the name she smiled even brighter; Drachus wondered how many relatives *she* had working there. This Laris seemed to be a real 'family' town.

The coach ride was comfortable and complementary. Dinner was fantastic. Drachus had eaten in some good places in the past (along with a lot of bad ones as well) but this was one of the best; little Chia was in heaven! "I've never even imagined food that could be this good" she'd said several times during the meal.

All during the ride back to the hotel she was still on cloud nine. As he helped her out of the coach she whispered "I am so glad you decided to keep me." That seemed to be an odd thing for her to say but before he could ask about it a barking dog startled her; she squealed and darted back into the hotel. Apparently the girl was a bit frightened of dogs.

Chapter 5

Why is a nice Trade City so verdamnt intense?

After a fine dinner Drachus and Chia had returned to their hotel. In their suite there were already a half-dozen packages from Tofferd's. If she wasn't still dreamy-eyed over the dinner, Chia might have started trying them on.

Drachus was about to see if the clothes were practical when there was a knock at the door. Outside he was surprised to see the blonde spell caster from before!

"Well it's about time, pervert" the angry young girl cried as she stormed into the room.

"Come on in; be welcome" he said sarcastically.

"Good Evening Priestess" Chia said with a curtsey.

"You know this little nut-job?" Drachus cried.

"Nut-Job!" squealed the blonde. "I am Sora Glarus, the High Priestess of the Sun, you ignorant deviant!"

"Wonderful - such a vocabulary; I haven't heard a girl talk like this since my last raid to shut down an underground brothel" Drachus responded.

Sora bristled at that but Chia spoke up. "Oh please don't be so rude to the High Priestess" she pleaded. "She is a most respected and honored person!" Sora puffed after hearing Chia say that.

"Are you kidding? Yesterday she nearly killed you with all those verdamnt lightning bolts she was dropping all over the place; just how *respectable* can she be?" Drachus called back.

He saw this surprise the blonde. It suddenly occurred to him that she hadn't actually seen Chia there – he had hidden her between boulders. Maybe the thought of hurting the little girl was shocking to her. Sora dashed over and hugged the surprised demon-touched girl.

"Oh dear, you were really there? I'm so sorry; I didn't see you!" she cried. Since Sora seemed genuinely sorry, he changed his tact.

"What brings the wonderful High Priestess of Sparkly Combat to our rooms this evening?" he asked.

Ignoring the mild slight Sora responded. "You stole all of my money and now I have no place to sleep. You need to let me stay here."

"You burned your money on the battlefield, when you were having your little ant barbeque" Drachus said.

"That was only because you stripped me you pervert!" Sora called back in defiance.

"I tore your fancy little lightweight dress off by *accident* while I was trying to save you from the bites of the poisonous ants that *you* sat on *yourself*" he said.

Sora: "That's because *you* were going to molest *me*!"

Drachus: "I stopped *you* from shooting star things at *Chia*."

Sora: "If *you'd* let me see her I wouldn't have shot them!"

Drachus: "If *you* had warned *me* you could have seen *her*!"

Sora: "If *you* weren't such a pervert *I would* have given a warning!"

Drachus: "I AM NOT A PERVERT!"

Sora: "YES YOU ARE! YOU STRIPPED ME!"

As the exchange progressed they'd gotten louder and louder as well as closer and closer; now they were face to face a few inches apart and shouting at one another.

"HEY!" screamed Chia. "High Priestess, please don't say so such bad things about the Dragon Lord; he really is such a very nice person. I've never belonged to anyone who treated me so well! Dragon Lord, please don't be so rude to the High Priestess; you should be nicer too, she is a wonderful person herself!"

Both were startled when the quiet girl had shouted; Drachus was especially taken aback. He thought it a bit odd when she said she 'belonged' to him but was even more shocked by how long she'd spoken.

"That's the first time I've heard you put more than two sentences together since we met" the surprised man said. Chia blushed at that. Drachus took a few deep breaths to calm his self then turned to the priestess.

"Why don't you have any place to sleep? I'm sure a city this big has a church you could stay at."

Sora hesitated before replying; apparently she felt the answer was somewhat complicated.

"I went to the church to have them heal my men. When the Bishop heard of our fight, he scolded me for going after you. He said that was the job of the High Priestess of The Moon. He spent a *lot* of time saying that my sister is the one trained for battle before he ordered me into seclusion to reflect on my errors" she said with irritation.

After a pause, she continued. "He sent my men to the capitol to explain their defeat to the Captain of the Holy Knights and to summon my sister to deal with you. I shouldn't have been locked up to reflect on errors ... because I did nothing wrong!" she finished with a shout of outrage.

Drachus was quiet for a bit: she'd just given him a lot to think about. Sora's magic lights had done plenty of damage to the bandits. If a High Priestess who was trained and specialized in combat was coming he didn't want to wait around to meet her. It could spell 'Big Trouble' for him if 'Big Sisters' magic *was* refined for battle.

Also, how does a *Bishop* order a *High Priestess* around? On his world there were Bishops in large cities but they were local officials; this entire *kingdom* only had *three* High Priestesses; the power balance was off.

He was also surprised that there even was a Bishop in a town this small; he hadn't seen anything like the cathedral that a Bishop would normally administer. A lot of the city was new; maybe they were still building it. Then he remembered how wealthy the place was; the church probably placed him to ensure they received their 'fair share' of tithes on the money flowing through the trade city.

As he sat thinking he noticed Sora was wearing a plain gray smock and some sort of draped headwear – he'd heard them called cowls in the past. Both were made of very coarse and probably cheap material.

'Oh, yes; she was in a penitence room. I guess a fancy outfit like the other one wouldn't be allowed there' he thought. Then he noticed she was squirming as if she wanted to scratch an itch; he grinned.

"Are your bug bites still bothering you?" he asked.

As a furious expression exploded on her face she shouted "I knew it; you are obsessed with my butt!"

But after a distressed whine from Chia she calmed herself. "No, actually I need a bath" the priestess said.

"Didn't they have one at the church?" Chia asked.

"Yes they did – and I did have one - but to escape I crawled through the garden ... when I left I ran into a cloud of ... of blowing sand and it got all over me" Sora said.

Drachus tried not to laugh. Even for a priestess, this girl was a terrible liar. Chia limped over and tugged on his sleeve. "Couldn't she have a bath and stay here? We have lots of room" she asked very quietly.

Something on Drachus' face betrayed him. He saw Sora sporting a gleeful expression that seemed to say 'I've Got You Now You Big Jerk!' She ran over and glommed onto Chia; during the hug she was practically gloating.

"I knew you were a wonderful lady who'd never force a poor lost and lonely girl like me out into the cold, dark night" Sora said. Chia seemed uncomfortable with Sora clinging to her but didn't try to get away from the embrace.

"Can't she stay, please?" she repeated. After a moment he gave in.

"OK, she stays. You may have to reheat the bathwater; it got cold earlier after took mine" he said.

"Hooray; come on Chia let's bathe together; just like real sisters! I've never stayed here, is the bath nice?" Sora asked, sounding just like a little kid

"Oh yes; it has very sweet-smelling soap" Chia said.

"I like your dress, where'd you get it?" Sora asked.

"Oh the Dragon Lord took me to this really nice shop today" Chia said. "They were all so sweet; it was a bit embarrassing when they took my clothes off to measure me but Miss Marla was so nice and all of the other ladies ..."

Drachus lost track of the conversation after the girls entered the bath.

"Oh! The water is still hot!" Chia called out a bit later.

"Yes, it uses magic to stay hot and keep clean" Sora called out just before he heard a loud splash.

"Don't jump in; the water spills out!" Chia scolded.

He heard Sora laugh loudly at that. "It's fine; the maids can use a Dipper Wand to fill it back up" she said.

Drachus guessed the silver dipper he'd seen the maid run off with was a 'Dipper Wand', a magic item that made water. 'This really is a high-end hotel' he thought. 'They can afford to use magic for a lot of comfort items.' Of course, considering how wealthy this city was he didn't consider it too strange. It suddenly dawned on him he actually seemed to be getting used to this magic stuff!

For the next hour surprised squeals from Chia, laughter from Sora and sounds of splashing water made it obvious that both girls were having a very good time. He hoped they were actually washing and not just playing.

After the girls' bath they were lounging in the sitting room wearing soft robes they found hanging in the bath. As they brushed their hair dry Drachus finally got a good look at Sora. Without all of the battlefield distractions he could see that the little priestess was pretty and probably a bit older than he'd first guessed. She had well-tanned healthy skin and bright brown eyes; she was just rather short, even more so than everyone else he'd met on this world.

"I have questions for you, Priestess" he called out.

"What?" Sora responded.

"Can you do anything for Chia's knee?" he asked.

Sora looked bit embarrassed before replying. "No, I did try while we were in the bath but it's been too long since she was hurt. Magic healing won't work if you wait too long after the original injury. But I did treat her with your Rosen Salve. Fortunately, that works no matter how long ago the injury was suffered. Unfortunately, it can't do a lot by itself though it will speed up healing and it prevents infections" she finished with a wide smile.

'Well that's better than nothing' Drachus thought. "Did you come after me or the bandits?" he asked.

"I came after you of course; I wouldn't waste time chasing all over the countryside after simple bandits" she said in a huff.

"How did you hear about me so fast?" he asked.

"It was the wanted poster" Sora said. "Did you think you could kill an entire village and no one would notice?"

Drachus choked on his tea. "I did what?!" he said.

"Karnet trading village; the two survivors said you killed all the guards with some sort of magic metal thunder wands and then summoned a pack of wolves to eat the rest" Sora said as if these were actual facts.

"I did no such things" Drachus shouted. "I knocked out one idiot who was bullying Chia and killed a wolf that had stolen a lamb. Where did you get that other crap from?"

Sora went over to her small purse; it was hanging next to her plain smock which was drying on the balcony after she'd rinsed the 'wind-blown sand' (bugs) out of it. She pulled a folded wanted poster from the purse.

"Count Bernard had those distributed as soon as he learned you'd destroyed his trading village. Of course, the church got them before anyone else so they could duplicate and send them out to the churches in other cites a lot faster than ordinary couriers. I got Big Sister Selena's before she did; she was out training with her knights" Sora said.

True enough the poster said he'd done a lot of killing at Karnet. There was a bad drawing of his face and a worse one of the embroidered dragons on his duster. It also said there was a 100 GC (Gold Crown?) reward, dead or alive. Oddly enough, it was being offered by this 'Count Bernard' fellow, not the church or the government.

Chia had been slowly reading the poster over his shoulder. He saw her lips move as she sounded it out word by word; she could read but only just. "Big sister, the Dragon Lord didn't do those bad things" she finally said.

Drachus caught it when Chia called Sora 'Big sister' and was about to ask why when Sora scampered over to Chia and started brushing her hair, just like a big sister would after a bath.

Drachus smelled a rat and when Sora stuck her tongue out at him from behind Chia's back he knew; the cunning imp had realized he doted on Chia and might not be able to say no to *her*. Since her two-colored eyes were only inches away Sora knew she was demon-touched.

He thought a High Priestess' acceptance of a demon-touched former slave and the wanted Dragon Lord as roommates was suspicious but felt that could wait until later to ask about. "One more thing" Drachus said pointing to his vest. "I know you hit me with some of those light things; I felt it when you did but there aren't any holes. How do those Diving Lantern lights you were throwing all over the place work?" he asked.

"Oh" Sora replied. "The *Divine Lance* only affects living things; like bandits, wolves, perverts and such. It passes through even the heaviest of armor like it wasn't even there. That's what makes it so effective."

Drachus had more questions but then he saw Chia yawn. "Isn't it bedtime?" he suggested.

Sora grabbed Chia by the hand and the girls headed to the bedroom. At the door Sora turned to look back at him. "You stay out; no perverts allowed!" she cried. "Big sister, be nice" Chia chided as she limped back to hug Drachus.

He kissed her on the forehead, they said their goodnights and Sora dragged her into the bedroom then slammed the door shut.

To check on something he'd heard Chia say earlier he looked at the bath tub. The water level was down by almost half – those two girls had done a lot of splashing. He also found the bath water was hot - and clean. The tub had some magical spell on it but he'd turned it off somehow.

After that Drachus spent an hour or so mulling over their options before deciding to get some sleep himself. Before that he checked in on the girls and saw them clinging to one another in their sleep, just like real sisters; Chia was smiling. That made the 'big brother' in him very happy.

As he closed the door, he decided that Sora could hang out with them as long as she was being nice to Chia - and as long as he didn't think she might be leading them into an ambush.

Early the next morning Drachus stood on the balcony watching the activity below. It all seemed perfectly normal; people were going about the normal daily chores of delivering foods, setting up stalls in the market and moving about. Strange as this new world seemed to be there were certain common traits with his old world.

His observations were interrupted by a soft knock at the door. The young maid from yesterday had arrived with a cart of breakfast foods. After a smile and a curtsey she transferred the trays and plates to the sitting room table. When she finished she left without even waiting for another tip; his Solar from yesterday was still considered adequate.

"Umm! That smells so nice" Chia called from the doorway to the bedroom. Before he could say anything she and Sora dashed over to the table. After a short, quiet prayer from the priestess both girls dived into the foods. Apparently, they were very hungry.

As he looked over the foods, Drachus easily recognized most of them as fairly standard fare just like on his old world; pancakes, fried eggs, bacon, ham, boiled eggs, toast and juices. He noticed there was no coffee but they did have several types of tea in various shades of red and green.

Sora poured cups for both herself and Chia – but not for him. It seemed she was still a bit upset for the way he'd treated her on the battlefield the other day. Even if it was an accident, he had torn her clothes off – a young woman was entitled to a few hard feelings about something like that.

He saw her spooning a yellow powder from what should be a sugar bowl on the tea service. Chia 'yummed' with a big smile at the dark red tea Sora made for her.

Pouring himself a cup Drachus added several spoons of the powder. It left the tea mild but not very sweet. Touching a bit of the powder to his tongue he could tell it had an aftertaste that reminded him of honey. He recalled a sweetener made from honey he once had in Siam; it wasn't as sweet as sugar but had a mellowing effect on bitter things like tea. Noticing a small pot of honey nearby, he added that instead; he preferred his tea with a bit of a bite.

During breakfast he watched the girls carefully; it seemed they were getting along very well, just like happy sisters. On the battlefield Sora had been angry, almost ruthless. Last night she'd been more than a bit arrogant. Now she seemed to be just an ordinary teenage girl, laughing and joking with Chia as they ate. But she tended to ignore him.

After breakfast Drachus gave the girls several of both sizes of his copper coins. As he counted them out Sora quickly took a small silver coin from his hand as well. Realizing she would know better what a morning outing would cost for the girls he let it go.

"You should show Chia around while I check out the shops. Be sure you don't overtax her knee and both of you meet back at the hotel for lunch" he told Sora, before he let them go off on their own. Sora seemed to be interested in what he was looking for but Chia was too excited to wait.

As they took off he felt a small twinge of ... jealousy! Chia seemed to be very happy as she and Sora chatted. With a grin he scolded himself. "It's good she has a girl-friend. There are some things a big guy like me could never help her with" he thought recalling how his little sisters had often told him that some things were 'girl stuff – none of a boys business!'

In fact, a High Priestess would have significant status here. Maybe she could take the girl in; that would be better for her than being dragged all over the countryside by a wandering mercenary. After he thought about it for a bit, Drachus realized he would miss her - but it was in her best interests all things considered.

Drachus spent the morning around craft shops to see what levels of technology - if any - were available here. He felt this was a good place to do that - a city this rich would have the best. As he headed back for lunch he knew what he had to work with and a few ideas that might be profitable.

If it went well, he'd introduce useful common items from his world these folks didn't have but would likely pay quite well for. He recalled how amazed some of the mine workers in Brazil had been when they were first introduced to flashlights; he couldn't do those but he was sure that a lot of easy-to-make common items he could put together would be just as surprising to the locals.

With luck, he'd just be a merchant, help out the locals and not have to do a lot of fighting. Things seemed to be looking up for him!

As Drachus approached the hotel he heard a noisy altercation. The Apex had a patio to one side for meals when the weather was nice, like it was today. The vine-covered trellis portico separated it from the noisy square outside while the lattice roof above gave nice shade.

Nearby were a dozen Holy Knights holding mounts. He recognized them by their silver armor but they had red trim on their gear; Sora's knights had gold trim on theirs. He recalled her combat-specialized 'Big Sister' the Moon Priestess had been summoned; these were likely her knights.

Their mounts had no lances; instead the carriers held halberds – 6' long axe-bladed weapons with spiked tips. Drachus saw several knights peering through the honeysuckle flowers at the side of the patio watching the encounter within. These men seemed to be shaking their heads and quietly laughing.

"I've got a bad feeling about this" he muttered. Hoping it wasn't anything serious Drachus approached with some caution. Hearing Sora's voice in an argument close to the wide front patio entrance Drachus decided to enter by the small side half-gate to avoid garnering any attention.

As he approached he heard the knights chatting; their comments seemed rather crude for 'knights'. It was more like the chat among common soldiers. Their lack of 'chivalric manners' meant they were likely recruited from common folk with a wealthy patron - a noble who could supply them with expensive gear. That or this world's nobility wasn't all that noble!

That's when it occurred to him that except for lance charges knights on this world fought on foot. Using mounts they could wear heavier armor and travel faster but they were still little more than mounted heavy infantry.

As he neared the gate Drachus heard a woman shouting. "What the hell do you mean, you captured a Dragon Lord? There's no such thing you little shit. Nobody was killed - Karnet is perfectly fine!"

"What do you mean you *captured* me - and by the way I am real - sort of" he muttered. Then he heard Sora shouting back.

"The Dragon Lord is real Big Sister and I did capture him because, because ... he's a pervert! In the middle of battle he tore my clothes off ... and fondled me. He followed me here and forced me to stay with him in his hotel; he's totally obsessed with ... with my butt!"

At that the guests inside began laughing. Drachus had reached the gate and could see the patio party in progress inside now. 'Big Sister' wasn't laughing; she was stunned. So was Drachus for that matter; all of what Sora said had happened, just not the way she said it.

Looking through the side gate he was sure the lady staring open-mouthed at Sora was the close-combat specialist High Priestess of the Moon.

She was taller than most women he'd seen so far; she was even taller than some of the men! Her long bright red hair formed a halo behind her shoulders as she shook her head in amazement.

She wore thick, polished white armor plates with red trim and red leather padding below. Sculpted as it was, her breastplate made it evident the lady had a nice figure. On the gorget below her throat were silver medallions with large pale gems, moonstones given her title. From the lack of leg armor and the armored side skirts she wore instead he assumed she was used to riding.

Her flat-heel boots surprised him until he recalled they didn't have stirrups here; since they didn't fight from horseback she wouldn't need tall heels to keep her feet lined up in them. With the color of her hair and armor padding Drachus now understood why her knights' armor was trimmed in red.

Impressive as she was, he wanted to avoid getting tangled up with her. Drachus hoped she was here to drag Sora back to the capitol; he rather liked that idea. The Dragon Lord couldn't see Chia anywhere so he hoped she was inside the hotel and out of the middle of this mess.

After a moment 'Big Sister' grabbed Sora by the cowl. "OK you little shit, when we get to the capitol your ass is so grounded that sweet *butt* of yours may not get out of the repentance tower until you turn 30!" she shouted.

'Big Sister' was foul-mouthed but that's likely because she hung around soldiers a lot. Drachus was surprised; for a moment he'd seen a glimpse of a worried older sister in her face.

Movement to his left caught the Dragon Lords attention; a waiter had moved to the patio corner. Ordinarily this wouldn't have registered; the restaurant was preparing for lunch so he was out here setting the tables. However, something about the bland look on his face was out of place.

Looking around Drachus saw three more waiters moving into position in the other corners of the patio. Again this shouldn't be odd but they looked exactly alike – not just the uniforms, all of their slack-jawed mask-like faces were identical too. When their lips began to move and their eyes to glow, he knew it was about to hit the fan.

"Ambush; get out!" he shouted diving back into the alley. As his shoulder hit the ground the patio was engulfed in an explosive burst of flames. The screams of the diners within mixed with the 'Whoosh' of the flames and the crashing noise of the collapsing trellis roof.

Scrambling to his feet Drachus saw the knights across the street had their hands full with their mounts; they had been panicked by the loud noise and flash of the explosion.

The knights who'd been watching through the trellis were down on the street and not moving; they were likely caught in the blast and might even be dead.

The Dragon Lord was pleasantly surprised to see Sora's 'Big Sister' getting to her feet outside the remains of the patio's front arch. Sora was on the ground near 'Big Sister's' feet. The tall lady had good reflexes; after Drachus' warning she'd got both of them out before the blast.

Rubberneckers who had gathered to see the show were fleeing in all directions. Almost all of them; there were a half dozen or so who weren't running. It was quickly obvious that they all dressed alike; even their slack faces were identical.

He was startled by a loud shout from his right. A tall heavy-set knight shouted "My Lady" and hurled a spear at her! When the lady caught it by the haft and spun it into the ready position Drachus knew it was her preferred weapon.

'This lady is strong and has good troops; maybe she can handle things without any help from me' he thought to himself.

As the doppel-ganger squad shouted "Death to the Priestesses!" their hands began to glow. After a second they threw balls of fire and sparkling light towards the sisters.

'Big Sister' acted with surprising speed for one

who'd just been blown up; her feet moved as if she were dancing as she spun her long weapon overhead like a cheerleader's baton. Now he understood why she didn't wear heavy armor below; she was agile and used mobility for defense.

The redhead shouted "Spin Dome" and a wave of light expanded out from the weapon covering her and Sora. When the incoming balls of magic hit that, they splintered into tiny bits of light as they disappeared.

"Clear the streets!" shouted the tallest knight as they ran towards 'Big Sister'. They'd given up on trying to control their frightened mounts and had grabbed weapons from their saddles. Before they could get into position the doppelgangers were chanting their next magic attacks.

As 'Big Sister' hit the ground with her weapon Drachus realized it didn't have a spike opposite the axe blade like a halberd; it had a flat hammer head. He recalled seeing a similar weapon called a Burgundian Poleaxe in a museum in Bavaria.

When he heard 'Big Sister' shout "Dispelling Surge!" a shock wave flew out from the weapon. As it hit the attackers their glowing hands, clothes and identical faces shattered into bits of light. They were now dressed in dark robes like the skeletons at the shrine; these were cultists!

'They can use magic to change their appearance' he thought to himself. 'I'll have to remember that'.

'Big Sister' shouted "Skirmish!" and her knights moved in front of her to fight. Unlike the last bunch these had no lances; half had drawn broadswords, the rest wielding halberds. They formed into a double line screening 'Big Sister' with swordsmen in the front rank and halberds to their rear. Drachus was impressed; 'Big Sister' was skilled and led good men. Maybe they could handle this.

Sora had recovered from the previous blast and now crouched on one knee. She'd drawn her golden scepter from under her robe and it looked like she was ready to give back up fire with her 'Light Lances'. Drachus gave kudos to the little blonde - she was more than just arrogant; the sharp-tongued girl had real courage.

The cultists shouted "We shall send the light of hope to the beyond!" as they drew short, almost toy-like bows from under their robes. The tall knight at the center of their formation shouted "Advance!" and her men began moving forward in a good skirmish line.

Seven child-sized short bows against 12 plate-armored knights wasn't even a fight. Drachus was sure he wouldn't have to get involved; these cultists were way out of their league, this 'fight' wouldn't last two seconds.

Then he spotted movement behind 'Big Sister'; a cultist had snuck out of an alley behind the fight. Drawing pistols he thought 'Full marks to whoever organized this. He made a back-up plan if the patio ambush failed.'

The sneaking cultist wasn't armed – all he had was a small silver coffer. Before Drachus do anything else the sneaking guy opened the box and some sort of black smoke sprayed out. It hit the ground and spread rapidly along the street towards the High Priestess' and Holy Knights.

As the smoke approached 'Big Sister' must have sensed it. She grabbed Sora by the cowl and shoved her away from it. "Sora, get out of here, that's miasma!" she screamed. The little priestess tried to run but before she got two steps she tripped on the singletree of a cart and fell face-first to the cobblestones.

Before she could get up the miasma scattering along the ground quickly engulfed all of the knights and both women. Thin tendrils slid upwards and wrapped around the victim's bodies like sticky netting. They must be very strong; those wrapped up were brought to their knees.

A second later, many of the knights joined Sora flat on the ground. 'Big Sister' was tougher but still on one knee in obvious distress; she could only stay up by using her poleaxe as a crutch.

Aiming their bows, the cultists repeated their chant "We shall send the light of hope to the beyond!" Since even a toy bow could be deadly in this situation, Drachus had to act and moved to flank the cultists.

A single tendril of the shifting black smoke tried to wrap his arm as he closed. When he swatted at it all of the misty stuff exploded in a cloud of red fire engulfing the cultists, guards and the girls; it even scraped Drachus.

It was a flash fire, over way too fast to cause any serious damage. However the flames had startled the cultists, singed their eyebrows and ignited the fletching of their little toy arrows.

The cultists' leader was the first to recover from the shock. Dropping his now useless bow he drew a silvered dagger and shouted "Scorch!" His hand glowed for a moment and suddenly flames burst from his dagger blade. The cultist charged towards 'Big Sister' who, leaning on her poleaxe, had still managed to stay up on one knee. The remaining cultists' followed his lead, all of them loudly shouting "Scorch!" to light their daggers as they charged.

By then Drachus had also recovered from the surprise of the sudden flames; he gunned down the leader and the next one in line with two quick shots from his pistol. As the lead cultists cried out and died, the others stopped and looked around in confusion for the cause of their demise and the source of the associated loud noises. It didn't take them long to connect Drachus and his smoking gun to the death of their leaders.

"He is helping them!" one shouted. The others hesitated for a moment then charged at him. Sweeping his pistol from left and right he fired almost by instinct; the four remaining cultist's were charging directly at him, not even trying to dodge and the range was only a few yards.

It quickly became obvious they were unfamiliar with firearms - they didn't realize just how dangerous large-caliber pistols were in close combat. The impact of the big .45 caliber slugs caused them to stagger; then they cried out and began to fall one by one.

The sound of the shots echoed off the nearby stone buildings making a huge roar – like a freight train. All of the cultists died before they reached him, though the last one did land right at the Dragon Lord's feet.

After that last one fell, Drachus quickly reloaded with a Prideaux Loader of lead rounds from his belt. Since these were humans, he had only used the lead bullet pistol. He could feel the pistol was hot from the rapid fire shooting but knew heavy-duty leather military holsters were designed to handle that sort of heat so he holstered it anyway once he had finished reloading.

Before he headed over to check on the girls Drachus stopped to pick up the empty Prideaux loader and spent shell casings. He'd dropped them out of habit but, realizing they were too useful to lose, he put them into his duster pocket. Once he figured out how to reload his empties, he could refill the loaders.

Walking back he saw many of the dead cultists' robes were burning and thought to his self 'I guess they landed on their own flaming daggers'. With that he realized he was beginning to take this magic stuff in stride.

The Swede had run into cultural oddities while working in new places throughout his old world. From all that exposure he had developed the ability to adapt, so all the strange new things became routine quickly. That way he could just filter out the odd and focus only on what might actually be dangerous. All of that experience was turning out to be quite helpful in this really weird new world!

'Big Sister' and her knights were flash blinded; they'd been inside the burning miasma cloud. As their sight recovered, they saw Drachus walking slowly towards them. His duster was flapping in the breeze and on the street behind were the burning bodies of six dead cultists. Drachus bent over to see if Sora was all right.

"Why-Who-What are you?" 'Big Sister' stammered.

"He's my great big pervert Dragon Lord" Sora murmured. Drachus smiled, realizing she was just dazed.

"Dragon Lord? You're real?" the tall lady asked.

As he moved over to check 'Big Sister' for injuries Drachus said "Yes I am real; are you hurt?"

"N-N-No" she stammered and blushed as he lifted her chin and turned her head from side to side. She had bright green eyes; her sun-bronzed skin made it obvious the lady spent a lot of time out of doors. She was also quite pretty even with a few old minor bumps and bruises. 'Big Sister' seemed more dazed than hurt.

Then he saw under her tan she was pale and trembling. 'Maybe that miasma stuff was a shock to her system' he thought to himself. Seeing she was also blushing at his attention and knowing tomboys could be helpless against girly flattery, he decided to keep her off balance.

That way he would have more time to get back to the hotel with Sora and wouldn't have to give a lot of explanations about everything that had happened. That would be especially helpful since he didn't have a clue of how to explain some of it.

Medieval-minded law enforcement officials in many countries on his old world didn't like it when they heard 'I don't know how all that stuff happened'. Those answers led to long interrogations that seldom ended well for those the police suspected of some sort of criminal activity. Drachus doubted authorities here would be any more understanding.

Thinking quickly he remembered some of the smarmy lines he'd heard other soldiers use on girls before.

"Good; a lovely lady like you should stay out of fights. It would be bad if that pretty face were to get scarred. You might have trouble getting married" he told 'Big Sister'. At that he could see she was trying to reply but was at a loss for an answer. Now that things were quiet, the locals were looking out through windows; several had already come over to help. Drachus also noticed that some of her men were beginning to stand.

"You should get her to a healer. I doubt she'll be able to use her own spells for a while" he told the nearest one.

As he picked up Sora 'Big Sister' asked "What are you going to do with her?"

"I'm taking her inside to have her injuries treated. You should see to yours too, pretty lady. It looks like you are about to fall down" he said.

With a flush of anger she quickly stood up. 'Big Sister' said "Hardly; I am fiiii ..." Drachus saw her eyes roll, her face blanched and she fainted. Fortunately the tall knight was close enough to catch her as she fell.

"Well done; now, get her to a healer" Drachus said.

"Yes Sir!" the knight replied as he carried her off followed by some of his men. Drachus carried Sora into the hotel to have her injuries seen to.

When High Priestess Sora Glarus awoke after being knocked out in a battle with cultists she saw she was lying atop a bed ... and wearing only her panties. Her loud scream brought a maid running from the bath with a pail of hot water to finish dressing her minor injuries.

"Did that pervert strip me, again?" she cried.

Before the maid could reply, Drachus called from the other room. "I asked the young lady to take care of you after I brought you in from the street where I saved your life from that miasma stuff and the cultists trying to kill you."

Chia was standing near the bed in a bathrobe nodding up and down in agreement as he'd been speaking. "It was amazing" she began with a grin. "We saw it from the balcony. When the bad men were coming for you the Dragon Lord breathed fire to destroy the miasma stuff. He was so angry he roared; the shock made them fall over dead!" Chia had apparently misinterpreted what she had seen take place in the battle below.

Sora glanced over to the maid who smiled as she nodded to confirm what Chia had said. The priestess was quiet for a bit thinking it over. "I guess I should thank you then. Is Big Sister Selena all right?" she called out.

"Her name is Salana?" Drachus asked in surprise.

"No, High Priestess of the Moon, *Selena* Rose" Sora called back in a most annoyed tone.

"Was she the tall lady who shouted all those bad words?" Chia asked. Sora nodded in embarrassment.

"She was a bit bruised and pale but otherwise fine. Her knights took her to get healed up." Drachus said.

He first thought the names were just similar. After a moment, he reconsidered; imagining 'Big Sister' with darker red hair, she would bear a strong resemblance to Salana, the warm and friendly auburn-haired Gypsy waitress from that last night he'd spent on his old world.

Sora was very quiet for a while. "Can we leave town soon?" she suddenly asked.

Drachus peered through the doorway asking "Why?"

Still clad only in panties Sora screamed "Pervert!" and threw a pillow at him. Drachus dodged it as he pulled back from the doorway.

"Sorry, I thought you'd be dressed by now" he called back. After he withdrew Sora jumped up to get dressed.

"I'd rather not be here when my big sister wakes up. She is going to be furious with me over all of that stuff out there today" she said.

"Oh yes, you knocked yourself out when you tripped over that cart. You're good against bandits but I guess you don't fare so well against those big evil C's; Cultists, Coaches and Carts" Drachus snickered.

"You Jerk!" Sora shouted back at him.

Drachus was quiet for a while. It might be a good idea if they were to leave while the place was still a bit disorganized after the cultists' attack. He really didn't want to have to explain a lot of things, especially the ones even he didn't understand. What the hell was all the fire about; what had made it explode like that? What about the cultist with the silver coffer; and what happened to that miasma stuff?

Once she was dressed Sora politely thanked the maid, hugged Chia and they joined Drachus in the other room. As the maid left he handed her a Solar and thanked her as well. Seeing that Sora smiled smugly

"I can see you now understand how important it is to take good care of me!" she snickered.

"The young lady took good care of *Chia* during the commotion - kept her from running down in a bathrobe to save her 'Big sister Sora' from the bad men. You I could have dumped a bucket of water on; it's not like I haven't seen most of it before" Drachus responded.

"You Jerky pervert!" Sora shouted sticking her tongue out. After processing what he'd said, Sora saw Chia blushing. She ran over, hugged her again and kissed her cheek making Chia blush even more.

Drachus was amazed at Sora's emotional range. The other day on the battlefield she'd been ruthless as she cut down the bandits; last night bathing with Chia she'd been like a little kid. Today she'd readied for battle against the cultists in mere moments but now she was like a little kid again. He was having a hard time figuring out just how mature she really was; he wasn't about to ask her age. Clueless as he could be about women he knew that could be a minefield where girls were concerned!

Under the circumstances, he would just ignore the tongue. "I think leaving is a good idea" Drachus said.

"Then let's get to my coach. A coach ride will be easier for Chia ... easier than walking, right?" Sora said with a wide smile.

"Any good ideas on where to go?" asked Drachus.

She thought for a bit before Sora replied. "Yes; I know a place where they won't look for me ... for us ... not for a very long while."

Sora seemed serious, so he decided to agree. "Good idea, let's go" he told her.

After Sora went downstairs to have a groom sent to the church to summon her coachman, Chia shed her robe so she could put on a new outfit. From the clothes scattered about the room Drachus could see she had been playing dress-up when the battle started. Drachus realized she was only in lacy underwear and quickly excused himself; this seemed to surprise her.

He recalled how shy Chia had been at the shrine; she now had no problem changing clothes in from of him. He wondered why.

When she came out afterwards, he was somewhat surprised when he saw her new outfit.

"That's really pretty and it looks very familiar; where have I seen one like it before?" the mercenary mused eyeing the clothes but didn't have the time to study it closer right now.

Chia's new outfit was a white blouse and red skirt that matched the cuffs, bow and collar with white stockings and red ankle-strap pumps. The shirt was a bit too short; he could easily see the tops of her stockings but at least her panties and garters were covered.

They loaded their goods into Sora's coach. When he saw the church's crests on it Drachus was a bit confused. Sora was a High Priestess. She had a lot of status and apparently considerable wealth. However, she said she had to 'escape' from the church to join them here.

Oddly, she didn't seem all that eager to get back there. As they loaded up he began to think that maybe the priestesses were treated like the harem ladies he'd seen in the Middle East. They wore expensive silks and jewelry; they lived in great luxury. However, they were treated less like important people and more like valuable property.

He recalled some of the daughters and wives in South America were in similar situations. While they were all pampered, they were more like prisoners. They had very little freedom (if any at all) and their lives were totally controlled. He was beginning to think that it might be the same with the High Priestesses here.

As he watched Sora directing the coachman and grooms with the loading, she didn't seem to very upset about running away. In fact – she seemed to be delighted!

If her church life was that regimented, she might not have enough freedom to be able to take Chia in – regardless of how close the two had become. In fact, the demon-touched might be sent away – or worse!

Drachus decided he would have to keep an eye on things before he decided to make any serious changes to Chia's future. They had a coach now, at least for a while. This would make travel much easier on them all – and let them get further away from possible complications.

They had lots to load. All morning they had received deliveries for Chia from Tofferd's, so they could finish quickly. Drachus offered a silent apology to the poor seamstresses who'd likely been kept at it all night long, sewing their fingers to the bone. Once it was all on board, he lifted Chia in and turned to lift Sora.

"No fondling my butt, you perv" she said as she climbed in while covering her butt with both hands. Once inside she knocked on the roof hatch.

"Take us to Karrat Kommons" she yelled.

At that the coachman opened the roof hatch with a confused expression on his worn and weathered face.

"Where did you say you wanted to go, Milady?" he asked. Apparently he was quite surprised at the destination.

"I said Karrat Kommons you ignorant oaf!" Sora shouted. After closing the roof hatch, the coachman began driving and they left Laris.

Chapter 6

Why am I babysitting a beautiful Nun?

Shortly after they departed Laris it became obvious that Chia had never traveled so fast. She was leaning out on the window ledge gasping every few seconds as new scenery flowed past. The coach wasn't moving all that fast – nothing like a car or train from his old world – but to one accustomed to walking it must seem amazingly quick.

Every so often she would lean so far out that Drachus was worried she might fall. When she did her short skirt would slide up just enough to expose her garters and sometimes her fancy panties. Tofferd must have supplied them: apparently these were common for wealthy girls here. Chia had said she'd never worn them before.

After about two hours he was about to scold her for it when she suddenly pulled herself away from the scenery. "Big sister, how did you become a priestess?" she asked. Sora glanced nervously at Drachus before replying.

"I never knew my parents – I was raised in an orphanage. Five years ago, I started to … to change. It happens to all girls, eventually" she said a bit awkwardly. Drachus realized she meant puberty. Sora seemed to be about the right age for that to start five years ago and it explained her nervous glance; girls were often reluctant to talk about that with guys around.

"On the spring equinox several church elders and the High Priestess of the Earth came to … to examine the girls who were going through that" she said with a grimace. Drachus figured that sort of examination was likely embarrassing for a young girl, hence her sour expression.

"When she looked at me, Maia Gravis' expression turned surprised. She grabbed me and hugged me close saying 'How wonderful!' I didn't think it was so wonderful; girls sometimes disappeared after these examinations" Sora added with a frown.

Drachus had heard disturbing tales about what sometimes happened to cute girls in orphanages. Sora was very pretty; being taken for something unsavory would definitely be possible. However, the priestess continued with a more normal expression.

"Then I was taken to a private boarding school and taught all about the church and magic" she finished as if that was all there was to say.

Drachus definitely wanted to hear more. "Just what is magic and how does it work?" he asked.

"Why don't I just tell you how the whole world works? That might be easier!" Sora said with a glare. As he shook his head she seemed to think for a moment then added. "Magic is all around. It is some sort of energy, like heat from the sun. Some people have ... an affinity to manipulate that 'heat'. They can turn it into other forms – to make it do things."

As Chia's eyes began to get wider with her explanation, Drachus glanced at the silk-wrapped magic scepter on the hat rack above.

Noticing his glance Sora shook her head. "No, the Scepter of Holy Light is a relic, left by the Angelus when they ... when they returned to the heavens after the Demon Wars - to watch over the world and protect us from further demon attacks" she said.

Drachus could tell she wasn't telling him everything but wasn't surprised; he knew church secrets weren't something she would be willing to just blurt out to a stranger, especially one she didn't seem to like very much.

"Very few can access the holy power it controls. That's why Maia Gravis was so happy when she saw I could" Sora explained. That seemed to annoy the priestess quite a lot but before he could ask about it she continued.

"The scepter can amplify the magic I can use in addition to its holy power. That way I can throw potent magic attacks against evildoers – bandits, perverts and such" she said with a grin.

"Is that why you are so powerful?" Chia asked.

With another glance at Drachus Sora said "I'm not all that powerful; I am still in training. I only became a priestess two years ago. It can take many years for a priestess to master her powers. Some never can and they end up marrying before they do" she finished with a slight blush.

"You said the scepter amplifies your magic; what kind of spells can you do on your own? Anything like that 'Spin Dome' your 'Big Sister' used?" Drachus asked.

"No, I can't do anything like that! I said her magic is *tailored* for battle; mine is not. I can work with light – I can make pretty pictures. I'm OK with minor healing and purifications. Other than that, it comes from the scepter."

From the look on her face Drachus could see Sora felt she was finished with her magic lecture. To make certain she pulled out her scepter and entertained Chia with pretty pictures of flowers and cute little animals made with light.

After another hour the coach stopped. The driver opened the roof hatch saying "Pardon sir, but I see smoke ahead." Looking out Drachus saw a hill on the left with a thick column of smoke rising above it. Ahead, he could see their road curved around to that side of the hill.

"We don't want to drive into something that makes a lot of smoke without knowing what it is" Drachus said as he stepped out of the coach.

"You girls stay here." Glancing at the driver he added "If anything comes close that isn't me, take the ladies back to Laris, as fast as you can."

As he climbed the hill the sounds and smells of a pitched battle became obvious. After cresting the hill on its right shoulder Drachus looked down and spotted five wagons trapped at a narrow point in the road flanked by small bowers of trees; a perfect ambush spot.

Two of the wagons, the front and rear, were on fire. There was fierce fighting in the roadway near each burning wagon between guards and two packs of scruffy bandits, one group to the front and a second to the rear. The guards were fighting well but were outnumbered and had no way out; there were already several wounded lying on the ground near the wagons.

Drachus didn't like bandits; he was already planning how to lend a hand. Descending down the side of the hill he made his way closer to the fighting, using trees and scrub brush as cover to avoid being spotted.

When he was about 10 yards from the rear fight he started to draw his pistols. He wished he had a hand grenade or two – there were rather a lot of bandits there. As his arm brushed the crossbow bolt pouches on his vest he recalled that he did have something similar.

Pulling a boomer from his vest he was trying to figure out how to trip the plunger to actuate the fuse without a crossbow when he saw the silver tips of his hat's chin strap. They were stylized claws; they might do the trick.

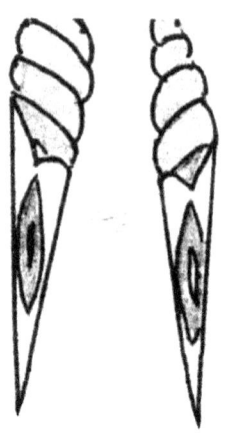

After a bit of working the tip into the slot in the nock he heard a 'snap'; a few sparks and a thin trail of smoke coming from the nock told him he'd lit it. Throwing the bolt like it was a stick and he was playing fetch with an old dog, he saw it land just behind the bandits at the rear. They were closest to Sora's coach and if they ran he didn't want them going that way.

Taking cover behind a boulder Drachus waited for the sound of the explosion. While waiting, he reloaded his silver bullet pistol with lead rounds. After some debris dropped around him he looked up; the explosion had killed several bandits and caused a lot of confusion in the rest.

The guards were holding their right flank just fine, the center of the bandit group was disorganized and trying to recover from the explosion. Since there were so many there, he opened fire on the left flank.

As he dropped the fourth one a bright flash of light off to his left caught his attention just as the boulder he had been using for cover exploded! The blast knocked him down; fragments from the boulder clipped his left arm causing it to go numb and he dropped one of his pistols.

Looking for the source of the blast, he spotted a lone figure on this side of the hill a dozen yards to his left. It wore a dark hooded cloak and was pointing a staff up into the air. As the staff began to glow Drachus realized it was magic; fortunately the spell hadn't hit him directly.

When the spell caster pointed the staff in Drachus' direction again he rolled for cover and a second explosion destroyed the boulder.

As the caster raised the staff up once again Drachus took careful aim with his remaining pistol and fired. Just as the caster went down, his staff fired a third blast up the hill striking a cluster of rocks. The impact caused a small avalanche to rumble in his direction. To escape it he had to roll far to the other side; he just did manage to avoid the wave of rocks.

By the time the dust cloud had cleared he saw the guards at the rear had finished off their bandits and the spell caster was down. When the bandits at the front saw some of the less injured rear guards moving forward to fight them, the bad guys retreated up the road, away from Sora's coach.

After reloading Drachus spent a minute searching the area for his other pistol as his arm recovered from the numbness. "Verdamnt!" he shouted when he realized it had been carried away by the avalanche. It took him several minutes before he eventually found it – but it was damaged!

The frame was cracked – it couldn't be fired but he decided to keep it anyway; the internal parts should still be good and he might need them to fix his remaining pistol.

Drachus walked downhill to check on the wagons and the surviving guards. He thought about getting Sora to heal the casualties when he saw her coach rounding the bend at a trot. After stopping, the coachman apologized.

"I'm sorry sir; they kept screaming at me to take them to help. She said she'd lance me if I didn't" he said, pointing at Sora. From the look on his face, he'd believed her!

"But we heard you roaring and breathing fire; then it got quiet. We thought you might be hurt!" Chia cried. There were tears on her cheeks; the girls had mistaken the battle noises for fire-breathing and roaring. Then Drachus noticed an older man with graying hair and a lined face stepping up.

"I am Virian, the caravan master" he began. The old guy seemed to be in the last days of the autumn of life; he'd soon be looking to retire to a quiet shop to spend his days spoiling local kids with candy and reminiscing.

"Many of my men are hurt. We have two priestesses with us in case healing was needed but they are exhausted from keeping our guards alive during the battle. We'll be heading to The Healing Shrine; it's only two hours away. Perhaps you'd accompany us..." he said.

Sora replied "That might be best; the nuns there do have healing magic and they are the ones who created the Rosen Salve. With this many injured, it would take me much longer than that to heal them all by myself."

It took over an hour to clear the debris of the burnt wagons, recover their panicked horses and ready the wounded for travel in the remaining three wagons. Drachus realized he'd never likely find another pistol on this world; he dismounted the left handed holster with the damaged pistol and stashed it in the coach. He replaced it with a silvered dagger he'd taken from the dead cultists.

When the guards gathered the bodies they found the spell caster's was gone; either he'd only been wounded or the bandits had carried his body away.

As the men loaded the wagons Sora tried to treat Drachus' arm - but her spells didn't work on him. Just like with her light lance spell he felt a tingling as she cast but it did no good - even if she amplified her own power by casting through the scepter! She eventually used Rosen Salve instead but warned him it would be much longer before it had any significant effect.

Drachus was concerned as he watched Sora treat Chia's knee with salve. The bruising was gone but the knee was distorted; it didn't move like normal. Her injury was worse than Drachus had first thought. He'd used the salve from Miss Gillian every day but her knee was still deformed. From Sora's frown, Chia's injury might leave her partly crippled for the rest of her life.

Once the gear was all collected, the survivors headed out. During the ride to the shrine Drachus spoke with Sora about the spells the cloaked spell caster had thrown at him.

"It sounds like elemental magic; it was likely just lightning." Sora said. "Dark elves use that a lot and they wear heavy cloaks in daylight. They are known to be evil, very dangerous creatures" she added with a sour expression twisting her pretty face. Chia seemed nervous hearing that.

Sora kissed her cheek telling her not to worry about the evil dark elf; Sora promised she' do anything to keep her safe. When she said 'keep' Drachus recalled something the demon-touched had said back in Laris that had been bothering him ever since. She had said something similar several times now but he'd never had a good opportunity to ask her about it. Well, now was a good time.

"Why did you say 'you were glad I kept you'?" he asked. Chia stared at him; she seemed confused.

"Just what I said – I am glad you decided to keep me. No one has ever been so nice to me before; I'm so glad I belong to you now" she finally replied.

As he noticed the odd look Sora was giving him, Drachus realized this could be something very important. Now he knew why she hadn't been shy about dressing around him; as his slave, she would be his to use as he pleased. It didn't take long to figure out what to say next.

"Look, I don't do the slave thing; you don't belong to anyone but yourself. You can stick around; I'll take care of you so long as you want me to – think of me like a big brother - but you are *not* a slave. And don't let anyone tell you that you are!" he finally said.

From the surprised look on her face Drachus realized Chia had really thought she did belong to him. As tears formed in the demon-touched girls' pretty two-colored eyes he saw a slight smile play across Sora's face; apparently she felt he'd handled things right, this time. The happy priestess went back to keeping the girl entertained with pretty lights.

They didn't arrive at the Healing Shrine until nearly sundown. They set up camp in the clearing outside its gates as usual and the nuns came out to tend to their injured.

Drachus saw that one rather plain nun was treating the three most seriously injured of the men; within minutes they were fully healed. Given this world had healing magic he just assumed she was very skilled with it.

While that was taking place the Mother Superior invited Sora to dine with her and to spend the night in their guest quarters but pointedly did not extend the same offer to the obviously demon-touched Chia.

"I'll spend the night in my coach with my dear little sister Chia, Thank You Very Much!" Sora said, quite upset.

The elder nun was surprised by her angry response but didn't pursue the issue. Drachus was surprised too; he'd seen that Sora and Chia had become close but didn't realize the priestess had come to feel *that* strongly about the adorable little demon-touched.

A bit later Drachus saw the plain nun again; she was in a heated discussion with the Mother Superior. "I'm certain it will help the child" he heard the nun say. Since Chia was the only child here, they were arguing about her - so he felt he should listen in.

"Sister Yuma, we shall not waste such a blessing on one of *those*" said the older nun. "It's too valuable!"

"But I'll be making more tonight" Sister Yuma said.

As she shook her head the Mother Superior saw Drachus listening. By the way he and Sora treated Chia it was obvious the demon-touched was precious to them. Knowing she'd gaffed again, the elder nun hissed. "Do as you must then!" and stormed off.

Curious about 'it', Drachus watched as Sister Yuma approached Chia and knelt down in front of her. "Does this pain you child?" she asked touching her distorted knee. Chia had been hobbling about helping wherever she could. It was obvious her leg hurt but she'd never complained.

When she hesitated to reply, Sister Yuma pulled a glass vial from her habit, rolled a honey-covered ruby-red berry from it and gave it to Chia.

"Here; I'm sure it will quiet the discomfort" she said with a smile. Accustomed as he had become to magic Drachus was wary of a strange red berry. Chia was such a trusting girl now she ate it without question. After saying 'Thank You' she turned to leave but the nun caught her arm.

"Why don't you take it easy for a bit; we can chat" she said. They talked about her new outfits for several minutes until Chia gasped and seemed to have trouble catching her breath. Alarmed, Drachus moved towards her as a look of surprise appeared on her innocent face. Oblivious to the men around her, Chia lifted her skirt revealing her very fancy new lingerie to everyone. As he pushed the shirt down to stop the perv fashion show Drachus saw her knee was perfectly fine!

Sora was amazed. "I know this shrine is famous for healing but I've never even heard of magic that could cure like this" she said. She and Chia were so excited they began dancing, laughing just like little kids.

Drachus turned to Sister Yuma to thank her. As he held her hands he felt a bit of a tingle in several of his fingers and her appearance changed. The plain pale, brown-eyed brunette became a beautiful dark-skinned woman with pointed ears, silver hair, golden eyes and long fingernails.

When she noticed the change, her face registered shock. With a surprised cry she snatched her hands away from him and fled back into the shrine, returning to her previous appearance as she ran away.

Drachus went looking for the Mother Superior for an explanation. It took a while; she was avoiding him but after dark he found her by the well.

"About Sister Yuma and her red berries" he began. The lady seemed resigned to the need for explanations. She asked him to come to her office. Once there she said "It's a long story; 30 years ago…"

A band of dark elves had raided the chapel and molested some of the nuns including Yuma's mother. She died after Yuma was born; the nuns chose to raise the half-blood child in secret. The former Mother Superior felt it appropriate; the circumstances of her birth weren't her fault.

Nine years ago the shrine saved a wealthy merchant who had fallen ill. During his recovery he learned about Yuma; she had done his nursing at night – she was vulnerable to sunburn and worked at night. In gratitude he later sent her a magic ring that could shroud its wearer in an illusory appearance, so she could blend in with the other sisters at the shrine making it less likely she'd be discovered.

"What about that berry" he pressed.

"Those are a closely guarded secret. Even the church elders do not know about them" the nun said defensively.

"Why" asked Drachus.

"If they learn about those, they'll discover the truth behind Sister Yuma. As a dark elf, she could be executed. There is no exception in law for mixed-blood children of those poor women who have motherhood forced upon them. And if not executed, she could be forced to produce berries solely for the wealthy nobles" she explained.

"Those berries are potent. They heal any injury, no matter how old; they even heal diseases! Only Sister Yuma makes them and only on the nights of the full moon. The golden ones she'll make tonight aren't as potent as the red ones but perform healing nearly as miraculous" she added.

As she paused in her explanation a pained expression crossed her face. After a few moments she spoke again. "I must apologize for my earlier words. As I have recalled Sister Yuma's past, I've become ashamed of my behavior. Just as Sister Yuma cannot be blamed for the circumstances of her birth, that child traveling with you is just as innocent. After all, she's not a devil-ling with an evil aura and dark demonic powers."

Drachus was about to ask about devil-lings and their dark powers when he heard his name being called; several of the guards were searching for him with some urgency. He went to find out what they were upset about.

There was a serious meeting around a campfire. "The guards stripped the dead bandits of armor, weapons and other valuables so they could be sold. As we cleaned them we saw that even though they'd been dirtied, the weapons and armor were new with no craft hall markings; there is no way to tell where these bandits bought them. That's not uncommon; some dwarven enclaves outside the kingdom will supply weapons and armor to anyone who will pay, no questions asked." Virian took a sip of his tea before he continued with a frown.

"However, each dead man had 30 new Lunars; that is an oddly consistent amount for bandits to have. These men were hired to attack my caravan! Mine is not a typical cargo. Few of my guards know but the locked chests are decoys, there only to explain having so many guards. I carry documents to the Noble Council. I don't know the details but I was told that a secret alliance may have formed between radical dwarves, dark elves and possibly even a demon. They may be trying to seize Whitewater Clefts!"

"What's that?" asked Drachus in curiosity.

Surprised at his ignorance, Virian explained. "At the north end of Hook Lake, the headwaters of the Snake River, Whitewater Clefts is an independent trade city. It controls the movement of commodities between the Snowfall Realms, Dwarven Mountains and Durakkon; most all traffic along the Snake River. If that huge walled city were to fall, it would take a massive force of arms to liberate it. Most mining and fine metals crafting occurs in the Dwarven Mountains; high quality fur and lumber trade is from the Snowfall Realms. Trade flowing though Whitewater Clefts is critical for Durakkon!"

"If you and all of your men are from the Clefts, why have you traveled so far north?" Sora asked.

"Actually, we're from Mere" Coramak said.

Coramak, the leader of the merchant's guards, was a lean broad-shouldered young veteran of many battles. Far from a dour hired sword, he had a boyish face and close-cropped bright red curly hair; he even laughed a lot. Drachus was struck by his resemblance to

Cormack, Arevalo's Scottish mercenary; like Salana and Selena, they were so close it was almost spooky.

From what Drachus had overheard from the other guards Coramak had reacted quickly when the bandits struck; if he hadn't split the men to the front and rear the caravan would have likely been wiped out in seconds.

When Coramak said they were from Mere, Sora was shocked. Seeing that, Drachus asked "Is that odd?"

"Odd doesn't describe it" she said. "The Clefts is 200 miles to the south west; Mere is 100 miles to the north east and the capitol is 30 miles south east!" she cried pointing in the different directions. Virian's face twisted in a grimace.

"I can explain" he began. "They were originally sent from Whitewater Clefts by barge to the port of Davrill. It was then to be sent by fast post rider to the capitol; they even engaged a Cromwell galley to take a second copy by sea. I came into possession of those after that ship drifted ashore." After a brief pause, he continued.

"As they battled a pirate both ships were caught up in a powerful storm; they barely made it to Mere in one piece. The original messenger was a senior merchant of my guild. He *claimed* to have been badly injured and unable to continue; I was assigned to complete the delivery."

Coramak spoke up saying "The pirate ship ran aground and some of the crew escaped. The guild thought that if whoever had arranged for the attack was still alive, they'd hire mercenaries to ambush us on the coast road heading to the capitol. They suggested we head inland and then follow the Midland River south to bypass them but they seem to have figured us out."

Drachus thought this explained the dark elf spell caster too. "I guess that spell caster was able to use magic to track us; someone does not want this news to spread before the takeover" Virian concluded.

"So, the villains must stop you from delivering the documents. We have to assume they'll kill anyone you may have passed them to along the way; so the sisters here are in danger now" Sora said.

"If that spell caster is still alive, with our reduced numbers, we won't reach the capitol" Coramak said bluntly.

"Dragon Lord, High Priestess, will you help us save Whitewater Clefts from evil?" Virian asked them.

"It is against church doctrine for clergy to take sides in a secular struggle, even for a High Priestess" Sora said.

"If you are attacked …" began Coramak.

"Yes, we can defend ourselves if we are attacked" Sora confirmed. "But if we placed ourselves in such a vulnerable position deliberately, it would cause great concern and distrust in future issues."

Drachus was hesitant for the wanted 'Dragon Lord' to show up in the very well-populated capitol before he knew more about this kingdom. He decided to ask about alternatives. "Is there another route you could take, one they won't think likely?"

"Instead of going thru Ingo, we could take West Wyrm Way: it's a rough road but we'd eventually reach the capitol via the Luminous Waterway. Or we could just take the old trade road along the Midland River" Virian said.

"Why would these be unlikely?" asked Drachus.

"Farther to the west is longer and slow going. It is also infested with bandits and occasional bands of marauding orcs. *If* we made it through, it would cost us a week or more, seriously delaying our arrival" said Coramak.

"And that old trade road?" Drachus asked.

"That runs right through cursed lands; there's little water. The Midland River isn't good in the best of times and it runs thin at this time of year" Virian said. "Even on this route we had to bring water barrels but they were on the front and rear wagons; they burned during the fighting."

"The trade road would be quickest" said Coramak.

"I really hate killing good horses ..." Virian began with a grimace.

After several minutes of arguing the various merits and problems of the routes, Drachus had an idea. "I saw some old wine barrels outside the shrine kitchen. You leave your decoy cargo here at the chapel, load those barrels, fill them with water, load the nuns and the wounded in the good wagons and move along the trade road. Without the fake cargo, you'll move faster than normal" he began.

After a moment he added "We take Sora's coach along the western route with your extra horses to disguise which group is largest. We don't need to worry about running into bandits and orcs. With extra horses we can move more quickly, we'll easily outdistance men on foot."

Drachus knew that even if these men were worth the money they had been paid up front, the survivors would know they couldn't catch up with the merchant to complete the job. Diverting to the Healing Shrine to get the men healed may have thrown them off. Virian and Coramak agreed with Drachus and began rearranging their wagons.

Drachus spoke with Sora while they worked. "I know you want to avoid running into your sister; can we get to your hide-out along the worm road?"

"That's West Wyrm Way and I am not hiding from her!" Sora cried. "I just don't want to talk to her till she calms down … sometime next year maybe" she paused as Drachus snickered. "But we can get there by that route."

After getting some general information about the new route Drachus walked back to their camp to get some sleep; it was late and they'd be leaving early. Along the way he heard a strange cry of a woman from a garden at the rear of the chapel. He went to investigate.

After a short search he found Sister Yuma collapsed on a blanket. She was in her dark-elf form, naked, sweating and apparently quite exhausted. Before he could approach to find out what was wrong the Mother Superior ran up and quickly covered the nun with another blanket.

She took four golden berries from Yuma's grasp which she carefully placed in a vial with a glass stopper. Drachus didn't even have to ask her to explain; she began as though relieved to be able to tell someone about it.

"Five years ago a Bishop was going to visit the shrine. There was no way Yuma could remain undetected during his visit. Once discovered she could be executed and the nuns' prosecuted for hiding her. Rather than cause harm to befall her sisters Yuma chose to run away. Not able to flee in a rainstorm, she had to wait until nearly midnight for the weather to clear. As she climbed the garden wall to leave the shrine grounds unseen an old wet stone broke loose and she tumbled down to the patio below. She awoke shortly after her fall; she was cut, bruised, had a twisted ankle and half of her dress had been torn by the thorny Rosen bush" the nun said as she pointed to a lovely flower nearby.

As the dark elf moaned a bit the elder nun caressed her head saying "It's all right, dear." Then she continued to explain. "The flower of the Rosen bush is lovely, bright red inside and a brilliant golden yellow on the outside. They grow everywhere, but the yellow berries they produce are poisonous." Shaking her head at the memory the Mother Superior continued.

"She couldn't run away now; she was out of options. Plucking one from the heart of a nearby blossom Yuma prayed and prepared to take her own life. Kneeling in the light of the full moon strange sensations began to build. These escalated until gasping and perspiring she screamed out loud and collapsed; her legs too weak to even continue kneeling." The Mother Superior paused for a moment to adjust the blanket.

"Hearing her cries I came to see what happened. As I covered the shaking girl with my apron Yuma swallowed the poisonous berry, expecting to die. When she awoke the next morning, and wasn't dead, she saw that the cuts, bruises and twisted ankle she'd suffered were healed." The lady paused as Yuma moaned again, then continued.

"When she told us of her injuries we were stunned; it was obvious that the 'poisonous' berry must have healed her. Fortunately, the rainstorm had cancelled the Bishop's trip. Night after night we tried to duplicate the event; we had no luck until the next full moon. After a half hour in the moonlight Yuma collapsed in a sweat with her heart pounding. I had cut my hand that evening preparing dinner; I ate the golden berry and my hand healed in moments"

Shaking her head at that miracle the elder nun said "Over the next year we worked to learn the details of this strange ... berry. They heal injuries regardless of how long ago they occurred! The injuries never become infected; if already infected, that is also healed."

She paused after hearing a call from the shrine. "I'll be there in a moment" she called back before continuing.

"On the second night, the true full moon, she can only alter two but these become a bright ruby red color. The aftereffects are far more severe – Yuma is so drained she doesn't awaken until morning." The elder nun brushed a small lizard away from Yuma before saying more.

"After months of testing we found these not only heal old injuries like the golden ones these can restore deformities. They will even heal the most severe of diseases" she said. With a snort the nun pushed the small lizard away from Yuma again. After watching the creature scamper into the brush, the nun continued.

"Where was I? Oh, Yes. Regardless of the color, both previously poisonous berries are perfectly edible. The altered berries lose potency quickly but by honey-pickling - immersing the berries in honey warmed by boiling water – they are good for up to three weeks. After a time we noticed the outer skin would often separate during honey pickling. Blanching them with boiling water removed the poisonous outer skin. After mixing the yellow berry pulp with warm honey we can make the Rosen Salve at any time." Wiping the smile from her face, the Mother Superior continued.

"As for those sensations ..." she paused for a moment before saying with a mild blush "I had some worldly experience before becoming a nun. They are *not* what they appear to be." At Drachus' skeptical look she explained.

"I assure you – there are certain – traces that are quite obvious when a woman has a ... an intimate experience; Yuma had none of these. I explained they must be ... just a reaction to the moonlight energy she channeled. Yuma would be humiliated if she learned what they seem to be!"

Drachus thought she might just be trying to save Yuma from embarrassment but decided he'd keep quiet about them anyway; after what she'd done for Chia it was the least he could do. By then

Yuma had regained her senses and needed to be helped inside before she caught a chill.

The next morning the Mother Superior approached the coach followed by Sister Yuma - in normal clothes and a bonnet. "A word please" the elder nun said. "Would it be possible for you to take Sis ... Miss Yuma with you?" Sora and Chia agreed immediately. Since she had healed Chia's leg, Yuma was their newest best friend.

"But why isn't she in her nun costume?" asked Chia.

"I'm afraid that Yuma can no longer be one of us" began the Mother Superior. "May we go to your coach so I can explain?" she asked. Once inside the coach and out of sight of the others, Yuma removed her magic ring revealing her true form; both girls were shocked.

"A dark elf" snapped Sora angrily.

"So pretty" cried Chia. Drachus agreed; seeing her in daylight, she was beautiful!

Sora was more concerned at the coincidence. "So, she's a dark elf; the dark elf sorcerer that nearly killed Drachus in that fight got away ..." the priestess said.

Shaking her head, the Mother Superior reassured her. "That couldn't have been Yuma; she has not left this shrine in all of her life. The closest thing she has to a combat spell is a flame we typically use to start cook fires! The ring provides fine protection for her out here but it will never withstand the scrutiny Yuma will face at the cathedral. Her aura would give her away almost immediately. She could be executed and the other sisters will stand before an inquisition for keeping her secret."

Bowing her head, the Mother Superior begged "Take her with you, to protect her and all the sisters." Sora was quiet but her expression said she wasn't on board with it.

"Appearance aside, she's been raised as a human" Drachus noted. Chia tugged on Sora's sleeve.

"Can't she come; she's really sweet and she fixed my leg for me?" After a moment the priestesses frown softened.

"Without the ring, it could be trouble" Sora told them. Apparently, she was just as helpless before Chia's innocent charms as Drachus. He had several reasons for agreeing, foremost was whether her berries would work on him since magical healing wouldn't; he still had a big bruise on his elbow from the magic lightning attack. The Rosen Salve seemed to work so he hoped the berries would too.

Chia absolutely adored the nice lady who healed her leg so she wouldn't be crippled and could run around like a normal girl. Drachus felt he owed her for that too.

As they left the coach Drachus remembered there was something else he needed to know about magic. He decided to ask the older nun. "Do you know about other magic stuff?" he inquired.

"I am familiar with a few devices" she said. "Is there one in particular you are interested in?"

Drachus showed her the silver wings in his vest.

With a shake of her head the lady replied. "Ah, I'm sorry; I've never seen anything like that. You might ask at an Enchanter's Guild. However, an item that small is quite unusual. It might be from an Elven Enchanter."

"Thanks for the information. I promise I'll take good care of Sis ... Miss Yuma from now on" he said.

Once they were all loaded up, the coach departed for their diversionary run to Sora's hideout – Karrat Kommons.

As they rode Drachus realized he now had *three* young ladies in tow. Before too long he would have to find some decent place to set them up in residence or he was going to end up traveling with an entire entourage of pretty girls in the coach!

Drachus and the ladies traveled the foothills for three days switching horses often to avoid tiring them. They even doubled back a few times to make it harder for them to be tracked. Drachus worried the mercenaries might not know who was in the coach and might still be after them. He didn't want to be tracked to Sora's hideaway.

Supplies weren't a problem. They had his refilling flask for water; Sora knew spells that could purify wild fruits, vegetables and even the nastiest water they found along the way. The ladies slept in the coach while Drachus and the coachman slept in shifts on top of it to keep watch.

By the third night Sora was not only used to Yuma, the pleasant former nun had become like a big sister; the three were the best of friends.

Yuma didn't even wear the disguise ring when outside the coach now. The coachman had no issues with her; he'd been made Sora's driver because of his remarkably tolerant nature in the first place. No one else could have put up with her spoilt and selfish nature for so long!

Chapter 7

Why are we running into orcs?

By the morning of the fourth day after leaving the Healing Shrine Drachus felt there was no further need for evasion. If they hadn't been caught by now there was no pursuit. He'd also been considering something for a while and spoke to Sora at breakfast.

"Until I learn more about this world I want to keep a low profile; traveling with a High Priestess is *not* low profile. The robes are bad enough; but this coach is a problem. Without the Holy Crests, it wouldn't be; removing those should be easy."

"I am the High Priestess of the Sun, Sora Glarus; I should not have to travel in a plain coach like a low-grade merchant" she said indignantly. Chia spoke up innocently.

"I think the robes are ... OK ... but they're not very pretty. You'd cute in some of the clothes Miss Marla made for me in Laris." A smile flashed across Sora's face as she recalled the clothes and accessories from Tofferd's now stashed inside the coach. Seeing that gave Drachus an idea.

"You're right Chia. Those outfits are pretty. It's a pity you can only wear one at a time. Of course if Sora weren't in robes it wouldn't look right to have that crest on her coach. So it won't happen" he said slyly. Riding in the coach was cleaner than walking so Chia had been wearing a new outfit every day on this road trip. He didn't think Sora would cave in so easily but he'd planted the seeds of the idea at least.

"You just want to see my butt while I change" Sora muttered.

While Chia and the others laughed, Drachus noticed something. "Chia" he said "open your mouth a bit."

"Why?" she asked in some confusion. When he looked in he saw that her cracked tooth was solid again – and the missing molars were back!

He'd previously checked Yuma and Sora's teeth; no surprise, both of them had good oral health compared to Chia. They were healers and had a healthier diet than the ex-slave but even they had a bit of yellowing.

However, the teeth being fixed was surprising until he recalled that she'd had a healing berry powerful enough to correct her deformed knee. 'Of course it would fix a tooth too' he thought to himself.

As he glanced around he saw Yuma smiling. Of course she'd know the tooth would be fixed. Sora on the other hand was amazed; after hugging Chia she hugged the dark elf and thanked her again for being so kind to Chia.

With danger no longer likely, they headed straight for Karrat Kommons. During the ride Sora and Yuma discussed their experiences with magic training. Sora had been taught a few spells by the church elders as she was schooled but they had seemed more interested in perfecting her ability to activate the powers of the scepter.

As Drachus listened to their discussions he realized that there wasn't any sort of organized training for magic here. Different church elders had taught Sora the healing spells, purification rituals and light magic she knew; no one of them was skilled with all of them. Yuma had similar patchy training; various older nuns taught her the healing, fire and purification spells that she knew.

Even though they were casting spells that did some of the same things, they were very different spells. Drachus realized there was no standardized training protocol for magic on this world. "Don't they have a common method they use to teach that stuff here?" he eventually asked.

With a sharp glare Sora replied in a rather testy voice; she felt the answer was blatantly obvious. "Fewer than one in a hundred has *any* magic potential at all. Most who know magic learned it from parents or neighbors as they grew up. Like Yuma, they can do small spells such as starting cooking fires, purifying water and other simple tasks that would be useful around a home."

As Yuma nodded in agreement Sora continued. "If someone has a lot of talent – and gets noticed - they *might* be taken in as an apprentice by a skilled sorcerer or maybe even get into a guild. Even then, the spells they'll learn will depend on a master's specialty or preferences. Very few ever learn a wide variety of spells here."

Around noon they were passing through a grassy valley when the coachman opened the roof hatch.

"Sir, Ladies, there is a pond up ahead. Would you like to stop for lunch?" Everyone agreed that would be a good idea. The pond was fed by a small stream of water that seemed to be at least marginally clean.

As they set up for lunch, Drachus noticed Yuma staring into the distance. She wasn't wearing her ring so he could see her ears twitching a bit under the loose sides of the big bonnet she wore to protect her face from sunlight; as a half-blood dark elf she was very sensitive to sunburn.

"What's up?" he asked.

"I hear something over there, people I think" Yuma said as she pointed along the stream leaving the pond.

"I'll go check it out. Just in case maybe you should wear the ring until we figure out who it is" Drachus said.

Nodding at the suggestion she put in on, once again becoming a plain human woman.

Walking about a half mile away from the wagon Drachus noticed the stream descending into a narrow ravine. When he got to the edge he saw the source of the noises Yuma had heard. There was a desperate struggle going on down below. Two people, adventurers by their outfits, were fighting a dozen ugly thugs with growling wolves in the mix. Drachus saw the fight was out of his gun range – he couldn't do anything from up here but draw the bad guys' attention for a bit.

As he looked for a way to get there he saw a ledge along the left wall of the ravine. He'd done some climbing for a job in the Alps; he was sure he could make it down but it might take a while. Hoping those two could hold out he pulled on heavy leather gloves and began his descent.

Krant and Romis were an adventuring team from the cold south; they found northern heat unpleasant and dressed light. He was a tall man with prominent muscles. The fellow was a master of the long rapier he used to open the throat of the orc closing in on his partner.

She was a beautiful sorceress in light leather that'd just launched an arrow-like mini-javelin of magical ice into the eye of the orc trying to stab her partner with a spear. Their tactic of taking on one another's opponents had confounded the orcs, leaving several of them lying dead as the two adventurers had retreated along the narrow ravine floor. However both their luck and stamina was running out; they couldn't keep this up much longer.

"Dammit! We go out for a salamander and find orcs! When we get back I'll beat that guildmaster half to death, have you feed him healing potions and do it again!" he said.

"You know I'd love to help with that" Romis laughed bitterly "but I don't think we're getting back" she said sadly as she sank to the ground.

For some reason the orcs had stopped attacking. Several larger ones were barking orders at the others as they reshuffled their line. Taking this chance to rest and catch their breath, the adventurers tried to make plans.

"Any ideas" Krant began as he noticed Romis sitting on the ground "about what's up with them?"

"Maybe they think I have to pee and are going to be gentlemen? How the hell would I know, I don't speak pig-face!" she said sarcastically

"Now is a good time to toss me a stamina booster. I could sure use it!" Krant gasped trying to catch his breath.

"I'd love to, but I don't have any left. No magic either" she said with a grim note of finality.

Glancing over Krant saw she'd flipped the crystal dagger she used to focus ice spells so its tip now touched the cleavage between her breasts. A cold knot formed in his belly. She'd once said she'd rather die than be taken alive by orcs. Having seen what orcs sometimes do to captive women, Krant knew she'd been serious. He was certain they were in real trouble now.

"Partner" Romis called out in a shaky voice "I'm not sure I can do this."

He saw her hands trembling on the dagger hilt. After considering their lack of alternatives, he swung his sword to the other side and sadly spoke up. "Don't worry; their dirty paws will never touch you. I'll take your pretty head off in one swing so fast you won't even feel it, partner."

As Romis closed her eyes and took a breath to thank him Krant started his swing but something stopped the sword. Looking to his left he saw a tall man was now holding the tip of his blade in a heavily-gloved hand; while Krant was focused on the orcs and Romis this stranger had come up from behind!

Drachus had managed to make it all the way down without being spotted and the adventurer's had held out until he got there. He used the spray from the waterfall from above to hide his approach so he was able to get close before the orcs noticed him and began to adjust their skirmish line. He stopped the blade before it could decapitate the lady by carefully grasping the tip with his gloved hand.

"Beautiful women with brains and guts are few and far between" Drachus said to the surprised Krant. "Don't write them off so easily. I've got this now; you two take a breather." With that Drachus advanced on the orcs while taking off his gloves and dropping them to the ground.

Krant joined Romis on his knees. "He's wearing a heavy coat, in this heat? Is he crazy?" Krant asked.

"Look at that hat; is the circus in town?" the amazed Romis asked.

As Drachus paused after a few steps a gust of wind fluttered the duster's cape; they saw the embroidery and recalled that new wanted poster they had seen the other day at the guild. "Dragon Lord?!" both cried out at once.

"Gimme a break with the Dragon Lord crap, will you" he muttered. Drachus saw the dirt along the base of the ravine walls was fine sand and loose gravel; dispersed by an explosion it would be a perfect smoke screen.

As he approached, Drachus heard the orcs talking. "Where did this human come from?" "Why isn't he running for his life?" "He only has a dagger!" "Loose the wolves!" "No, the boss will want the woman alive!"

'How is it I understand them?' he thought to himself.

Walking towards the orcs he drew a boomer from his vest. After tripping the fuse with his chin strap tip he tossed it to the right of the orcs. Then he drew his pistol; as an afterthought he pulled out a Prideaux Loader - there were a lot of orcs and he might have to reload quickly.

The orcs were even more confused now. "He threw a stick?" "Is he gonna play fetch with the wolves?" "He must be suicidal" several laughed.

When the boomer went off, it kicked up a storm of blinding sand, flying gravel shrapnel and killed several of the orcs on the right side. The detonations caused howls from the wolves and some of the orcs as well.

Then Drachus began shooting the orcs, moving from left to the center. On top of the echoing explosion the sound of the gunfire in the narrow space was deafening! After 20 seconds enough of the dust had settled to reveal more dead orcs. He could see the survivors shouting and running for their lives alongside their panicked wolves.

Up at the coach Sora and Chia had been preparing lunch when they noticed Drachus and Yuma were missing. "The Dragon Lord went off in that direction" the coachman said pointing north. "The dark elf lady followed him."

After heading out they found the distressed Yuma at the edge of a nearby ravine looking down at a band of orcs about to fight with the Dragon Lord. Suddenly smoke exploded around the orcs; immediately afterwards Sora and Yuma were shocked when they saw red and yellow flames flash in the dust cloud as the roaring Dragon Lord 'breathed fire' on the orcs. Chia wasn't surprised; she had seen some of his fight with the cultists in Laris.

"Isn't he magnificent?" she said. "Let's go get ready; I'm sure he'll bring those two back to help them once he's done with the orcs."

The shocked ladies followed her to the coach and began laying out supplies to feed the newcomers and take care of any of their injuries.

Drachus reloaded and holstered his pistol, and then he picked up his empties and gloves.

"Are the Dragon Lord?" Romis asked hesitantly.

Before he could respond, Krant gestured at the dust settling over the dead orcs saying "Who else could he be?"

"Yeah, right" she said. The lady who had been mere seconds away from death finally accepted that she was safe once again and called out loudly in a very relieved and sincere voice. "Thanks, we owe you for this. If you ever need anything, just ask!"

With a smile Drachus asked "Can you two walk? I have friends up there" he said indicating the head of the ravine with a wave of his hand. Krant got to his feet; he was able to stand though a bit unsteady, having lost the adrenaline-rush of combat.

Romis' knees collapsed before she could even get her feet under her; she was exhausted both from spell casting and from the fear of being seconds away from death. The lady wasn't ready to do any climbing yet.

Before she could try again Drachus cut in "No, you can't walk yet. Let's wait a bit, at least until she can stand" Drachus said to Krant, who was also very grateful for the chance to catch his breath too. While they waited, the adventurers explained how they had ended up here. After their explanation, the exhausted Romis could finally stand without leaning on anything. Drachus pointed to the ledge. "We'll go up that way" he said. When he saw Krant scowl as Romis giggled he "Something wrong?"

"No, it should be fine" Romis said with a wide grin.

Pulling his gloves on he began to slowly climb the side of the ravine with Romis right next to him. Every so often she would grasp his shoulder saying "Can we wait a bit?" as they reached a wider spot on the ledge.

After the third time he asked "Are you really OK?"

"Yes, I'm just a bit tired" she said. "He's the real problem here" she laughed glancing back. Drachus saw that Krant was still far behind them; his eyes were squeezed shut as he felt his way up the ledge inch by inch.

"He may be tough in a fight but he's absolutely terrified of heights" Romis said with a grin. Now understanding the earlier scowl the Dragon Lord grinned.

"That doesn't scare you?" he asked.

"Nope, the only thing that scares me is falling ... falling in love with some big pretty hunk with no brains. I'll only love a man who is my mental equal" she said with what sounded like a long-running half-hearted joke.

"Oh shucks" Drachus cursed with a laugh, playing along. "I guess that leaves me out; I'm as dumb as a box of rocks." Romis giggled as she stood to continue climbing. Panic flashed across her face as she lost her balance and began to fall towards the edge of the ledge. Reaching out quickly Drachus managed to grasp the young woman before she fell and pull her in close.

"Whoa; you are still tired, aren't you? Let's rest a bit longer" he called out as the two of them leaned back against the rocky face. Safe in his arms Romis took several deep breaths to recover and calm her racing heart; a fall from here would have surely been fatal.

Confused for a moment she first thought her racing heart and deep breathing was because of how close she had been to death twice recently. Then she realized she'd been at risk of dying before but it never took her this long to calm down afterwards. As she leaned her head onto Drachus' chest Romis noticed he had grabbed her shoulder and her butt to steady her. Normally she reacted rather badly when a man grabbed her butt; the lady was surprised to realize she was actually happy about it this time!

After they had stood there like that for a few minutes giving her time to rest Krant caught up. Opening his eyes he groaned and closed them again as he saw how high they were. "Is something wrong?" he asked through clenched teeth. Before Drachus could answer, Romis spoke up.

"No, I tripped. We're fine; let's get moving!" As she hesitantly pushed away from the Dragon Lord he smiled.

"Right; let's go. Lunch is waiting!" he said. However, he didn't let go of her the rest of the way, holding on to her shoulders just in case.

At the top Romis broke into laughter and tears of relief as she sat on the ground to rest. As they waited for Krant she could tell her breathing was still heavy. Scolding herself silently she thought 'Get a grip! You've been near death before; why is this time freaking you out so much?' As she glanced at the Dragon Lord she saw he was putting his hat on straight and his gloves in his belt. The lady suddenly realized it wasn't fear from nearly dying; she was aroused!

Romis was no blushing virgin; ever since her figure had blossomed several years ago she'd had no trouble attracting male attention when she wanted it. She even had to discourage aggressive guys with a well-placed kick from time to time. Not that she slept around a lot either but she was fond of big, tall men and this Drachus was both. He had also just killed a bunch of orcs to save her life and kept her from falling to her death. With that plus his amazing aura, it was no surprise she'd find herself attracted to him.

However the strong feelings sweeping over her were near-overwhelming. Making certain he was watching Krant climb up the ledge and wouldn't see her do it, she pinched herself. "Get a grip; you're no panting tween facing her first crush, you are a grown woman - behave like one. Cut out the gasping and the sweating right now!" she muttered.

Once Krant caught up they walked to camp. After they recovered they all had a late lunch. Neither adventurer asked why the wanted Dragon Lord and a High Priestess in penitence robes were traveling together. Both were experienced enough to know that the church sometimes engaged in activities that were best kept secret. Sora did explain the crimes on the wanted poster were exaggerated and given what he had just done for them, the adventurers believed her. Yuma was wearing her ring so they had no idea what she was. Romis noticed Chia was staring at her.

"Do I have something on my face?" she asked. Chia blushed and stammered a bit.

"Why do you dress that way, in so ... little? Isn't it embarrassing?"

Glancing at her little leather outfit – boots, bracers, a halter top, thong, leggings and a garter belt - her small skirt was still drying so she wasn't wearing it right now. Romis had chosen not to put it on after seeing the other ladies – she wanted Drachus to pay attention to her! Scolding herself again for her lack of self-control, her mind raced for an explanation other than jealousy. "It's really hot here" she finally said.

"Hot?" Chia asked.

"We're from the Snowfall Realms. It's cold there; you dress warm if you want to live to see spring. Here you don't have to. Plus dressing light is cheaper – wash-women charge too much to clean blood from clothes!" Krant laughed.

Chia blushed deeper as she glanced at him. His lean form was clearly visible to all in the camp – he was almost as tall as Drachus and much more muscular. His tattered kilt was little more than a loincloth and his shirt was drying; he was half naked.

When talk got back to the orcs, things became serious. "We never got a look at their whole band" Krant said."

"Is it common for a band that big to be here?" Drachus asked.

"Absolutely not; the army must be told" Sora shouted.

Drachus looked at her. "Do you really think it's a good idea for *us* to do that right now?" he asked quietly.

Romis was shocked as Sora whispered "Maybe not."

'There is something odd going on here' she thought to herself. If a priestess was hesitant to carry a warning about something this dangerous, she assumed they were on a very important secret mission for the church.

"If we gave them two spare horses, couldn't they ride bareback to carry the word?" the coachman suggested. Krant and Romis looked at one another then both shook their heads.

"Sorry, it won't work." Krant said.

"Why not; don't you know how to ride?" Sora asked.

"She'd be OK if there was a saddle. Bareback riding, at more than a slow walk she'll fall ... a lot. She climbs like a monkey but she'd eventually break her neck" Krant said.

Before Sora could ask more Romis blurted out in a rather annoyed tone "And if he goes alone he'll get lost, saddle or not." When it looked like Krant was going to refute her she added "You got lost inside that little crossroads inn just looking for the bar that one night!" Grinning in embarrassment Krant decided not to argue.

"So you would need to ride double?" Drachus said.

"But all we know is there are a lot of orcs" Chia said.

"Good point," Drachus mused. "Weak Intel can be worse than no Intel at all." He recalled that's what had killed the American General Custer. In the dark of night, his 7th Cavalry Regiment scouts had found the camp of a band of a few hundred renegades he'd been chasing. In the morning when he attacked he found they had joined up with a bunch of others; there were actually thousands of them there. The General's day did not end well.

The group had fallen silent while thinking.

After a bit Drachus saw Yuma waving at him. After he walked over she whispered "I can find them."

"No way are you playing Girl Scout!" he hissed quietly. She shook her head and continued.

"I have a spell, of sorts; I can do it by magic. I won't even need to leave the camp. I can count them as well as find out where they are. But there is a really big problem though; I can't wear it and do the spell." she said.

Thinking about how she made berries, he asked "You have to be naked to do it?"

"No, this!" she exclaimed, pointing to her disguise ring. Drachus glanced at the adventurers then pointed to the coach. "No, I can't do it from in there; I have to be out here. They'll see what I really am" she said before he could ask.

Krant saw the two of them in a serious quiet conversation. "I think we're causing a problem" he said.

"Yeah, I noticed" she said. As Drachus headed towards them Krant and Romis tried not to look concerned as he approached.

"You said if I ever needed anything ..." he said.

Krant looked from his partner to the distressed Yuma, back to the very pretty Romis and then at the coach. "Oh; I get it, she likes you; have fun with it! That coach is plenty private and we've got time" he said with a barely concealed grin.

"Jerk" Romis shouted. "You know I'm not like that."

"Oh, please. You take so long in the bath you must be looking for company. You're such a tiny thing; it can't take you that long to get clean." Krant was right about that. Romis was shorter than average, barely taller than Sora but unlike the slender priestess Romis was a fully grown and well-filled out young woman.

"I have never ..." Romis started indignantly.

"What about that elf?" Krant cut her off slyly. As Romis stopped in mid-sputter he added "The one with that spell you wanted so badly?"

At that she turned beet-red and looked to make certain no one else could hear. "Look that was different. We NEEDED that spell and she didn't want money ... or anything else we had to trade."

Drachus coughed as he realized the lady had just admitted to an embarrassing Sapphic episode in her past.

"Yeah well you did get that spell all right. It took you two days and nights and your head was in the clouds for a week after. Plus, some of the things you've been saying in your sleep ever since are just plain strange ..." Krant added.

"I'll kill you" Romis shrieked at the top her lungs as she tried to punch him in the head. "You know I didn't have a choice; you swore you wouldn't bring it up again!"

Krant seemed to be toying with her, not in a mean way. Her yells didn't seem serious either so Drachus assumed they were relieved to be alive after nearly dying, needling one another over a past embarrassment. A girl with personal secrets who talked in her sleep would be accustomed to her partner hearing embarrassing things from time to time. He assumed Krant made a point of only bringing that up when she was the only girl there.

"That's not it" Drachus interrupted.

Romis ended her mock assault on her laughing partner and went back to listening. Everyone else wrote it off as two friends having a good-natured scuffle.

"What do *you* want?" Romis asked quietly as her heart fluttered imagining what he might want fom her.

"Not what you think. Forget what you are about to see. Never tell anyone; don't ever bring it up again" Drachus said with all seriousness.

"Is that all?" Krant asked. "Forgetting is easy; remembering takes work. To forget something you don't work to remember it, right?" Romis nodded in agreement.

Since they were both on board Drachus gave Yuma thumbs-up. As she nervously took off her ring they saw her suddenly become a beautiful dark elf. Krant sat bolt upright and Romis' jaw dropped from the shock.

They watched as Yuma took a cushion from the wagon, sat down facing the direction the orcs had run off to and began meditating.

Everyone else in camp was very quiet while she did. After a minute, Romis sat up straight in surprise. "That's Flying Eyes" she whispered.

"Huh?" grunted Krant.

"It's an elf spell. I've heard they can cast their minds out to see things at a distance" Romis explained.

"Is that's why she changed; she can't do it if she is disguised?" he asked.

"Maybe; I don't know all the details" Romis said.

"It sounds useful. Could you learn it?" Krant asked.

"I've heard only elves do it. But if she *could* teach me, maybe ..." Romis began but Krant cut in.

"Well you know she's interested in your tiny self. THAT would be the best way to ask. It's not like its anything new ..." Romis must have known what he was going to say; the kick was on its way before he even finished his sly joke.

Yuma flew her eyes around until sundown. The camp was quiet, not wanting to disturb her. The only one moving was Drachus. He paced behind Yuma between her and the camp, careful not to get too close.

After a while, Romis wiggled her cup at Chia and the girl came over with a pot of tea. As she poured, Romis asked "Are they a couple? He seems awfully worried about her."

Chia shook her head no as she replied "The Dragon Lord doesn't know much about magic and that makes him worry. Plus, he really worries about us girls anyway. Besides, I've never seen her work a spell for so long either. But Big sister Sora says it's OK. She's watching with her own magic, making sure nothing bad happens to Big sister Yuma while she's using her spell to look for all of those mean orcs who tried to kill you" Chia said.

Romis wasn't sure why but knowing they weren't a couple seemed to relieve her. She was quiet for a while longer. "Why are all of you traveling together?" she asked.

Chia was happy to spend lots of time telling Romis all about how the wonderful Dragon Lord had saved her by killing that demon at the shrine, protected her from mean people at Karnet, helped Big sister Sora when she was in trouble with cultists, blasted the bad bandits who were trying to hurt the merchants and saved Big sister Yuma when she was going to be seen in the capitol and killed.

The two adventurers were increasingly amazed the more they heard. Then Chia started going on about how Big sister Yuma had cured her bad leg and how she could walk and run now just like a normal girl. Eventually Sora came over and interrupted.

"Please take tea out to the perv" she said.

"Sure thing, big sis" Chia said and dashed off.

"Lady Sora, I hope you won't be offended; I would like to ask you rather odd question" Krant said.

"I may not answer if it's *too* odd" she said.

"In all seriousness, why is a High Priestess in penitence robes traveling with the wanted Dragon Lord, a demon-touched and a magically-disguised dark elf sorceress?" he asked with a confused frown. Romis was surprised at the depth of the question from her muscle-bound partner; he had noticed Chia's heterochromia iridum just like she had.

Sora hesitated for a bit before answering. "Chia told me about something that Drachus had once said to her and it affected me, deeply. It made me rethink a lot of things I'd always accepted as normal. He told her that no one can choose their parents; holding that against them is just plain wrong. It seemed to be quite a … a fine way to think about people. Maybe I'm not saying it as well as he did but that's why." Romis saw the priestess was blushing.

"Do you love him?" she asked. Even Krant was surprised at that one. Sora turned beet-red.

"That-that butt-butt obsessed pervert? He's such a jerk! Just because he saved me, saved Chia, saved you, s-saves everybody? How-why-why what would make you even start to imagine that I might have fallen in love with a big butt-petting jerk like him? Don't stare at me in that ... that tone of voice; I am *not* in love ..." she sputtered.

As Romis worked to hide her grin at the obviously love-struck girl's embarrassment Yuma suddenly let out a cry of pain and collapsed. Drachus was on her in a second, checking her for obvious injuries before carrying her over to the coach where Sora checked her out a bit more carefully. After a few moments, she came around.

"I'm fine; it just a headache. They spotted me. That's the weakness with Flying Eyes" she grimaced. "Most spell casters can see it; it is vulnerable to direct attacks and these can cause a backlash to the caster." After a few minutes rest and a cup of tea she explained.

"I found them and there are a lot; four groups of 15-20 on foot, each with several trained wolves plus there are 20 or so goblins riding really big wolves. They're camped about nine miles that way" she said pointing north.

"There were also three wagons and a coach. The wagons hold supplies and the coach windows were shuttered; it's not easy to see inside. When I got close enough to try, a spell caster must have spotted me. A flame spell hit the Flying Eyes and destroyed them; it hurt!" she said then finished her tea.

"So they have a sorcerer with them?" Romis asked.

"No, the spell wasn't from the coach – it came from among the mounted goblins" Yuma said.

"That means a shaman" said Krant.

"Then this isn't just a raiding party, it's a war party. They're going to hit a village or maybe even a small town somewhere" said Romis.

Speculating on targets, who was in the coach and other particulars went on for a few minutes before Drachus ended it. "Sora is right, the army has to be told right away" he said in a loud voice.

"Quiet!" Chia hissed. She pointed at Sora gently massaging Yuma's temples to help alleviate the pain of her headache. After a bit the dark elf fell asleep and Sora covered her with a light sheet before going to the now sleeping Chia and doing the same for her. Then the priestess curled up alongside Chia to get some sleep herself.

Drachus took the opportunity to clean his pistol. He had no cleaning kit so he used the same methods needed to clean guns in some of the backward areas on his old world. Pushing a bit of wet rope through several times with a punch from the coachman's tool box swabbed the powder residue from the rifling grooves and the cylinder chambers.

Pouring boiling water through the barrel and cylinder washed it out pretty good and a second small piece of rope soaked in the grease from the wheel axles provided corrosion protection. Later he would see about having a real cleaning rod made by a blacksmith somewhere.

On the other side of the camp Romis was astonished at everything she'd seen today. A High Priestess had offered comfort to a dark elf and a demon-touched. Dark elves could be killed for being in the kingdom! Rumor said this girl was the most arrogant and selfish High Priestess there had been for generations; someone had worked a miracle.

The demon-touched had an obvious case of hero-worship; after all this Drachus had done for Chia, Romis didn't think that was odd at all. But even with everything he'd done for the priestess her falling in love as well was strange. Maybe his aura had something to do with it.

She turned to Krant to ask his opinion but he was already snoring. Shaking her head she decided it could wait until morning. As Romis lay there watching the Dragon Lord clean his orc-killing gadget, she realized she was breathing heavy and her heart was beating fast – again!

The adventurer was surprised to notice she was also tingling a bit in sensitive places; she was very aroused - *again*. For a moment she wondered if the others would notice if she went over to him so they could...

"Stop it; you are being a fool!" she muttered to herself. True, she did like tall men and this Dragon Lord was taller than anyone she had ever seen plus he had just saved her life – twice. But she was a mature woman, not some adolescent infatuated with a man she had only just met.

With some effort she overcame her urges and calmed down. It had been a long day and she was rather tired.

Sora's comment about problematic parental backgrounds had reminded her of her own childhood. Her mother worked in a tavern; despite her beauty and desirable physical appearance – Romis was much like her in those respects – her mother always spurned the advances of men.

Romis eventually learned her father and his three friends had not been very nice. The rough drunks had dragged her into a stable and treated her quite harshly all night long - Romis' conception had *not* been consensual.

That was part of the reason her mother and the tavern owner's half-elf daughter were a couple. Elian was a sorceress with some skill in ice magic; the ice cold drinks they served made the tavern very popular in summer. She had taught Romis quite a bit about ice magic.

After the teen had forcefully repulsed the advances of a drunken noble it was felt Romis should begin a life of adventuring – somewhere else.

Despite camping near a pack of marauding orcs, and the silly urges she was feeling to the Dragon Lord, she felt safe enough to fall asleep easily. That night, Romis had a dream about herself, an amorous dark elf sorceress, the tall Dragon Lord and many Flying Eyes watching as they frolicked in soft, fluffy, cloud-like bed sheets. This was a dream that she would not tell anyone about for years.

Upon waking she realized she'd squirmed about so much in her sleep that her top had slipped off. As the blushing lady put herself in order she was glad to see no one else was awake. When they all started getting up for breakfast she saw Drachus was missing, so Romis asked about him.

"He went down into the ravine to collect gear he said you'd need. He said we should start breakfast without him" the coachman said.

As they ate Drachus returned with an orc's cloak filled with belts and odd bits of armor. He didn't speak until after he'd finished breakfast.

"The best option is for you two" pointing to the adventurers "to ride to the army to warn them about the orcs; the rest of us will continue to our destination. You need to go fast so take all four of the spare horses; the coachman told me we can reach our destination without them."

As the coachman nodded Drachus continued. "These are draft horses; they're not fast but have lots of stamina. Krant, you swap out among three of them every hour or so. That should keep them from playing out before you reach Midland Crossing; the coachman said there is an army post there. Romis, you are a lightweight: I doubt you'll tire out one horse the whole way."

She grumbled at that and raised her hand. "Speak" Drachus said.

"Riding that fast with no saddle, how do I avoid breaking my little neck when I fall off every few minutes?" Drachus held up a finger towards her and turned to Sora.

"By the way Sora, didn't you want to try on some of the new clothes Chia got in Laris?" he asked. Everybody was shocked by the sudden topic swap.

"What are you going on about? Are you really that desperate to see my butt again?" she cried.

"Hardly, I've seen it – twice" Drachus snickered.

Romis and Krant were surprised by that; were these two actually lovers? Romis was shocked that she wasn't jealous; the adventurer realized that thought just seemed to make her wonder if he wanted to see hers – and if he would like it if he did!

"Given what we'll be doing soon this may be your last chance. It will take time to get these two on the road but after that we'll all be in the coach together so unless you want to do it then ..." Drachus continued.

"Why not do it, Big Sister? You'll look really nice in some of those pretty new clothes we got in Laris; I'm sure of it!" Chia stepped up to say. Sora held out for two more heartbeats before both girls ducked into the coach for their private fashion show. As she turned to close the door she opened her mouth but Drachus beat her to it.

"Right ... No peeking for the perv!" he shouted. She glared at him, slammed the door and closed the shutters. By the time Drachus walked back to the adventurers the 'Oohs' and giggles of both girls could be heard clearly.

"You should make Midland Crossing by evening to report the orcs to the army post" he said. Romis held her hand up to stop him again.

"Look, you still haven't told me how I'm to stay mounted with this directionally challenged, half-naked skirt lifting hound when I can't ..."

Being 'mounted' by a man could have a very different meaning than what she had intended to say; Romis realized she hadn't used the best wording. Blushing beet red she was about to re-speak herself when Drachus held up his hand again and walked back to the coach. Krant couldn't hold back and burst out laughing.

"What you said!" he snickered.

"You lousy beast; as if I ever would with a leg-fetish freak like you" Romis cried and kicked him in the shin.

They were adventuring partners but not lovers. The ever-jovial Krant liked his women tall, slender and inexpensive – Romis was short and blessed with a curvaceous figure that could *never* be called slender.

While the adventurers had their scuffle the Dragon Lord approached the coach and called out "Sora!"

"What?" came her irritated reply as she threw the shutter open.

"I made a gadget so Romis won't break her neck riding to warn the army but I need more parts to make it work" he said.

"Well, you're certainly not going to find them in here are you?" Sora challenged.

"Well, actually yes; what I need is two pieces of stiff woolen fabric. A long thin piece, like your cowl, to pad the gadget so it won't chafe the horse's neck and a wider one, like your smock, to pad the horses back so it won't chafe her trim and delicate ..." Drachus said.

"Butt!?" came Sora's outraged response.

"Yes" he said simply "her butt."

Sora stuck her head and shoulders out the window so she could yell at Drachus. His eyes opened wide in surprise as his glance darted down. Sora realized she wasn't wearing a top right now and was leaning out far enough that her lacy bra and a surprising amount of cleavage were exposed.

Ducking back inside with an outraged cry just her head returned moments later. "Even if it is a penitence robe, you want to turn a Holy Raiment into a BUTT PAD? ARE YOU INSANE?"

"No" Drachus replied calmly. "Without this they'll never make it and those orcs will kill a lot of innocent people." Seeing how serious he was quieted the girl.

Her eyes flickered over to the two adventurers for a moment. "Why can't you use the orc's cloaks?" she asked.

"Those have too many ticks, fleas and such. I wouldn't want to infest her delicate ... region ... with such vermin as that" Drachus said.

That was true but what he wanted was to separate Sora from her holy garb to make it easier to convince her to get rid of the coach's crests; eliminating the holy emblems one at a time like this seemed the best way. From the look on her face, he knew he might need one more push.

"Of course you could always take the coach there yourself to deliver the news. I'm sure your Big sister Selena really wants to see you again. You two didn't get to chat very much before we had to leave Laris in such a hurry after that big fight with the cultists' ..." he added.

Sora ducked back and slammed the shutter. Drachus stepped to the side and waited. After only a few seconds the shutter popped open and her cowl flew out followed by her raiment; then the shutter slammed shut again. Drachus had anticipated where they would land when the left-handed girl threw them out and was right there catch them.

As he approached the adventurers Krant dropped to his knees and kowtow chanted "Oh Great Master Manipulator; we're not worthy!"

Romis kicked her comedian partner in the leg and stood waiting silently with her arms crossed – which only caused her breasts to be even more evident. Once Drachus drew near enough to hear, the annoyed adventurer looked him in the eye.

"You know, you are such a ..." she started.

"Jerk" Drachus interrupted. "Yes I know; you are not the first woman to tell me that since I got here" he said as he walked past not even slowing down.

After Drachus installed the makeshift stirrups he'd fabricated he showed Krant how to lift Romis onto the horse's back. Without being attached to a proper saddle these couldn't be used to mount up. Besides, draft horses were big; diminutive Romis would have had trouble even if it was a small pony with a real saddle.

As Drachus lifted her up the first time to demonstrate her little leather skirt hiked up - a lot. She shoved it down quickly while he glanced away like a gentleman should and Krant laughed at her blush. Then Drachus showed her how to swing her leg over and put her feet into the stirrups.

After practicing a bit they seemed to have it down. Fortunately her boots had high heels so her feet wouldn't slip through the stirrups causing a fall. The lady was apparently self-conscious about her lack of height. After she was securely in place, Romis frowned.

"How are these things going to make sure I don't fall off?" she asked as she looked the odd contraption over. She recognized the steel cups holding her feet as helm armor parts from several of the dead orcs but didn't understand the strange way they were attached with straps.

"If you feel yourself falling, stand up with both feet in the steel cups – the stirrups" Drachus said.

After standing she shifted side to side a few times and realized they didn't slide much; they were connected between the horse's legs. They were attached at the center with loose leather loops wrapped around the horse's front legs at the shoulders and another strap going up over the horses' neck; they wiggled but would keep her from falling.

"Knights would pay a fortune for these!" she cried.

"Yes, I'd planned on selling them but, it's whatever. You need them here and now" Drachus said. "Just keep them hidden if you can once you get to the crossing. That or just drop them in a deep hole before you get there."

All the while the two adventurers were practicing getting her up into the saddle Krant noticed Romis seemed preoccupied. The lady knew there was something she had to do, just not what. When they went to mount up to leave, she saw the shadows cast by the morning sun and it suddenly came to her.

"You go first" she told Krant, then led her horse out of camp. After spending some time to stand it in the right spot she called out. "Drachus, hoist me up please." When he did her shirt hiked up again but she didn't push it down.

"You need to swing your leg over" he said.

"I know" she replied "but I have to say something." Romis hadn't been able to think clearly for a while now so she hadn't planned on what to say - but words just suddenly started tumbling out.

"I always pay my debts. When I owe someone I pay them back as soon as I can so I don't have to worry about any debts coming back on me later" she said.

Glancing down she shifted her legs; the simultaneous movement caught Drachus' eye. By reflex he looked down to see what was going on and realized that where the horse was standing the morning light of the sun perfectly illuminated the space under her lifted skirt!

The surprised man looked her in the eye and saw that she was deliberately facilitating the exposure. Despite her red face this wasn't an accident; the lady apparently thought this was an appropriate compensation for his saving her life yesterday – twice.

Drachus had been concerned the orcs might come back so he had kept a careful watch from that direction most of yesterday; the womanizer had noticed Romis' revealing attire but decided the orcs were too big a threat to direct too much of his attention towards her. Then with all the concern over Yuma's injury and normal camp activities he hadn't had too much time later in the evening.

Now realizing she had created this made up excuse for a bit of blatant flirting he accepted her offer to even things up between them. For several seconds he looked as she gave him a clear view of the mysteries typically hidden from view under her shiny black leather miniature skirt.

Romis knew that with her sitting on the horse he couldn't see her butt; however she was determined to give the Dragon Lord a perfect view of everything else down there. For a moment she fantasized about him lifting her off the horse and carrying her to the coach where they could…

"That was lovely, most appreciated. I wish we had enough time to explore all of the possibilities; maybe we'll have another chance sometime in the future" he said. He meant it - she really was a beautiful young woman; she seemed to be interested in him too. If they met up later the lady could express her gratitude a bit more thoroughly.

Krant saw Romis and Drachus chatting for a bit after he hoisted her up. Then she lifted her leg over, put her feet in the stirrups and rode over.

"What's up, your face is bright red?" he asked.

"Nothing" she snapped back "forget all about that." Krant just laughed when he realized why she was blushing.

"I get invited to the wedding, right?" he asked. Romis didn't rise to the bait this time - which was unusual.

"When you talk to the army, tell them all about the orcs but don't even mention them" she said indicating Drachus and the other ladies.

"You're right." Krant agreed. "We owe them ... wait, you said when *I* talk to the army. Where ..."

"I'll be staying at the crossroads" Romis said. "Even *you* can't get lost on Army Post Road and I need to hide these stir-up things." Krant understood immediately.

"Yeah, they are worth a fortune and Drachus deserves to be the one who collects on that fortune ... but there's something else going on here, I think. Are you really all right? You sound odd" he said.

"I don't know. I feel ... weird" Romis whispered back. Krant was quiet for a moment before he added more.

"Speaking of weird, you said some stuff in your sleep last night that was even stranger than your usual mutterings. I always thought you hated it - since when do you *like* it when a man squeezes that trim little butt of yours?" he asked slyly.

Romis practically choked as she swung at Krant with the riding crop Drachus had made for her but he ducked it; just like the rest of her diminutive self, her arms really were short.

As Krant laughed Romis slapped her horse's rump with the crop and rode ahead. He spurred his mount on as well and they headed for the Midland Crossing to find the army and report the orcs.

CHAPTER 8

WHAT IS UP WITH ALL THE BUNNIES?

Shortly after noon the coach arrived at Karrat Kommons, a small farm community in a slightly less desolate valley deep in the cursed lands.

"It officially belongs to me but it's actually run by a church-appointed overseer" Sora explained as they arrived.

As the coachman was moving the horses to water a short and very annoyed human rushed out from the largest of the buildings. The overseer was surprised to see how Sora was dressed; she wasn't wearing a holy raiment. Her new attire was ... a bit risqué.

She sacrificed her holy raiment yesterday to make a riding pad for Romis. Sora was wearing one of Chia's cute new outfits instead. The sleeves and skirt were very short; diminutive as she was Sora was still about 4" taller than Chia.

Like Romis' boots, Sora's new ones had high heels. However they'd been intended for Chia; as Drachus wondered how Sora fit into them he saw they laced in the rear making them adjustable; Chia had to use several pairs of extra socks for the shoes she wore so they would fit her tiny feet anyway.

Noticing her short skirt Drachus thought 'Maybe Sora took some fashion tips from Romis?' As a priestess she would likely be unfamiliar with normal women's attire. However, Romis had been a bit on the flagrant side; maybe he should tell Sora that letting your stocking tops show under your skirt wasn't very lady-like!

"Oh my" the overseer started. "High Priestess Sora, I was not notified you were coming for a little visit. I hope all is well." The Dragon Lord spoke up before Sora could reply.

"Sora is the lady who rules this village. Why would she need to pre-arrange a visit to her own lands?"

The overseer looked as if he were going to swallow his tongue. As the nervous man paled after seeing the embroidered dragons on his duster Drachus thought 'He's seen that verdamnt wanted poster too.'

As Drachus considered Sora's new fashion sense, two pretty girls in work clothes – and a pair of bunny ears - hurried up, curtsied and greeted the High Priestess. From the overseer's sneer they were likely his assistants and he felt they should have been here quicker. Drachus expected they were in for a chewing out.

A moment later he amended that to a backhand when another bunny-eared girl with a bloody lip and a very new black eye scampered out of the door the man had just used. She was obviously trying to not be spotted by the overseer. They hadn't even met yet but Drachus already felt that he had disliked this guy for years.

Sora ignored the overseer as she spoke with the out-of-breath bunny-girls. "Hello, I remember you from my last visit. Isn't your name Miyun?" she asked one, a nice looking girl with long brown hair (and ears).

"I'm Mion milady. I'm honored you remember me!" Pointing to the other girl she said "This is my cousin Surra."

"I am much honored to meet you milady" Surra said as she curtsied. Surra was a lovely girl with short sandy-colored hair (and ears).

Both were about the same height; about 4" taller than Sora (not counting their bunny-ears) and had bright violet eyes. They were among the taller girls Drachus had seen so far. There were several bunny-eared men around who were only a few inches taller than these girls.

He first thought the 300 or so folk here were just wearing cute costume bunny ears for some reason. As Drachus looked closer he saw the ears were real; so were the fluffy cottontails! Otherwise, they seemed perfectly human. 'Well, I've run into demons, dark elves and orcs; why not bunny-folk. At least they seem to be friendly' he thought.

None of the bunny-folk looked very healthy; they were all a bit thin and pale. The Dragon Lord didn't like jumping to conclusions but he thought they looked malnourished. Mion and Surra seemed tired as well. As Sora chatted with the bunny-girls, Drachus noted they were very conscious of what they said, always glancing at the overseer before answering questions. Thinking it would be best if they could speak freely, he interrupted them.

"Sora, I wouldn't want us to keep the manager from his important duties. Why not have these lovely young ladies do the tour instead?" Drachus suggested.

"Oh no, escorting the High Priestess is far more important than any task I have in my office. I would enjoy personally conducting the High Priestess myself" he said with a touch of anxiety. Both of the bunny-girls went a shade paler as the overseer replied. Sora was beginning to smell a rat and it showed.

"I would rather catch up with Mion and learn more about my new friend Surra than infringe on your valuable time" she said with a thin smile. The overseer could tell she didn't want him conducting the tour.

"I'm sorry, High Priestess, but I have strict orders to ensure any visitor is given a proper tour by me, myself. I'm afraid I must insist." The tone of his voice made it evident he expected her to back down. Drachus saw hesitation in Sora's face; she likely wasn't used to going against orders from the 'Main Office' of the church so he spoke up.

"You know, from what I've seen it's good we came here today. From the looks of it, whoever has been running this place doesn't know a damn thing about farming." At that, Drachus saw a grateful look flash from Sora. The overseer seemed offended and straightened up a bit.

"I doubt you are qualified to make that assessment, SIR! I am an expert appointed by the church to manage and protect the High Priestess' lands and I will do so as *I* see fit" he replied with some arrogance. As the manager ranted Drachus saw the bunny-girls go paler and cringe away from him. They appeared to be accustomed to physical abuse when he was upset; that settled it as far as the Dragon Lord was concerned.

"Sora, I don't believe this 'person' can manage a flowerpot. I suggest you send him back to his 'superiors' to report that you and I will manage this land from now on *without* his dubious assistance" he said with some irritation.

At this point the bunny-girls had wide, happy smiles. Apparently having the dangerous Dragon Lord here was preferable to this guy. Sora now had a happy smirk on her face too but the overseer wasn't giving up just yet.

"Now see here Miss Sora" apparently the formality of her 'High Priestess' title was no longer needed "it would be the height of ... foolishness to do something that ... foolish. This person can't possibly have the skills and experience necessary to control these beastly creatures, to keep them properly disciplined and producing profitably as the church has decreed is required. He should be ..." The overseer's voice trailed off as he noticed Drachus' glare.

"Perhaps I should demonstrate the skills I do have and what I can do with them" Drachus said quietly. He didn't like what he'd heard about 'discipline', especially when Mion and Surra cringed on hearing it. As he stepped towards the overseer the smaller man paled, recalling this was the dangerous Dragon Lord he was mouthing off to.

"That's enough, Dragon Lord; I shall deal with this" Sora said. The angry priestess pointed her finger at the manager's face.

As she whirled to face the overseer Drachus realized that her skirt was so short if she moved quickly it would flare out enough that you could see her panties quite clearly; apparently she had taken a *lot* of fashion tips from the very flagrant Romis! He was pretty certain she knew how exposed she was with a skirt this short; at least on his old world women seemed to be quite cognizant of that. He wondered why she was being so obvious; maybe she thought Romis-like fashion was normal?

"Your services are no longer required! As of now you are no longer employed here; gather your personal things and depart. You have 10 minutes" Sora shouted.

"But milady, High Priestess, that isn't enough time ..." the now-sweating man began.

"9 minutes" Drachus said quietly, staring into the man's eyes, with that same sneer on his face. The fired man glanced at Sora but she was already talking with the bunny-girls about the tour. The overseer looked back at Drachus.

The Dragon Lord had pulled his watch out and was looking at it with a sinister laugh. "You're wasting time: you have eight minutes until I consider you a criminal trespasser and take ... appropriate actions." The pale, sweating ex-overseer spun around to run back to the large building.

"Hitch up the wagon, immediately; I'm leaving right away!" he shouted to several bunny-men working at the nearby barn as he literally ran away.

Some minutes later the frightened toady left the main building carrying a coat and a large bottle. Two small leather bags tied to his belt jangled and bounced back and forth as he ran towards the stables. Seeing the wagon wasn't hitched up yet he looked over at Drachus. The Dragon Lord was putting his watch away and laughing as he walked towards the barn.

The now terrified man ran over to the horse being brought out to the wagon. Dropping the coat as he clambered up onto its bare back, he grabbed the lead from the groom and kicked the beast's sides. When the animal jumped he lost his grip on the bottle; it hit rocks on the ground and shattered. Cursing, he clumsily headed the horse to the gate. It was obvious he didn't know how to ride.

"You bully" Sora said with a wide grin as she looked at Drachus. The overjoyed Mion and Surra started the tour.

Despite his earlier statements, Drachus was out of his depth here; he'd been born and raised on a family farm producing fruits, vegetables and livestock in small quantity for their own consumption. They'd sell off any excess for a little extra cash to buy things you couldn't grow on a farm.

Yuma could not be much more help. She was only familiar with gardening, growing just enough to feed the sisters at her former shrine with a little left over for guests.

This was a production facility growing three vegetables in quantity on 300+ acres for distribution and sale; the scale was very different. However, even without production-level experience they could both see some of the more obvious problems. The biggest issue was the well; every bucket pulled from it yielded as much mud as water.

"We spend so much time drawing up such dirty water" – "and filtering out what we need for cooking and drinking" explained Mion and Surra. Drachus noticed the two of them had a habit of finishing one another's sentences in perfect tandem. It actually sounded very cute!

"This area is now very dry, almost barren. From the old fields we've passed it was once good farmland. What happened?" Drachus asked.

"Don't you remember Dragon Lord? I told you how that demon you destroyed cursed the lands before it was sealed away" Chia prompted him.

At the mention of his destroying a demon both bunny-girls caught their breath and went wide-eyed in shock; killing a demon must be a big deal on this world. Drachus recalled some of the details of that conversation but back then he wasn't too sure about magic and curses. Given all he had experienced to date, he was taking them a bit more seriously of late.

Examining the well he had noticed something odd at once; it was right out in the open. There was no shelter and it had no crank; buckets were pulled up on a rope, by hand. There wasn't even a lid to keep wind-blown dirt and debris out. Seeing a small dust devil spinning a few miles away, he spoke to Mion and Surra.

"How often do you ladies get dust storms?" he asked.

"We have small ones all the time" – "every so often we get a pretty big one" – "yes, every few weeks" – "there's a lot of clean-up after those" – "it gets everything so dirty" came their tag-team response.

He thought for a few moments remembering some of the issues he'd seen with small wells in Algeria and how often they'd had to dig debris from them so they could get enough clean water to be of any use. Drachus glanced down into the well; it was so dark he couldn't see more than a dozen feet down.

"Do you have a spotlight … umm … a large mirror" spreading his hands to about 3' across "or a shiny metal plate that will reflect sunlight?" he asked. Mion and Surra glanced at one another each holding their own hands about three feet apart.

"There is a big mirror" – "in the manager's room" – "ex-manager's room" – "will that work?" they tandemed.

"Can you bring it here?" he asked. When both nodded yes, Drachus had to stifle a laugh; the bouncing bunny ears were too cute for words. After they scampered away to fetch the mirror he found a long-handled rake and leather ties in a nearby shed.

When they brought the mirror he tied its frame to the rake's handle so they could lean it out over the well and reflect light down inside so he could inspect it. Even with the extra light it was too deep to get a good look from up here but he did see it had ladder rungs embedded into the sides. He sent the bunny-girls to fetch a large pair of oiled boots, some coveralls, a bucket and a small shovel.

Once he was properly dressed he slung his gun belt over his shoulder. Then he recalled that the mirror didn't shine enough light to work with.

"Do you have a lantern?" he asked. The bunny-girls seemed confused at that too.

With a snort Sora pulled a copper coin from her purse. She muttered a bit while her hand glowed and handed him a glowing coin. That's when he recalled she was good with light spells. He took it and as he was about to thank her, the light went out. As Drachus snickered she glowered.

After a moment she picked up a twig; repeating the muttering it began to glow. Instead of giving it to him she poked it through a buttonhole in the coveralls as she glared.

"Do - Not - Touch!" she said quite miffed. The grinning Drachus climbed into the well as Sora fumed.

By the light of the glowing twig Drachus was able to climb to the bottom of the very deep well. Once there he dug at the edge; as expected he could go down more than a foot under the water level and find wall bricks below the mud; it was choked with years of wind-blown dirt. To be sure he repeated the test in other places with the exact same results.

"We can get your well working a lot better than it has been in just a few hours" he told them once he was back up top. The bunny-girls jumped for joy. That's when he noticed their cottontails bounced as they jumped up and down, almost as much as their breasts. Bunny-girls tended to be slender but that part of their anatomy was generous. Their loose farm dresses had disguised that until now.

"We can also fix it so it won't ever get this bad again" he added. Drachus asked them to collect several boys about Chia's size and a grown man to supervise. When all of them were gathered he gave them the same lecture on water tables and well digging his uncle had given him years ago as they dug a new well on his family's farm.

He didn't know how much the bunnies understood - Drachus didn't get most of it himself back then - but he knew that after dredging out three or four feet of dirt and debris the well would bring in a lot cleaner water.

After he changed to normal clothes he saw that Sora and Chia were gone.

"Sora saw something and took off; Chia ran off following her" Yuma said. He assumed they'd gotten bored and were off playing with bunny-kids. Continuing on with the tour without them he noted issues with how they distributed fertilizer, didn't rotate crops or use extra earthworms in their composting. He explained a few improvements to these processes

Drachus was happy to see the bunny-folk were fairly fastidious with their toilet practices. The bunny-folk had several outhouses distributed among their fields and in the area near the main buildings. In many places on his old world, he'd seen local farmers just 'cop a squat' anywhere - whenever the urge hit.

Mion and Surra tandemed telling him they used chamber pots inside at night or during inclement weather.

He did make mention that they should wash their hands afterwards – especially before they ate meals. With that he saw nothing else significant on the outdoor portion of the tour. Drachus asked them to show him where the manager's office was so he could check to see if he actually had kept any records.

Along the way he thought that Sora should be there for this and asked Mion if she could locate her. He noticed that her smile wasn't as happy as it had been; he'd ask her about that privately a bit later.

In the main building the large kitchen was reasonably efficient. As they moved on Drachus glanced through a window and saw a cemetery off in the distance. Mion was standing at the gate and further in he could see Sora kneeling at a gravestone with Chia holding her from behind.

After seeing that, he suddenly understood all too well. On the trip out Sora explained she'd only been here once, when the land was granted to her. She was certain her sisters wouldn't even consider looking here and remembered Mion whom she'd only met once. Obviously something pretty horrible (apparently fatal) happened on that visit and it still brought up bad memories for Sora.

He figured this was a personal thing for her and unless she decided to bring it up, he wouldn't pry.

In the fireplace of the manager's office were warm ashes from a recent fire; there were several dustless gaps on the record shelves and an empty cashbox. That explained the ex-overseer's slow departure; he was burning records (probably to hide crimes) and looting the treasury.

While waiting for Sora, Drachus made a drawing of a roof to protect the well, a lid to cover it and a crank for raising water. "This will keep the well from being choked up with dirt like it has been. The crank will make it easier to pull up more water with each draw" he explained to Surra.

While drawing he'd sent Yuma to check out the dispensary since she was best qualified to handle that. As he headed there Sora, Chia and Mion rejoined him. It was obvious they'd all been crying but he deliberately did not mention it.

At the dispensary they found Yuma with tears in her eyes too. As Drachus brushed them away he muttered "Is there something in the air?"

"It's so sparse; there's almost nothing in there!" Yuma cried. Drachus looked in - it seemed normal to him – but most of his experience with dispensaries was as a patient.

"Who normally takes care of your dispensary when there are injured to treat?" he asked Surra.

"Arlen, Trey and lately Miso" she said.

"Have them meet here with Yuma" he added. Turning to her he said "Talk it over with them and make a list of what you think is needed to make the place useful."

"I'd love to, thank you" Yuma said with a smile.

Drachus took a second look and realized there *was* something not right. As the bunny-medics arrived it hit him; there was no water. There was no sink for washing hands, no stove for boiling water, not even a bucket.

"When you need to treat someone, where do you get the water from?" he asked the three newcomers. They seemed confused at his question.

"If we need water we just get it from the well" Arlen, the oldest of them, replied.

It suddenly dawned on him that knowledge of bacteria and infections was 20th century medicine; from what he'd seen this was a 10th century world at best.

"How long before the cooks begin dinner?" he asked.

"It will still be a while" – "the afternoon work isn't done yet" Mion and Surra replied in tandem.

Assembling them all in the kitchen was easy; it was a large area that cooked for 300+ at each meal. Drachus went through the basics of sanitizing and cleaning injuries with filtered water sterilized by boiling it for three minutes before it was used. At their confused looks Drachus realized he hadn't seen any clocks.

"Do you ladies known any songs?" he finally asked.

"There are nursery rhymes" – "and lullabies" the bunnies tandemed. Rather than have them take a lot of time singing a selection of those Drachus pulled out his watch.

"Is there one you both know that is about this long?" With that he clocked three minutes. After a short discussion they decided a nursery rhyme about a mischievous but adorable kitten named Sally was just about that long.

"Once the water starts boiling with bubbles the size of a pea recite that rhyme at a nice, normal pace; that's how long you need to boil it to make certain it's safe to use for cleaning injuries" Drachus finished.

After a few minutes explanation most of them knew how to properly wash their hands and clean patients' wounds with previously boiled water. He also explained they should boil all bandaging materials too. This would reduce the chances of an injury becoming infected.

Even Yuma had never heard of this; she finally asked "Why?" Drachus didn't think he could explain the medical science of his world to healers from this world; he didn't fully understand it himself. After a bit of thought he finally just told them straight.

"I don't know the details; I've been told this by some ... some well-schooled healers who didn't have magic. I have found over the years it works. Most who die from injuries ... without stuff like Rosen Salve or magic healing ... usually die from infections - not from the injury itself, right?"

They thought for a bit before agreeing that was the case. Drachus already knew it was true. The many lectures he'd heard from battlefield medics over the years said it was infections that killed most wounded on the battlefield; some said pneumonia, influenza, gas gangrene and trench foot had killed as many soldiers as bullets in the Great War!

Ordinary injuries, even minor ones that became infected could easily kill – especially in a world without magical healing. The assembled healers were uncertain but promised to follow those procedures in future.

It had been a very long day for Drachus. An hour after sundown he was preparing for bed when there was a knock at his guest room door. It was Mion.

"Is there something you need?" he asked.

"Yes, I've come to see to your comfort for tonight" she said. Then she stepped in, closed the door behind her and began to unbutton her dress.

"Just how much comfort do you mean?" he asked with a sly grin.

"Just as much as you wish" she said as her dress slid to the floor. Drachus immediately saw that bunny-girls didn't wear underwear. Despite their bountiful breasts, they didn't even wear bras!

Once nude she stepped forward, slid her arms around his neck, stood up on her tip-toes and kissed him lightly on the lips. Mion seemed genuinely happy to be there, the fully-grown and well-formed young woman was not hesitant at all, so he decided to accept her offer; it had been weeks since his night with Salana.

As they embraced he noticed something ... odd. Since bunny-folk farmers distributed fertilizer raw, his sense of smell had pretty much been hammered to death during the tour today. He'd spent an hour checking records the ex-manager hadn't burned; his nose had recovered enough to let him notice smells, especially close up like this.

"Don't be upset when I ask" he began "but just when was your last bath?"

"Baths are for humans. If we need to, we just wipe one another down with a wet towel" she said with a bit of surprise. Then an alarmed look appeared on her face.

"But if you find it offensive..." As she started to back away he pulled her close again.

"No, smelling a bit ... sweaty ... isn't offensive, but I'd rather share my bed with a sweet smelling bunny-beauty." As he thought about it, he hadn't seen a bathing area anywhere in the compound today.

"Have you ever had a sponge bath?" he asked the confused girl. She shook her head 'no'; her ears wiggled adorably.

"Get a small pot of hot water, another of cold water, an empty bucket and a few towels; there's some nice soap in Sora's coach. Once we have it all here I'll show you how. Don't worry; I think you'll love it!"

Giving her a sponge bath was great foreplay.

"I do like spongy bath-ing ... before coupling" she whispered as they cuddled a bit later. As Drachus began to drift off to sleep, she added something that seemed odd.

"I hope Shara can have one someday." Something about the way she said that seemed to set off an alarm in the back of his head waking him.

"Who is Shara?" he asked.

"Oh, that's Surra's younger sister" Mion said.

"Is something wrong with her?" Drachus asked.

After a short hesitation, Mion eventually replied. "She was ... injured ... several days ago. The manager – ex-manager – always says it is too expensive to summon a healer all the way out here so she's in one of the recovering rooms. Surra hoped Lady Sora could help her but I'm not ..."

"Of course she'll help her" Drachus interrupted. "If she can't, I'm sure Yuma can. She's a healer too." He was now wide awake and rather concerned.

"Take me to see this girl, please" Drachus asked as he started to get dressed. Mion was dressed much faster than him - not wearing underwear made getting dressed quick. She led him to a second floor wing of the main building. He realized this area hadn't been on the tour today.

"What could that beastly man have been thinking?" Sora's annoyed voice was easy to hear through the door as they approached.

After Mion knocked Chia opened the door to a candle-lit room. Face down on the bed was a petite bunny-girl with most of her body covered by small white cloths.

On a table next to the bed Drachus saw a glass jar of water and a ceramic bowl of bandages both marked 'Boiled'; he was happy to see that Surra was using what he'd showed them earlier about preventing infections.

When Sora was about to lift a towel covering the girl's derriere she noticed Drachus. The lady stormed over and pushed him out of the room. "No free peek for you, butt perv" she said as she closed the door.

Once they were both outside, he spoke to Mion. "I thought you two looked tired. You've been working during the day and taking turns caring for her sister at night." Mion nodded and seemed about to speak when he noticed several women gathering in the hall nearby. Drachus was going to ask them to disperse when he saw that several had bandaged injuries.

Now he understood completely; these rooms were right above the dispensary. "Those recovering rooms you mentioned; this is where the injured are sent to heal" he said to Mion. As she nodded Yuma and the young dispensary attendant Miso came up the stairs.

"Yuma" he quietly called to her "some of these girls have injuries. Will you see if you can do anything for them?"

"Of course" she said. As Miso showed her and one of the bandaged girls into a nearby room the door to the first room opened and Surra spoke with Mion quietly. Afterwards, she approached Drachus.

"Lady Sora asked if you could ... arrange for more boiled water" she asked; it was almost as if she were trying to apologize.

"You mean she said to keep me out the way because the girl will be naked and she's afraid I'll peek?" he replied after he figured it out. Mion's blush answered for her.

"OK" he said "no worries. Let's wait in the kitchen. I think a cup of hot tea with honey sounds great right now."

Drachus spent the next half hour down in the kitchen staying out of the way until Chia came down to fetch him. In the recovering room the girl was now covered with a sheet and sleeping comfortably. Sora was sniffing a small vial.

"But it's the only pain medicine we've ever been allowed to use!" a very distressed Surra was saying.

"It's fine; the concentration isn't so high as to be an issue" Sora said with a smile; that seemed to relieve Surra.

'I guess it is something that might be addictive, like Morphine' Drachus thought. Sora moved to Drachus with a very sour expression on her face.

"What the hell is going on here?" she quietly hissed

Motioning her out into the hall he waved for Mion to come along. Once they were down in the kitchen he asked Mion to bring Sora up to date on the old manager's policy for treating the injured here. What followed was a nasty review of the neglect the bunny-folk were subject to.

"If it will cost more than a few coppers, we are expected to heal on our own" Mion explained. By then both Sora and Chia were literally in tears.

"I'm sorry, I didn't know; I'm so sorry" Sora said over and over as she embraced Mion.

Yuma eventually came downstairs. "The other girls have mostly healed previous injuries. Only one is of any serious concern. She has several broken fingers that have become slightly infected. It also looks as if many have been ... whipped, recently" she said quietly.

As Drachus sneered he recalled the ex-overseer saying he had to 'discipline' the workers to make them productive; that explained the short whip he'd found in the office desk and the well-oiled manacles hanging from the rafters in the barn!

Now that he thought about it, it also explained Shara's injuries too. Drachus was very glad that bastard was gone; now he didn't need to kill him.

"In their condition, how long will it take you and Yuma to get these girls fully healed?" Drachus asked Sora. She was still sniffling back tears.

"I'll take care of the fingers in the morning. They don't even have Rosen Salve. Fortunately we had some left out in my coach. We'll have them recovered enough for natural healing to finish by lunch tomorrow. So long as they get rest and good food, they'll recover even if we have to leave. Otherwise, by day after tomorrow we'll have all of them healed." Yuma nodded in agreement as Sora finished.

Pointing to Sora and Yuma he said "You two into bed right now. Get rested so you can deal with that in the morning." Both girls nodded and headed out.

Drachus went back to his room and undressed. Just as he was climbing into bed there came a light tap at the door. He found Mion outside waiting and let her in. She quietly slid out of her dress and back into bed. After he climbed in beside her, they kissed and curled up together.

"What really made you come to me?" Drachus asked.

"If a visitor wishes for company, he'll ask for one of us to be sent to his guest room" she began. "The ex-manager said we were to provide whatever they wished - to make them feel welcome. Sometimes it's not pleasant; often it's quite painful" Mion added with a frown. Her ears drooped as she likely recalled some of the nights she'd spent with visitors. After a bit, a small smile returned to her pretty face

"You didn't ask for company but you did spend most of the day with Surra and I so we assumed you would be interested in one of us" Mion said.

"And since Surra was busy taking care of her little sister, you volunteered" Drachus concluded. After a few moments Mion nodded and continued.

"I also hoped I could convince you to ask Lady Sora to help Shara. I'm sorry; I know that sounds like I was trying to manipulate you but ..."

"Don't even worry about it!" Drachus interrupted. "In future, if you ever need anything else like that, just ask. Most people are willing to help someone in trouble if you need it!" Mion leaned up with a surprised look on her face.

"But we're not human, we're bunny-folk! No human will help one of us!" she cried.

Drachus suddenly realized the only people he'd seen here in this world up to now *were* humans, other than Yuma and she'd had to stay hidden. But in Karrat Kommons there had only been the one human.

This was some sort of reservation for non-humans. Not only that, the ex-overseer had run it like an underground brothel – one where you could do anything you wanted to the girls! On a hunch he asked "Have you ever traveled outside this village?"

"No" Mion replied quickly. "It would be a crime for us to leave."

As he lay there watching Mion nuzzling his shoulder, her bunny ear grazed his cheek. It suddenly dawned on him he was cuddling  with a girl who wasn't totally human. On his old world he'd never had issues with women of differing regions; Asian lovelies, South American cuties, dark Moroccan ladies and playful Caribbean women had all appealed to him. Thinking about it he realized that he found bunny-girls and dark elves to be just as attractive as human ladies; maybe even a bit more so!

With a grin he wondered if this attitude was also something his summoner had arranged for. After a bit he decided it didn't matter; he was here now and the lady certainly seemed happy to be with him.

Mion let out a squeal as Drachus squeezed her cottontail. "They do feel like a big ball of cotton" he said. Mion smiled and kissed him, both her sad mood and his curiosity dispelled. They eventually did sleep, but not until much, much later.

In another Guest Room Sora was curled up in a ball on the bed still sniffling. Chia climbed into bed after undressing. Sora hugged her and after a few minutes starting talking about her first visit to Karrat Kommons.

"It was the day after I was given dominion. The previous overseer was giving me the tour. Mion was with us. Her little sister was tagging along too. Tion was such an adorable little girl with soft brown hair and green eyes, so much like you but with adorable bunny ears" she added while caressing Chia's head.

"She was only 7 years old and wanted to be just like her wonderful, smart big sister. When she asked to go along so she could learn I said it was fine, much to the overseers' annoyance. Since there were other church administrators with us he was treating me with a bit more respect than that last one so he had to let her come along."

After a few more sniffles Sora continued. "It was a hot day and I'd asked for a glass of cold tea; Tion ran back to fetch it. Craftsmen who had come with us were repairing the roof of one of the outer buildings. As she came back a worker slipped and dropped a bundle of wooden shingles ... right on top of her; Tion was hurt so badly! That day I was the only one in the village who could do magic healing." After another grimace the priestess continued.

"Even now my magic healing isn't very strong but back then it was pitiful. Despite everything I tried to help ... little Tion ... she died in my arms! The last thing she'd said was 'I'm so sorry ... I spilled your tea.' I haven't been back here since." By now both Sora and Chia were crying openly. They cried themselves to sleep in one another's arms.

In the morning, Drachus asked Mion about Sora's cemetery visit. When he heard about little Tion's death he felt like a heel for pressing her about it. He apologized over and over until Mion finally asked him to stop.

At breakfast a red-eyed Sora made an announcement. "Any injured bunny-folk are to see me after breakfast in the dispensary." She and Yuma were busy there most of the morning; even though they had refilled it from the stock at the Healing Shrine they ran out of Rosen salve from the medicine chest in her coach treating all of the injured. Yuma knew the recipe; after all she helped create the stuff. She went out with bunny-girls to collect Rosen berries to make a large batch.

Drachus realized he needed to have a talk with Sora after she and Yuma had finished caring for the neglected bunny-folk. There were issues here that Chia hadn't known and he needed to learn all about them. That angel had said 'These people wallow in despair. Death is often their only escape'. He was only just now realizing how bad things were here!

Chapter 9

My First History Lesson

Meeting in the manager's office after lunch, Drachus and Sora discussed the medical status of the bunny-folk.

"Yuma is teaching them to make Rosen Salve; she'll also show them how to make soap. That miserable pig didn't even let them have that" she said shaking her head in disgust. The Dragon Lord could see Sora was still depressed about the injured bunnies so he tried to change the subject.

"Mion said the bunny-folk are here under the churches protection but it looks like they're prisoners. What is really going on here?" he asked. With that question, Sora began his first *real* history lesson.

"Demons arrived on our world during the Great Catastrophe 500 years ago. They had opened a gateway direct from the deepest pits of Hell; it was a time of violent shaking, strange glows on the west horizon and skies darkened by choking clouds of dust."

Drachus thought that sounded more like volcanic eruptions in the distance, but he didn't mention that. From the way she was speaking He felt it likely Sora was repeating a history lesson from her time in school. Recalling how some backwards areas taught history by rote memorization, he figured that was how she'd learned it too. Until books became common this was also how *history* could so easily become *legend*.

"Demons started raiding Durakkon about 400 years ago. After more than a century of destruction the Angelus descended from heaven to aid the mortal world. They organized an army from all of the eastern realms. The demons were defeated and the Demon

Warlord Kreeger sealed in the specially constructed Shrine of Hope" Sora said. After a short pause she continued.

"That forest had been the bunny-folk's home and they were forced to abandon it. Before returning to the heavens Angelus Solus ordered the bunny folk be cared for by the church in recompense for losing their homes."

"That explains the orchards there" Drachus muttered.

"You've seen them?" she asked. After he nodded she continued. "Ever since the plagues that swept through last century the kingdom has become almost entirely human. The plagues only afflicted humans, rumors blamed demi-humans for causing them; demi-human races are hated, subjugated or even killed on sight. It's only because of the Angelus Solus' command that the church even lets the bunny-folk live. From the look on your face I can tell you really hated that story."

"Are you happy about it?" Drachus said. After a few seconds hesitation, she spoke again.

"I've never liked it; there's nothing I could do about it by myself." Drachus was lost in thought for some time after she said that. Afterwards, he decided to ask for some clarification on several things that had bothered him ever since he got here.

"You're a High Priestess but church officials don't seem to treat you very well. Any 'respect' they show to you is only lip service. The Bishop in Laris took your escort away and locked you up; that rotten overseer thought he could order you around. What is the story here?" he asked.

"I don't know. The only one of us who gets any real respect is Big sister Selena - because she's likely to beat them up if they try to push her around" Sora quietly replied.

Drachus grinned imagining that foul-mouthed red-head pounding some pushy noble with his own padded chair as Sora continued with her explanation.

"She's popular with the common folk because she hunts bandits and marauding orcs. The nobles and high church officials are nice to Big sister Maia; she is in charge of protecting the capitol and warding it from evil. But she rarely gets to leave the Holy Cathedral; she is always surrounded by church officials. The people only see her on Holy Days; she gives blessings from the cathedral balconies to ten thousand or more in the courtyard." With a sneer she added even more unpleasant details.

"Our servants, our maids and even when we can hold services are selected by the church elders; we have almost no say in our day-to-day lives. They even tell us when to … when to marry" she finished with a blush.

Now Drachus understood why Sora had been happy with running away from the church. She really was treated like valued property – held in virtual slavery, though in a comfortable 'cage'.

"You're fancy figureheads for the public to adore; Pretty Princesses! You're supposed to be in charge but the real rulers are nasty little men in the shadows. I'm surprised other priestesses don't give you more support; you ladies do stick together when men are trying to push you around" he said.

"There are no priestesses in the church" Sora said.

"What?" Drachus asked. "Virian had two with his caravan, plus Yuma was a priestess in that Healing Shrine." As she shook her head Sora explained in a bit more detail.

"Virian had hired *adventuring* priestesses. Women who can cast healing spells can be priestesses but they can't hold any significant positions in the church. The church doesn't even pay them; they earn a living by aiding adventurers with quests. They can stay at shrines between adventures giving healing but they can't hold services. The Healing Shrine was not a church; shrines are run by nuns and supervised by a Mother Superior. You can't get married at a shrine because there is no priest" she finished with a sour expression and a sullen voice.

Drachus suddenly realized he'd goofed. He'd tried to distract Sora from her own sadness only to bring up the sadness of an entire sick society. Then it hit him – despite that first day, the angel who summoned him didn't bring him here to fight demons; he was here to show these people how to *live* better. She'd said his *knowledge* could save them; he was no scientist but he had 1,000 years of basic information that the locals didn't.

Just like boiling water to prevent infections, rotating crops and covering the well to prevent dirt from building up; on his old world that was common knowledge but here they didn't seem to know about it.

The angel also said his *skills* that would make it happen. He was a soldier, and a pretty good one. If he could stay alive long enough to pass on what he knew that would certainly improve the lives of the locals. Well, here was a perfect place to start!

"Look, do you remember the stirrups I made for Romis?" he asked with sudden excitement in his voice.

"What's that have to do with anything?" Sora asked sniffling back her latest round of tears.

"It has everything to do with everything. Those are not the only items from my land I can introduce; all of it will be valuable if done right. If you OK it, I'll set up shops here to make them. We're remote, there's room - it won't take much - and the bunny-folk can help. Before long, your little village of cute bunnies will be so wealthy the world will *have* to respect you" he finished with a wide smile.

"Are you serious?" Sora asked.

"You bet; it won't be overnight but it will happen" he said. Then she asked a question Drachus never expected.

"Will it really help the bunnies live better?"

"It will make them happy, keep them healthy and protect them from being abused by pigs like that overseer" he practically shouted.

After she though it over for a bit, Sora answered. "OK, do it. Just don't let me see you petting their butts whenever you feel like it you perv!"

"Can I fondle a few cottontails if I do it where you *can't* see it?" he replied with a wide grin. With a laugh and a tearful smile Sora kicked him in the shin before he left to get some very important work started.

The rest of that day Drachus checked out the farm, compiling a long list of the materials and tools needed to fix the worst of the problems. Before establishing a crafting enterprise he had to secure their food production. With Sora taking over direct management, the church was likely to make commerce with the village difficult to punish her.

Drachus also made a point to ask the bunny-girls about their diet and food supply.

"Oh don't worry about that" Mion told him.

"Yes, we have a garden just for our own food; we get plenty of veggies to eat" added Surra.

"You work outdoors all day but you're all so pale" Drachus noted.

"That's natural" – "most of us are like that" replied the Mion-Surra duo.

"And you're always so slender?" Drachus added.

"Oh yes" – "there's no such thing as a fat bunny." – "But these are always plump" – "oh yes, nice and round" said the Mion-Surra team, smiling as they indicated their breasts. Mion had apparently told Surra how Drachus had paid a lot of attention to hers last night. Like many men he found large breasts on pretty women to be very desirable!

While organizing his lists before bed he heard a knock at the door. Images of sponge bathing with Mion again flashed into mind. He was surprised to see it was Surra at the door this time.

"May I" she said pointing inside.

"Sure" he responded.

"I want to thank you for all you have done for us. The well is practically gushing with clean water now. I am also very grateful for everything you asked Lady Sora and Lady Yuma to do to help Shara. And for all you did for the other girls and those new things Lady Sora said you are going to do to help the village."

Before he could stop her she went to her knees and touched her forehead to the floor in a very deep bow.

"Please don't do that" he asked. By the time Drachus stood her back up he could see where this was headed. He was about to tell her they were welcome and send her away.

"Mion also told me about this spongy bath thing. She was raving about it all day and she smelled so nice - all over! I'm very curious to see for myself if that sort of thing is really as wonderful as she said it was" Surra said.

Right then there was a quiet knock at the door; Mion had come to deliver bathing supplies for them. She kissed Surra's cheek saying "Good night" as she left. Since they had set things up Drachus decided not to fight it.

He was surprised at how much Surra enjoyed having her sponge bath - even more that he enjoyed giving it to her! He didn't get a lot of sleep that night but he certainly wasn't going to complain.

On the way to breakfast Drachus was looking for Sora; he would ask her to have the bunny-folk carpenters pull the crests from her coach and repaint the doors. Before he could say anything she and Chia cornered him.

"What did I say about not molesting the bunnies?" Sora yelled. With tears in her eyes Chia pushed at his chest.

"I thought you were so nice! I heard you made them come to your room to ... so you could ... you could make them ... how, how could you?" she cried.

Stepping back from the angry girls the surprised man raised his hands saying "I didn't drag them into my room; *they* knocked on *my* door."

"Of course they did; they don't know any better. That miserable manager ... ex-manager ... made them do that for any visitor!" Sora yelled. Before he could say anything else Mion and Surra hurried up.

"Please don't be angry" – "It's not his fault" – "We did go to him on our own" – "He didn't drag us anywhere" they tandemed. At that Mion and Surra took Sora and Chia by the hands and led them to a corner table where they had a fierce, quiet discussion for several minutes. Once they were done Chia came over with a shy grin.

"I'm sorry I said mean things; they said it was OK, that you didn't do anything wrong. In fact, they said it was – all right." Sora came up a few seconds later with a frown still on her face.

"I suppose if *they* say so, it is all right. Like I said before, just don't go grabbing bunny-girl butts at random!" she said glaring at him.

While the carpenters removed the crests from the coach Drachus had the blacksmiths make a cleaning rod for his pistol so he could keep using pieces of rope, boiling water and mineral oil to keep his weapon cleaned. That piece of technology from his world was just too valuable to lose to rust.

While they were making that, he had a long discussion with some of the older bunny folks about typical wind direction. Then Drachus drew a rough map of where the craft shops should go and asked them to clear the crops from those areas. The spots he were usually down-wind of the fields and village buildings.

He'd seen in Laris that they burned coal for the forges here; he didn't want the bunny-folk to have to deal with smoke in their homes or soot contaminating their crops and this seemed to be the best way to avoid it without using really tall smokestacks. He hadn't seen any brick works that high on this world – they might not be able to build them.

At lunch Sora asked "How are you going to pay for the stuff on your huge list? That creep ex-overseer took all the money and I don't have much."

"Don't worry" he smiled. "I won't have any problems convincing donors to provide all the funds we need."

She smiled for a moment and then with a shocked face shouted "You're not going to threaten them with fire and death are you? Like you did to the orcs and those cult-creeps in Laris? I mean, they are only merchants; that would just not be right!"

"Quiet, you'll scare the nice bunnies" Drachus scolded. "I'm not threatening anyone. I planted the seeds of a business opportunity in Laris; they should be blooming quite nicely in the capitol by now" he said.

That evening he heard a knock at the door. Was it Mion? Or Surra? Or Both! No, it was just Sora here to complain. "Why are we leaving so early? The sun won't even be up" she whined.

"We have a lot to do; I want to get in early to get started. Now go get to sleep so you can get up early enough" he said.

Awake at 4 am Drachus dressed and went outside; he'd told the coachman to be ready well before dawn. He was there hitching up the horses.

Drachus saw Sora leaning on the coach. Seeing him she whined "Why are we leaving so early?"

"I told you last night" Drachus growled.

"What do you mean? It's STILL last night!" she complained loudly pointing up at the dark sky.

"Don't worry Big sister, we'll nap inside" Chia said.

"I can't sleep in that rocky, rolly coach" the priestess whined as they got in. As he waited for them to board Drachus realized that Sora was not only sharp-tongued, she could be whiny at times too. The little lady had a variety of emotional states; she was definitely a teen-aged girl!

Drachus was a bit surprised when Yuma came out to the coach wearing a traveling cloak. He'd assumed she would remain here to make sure the bunnies stayed healthy. Apparently she, Sora and Chia had become even closer that he'd thought. As Yuma walked up she seemed fine until he saw her glazed, unfocused eyes.

Drachus stopped her and asked "Are you all right?"

"Oh yes Reverend Mother, I'm fine. I'll have the goats milked well before breakfast, then to bed" she said; the lady was sleepwalking!

'Some people can't handle early rising' he thought to himself as he guided her to the coach. Then he recalled that Yuma had worked mostly at night at the shrine; she was sensitive to sunlight. She was now trying to adjust to being awake in daylight; her day/night schedule was rather confused right now.

Mion and Surra walked from the kitchen carrying two lunch baskets which they put on the coach's rear luggage shelf. Both kissed him good bye in turn and wished him well.

After he climbed into the coach he saw Sora and Chia already asleep with their pretty little heads on one another's' shoulders. Yuma was curled up almost in a ball on the other seat also sleeping. As he settled in next to the former nun for what Sora had warned would be a boring half-day trip to the capitol he muttered "This will be a really weird ride."

Despite her complaints Sora and Chia were asleep on each other's shoulders well past sunrise. Drachus thought that was surprising. Sora was right about the rough ride; he'd never noticed before but her coach had no real suspension. Vehicles on his world had leaf springs to smooth the ride on rough roads. Fancier cars also had hydraulic shock absorbers.

Here they used leather straps reinforced with oiled rope. Though it did smooth out the worst of it, it was still quite bumpy.

Drachus was uncomfortable for other reasons. After sunrise a bump caused the sleeping Yuma to roll to the side. Her face landed in his lap and she stayed there.

As he looked up to avoid staring at her he could see Chia and Sora were dressed the same, wearing what had become Chia's favorite new outfit; a long-sleeved white blouse with matching collar, bow and cuffs, a short red pleated skirt, white stockings and red ankle-strap pumps.

Drachus was surprised to see they both wore skirts so short their stocking tops were exposed. 'I'll have to make certain to warn them that is *not* lady-like' he thought.

He suddenly recalled where he'd seen an outfit like it before – it was similar to uniforms worn by girls at private schools on his old world. He had commented how pretty it was, mainly because it looked so familiar; it had likely become Chia's favorite because he had noticed it.

Drachus realized that she seemed to have acquired a bad case of 'Hero Worship'. Of course, he had saved her from the demon, saved Sora and her sister from the cultists in Laris and saved Romis & Krant from the orcs. The impressionable girl had seen him doing a lot of 'heroic' things since they'd met; a bit of hero worship wasn't all that odd. He'd have to make certain it didn't go too far though.

Tofferd only made the one outfit; Sora likely had the bunnies make her one of her own, so the two could dress alike. She and Chia had become comically close of late. Their hair was even done in the same style now!

As Sora wiggled in her seat to cuddle closer to Chia he could see her white lace panties and garters. The Dragon Lord had never asked her about it - because he was sure that would convince Sora he *was* a pervert – but based on what he'd seen, lingerie was a status symbol for women here. The high-status priestess wore very fancy ones, the working class adventurer Romis had worn durable, plain ones and the virtually-enslaved demon-touched and bunny-girls didn't wear any at all.

Realizing that if Sora woke up she would never let him forget she'd caught him looking up her skirt to see her butt, he focused his attention back on Yuma instead. She usually wore a durable dress suitable for working around the farm and a large bonnet to protect her from sunlight. What she wore now was much prettier.

When she'd walked to the coach earlier she'd worn a traveling cloak so he hadn't noticed. That cloak had apparently fallen off; looking around Drachus couldn't see it anywhere, so it was probably lying on the ground back at Karrat Kommons.

With the morning sunlight shining in he could see Yuma now sported a white long-sleeve lace-up blouse with floppy cuffs long enough they could even cover her hands, protecting them from sunlight if you unfolded them.

She also wore a short maroon skirt with an asymmetrical hemline. A Parisian dancer he'd once spent time with had called it a 'Can-Can high-low'; the front hem was higher than the sides or rear. She'd told him it made dancing easier – it also displayed your legs and often your lingerie; that's how she attracted the customer's attention. It was also why he had noticed her.

Yuma's striped leather vest was cinched by a wide belt accentuating her ample bosom, another nice facet of his traveling companion Drachus hadn't seen before now. On the floor was a matching leather hat with a very wide brim to shade her face and décolletages from the sun.

Feeling like he was in the middle of a traveling peep show, Drachus decided to review his shopping lists, to focus on something other than girls in sexy clothes. As he lifted one of Yuma's legs to get his valise the Dragon Lord saw she now wore silk tights and black riding boots with the tops folded down, pirate-style.

The shirt-tails were long and showed under her skirt hemline. With her leg lifted it slid up showing smooth thighs and a trim derriere covered by sheer black silk – she wasn't even wearing panties!

'Where the hell do girls *find* those kinds of clothes at a farm?' he thought. The bunny-folk wouldn't have any so his mind raced; the man almost thought he was having a dream right now but the rocking of the coach felt all too real.

As Drachus focused on his lists to distract himself he realized Yuma's outfit looked like it had been put together from some of the clothes Tofferd had supplied for Chia. After a bit he finally figured it all out. Sora likely had the bunny seamstresses alter one of Chia's dresses to make Yuma's new blouse, another to make her vest and a third to make her skirt. The floppy cuffs were probably added to make up for the short length of the sleeves.

The tights had likely been a pair of slacks. No wonder the fit was near-skin-tight; the dark elf half-blood was several sizes bigger than Chia. It also explained the wide décolletages of her new 'blouse'.

Though they fit Chia and Sora, the lace panties from Tofferd would be far too small for the former nun. 'That's why she isn't wearing them; the bunnies don't any to begin with' Drachus assumed. He'd had never seen what Yuma wore under her dress, so these were probably her own boots; though he didn't know why a nun would even have a pair of boots like those.

As the Swede shook his head from side to side he thought to his self 'This is going to be an even weirder ride than I first thought!'

Chapter 10

What is Going On Here in the Capitol?

An hour after sunrise the coach lurched to a stop. The jolt threw Yuma off the seat and would have plunged her face-first to the floor if Drachus hadn't caught her. Chia and Sora in the front seat didn't have to worry about falling but were jolted awake.

As they looked about in confusion Chia blushed and Sora's eyes narrowed as an angry expression crossed her face. "Pervert!" she muttered glaring at Drachus.

The baffled man heard Yuma shyly say "Um, excuse me?" As he looked down he saw that when he'd quickly grabbed her to stop her fall he hadn't been too concerned about *where* he grabbed her. With one hand firmly holding her breast and his other buried high under her skirt gripping her thigh he knew exactly what it looked like.

With the damage done Drachus didn't even try to make an excuse. He pulled the lady into an upright position depositing her on the seat next to him. Then he called out "What's going on?"

The coachman opened the roof hatch and called down "We may have a problem here."

Sora went to lean out the window to see what was happening but Drachus grabbed the back of her skirt to stop her. This earned him another glare that would have been followed by her trademark hiss of 'pervert' if he hadn't motioned her to silence; she still stuck her tongue out.

He leaned his head out and saw they were in a shallow, narrow ravine with sheer sides where the road bed had been cut through a low hill. Coming around a curve up ahead were several riders and a line of at least three big wagons; there was nowhere near enough room on the road for them and the coach to pass one another side-by-side.

Seeing one well-dressed man, a scruffier one and an armored guard were walking towards the coach, Drachus pulled back to think things over.

After a moment he motioned to Yuma saying "Ring! You two, quiet" the last directed at Sora and Chia. Seeing from his easy-to-read face that he was worried, they all quickly complied without arguing. After Yuma had donned her ring, once again becoming a rather plain brunette human woman, Drachus whispered to her.

"You are a maid looking after your mistress' daughters. You are all on your way back to the capitol after visiting family on a country estate to celebrate … an elderly aunt's birthday." As they heard the crunch of footsteps coming closer Drachus went silent but pointed to himself and shook his head. Yuma was confused for a moment until she nodded as she realized he wanted her to not mention him to the men outside; if they were up to no good, not knowing about the Dragon Lord could expose their intent.

Then she leaned out the window to talk to the men … and block their view of the inside of the coach. When she did Drachus saw that the longer hem on the rear of her shirt prevented anything underneath from being seen; she could bend over as far as needed without exposing anything!

Yuma and the coachman spent some time arguing with the merchant over who should back up. After a lot of back and forth it turned out the merchant had nine big wagons and it was a half a mile back to a wider point of the road at their side. The merchant pointed out an easily seen wide spot on the coaches' side only a few hundred yards back around an S-curve. Drachus had hoped they'd give the coach priority. While it no longer had church crests, only the wealthy traveled by coach. But once he got a look at the merchant's wagons he understood why they wanted the coach to back up.

Unlike most of the wagons he'd seen so far here these heavyweight things were huge ox-drawn affairs; they were practically cabins on wheels! The wheels didn't steer at all so it would be almost impossible to turn them around in the narrow ravine. Plus, the heavy yoke for 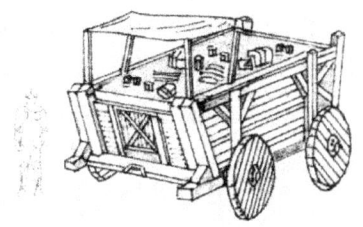 the two oxen might take a lot of time to be switched to the rear to pull them backwards.

Drachus had been confused as to why so many of the roads they had walked had been leveled out; rather than go around hills the locals cut passes and small ravines through them – like the one they were in now. These big wagons would have a tough time turning much less climbing hills.

While the merchant was being polite, it was obvious reversing his caravan would take longer. Shucking his duster, Drachus pulled the tails of his shirt out and draped them to hide his pistol – the dangling dagger still showed. Tapping Yuma on her shoulder he motioned her back. His exit from the coach startled the merchant; he hadn't suspected that such a tall man was in there.

Drachus hoped the merchant and his crew would assume the big guy with the dagger was a bodyguard and behave. If things went south, he still had his pistol but he really didn't want to use it. He doubted the oxen pulling these big wagons were more stable when confronted with 'thunder' than the horses he'd seen so far. If it came to shooting, most of them would stampede – and the coach with the girls in it couldn't get out of the way!

Once on the ground he pointed to a grassy patch off to the side of the road where they would be safe from a stampede. "Miss

Yuma-*rr* perhaps you and the little ladies should take a break over there while we deal with the roadway situation" he said.

Ever since an incident in Peru Drachus had come to realize that sometimes things of a religious nature should be kept secret. Every so often an alarm would go off in the back of his mind telling him that a bit of information might cause problems if others heard of it.

In this part of his new world it seemed likely that many travelers may have been treated at the Shrine of Healing; one might remember the skilled but plain human nun named Yuma and wonder why she was now traveling around dressed like a lady pirate. To keep her from being recognized he thought a pseudonym was a good idea.

Taking the hint Sora spoke up in a spoiled little-rich-girl voice. "Yes … Yes, Miss Yumar, I think a picnic sounds nice. It's too cramped and hot in here!" she cried. The girls came to the door and Drachus helped them down. He saw Chia holding his duster, folded to hide the embroidered dragons. After he had hoisted "Miss Yumar" down, she winced and shaded her eyes from the bright sunlight.

Even if the disguise ring made her look human, dark elves were sensitive to sunlight; Yuma usually wore a bonnet with a big brim. Drachus worried that would not match her current outfit. Sora reached back into the coach and pulled out a floppy hat that did match her outfit. As she shot Drachus a smile she handed it to the 'maid'.

"Don't forget your new hat, Miss Yumar" Sora said.

After donning it, the 'maid' went to the rear of the coach and extracted a lunch basket. When the ladies went to have their picnic Drachus saw the men's eyes were glued to the shapely 'maid' as she strutted away. He couldn't blame them; her skirt swished a lot as Yuma's hips swayed wantonly from side to side; fortunately, thanks to the longer rear hem of the skirt, nothing showed from behind!

He suddenly had a thought; 'how the hell does a nun learn to strut like a Parisian model at a fashion parade?' He also noted the tall heel of her boots made her stride seem even more lewd.

Meanwhile the coachman had negotiated the loan of some ropes to tie their horses to the coaches' rear axle so they could drag it backwards. Drachus and two of the merchant's drivers manhandled the singletree to steer by the coachman's directions shouted from the roof.

Manhandling a rear-steering coach around an S-curve was neither quick nor easy. After two hours of hard work, they finally had the coach far enough back so that the merchant's wagons could pass without further problems.

It took another hour but the slow merchant wagons were finally out of sight. Drachus took off his sweat-stained shirt and wiped himself down with a wet cloth. As he did Yuma suddenly gasped and looked away. Once finished and dressed again they boarded the coach heading towards the capitol. When they were on their way again Yuma took off the disguise ring as she let out a deep sigh.

"I have never been so frightened in all of my life – and this was all SO embarrassing" she gasped.

"Where did a nun learn to walk like that? I was worried we'd some trouble with those men – not that I could blame them. That wiggling skirt was ... really nice" he said.

At his comment Sora burst into quiet laughter. After a moment Yuma blushed to a deep crimson pointing at Sora. "She said I could distract them and keep them from recognizing us if I crossed my feet in front of each other as I walked. It sounded odd but she swore it would work. Was it truly that lewd?" the former nun whimpered. Sora was now laughing so hard she almost fell off the seat.

"It's not funny Lady Sora!" Yuma whined.

"By the way, how does a High Priestess happen to know that trick?" Drachus asked while shaking his head. Wiping the tears from her eyes, Sora replied.

"I overheard my maids complaining about a co-worker using 'The Strut' to get the attention of a handsome knight; I watched the offender. She did have a lot more wiggle in her walk than the others; the men obviously liked it. When I heard she had a very active night life I made a point of learning *all* about it!"

Shaking his head Drachus saw Yuma was nearly in tears. Then he asked "About her pirate costume; was that your idea too?"

Yuma gasped and stood up in the coach "You said this was proper to wear in the capitol!" she shouted. As she stamped her foot Drachus recalled her unusual footwear.

"Where did you get those boots anyway?" he inquired. Yuma looked down and calmly explained.

"Oh, these? Two years ago a nobleman's daughter came to the shrine for bridal training. She went home after the marriage was cancelled; she left these and other rather odd leather attire behind – much of it like the things Romis wore. The Mother Superior thought these boots would be better for travel than my old work shoes; they are made quite well and they do fit me. Why, are they inappropriate too?" she whined at the end.

"Yuma, you are just too serious! You need to lighten up a bit or you are going to lose your mind in the capitol" the priestess said with a grin.

Poor Yuma was actually crying at this point and Sora was giggling uncontrollably as Chia scolded her for being a meanie. However Drachus realized Sora did have a point; Yuma was too uptight. That could attract the wrong kind of attention in a crowded city. To calm the sobbing former nun he pulled her towards him.

"We'll pick up a cloak and more appropriate clothes for you once we arrive at the capitol. That should help out quite a lot" he said quietly.

"Thank you, Dragon Lord" Yuma said as Drachus used his handkerchief to wipe her tears away.

"By the way," he said "Sora is right about that; you do need to lighten up around people; you are so skittish that it will attract the wrong kind of attention. And please don't call me Dragon Lord; it scares people!"

Due to the delay caused by the merchant caravan they had arrived too late in the day for any serious shopping. They were going to stop near a market square so he could buy a new traveling cloak for Yuma until Sora admitted she had brought along a nice dress with a long skirt and high collar that Yuma could wear to hide the other more revealing clothes she had been tricked into wearing.

As the coach moved slowly through evening traffic at the market square, Chia spotted a vendor selling sweet cakes. "Oh Please, Please; they look so good! I've never had something that looked and smelled so sweet" she pleaded.

Sora told the coachman to stop as she grinned from ear to ear watching the uber-powerful Dragon Lord give-in to little Chia's wheedling. After receiving a few coins the two girls darted away to buy the treats. Now aware that her outfit was provocative Yuma, the shy former nun, felt it embarrassing for him to watch her pull on her new dress; she asked Drachus wait outside until she felt she was appropriately attired.

Outside he spotted a nearby tent with a small banner showing what looked like a crystal ball hanging at the entry. 'Might be a Fortune Teller' he thought. He'd always found these interesting, so he went to check it out.

The older woman in the tent gave him an odd look as he entered. After she looked him up and down the lady motioned for him to sit. "Have you concerns or do you merely wish a reading?" she asked.

As he placed a Lunar on her table he said "I just decided to stop by out of simple curiosity."

"As you wish; an ordinary reading it will be. I shall consult the cards to see what the spirits may reveal to me of your past and what the stars have to say of your future destiny" she said with a thin smile. She spent a few moments making a five-pointed star of face-down cards; then drew one from the stack placing it face up in the center.

"You have traveled far" she began.

'A standard and safe opening' Drachus thought to himself; he was a bit dusty. He was familiar with the Tarot of his old world and wasn't surprised to see similar elements in the cards she was using. After she turned the card above it she seemed surprised.

"You hail from a land so distant it sees the light of a different sun!" she said.

'OK', he thought, 'that was a direct hit.' She passed her hands over several cards before exposing one.

"You have received a blessing from a great power." Remembering the angel at the Shrine of Hope, Drachus gave her credit for another hit.

Turning a third card she said "Your blessing is like that coin – while valuable it has two faces. One shines with great beauty but comes at great cost. The other shines with wealth but carries responsibility."

'OK, that was a bit esoteric' he mused. After a moment he realized that since he was stuck here with no way home and was supposed to save the world, it did make some sense. This old lady just might be the real thing!

"You will attract loyal followers who give much of themselves; their devotion will be without measure" she said after turning aver another card.

Drachus wasn't sure why but his mind suddenly flashed on his bunny-girl lovers, Mion and Surra as well as the adventurer Romis; that little beauty had made it obvious she was more than a just a bit interested in him. With those ladies on his mind he interrupted.

"It seems that I do have a question after all" he said.

"Speak" said the old woman.

"Will I marry well?" he asked with a smile.

"A common but important inquiry" she said. Passing her hands over the face-down cards she turned one over.

"Marriage is indeed in your future" she said. Turning a face-down card next to the last she seemed surprised again. "Your matrimonial bounty shall exceed all bounds; the coffers of heaven shall deliver unto you blessings never before seen in this world!" she said with wide eyes.

'That was a bit theatrical - but then so is fortune telling' he thought.

"One last question; I've come to the city on a business endeavor. Can you tell me if it will be successful?" he asked.

"An even more common question" she replied, sounding just a bit disappointed with it. She picked up the deck, fanned it open and extended it towards him. "The results of such actions are most always determined by one's own hand. Choose and we shall see what the cards predict yours will accomplish" she said.

Drachus slid a card from the middle, turned it over and put it in the last open space on her table. As she saw it a curious smile crossed her face.

"The cards predict strife and success, both in great quantity." She turned over the card below it and said with a voice that seemed both curious and impressed. "Despite the strife, so long as your profit provides a benefit to others, great bounty shall befall you."

Drachus would have liked to continue but heard the voices of Chia and Sora chatting as they returned from the sweets cart. "Thank you. That was most entertaining" he said after standing.

"The cards did not choose to entertain you, great power from another realm. They wished to forewarn you; take care with your work! There are many who will be affected by it." That startled Drachus as he took his leave, returning to the coach.

Inside he found a tearful Yuma and a laughing Sora once again being scolded by Chia for being such a meanie.

"Now what?" the exasperated man asked.

Yuma stood up suddenly saying "Look at this!" Her movement revealed the skirt of the new dress had a side slit all the way up to the waist! When open, you could see her painted-on tights and leather riding boots.

"I'm sorry" Drachus groaned as he knelt to study the slit. "It was sewn with a lot of overlap, so I think if you move carefully it shouldn't open up" he said after examining it.

"Are you sure?" she practically begged as the girl closed in to cling to him.

Drachus saw that while the bodice did have a high collar it was also tight-fitted. Yuma wasn't wearing her disguise ring right now so there was a very beautiful and buxom dark elf in a sexy dress plastered up against him. He also noticed she was wearing a very sweet perfume; no, a former nun wouldn't wear perfume. That must be her natural body scent.

Then he realized there was silence in the coach. Glancing over he saw both Sora and Chia staring wide-eyed. Seriously wanting to paddle their suddenly childish bottoms, Drachus grasped Yuma by her shoulders and gently pushed her away for some breathing room.

"I'm certain if you move slowly and don't draw attention to yourself everything will be just fine." He wiped the tears from her cheeks and continued "Now, we don't have time to do any real shopping. We'll check into a good hotel and then head out to have dinner somewhere."

"Oh yes" cried Sora. She tapped on the ceiling hatch and when the coachman opened up she shouted.

"Stop by the Golden Pavilion and check us into their best suite. Have them send a runner to the Silver Table to let them know we are on our way for dinner – make certain they know we want a balcony table. Then drive us there as fast as you can – we're starving in here; I've never been so hungry in my life!"

As they rode through the city Drachus was surprised at how old it was. The worn stone buildings had a wide variety of architectural styles and showed a lot of rebuilt sections; it was nothing like Laris. When he mentioned that to Sora she glared at him as if he were an idiot. While shaking her head she explained.

"Luminas is over three thousand years old. Even stone buildings don't last that long. The lower walls are quite thick with columns to support the brick works of the middle floors; the uppers are mostly wood. That's why most of the living space is high up. The floors are wood framed and must be replaced often but covered with ceramic tiles they wear quite well."

"My, our little High Priestess seems to be a very skilled architect" he grinned.

As Chia giggled Sora blushed and snapped back. "They were redoing one of the floors in the chapel where I took early training. I overheard the craftsmen talking while I was skipping out ... waiting between some of my classes." Drachus was about to remark on her gaffe when the coach stopped. The coachman went in to make the arrangements Sora had ordered.

"I'm curious" Drachus said. "This is the capitol, so I assume you have a mansion or a palace here; why are we checking into a hotel instead?" Sora hesitated as though the answer was embarrassing. Suddenly Drachus remembered their household staff was chosen by nobles; the movements of the High Priestesses were likely well-watched. 'That's why she went to Laris to have her men healed' he thought.

"You don't want your sisters to know you are in town, do you?" he asked. Sora's bright red face answered before she could.

"Don't you like your Big Sisters?" Chia asked.

Fortunately for Sora the coachman returned with word they were in the top suite and they headed for the restaurant so she didn't have to answer that apparently awkward question. Instead of explaining her sibling issues, she started bragging about the dinner they were going to have at the best restaurant in the capitol.

The Silver Table was a fancy place frequented by nobles and the wealthy so Drachus couldn't go in with shirt tails out to cover his gun belt. Fortunately as they rode to the restaurant he'd seen several men - and a few women - wearing dark dusters with embroidery on the cape. Apparently the dangerous Dragon Lord was now a fashion statement among the wealthy.

Sora and Chia wore matching school-girl outfits; they were unusual but likely to be seen as fancy play-clothes. As short as the girls were he felt most would assume they were children playing dress-up. If they didn't do a lot of jumping, the short skirts wouldn't expose their panties.

Yuma was wearing her ring and the new dress; she wouldn't have to dine looking like a pirate lady. They shouldn't draw too much attention.

Their first stop was ground floor washrooms where attendants tidied them up before they entered the restaurant upstairs. His maid asked "Which would you prefer?" as she pointed to a short table with numerous scented soaps on it. That's when Drachus realized 'soap' on this world wasn't usually for cleaning; it was normally used only as a fragrance.

"My, this is the nicest one I've seen yet!" she said while brushing dust smudges from his duster; that implied they had become common among wealthy diners. This was such good news Drachus tipped her a silver Sovereign.

Suspecting the place might have a cloak room or at least attendants to hang coats and sword belts for the diners, before he left the washroom Drachus tucked his pistol in his waistband – covering it with his vest. Now he wouldn't have to draw attention to it by insisting on wearing the belt.

As they walked in Drachus was careful to caution Yuma. "Make sure you don't move too quickly" he told her.

"I'll remember" she whispered back.

"Also, try not to breathe in too deeply" he said. At that Yuma suddenly noticed how tightly the bodice of her dress clung to her ample breasts. As her tiny squeal of distress made it appear the former nun might turn and run out, Drachus held her arm in a strong grip.

"Don't worry, if they notice most will assume you're just a courtesan who ... umm" he stopped as he saw her confused expression; of course a cloistered nun would not know what a profession mistress was.

"They'll assume you are ... an adventurer meeting the restaurant's dress code. And I promise I will give a stern lecture to our suddenly childish Prankster Priestess once we get to the hotel. You are not skipping dinner!" he added with emphasis. At that she blushed again.

'This girl sure blushes easily' Drachus thought; he hadn't realized that she wasn't accustomed to dealing with men – she had been a nun and close attention like this from a man was still quite new for her. He also hadn't realized that the former nun was developing her own case of hero worship due to all she'd seen him do.

Sora had asked that they be seated on the balcony overlooking the city's center for the sunset view. It was almost full; they were seated among dozens of well-dressed nobles. As expected, an attendant took his duster and 'sword' belt to hang them on a nearby coat rack as they were seated at their table.

Their wonderful meal had several courses. After the lovely dinner a fine dessert was served. While enjoying that a well-dressed middle-aged woman stopped by their table for a chat. "It's been so long, little Sora. And now you're here with new friends" the woman said with a wide smile.

"Oh, Lady Eva; it has been such a long time - how have you been?" Sora asked nervously. The familiar way they addressed each other led Drachus to believe they were more than just casual acquaintances.

"We are just now having dessert, Lady Eva. Will you care to join us?" he asked.

"Charmed" she said. "Invited by the true Dragon Lord I'd be a fool to say no. I had finished dinner when I saw little Sora and decided to stop by and say hello. I seriously doubt that a second desert will hurt!"

The lady was carrying a few extra pounds so Drachus assumed she indulged in second deserts often. Lady Eva's maid removed her wrap and limped over to hang it up.

"She is very influential; she knows everything about everybody. She terrifies the nobles; they call her 'Lady Evil'. She can be a bit overbearing but ... she's actually quite nice" Sora whispered. Since nobles ran the country Drachus knew she could be a valuable ally - or a powerful enemy.

"Everyone, be polite" he quietly cautioned.

After a bit of small talk about the weather Lady Eva had a question for Sora. "By the way dear have you spoken to your eldest sister lately? Maia Gravis has been quite worried about you since that awful business in Laris."

As Drachus glanced at Sora he saw her face twisting with a nasty grimace, like she had just swallowed a bug! The priestesses were referred to as 'sisters' even if not related by blood. He'd already met one Big Sister and saw how badly she and Sora got along. He hadn't known it was this bad between her and the oldest one.

"Ah well," Lady Eva said. "I'm an only child myself, so I can't give you any good advice I'm afraid."

Drachus wondered what the eldest High Priestess was like. Sora had only mentioned her in passing before now and her reaction here was so bad he assumed there must be some pretty serious issues there. Unfortunately, it really was a 'family' matter and he didn't have the skills – or inclination - to get in between something like that.

All during the dessert Yuma had been nervously glancing out over the city. Drachus had to admit the view was nice but that didn't seem to be why she kept looking out there with such a concerned expression.

He was about to ask her what she was looking for when the doors to the dining area opened suddenly. Several men in various noble liveries quickly scattered among the diners, heading for their employers. Among them was Sora's coachman. Most alarming, he had her silk-wrapped magic scepter - which she'd deliberately left in the coach.

As Drachus thought to himself 'This does not bode well' he spotted a huge burst of flames in a distant part of the city. After a longer look he realized there were a lot of small fires all over as well as bright flashes of light - likely magic spells being cast!

Suddenly one of the nobles stood up shouting "Demon cultists are rampaging, here in the capitol?!" causing panic among the nobles.

When the coachman reached their table he handed Sora her scepter. "Yes sir, ladies. It seems a lot of them snuck into the city during the day and began killing at sundown" he said. Lady Eva seemed shocked at that

"How could they get in; the City Guard watches out for their kind!" she exclaimed.

"They have a method of using magic to disguise their selves – that's how they did it in Laris" Drachus said with a frown. Suddenly glaring at him, Sora spoke.

"Speaking of that, how did *you* sneak into Laris? A pervert as big as you are should have been easy to spot."

"When we walked in, Chia was sitting on my shoulders" Drachus explained.

"Oh! So they couldn't see the dragons on your coat. I suppose that also explains why they didn't realize how absurdly tall you are" Sora muttered.

"How did you find us, Big sister?" Chia asked.

After a short pause the annoyed priestess replied with some heat. "The maids were talking about a gigantic rich pervert in a ridiculous hat buying clothes for a tiny little girl and paying with *my* Holy Star; it had to be him!"

Even under these circumstances Drachus had to grin. He was about to ask how she knew it was her Holy Star he was spending when he recalled a line of strange glyphs along the edge of the coin. Nolemande had mentioned that Holy Stars could be connected to famous clergy.

"I guess they are engraved with the name when they are issued. It would be a lot easier that using a passport or something similar to identify genuine high-ranked clergy" he muttered to himself. It would also give the possessor funds if needed while traveling. Then he suddenly realized he'd never thought to ask Sora about this before.

"By the way, other than escaping from the 'penitence room', why did you come to our hotel?" he asked Sora.

From the growing blush and confused expression on the little priestesses' face Drachus thought she might refuse to answer. After a few seconds she finally looked up at him.

"I had a dream about you killing demons ... and you were killing them to protect me. It was a vivid dream ... it actually felt more like a memory. I also needed to know why I was holding a ... during the dream ... it felt like I was ..." As Sora tried to work up the courage to mention the very big baby she'd been holding in the dream – which she somehow knew was theirs - more flames flashed in the night sky.

"This is insanity; they must know they'll all be slaughtered!" Lady Eva cried.

"They'll die anyway. That Laris job was well planned; they do have a good tactician. It only failed because I disrupted their scheme. After Laris they know the army will be after them hardcore" he explained. After another flash of flames drew their attention he continued.

"They only had two options. Rather than hide out and be picked off a few at a time over several months, they massed for a big strike hoping to seriously damage their enemy before their numbers are too depleted."

Drachus walked to the ledge and looked out over the city. Along with the flashes of light indicating magic spells were being cast, he could see a lot of small fires all over the place. Concentrations showed there were three main areas of conflict. After a bit, Yuma came to stand next to him.

"Why didn't you say you knew the attack was going on?" he asked.

"Oh I didn't know about an attack" she said. "I kept hearing strange sounds; I didn't know what was going on."

'Of course', he thought. Even wearing her disguise ring, her elf ears could hear the battle sounds but a cloistered nun wouldn't recognize them.

"Sora, Lady Eva, I'm not familiar with this city. I need you to tell me what is there, there and there?" he asked as they joined him, pointing to the concentrated firelight and spell casting; the three main areas of conflict.

As the women looked where he'd pointed their faces fell, Sora's most of all. Lady Eva pointed to the last one he'd indicated. "That is the palace of the High Priestess of the Moon, Selena Rose. That" she said pointing at a hill in the middle of the city some miles away "is the Holy Cathedral, home to the High Priestess of the Earth, Maia Gravis."

She stopped while looking sadly at Sora. Though he'd pretty much figured it out by now, Drachus glanced at Sora as he pointed to the closest.

"That is the palace of the High Priestess of the Sun, Sora Glarus." As Sora's mutter confirmed his suspicion a huge fireball erupted there.

"Oh dear" Chia, Yuma and Lady Eva said at once.

"I have to go" said Sora.

"No" said Drachus "you need to stay here."

As she started to argue he added "Look, this is a replay of Laris. They were after you and your sister there" sweeping his arm towards the combat zones he added "and they're after you here; they want you priestesses dead. Your place is already a pile of ash; the other two seem to be holding their own." It looked like Sora was still going to argue so he pressed on.

"Do you think that hot-blooded red-head is going to roll over and die just because some cultists tell her to? I bet she and her knights are kicking their asses halfway to the moon ... to the moons ... by now!" Lady Eva chuckled at his unintentional joke; even Sora grinned.

"And this Holy Cathedral sounds like it would be well defended. Isn't your eldest sister the 'Priestess of Protection' herself?" he pressed on.

"But there are people there who depend on me" she said pointing to the big fire at her palace. "I can't abandon them. Even if they were picked by others, I have a duty to protect those in my service" Sora added seriously.

Drachus was quiet for a moment. The look on her face was quite determined. The childish Sora was gone; now she really was acting like a true lady. While emotionally volatile, she was reliable when it mattered; some of his respect recently lost to her childish side had been restored.

"I'll go instead" he said. "I doubt the creeps expect to run into me again." The other ladies sounded a chorus of agreement but Sora's pretty face still had a stubborn set so he added more.

"Someone has to guard Lady Eva, Yuma and Chia. They don't have any soldiers here yet" Drachus pointed down over the ledge of the balcony and added "Look what they've got to protect them here; a dozen bodyguards and a bunch of grooms on the doors downstairs."

He'd noticed the men as they moved into position and with that argument Drachus could see he struck a nerve. Sora didn't even look down; she knew he was right.

"The Dragon Lord has a point, Sora" Lady Eva added. As she spoke the odor of burning wood wafted in and they could make out the sound of nearby fighting.

"Besides, if you go waving that stick and shooting off lights every cultist in the city will know exactly where you are" he said. That plus saying she had to protect Chia and Yuma seemed to have convinced her. Then she glanced at the burning ruin that had been her home.

"I'll go to your place first, I promise" Drachus said. With that, her shoulders slumped; she knew he was right.

"All right, I'll protect them here" she agreed quietly.

As he put on his gun belt and duster Yuma gave him a glass-vial with the four golden berries she'd made before they left the Healing Shrine. "Just in case" she said.

"Thanks" he said. "Look after those two will you?" he said quietly, glancing at Sora and Chia. Yuma nodded with a smile.

As Drachus walked to the edge of the balcony he moved his pistol back to the holster; his exit method would be safer with it there. He'd seen wide canvas awnings on their way in and after his grand talk he felt he needed to make a grand exit – his talk with

Sora had been pretty loud and many diners were watching him closely. After all, he was the Dragon Lord!

Besides, he wasn't sure he could remember which of the winding stairways here led to the exit; this place was a labyrinth. Back on his old world he'd used this method to escape from more than one brawl - and brothel raid - he was pretty certain it would work here too. Stepping up on the short wall surrounding the balcony he looked around.

"I'll be back" he said loudly and then stepped into the darkness. Most here gasped; the balcony was on the third floor! A few nobles close to the edge ran to the short wall and looked down. They arrived in time to see him disappear as he tore feet-first through the red canvas awning below.

A bodyguard and two grooms at a side door practically jumped out of their skin when he plunged through the sunshade landing on his feet. With a smile and a wave Drachus headed to what was left of Sora's palace.

The Dragon Lord felt this wasn't really all that risky; the awning drop was chancier. He knew he was pretty much immune to the cultists' spells. During the ride here he'd worked with Sora and Yuma; they cast various spells at him to verify he was immune to the magic of this world.

Nothing they used affected him at all. Like when the boulder had exploded, if the cultists hit him with a flame spell, his clothes might catch fire but the spell wouldn't affect him; he would just felt a slight tingle.

Not even healing magic worked on him; that was bad news but he hadn't tried Yuma's healing berries yet so there was still hope. After all, the Rosen Salve worked on his elbow; over the past few days it had fully healed.

While the cultists had a good tactician, only a few that he encountered were spell casters. The rest were close combatants –

and pretty poor ones at that. Drachus didn't bother sneaking; he strode through the streets as quickly as he could, gunning down cultists he caught swinging torches to light fires and burn townsfolk alive.

He couldn't tell which brought out the louder shouts as they died; the sound of the gunshot, the bright muzzle flash or the impact of the big .45 caliber bullet! On the way to Sora's palace he killed a dozen. Even at a good pace it took half an hour to get there; this city was big.

Drachus arrived at the burning remains of a mansion with Sora's crest on the broken gate outside. After checking the grounds he was surprised to find only two armored bodies near the gate. From the trampled plants it appeared the others fled out the back gate once the attack started. After only a few glances it was obvious that there were no survivors in the remains of the burned building so he headed to the cathedral.

A half a block from the ruins of Sora's palace Drachus heard sounds of battle from around the corner. In the light of several burning carts he saw two men fighting with cultists at the bottom of a small rise. He thought they were adventurers – they were not dressed like soldiers.

It seemed odd they'd made a stand in the middle of the road. They had a pile of debris from a toppled statue at their rear but it wasn't a good defensive position. Then he saw townsfolk who'd taken shelter behind the debris in a cul-de-sac with no way out.

'That's why they're making a stand there; to protect the civilians' he thought as he went to help them out.

He recognized Coramak, Virian's guard leader, as one of the men. 'Small world isn't it?' he thought. Neither he nor the other man was on the offensive; Coramak held off two cultists with a broadsword while using a barrel-lid as a makeshift shield.

His tall partner swung a long halberd in wide arcs to both sides holding three back. From the tattered ribbons fluttering on its shiny blades Drachus deduced it was actually a decorative piece likely from a nearby shop. From the whistling sounds it made the man swinging it was strong; even if it wasn't weapons-grade, it would likely kill at least once if it connected.

The dark-robed bad guys were using short swords and had no shields; the broadsword and halberd had an advantage in reach. The cultists couldn't get close enough to strike effectively without getting killed. Drachus saw two of the bad guys with their ridiculously small bows step from an alley to his right. Before he could shoot them, they let fly.

As he muttered 'Verdamnt' the Dragon Lord saw a flash of light from the statue debris; the arrows sparked as they flew back at the cultists who scrambled to avoid the returning projectiles. Looking close he saw a young woman pinned by the legs under the debris. She held a short staff similar to Sora's scepter; the bright silver magic symbols embedded in its surface were illuminated in a fading glow.

"She must be a spell caster, deflecting the arrows" he muttered. From the several dead cultists littering the road around them the defenders had been doing just fine. However, Drachus knew they were outnumbered and it was only a matter of time before they'd be overwhelmed by numbers or exhaustion.

Even though the arrows looked like a child's toy, from way they had scampered to get away from the returning projectiles the cultists certainly considered them dangerous. Deciding it would be best to deal with the archers first, he headed to the alley where they were hiding.

Before Drachus got there he spotted another group of cultists emptying kegs of lamp oil from a nearby burning shop. He could see it was going to flow down the slope into the cul-de-sac; burning people alive seemed to be the cultists' favorite trick.

"Well, I have a favorite tactic too" he muttered. Pulling a boomer from his vest, he triggered the timer with his chin-strap tip and threw it through the open door into the shop. The flickering orange light inside made it obvious the cultists had already set it on fire.

The detonation shattered the windows, turning them into razor-sharp shrapnel. Embers from the fiery debris of the burning shop ignited the oil the cultists were dumping into the street, turning several of the fiends into wailing human torches roasting in an inferno of their own making.

As he walked towards the fight, Coramak recognized him. "Raledon, the Dragon Lord is here!" he cried.

"What? You mean he's real?" the tall man called back in a high-pitched voice that cracked. The remaining cultists looked at Drachus, standing transfixed for a moment.

Suddenly one of the cultists shouted "Our time has come!" Drachus stared in surprise as the cultists fell back, dropped their swords and joined the archers in the alley. Once there drawing their long silvered daggers they faced one another in pairs and started chanting.

The obviously tired and sweating Coramak staggered up. "We've got to move, now; this is dangerous!" he gasped.

Uncertain how many more cultists' were nearby Drachus decided it would be best if they left instead of engaging them. After all, so long as they were just chanting they weren't a serious threat; the Dragon Lord still didn't fully understand magic yet.

He saw Raledon trying to lift statue debris off the young woman. "We should help him" he said, holstering his pistol and pointing. The debris had once been a statue of an angel. Putting shoulders under overhanging parts of a wing both of the taller men shoved up as hard as they could.

When the stone shifted Coramak pulled the woman out by her arms. At that she screamed in agony and fainted. Looking down at the young woman Drachus couldn't blame her – one of her legs was badly mangled. Realizing that the medical help she needed was likely too far away and she might end up dying before they could get her there he pulled out the vial of healing berries Yuma had given him.

He hoped that a golden berry could at least stabilize her until she could get healing spells. Drachus mashed one between his fingers, smeared it on her tongue and held her mouth closed for a few seconds.

The cultists' chant had reached a crescendo. He looked over and stared in shock as they thrust their daggers out, stabbing their chant partners' through the hearts!

"Oh no," moaned Coramak "it's too late." Somewhat confused, Drachus looked back at the dying cultists and he saw their flesh dissolving into a greenish-black smoke, leaving only collapsing robed skeletons behind.

'Well that explains why the cultists' skeletons at the shrine were so clean' he thought. Instead of sacrificing innocent girls, here the cultists' sacrificed themselves! At first he thought this was rather stupid.

As the swirling cloud cleared the folks in the cul-de-sac began to cry out in despair – a 12' tall demon had emerged from the coalescing smoke with a rumbling roar.

Now it made sense; recalling how pitiful their combat skills were Drachus saw that, at least from their perspective, sacrificing a dozen inept soldiers to summon a powerful combatant was a very viable strategy.

This demon had curved horns like a bull and wore an odd metal breastplate. Like the first one it had cloven hooves instead of feet and was muscled like a weight-lifter. Its wickedly curved claws were short but looked very deadly.

After laughing like a maniac, the demon called out in a rumbling voice that sounded like an avalanche of rocks sliding down a hillside.

"I've been invited to a feast! Look at the little human children; young flesh goes down so easily, like tender veal. As their screaming parents beg for mercy, I'll savor the crunch of their tiny bones." At that the demon spread his arms wide and began to slowly approach the frightened townsfolk.

Initially feeling confident, he had killed a bigger one before, Drachus smiled. The smile froze on his face as he recalled his pistol was loaded with lead rounds, not silver ones; he doubted he could reload fast enough to avoid being attacked. Plus he saw this one had no gem-thing in its forehead: that trick wasn't going to save anyone this time. His mind raced for a way to kill this thing quickly.

The Swede suddenly recalled an incident in Argentina. An older man had faced down a crowd of angry villagers armed with only a rifle; as he'd cycled the bolt to scare the crowd Drachus had noticed that the Mannlicher 95 was empty! Van Neumann had intimidated them by playing on their fears. "Mobs are like bullies; scratch a bully you'll most always find a coward" he'd told Drachus later.

This demon sounded like a bully, bragging about eating children and it had gone after the civilians instead of the armed men. Plus the look on its face seemed to be forced; as if uncertain it could kill everyone here. The Dragon Lord decided he'd try and intimidate it to save the civilians - at least until he could think of some way to kill it. Intimidation didn't work so well when the target is twice your height but he didn't have a lot of choice.

Coramak had also been desperately trying to think of another way out; he was startled to hear the Dragon Lord begin laughing. The baffled man could only stare as Drachus pointed to the young woman.

"Coramak, help take care of her; I'll deal with this ridiculous thing myself" he shouted. With that the demon turned to face the Swede. Drachus started slowly walking towards the demon with a snide grin on his face.

"You realize you are little more than a bad joke? Your voice sounds like gas escaping from a horse's ass. Those silly claws must make it awfully tough to pick your nose" he called out. The demon seemed a bit perplexed by his words.

"Well this is new. Usually humans run away or beg for their lives; I've never seen one just walk right up to me before!" it grumbled in confusion.

"Who said I was human, you side-show reject?" Drachus snarled.

At that a look of concern crossed the demon's face. "Well you look human" it growled.

"Wipe the pig shit from your eyes and you might see clearer, dung breath" Drachus added as he continued with his slow approach. Obviously sniffing the air the Dragon Lord added.

"Speaking of pig shit, just how much of the stuff is stuck between those silly hooves? Or do you just naturally smell that bad? I guess that drape on your belt is toilet paper; your ass must be so rough you have to bring your own. And I won't even start on those silly little claws!"

At that the confused demon shook its head as it looked at its claws. Drachus had a sudden inspiration; this demon was either too confused or just too stupid to react to his insults – either way it would be likely to make a bad decision if he forced it to think quickly. "Now that I see you close-up I don't think a pig as weak as you can even offer me a fitting challenge" he called out.

Drachus pulled a boomer from his vest and showed it to the demon. "A gift for you" he shouted. Continuing forward he added "With this you might, just might be able to give me a fight worthy of the name." Drachus knew he was on the right track when the baffled demon stepped back from his approach; it was a coward.

Bringing the boomer near his face Drachus popped the plunger with his hat's chin strap tip and pretended to sniff the trail of smoke from its burning internal fuse.

"Ah! Brimstone! This might help!" he exclaimed tossing it. With no idea of what it was, the demon caught it.

After sniffing the smoke its gravelly voice rumbled "Yes, it smells just like brimsto ..." Before it could say more the boomer exploded, blowing fingers, claws, teeth, eyes and bit of horns in many directions.

After another second it fell backwards with a thud. A red glow engulfed the now dead thing and just like the first one it burst into swirling red flames leaving only a scorch mark on the cobblestone road.

A few seconds of silence followed the echoes of the explosion. Then a roar of cheers erupted from the trapped townsfolk. Playing up the Dragon Lord shtick, Drachus turned and waved his hat to the crowd.

Checking on the others he saw Coramak was laughing and Raledon was on his knees next to the injured woman; his face was twisted in a look of utter disbelief at what had just happened.

"Are you two all right?" he asked after walking back.

"Just tired; where did you learn to speak Demon?" Coramak said. Ignoring the weird question Drachus glanced at the unconscious woman; he was glad to see her leg injuries were partly healed.

"Raledon was it? Get her to healers as fast as you can. Coramak, you lead the civilians out of here" he said.

"Come on Big sister; let's get you home. Mom can take care of that leg for you" Raledon said to the unconscious sorceress. Seeing his face up close Drachus realized this kid was young; despite being tall he couldn't be more than 12 or 13 years old! His face needed no shaving and his voice had a high-pitched innocence that proved he hadn't even reached puberty yet.

'That's why he was swinging the halberd like a big stick' Drachus thought; 'a kid wouldn't even know how to use one in a real fight.' Coramak called back to the civilians.

"You should all go that way" pointing in the direction the Dragon Lord had come from. "I'm sure there won't be many left there!" he shouted. As they filed past him, they shouted cheers and thanks to the men. As the last of them passed, Drachus turned to Coramak.

"I have to be somewhere else. Can you fellows take care of all of this?" he asked. Raledon cradled his injured sister and nodded as he jogged away.

"I'll get the townsfolk to the guard station at Alachua Way; it's big enough that it should still be standing" Coramak said.

"Fine but be careful. I don't know how many are left and some of them got away" Drachus said pointing to the smoldering corpses that had been dumping oil in front of the oil shop.

Looking towards the hill rising from the city center he could see the tall cathedral wasn't on fire yet so they were still likely safe. Hoping it could hold out at least a bit longer he headed to the Holy Cathedral; maybe the good guys over there could win before he got there and he wouldn't even need to help out.

Chapter 11

How the hell do I beat the Devil himself?

In the treasures room of the central tower of the Holy Cathedral the High Priestess of the Earth Maia Gravis was dressed in her finest ceremonial raiment, the one she wore to give annual blessings at festivals. As she prayed the braids of long dark hair hanging from her bowed head lay unmoving below the smoky trails of the incense that filled the upper half of the room.

Some four hours after sundown, the sounds of conflict still occasionally penetrated deep into the sanctuary. Her maid entered the room and cleared her throat.

"Is there news, Laika?" the priestess asked quietly.

"Yes my lady" the maid said. "Lady Selena didn't wait for the cultists. She assembled the knights at her training hall and sought them out."

'Just like you, Selena' Maia thought with a smile.

"After destroying many she joined forces with the Grand Marshal. He'd rallied men of the army and their forces were to execute something called a 'wide sweep' through the north of the city. Though I don't know what that is, I'm certain she'll be fine."

"What of little Sora?" she inquired quietly.

"Lady Sora was seen dining at the Silver Table before the attack but no word has come since." Laika seemed to hesitate before continuing.

"Is there more?" the High Priestess asked.

"Yes, My Lady. There have been demons seen taking part in the attack. The rumored Dragon Lord may also be here. In addition, while the gates and doors are secure now the cultists swarmed the courtyards before any alarm was raised; all of the guards on duty outside were slain."

The priestess grimaced as she offered prayers for the souls of those men. There had been reports the demon cult was growing in power but for them to be capable of mounting such as assault as this was shocking!

Maia Gravis had never been frightened before. As the pampered daughter of a powerful noble she had been raised in comfort and complete safety for her entire life. The only time she had even been nervous was when Cardinal Trent had attended her 13th birthday party nine years ago.

After the old clergyman had patted her head and wished her "Happy Birthday" a strange look had crossed his face. Turning to her parents he said "Please convey the young lady to the treasures room of the Holy Cathedral tomorrow morning. There is something I must verify."

While her family had been to the cathedral many times this was the first time she saw her parents were nervous about it. In the treasures room there were so many beautiful artifacts that the girl wanted to touch, but her mother kept quietly saying 'No dear, behave yourself.'

The cardinal arrived with the previous High Priestess of the Sun. That lovely lady grasped the prettiest thing in the room – the Staff of the Angelus. She smiled brightly as she presented it to the nervous girl.

Maia Gravis had hesitated to touch it, looking up at her mother's concerned face. When her mother smiled and nodded the girl reached out. As she touched the golden haft she felt a tingling in her fingers; the three lovely jewels mounted in the headpiece began to glow. At that all the others in the room let out a collective sigh.

After her mother kissed her on the forehead with tears in her eyes, Maia Gravis was led away by several priests. She did not return home that day or for several months afterwards. She was to begin schooling to become a High Priestess.

Though her mother visited many times, she was never as close as she had always been before; her beloved daughter was now a High Priestess candidate and had to be treated with reverence. Her father had never come to visit; he was very unhappy she was to be a priestess. He knew what her life was about to become. She did not see him again for many months; her next – and last - view of him was at his funeral.

For the first time in her life, Maia Gravis was afraid.

"Cultists have gathered in the east courtyard" Laika was saying. "The Captain of the Holy Knights feels they have a plan to breach the gates."

Closing her eyes in near-despair hearing this, the priestess said "We can only pray at this point."

Moments later both heard a loud shout of 'Our time has come!' before an evil chant began outside. The High Priestess grasped the Staff of the Angelus with shaking hands and walked towards that sound with a determined look on her lovely face.

Back at the Silver Table Yuma, Sora and little Chia were worried sick; despite their total confidence in the Dragon Lord, they were scared. Lady Eva spent the time among the diners quelling fears with a calm voice.

"Don't worry; there are strong men downstairs on the doors. Plus we have the High Priestess of the Sun with us here. And if that weren't enough the Dragon Lord himself is out hunting the scum; I daresay he's thrashing those fools here as thoroughly as he did in Laris! This terrible noise should all be over soon." Despite the danger her efforts were keeping things calm in here.

"Don't worry Chia" Sora assured her. "That pervert is so much stronger than any cultists could ever be. You've seen what he can do, when he's not molesting girls and petting their butts." Chia smiled hearing that.

"You know he isn't really like that ..." but before she could say more a man in a cultists' robe jumped down to the patio from the roof, landing atop and then crashing through a nearby table.

"Death to the Priestess!" the fanatic shouted as he stood from among the debris to attack Sora.

Unfortunately for him Sora was still carrying her silk-wrapped scepter. Before he could even get out of the debris of the table that had broken his fall she'd uncovered it, aimed and shouted "Divine Lance!"

He was determined however and managed a step towards her, screaming in agony before dying.

The attack had unfolded so fast the wait staff had barely paused in their serving; the noble diners didn't even have time to drop their forks. Lady Eva recovered first. Pointing at the dead cultist she called out "See, even if the evil creatures do get in ..."

Before she could finish a silver flicker flew in from Sora's left; a throwing scythe shattered the girl's wrist. Screaming in pain Sora dropped her scepter as a man wearing a cultists' robe entered from the kitchen. "Death to the Priestess" he muttered as he drew a silvered dagger

Yuma moved to get in his way while the other diners ran across the room to get away from the fanatic. Rather than simply run around her the cultist stopped and smiled.

"What do we have here - a little lady hero?" he sneered. Looking to her right Yuma saw a serving cart. Picking up a large carving knife she stood her ground to protect the helpless Sora.

The cultist didn't seem to take Yuma seriously. The man with the black eye patch was tossing his dagger from hand to hand while occasionally stamping his foot to make the frightened woman twitch; he enjoyed scaring her on his approach. The priestess was kneeling on the floor in tears, trying to focus through the pain to cast a healing spell. Chia was trying to get her away from the killer but the small girl just wasn't strong enough to pick her up.

"Yuma, don't" Sora whimpered. "He's a fanatic; he'll kill me anyway. Don't throw your life away" she cried. Her hands glowed for a second before she moaned as the pain from her broken wrist made it impossible for her to finish casting her spell.

Once she saw the throwing scythe on the floor, Lady Eva shouted "Lady Yuma; that's a Skerne; this one is no cultist, he's a guild assassin!"

Yuma's heart froze at that; she knew nothing about fighting but could tell this guy wasn't behaving like the first cultist. As he drew close she was trying desperately to think of something that might scare him away.

Yuma had been raised as a nun. Even at the shrine her duties at night had kept her quite isolated; she rarely had more than a few words with the other nuns at breakfast and dinner. She had never even been in a shouting match with one of them!

She was no match for *anyone* in a fight and unless Sora recovered soon, he'd be on top of them. The bodyguards and grooms were downstairs guarding the doors; the nobles had fled to the far side of the room. 'If there was just someone, anyone, here who really knew how to fight' she thought.

The robed assassin moved around a large table to get an easier approach to Sora. As Yuma shifted to stay in his way her dress swished with a sound that seemed unnaturally loud; the assassin looked down and leered.

Glancing down Yuma saw her tights and boots were visible through the now open slit in her dress.

'Oh God, I'm going to die from humiliation before he even cuts me!' she cried in her head. Then she recalled something Drachus had said about her outfit.

Taking a risk Yuma reached up and pulled on the collar. As it tore the dress fell to the floor exposing her 'pirate lady' outfit – the one Drachus had said looked an adventurer's clothes.

She heard several in the crowd behind her shouting things like "She's an adventurer!", "Who is she?" and "A secret bodyguard for the High Priestess!"

Yuma tried to give a confident smile as she took her hat from the nearby cloak rack and put it on her head. From the assassin's scowl she knew that he didn't like what he saw. "They didn't mention someone like you being here. Even if this was short notice I should have known it wouldn't be all that easy" he sneered. He stopped his scare tactics and now approached in what Yuma assumed was true fighting stance.

She'd hoped he'd run away when facing an adventurer; while not soldiers or mercenaries, they had a reputation for being tough in a fight.

When he was only one step away she clenched her fists anticipating the fatal sting of a dagger thrust; as she did she felt the disguise ring on her finger. At that she must have unconsciously smiled.

"What, did you think of something impressive to say before you die sweetie?" the killer sneered.

"Funny, I was about to ask you the same question" she said quietly – imagining that's the kind of thing Drachus might have said in her place.

Surprised at her own courage Yuma slipped the ring from her finger. Sora and Chia could see her change from their place nearby on the floor but everyone else was far behind her. The only other one who saw Yuma suddenly become a dark elf, a race of dangerous spell casters, was the now wide eyed assassin in front of her!

Suddenly another idea occurred to her – she must be learning a lot from Drachus. As she smiled even wider the former nun began casting a spell used for starting cook fires; it wasn't going to be very helpful in a fight but she knew her hand would glow and an assassin wouldn't know what spell she was casting!

"Of course they'd hire someone tough for this but why would one of *you* people take the job - that is bizarre" muttered the assassin as he stepped back in surprise.

The murmurs from the crowd showed that they all knew something about the stand-off had changed drastically. After glancing at her glowing hand twice the assassin stood up straight.

"You know, they didn't offer near enough to deal with the likes of one of *you* on top of a priestess. Even that old bastard guild master couldn't hold this against me." Tossing the dagger aside he ran to the edge of the balcony and laughed as he jumped off into the darkness.

The surprised Yuma ran to the edge and looked over. A genuine adventurer would have known it could be a trap but she really was an amateur. She got there in time to see the assassin drop over the awning, throw the cultists' robe at a groom and run off into the night. She canceled the fire spell as she turned to walk back to the others.

"Ring, ring!" Chia hissed. Yuma slipped it back on, hoping she did it quickly enough that no one had seen what she really looked like. Sora was massaging her wrist after finally casting a healing spell.

"Thank You!" the priestess cried as she hugged her. The crowd was cheering with other comments too.

"She's a tough one."

"That's smart having an undercover bodyguard."

"Damn what a body; does she do 'bawdy' work too?"

Hearing that one Yuma realized she was now very exposed. With a small whine she pulled her dress back on. Unfortunately, when she'd pulled it down the collar buttons had been torn free. Lady Eva saw her distress and called to the maitre'd.

"Summon a maid from the ladies' lounge; the poor girls' dress wants for repairs." Turning to Yuma she patted her hand saying "There, there dear. It will all be fine." She quietly added "And I'm sure no one else here noticed" though she didn't elaborate on *what* no one else had noticed.

A curving colonnade stood on the opposite side of the East Courtyard from the Holy Cathedral gates. 108 gaslights burned on the 108 columns that supported its flat roof and wide eaves.

Sitting atop the roof was a small girl in a tattered black dress with long, unkempt blonde hair. Her knees were drawn up close to her chest and her chin rested on her crossed arms as she considered what to do next.

She had been sent by Luther, the Grand Master of the Cult to deliver a silver coffer of miasma to those battling the High Priestess; the coffer sat – unopened - nearby. The cult leader told her often and quite loudly the only reason he tolerated the presence of a worthless devil-ling like her was her ability to fly – and to handle miasma safely.

As she left from the temple roof she'd seen Luther's coach heading to the port. Curious why he'd leave his headquarters during the cult's biggest battle she flew down. Near the window she overheard Luther shouting inside.

"It will be years before we can rebuild after this; we won't even be able to keep our secret temple! Damn that Dragon Lord!"

"But we may be able to eliminate a High Priestess; our brethren will be slaughtered anyway, after he perpetrated that fiasco in Laris where we lost half of our spell casting brethren. We have the treasury and the book of golden scrolls with the original magic disguise spell; we can rebuild. Besides, sacrificing so many will bring forth a powerful demon. With that we may be able to destroy the Holy Cathedral itself!" Kelleg replied quietly.

Kelleg was a former Army Knight; before his dismissal for demon worship he'd been Captain of their spell casters. He had been known as a skilled tactician and a cunning planner. He had originally felt sacrificing a dozen men and one third of the entire miasma supply the cult had painstakingly collected over many years was a reasonable price to pay to eliminate a High Priestess in Laris.

Thanks to the Dragon Lord's interference, the Laris attack had failed miserably; they hadn't even killed a single Holy Knight! Now, with the majority of their men at risk he'd decided they should expend the last of their miasma to eliminate the most senior High Priestess and maybe destroy the Holy Cathedral itself.

Of course, if this failed Kelleg would denounce Luther, kill him and then become the new Grand Master; Kelleg really was quite the schemer.

Rather than confront the cult leaders the girl had flown on to take the time to consider what she'd heard. If they were abandoning the temple, they must not have any members left there. If that was the case, she could be free!

For the first time in her life she wouldn't be a slave; there would be no more beatings, no more abuse and no more pain. If she just waited a bit longer to use the miasma she might ensure her tormentors were all going to die.

Selena Rose had not accompanied the Grand Marshal to sweep the cultist's from the city. Knowing the Holy Cathedral would be the cultists' main target she had ordered her knights to go with the army and she headed there to help her older sister.

The only child of a renowned knight, demon and dragon slayer the tomboy wanted to become the first woman the kingdom would recognize as a knight! Her mother had passed shortly after her birth and her heartbroken father had been determined to raise her as one.

Seven years ago when young Selena was told she might be a High Priestess candidate, she'd naively asked if she could decline. After being told she couldn't, Maia Gravis had shown the pouting girl to a velvet-covered altar with a golden scepter and a silver plate with two large moonstones. As the 13-year-old looked at the artifacts she saw a sparkle seemed to appear from the heart of the two moonstones. She reached out and touched them almost by instinct. As they began to glow brightly a feeling of warmth washed over her body; the teen heard many gasps from those behind her.

Looking back she saw her father's face was beaming with pride. From that day on, Selena Rose began training to become the High Priestess of the Moon – the closest thing a woman of Durakkon *can* be to a knight!

In the eerie illumination of gaslights the High Priestess of the Moon arrived just in time to see a hundred cultists become skeletons as they murdered one another to summon a demon. The smoke swirling high above quickly dissipated to reveal a tall man with black feathered wings. From the powerful aura surrounding the villain it was obvious they had summoned a full-blooded devil!

"We might be in trouble here" Selena muttered. Spotting movement high on the cathedral she saw High Priestess Maia Gravis on a balcony with the Staff of the Angelus, the most powerful holy artifact in the world. 'Big Sis' thinks we're in trouble too" thought Selena.

As she saw Maia Gravis cast a spell three glowing lights appeared from the gems mounted in the staff. Each grew larger until the three combined into a single sphere as big as the priestess herself. With a shout she swung the staff overhead, hurling the bright orb at the hovering devil.

As the magic sphere flew toward him the devil raised a hand creating a black disk floating in the air between them. When the sphere struck the disk, both scattered into thousands of sparks which vanished. Maia Gravis fell to her knees, weakened by the massive amount of mana she had expended. From the devil's sneer it was obvious she could not drive him away with only her magic.

"We are definitely in trouble here!" Selena muttered as the devil turned to face her with a truly evil laugh.

Meanwhile Katarina Aries, an infamously reckless adventuring priestess had come to the Holy Cathedral knowing that would be the cultists' main target. She arrived in time to see the devil dispel Maia Gravis' spell; that's when 'Trina' knew they were in trouble too.

Trina's mother had been the personal maid to Lady Althea Rose. As the lady lay dying shortly after Selena was born she begged her maid to make certain her daughter grew up well. Having recently given birth herself Trina's mother became wet nurse to infant Selena.

The two girls grew up as the best of friends, as close as sisters. During preparations for Selena's 13th birthday the girls were playing in the garden when a wild dog charged at them. Knowing Selena wouldn't even recognize the danger – her best friend absolutely loved doggies - Trina picked up a large stick and hit the offending beast with it. When she did a small burst of light engulfed the animal with a crackling sound; the dog yelped once before running away.

When told of that Selena's father had Trina evaluated by a sorcerer who confirmed the lady had exceptional magic talent of a most unusual nature. Once Selena Rose was ensconced for High Priestess training, Trina went to convent where a retired nun saw to her priestess training. Four years ago she stood with her bestie as Selena was ordained officially as High Priestess of the Moon.

Belleck, the highly skilled and most loyal leader of the Dark Horse Phalanx of the Cult of Demonic Transcendence was having a very bad night. His group had been successful at first, killing townsfolk and guards once they broke cover at sundown just as Grand High Priest Luther had ordered.

However, that bastard hadn't told him there was an Adventurer's Guildhall in his area. By the time they'd finished with those fighting fools his men were all dead and he had barely escaped alive. Belleck had come to join with the storming the Holy Cathedral but he was too late; he arrived just in time to see the other gathered cultists sacrifice themselves to summon a demon. Now he hid behind a pillar deciding what to do next.

The dark angel floated above on unmoving wings. He sneered at the red-haired priestess below as they exchanged volleys of magic back and forth; he firing bolts of black light and her shooting streams of red flames. Neither caused noticeable damage to their opponent through their inherent and opposing magical defenses.

The devil sneered and smiled as he descended towards her; it looked like he wanted to get close, to engage her in melee combat. Spell casting wasn't really her forte, so that was fine with Selena Rose.

She drew the poleaxe from her back; the two moonstones on her gorget glowed brightly while she prepared to do battle.

As the black-winged devil neared she realized what she had taken for a fur wrap around its waist was a collection of scalps and the bones of human hands!

Then she saw the colorful ribbons making up the skirt of its perverse raiment were noble pennants. As it touched down she recognized the emblems of the Prince of Ancien and Duke of Strolls; according to the history books both those royals and their personal guard were slain by the same powerful demonic foe.

"Oh my god" she cried. "Those damned cultists' actually summoned Adeya-khan himself!" With an evil grin the dark fiend issued a cruel laugh when he heard that.

"You recognized me? I cannot help but feel touched" he sneered with obvious contempt as his hand moved to where his heart should be. Then he touched his scalp collection saying "Your flaming locks will blend in nicely; I can't wait to shave them from your skull as you die!"

As the devil closed in on Selena, Trina used quietly-cast magic spells to bend the darkness surrounding her to hide her approach.

Moving up behind the Devil who was focused on her childhood friend, Trina waited so she could attack from surprise.

As the devil readied to swing at her Selena saw a flash of magic light. The fiend was engulfed in a powerful electrical discharge which caused loud gasps of pain through his clenched teeth. Recognizing Trina's power even before she could see her best friend she laughed loudly.

Dispelling her bent darkness, Trina smiled at the High Priestess. Selena was surprised that she'd managed to sneak in; she hadn't even noticed her besties approach. With a smile Trina glared at the devil.

"My beloved staff is imbued with power drawn from the heavens; the cost in gold and favors to the old perverts of the enchanters' guild has been prodigious. But it can now deliver unto your vile kind pain so great that even one such as you cannot endure it" she bragged.

Selena smiled at those words; now she was certain that she and her best friend could take this thing down.

Behind the pillar Belleck had been trying to think of what to do next. When Maia Gravis' spell failed to reach the devil, he grinned. His glee vanished as Trina Aries appeared on the scene. Grumbling in dismay, he heard girlish laughter from above; looking he saw the filthy devil-ling Luther kept for errands - and to abuse most viciously when he was in a bad mood.

Belleck knew she was to deliver miasma to help defeat the priestesses; he couldn't understand why she hadn't used it yet. "If that disgusting little bitch won't do it, then I will" he muttered looking about for a way to get on top of the colonnade.

Drachus arrived through a small gate leading into the courtyard near the Holy Cathedral. Along the way he'd reloaded his pistol with silver bullets – now that he knew there were demons to fight here.

Carefully entering the courtyard he was first shocked at how big the church was; perhaps it was the dark night that made it look so huge but it seemed to be even bigger than the Notre Dame in Paris!

Movement to his left brought his attention to Sora's bad-tempered big sister and a lady with dark hair closing fighting with a very tall man with black angel wings.

The lithe way the leggy lady moved plus her fancy shining armor told him she was very skilled in close combat. The head of her staff was sparkling with an obvious magic spell of some sort.

Drachus already knew that the red-head was quite good. Maybe it was because this fight was at night and the Laris fight had been in sunlight - he hadn't noticed then but the moonstones in Selena's gorget were glowing brightly.

The bad guy wasn't moving much, just standing between them glancing back and forth as he waited for them to close. Despite the evil leer on his pale face, Drachus wasn't sure of how tough this thing really was. He decided to hold back for now, hoping the ladies could handle the dark-winged dick on their own.

At first they did well; both had long weapons allowing them to stay out of the winged freak's reach. They alternated closing and executing quick attacks with their magical weapons; apparently they had fought together in the past and knew how to coordinate their attacks.

Every time Big sister Selena stuck there would be a flash of light from the moonstones at her throat. Whenever Lady Legs struck there was a flash and crackling of lightning from the headpiece of her staff.

However, it soon became apparent they weren't doing any damage; the black-winged jerk would parry their strikes quite effectively. Watching closely Drachus saw his hands had a pale glow that flared each time he batted their weapons away. Their magic weapons and his magic defenses were so well matched neither had an advantage.

The buff bad guy was standing still blocking their weapons while they were charging in to attack and then pulling back to stay out of his reach; they were much more active. If the fight went on too much longer Drachus worried the ladies might tire before the nasty dark angel did. He began trying to come up with ways to intervene effectively if it became necessary.

Atop the colonnade the little blonde was leaning forward praying for the two women fighting the devil when she heard someone behind her. "There you are, you filthy little mongrel" Belleck shouted. Glancing back she saw he'd climbed a ladder leaned on the roof of the colonnade. The cultist grabbed the silver coffer of miasma.

"I shall send the light of hope to the beyond - with my own hands!" She jumped up and grabbed at his arms.

"No; I want to be free!" she screamed.

As the two struggled Belleck backhanded her so hard it knocked the tiny girl down and left her senseless. However, the force of the blow put him off-balance; he stumbled when a shingle broke underfoot. As he fell from the roof the coffer opened; miasma spewed forth engulfing him. Belleck screamed as the thin tendrils wrapped his body and began draining him of life.

"I shall send the light ..." he shouted but landed face first on the cobblestones below, dying before he could even finish his last words.

A stream of glistening darkness falling from the roof of the nearby colonnade drew Drachus' attention; it was obviously miasma. Like before it skittered across the stone to surround the women; the tendrils slithered up around them. Once wrapped both women were dragged to the ground by the sticky mess.

During the ride from Laris, Sora had told him that miasma could drain the life from a priestess in only a few minutes. "Of course it couldn't be that easy" he muttered as he began moving in, hoping he could approach without being seen. As he walked towards it Drachus saw the black-winged demon wade through the miasma without being affected. 'So, it doesn't hurt demons' he thought to his self.

The devil stood over Trina Aries with an evil leer as he gloated. "Well, crawling down there you can't make much use of your beloved staff, now can you worm?" he sneered with glee. Then he kicked her in the ribs; wrapped in tendrils she couldn't even squirm out of the way.

The devil seemed to enjoy her screams of pain, laughing as he viciously kicked the helpless woman again and again. His last kick didn't get a scream from the now motionless woman. "How unfortunate; this one died far too soon" he said.

With that, he turned his attention to Selena Rose. "But this bug looks like it will provide me with much more entertainment" it said as he walked slowly towards her.

Selena realized that tied down with miasma she was helpless. Lacking any other means of resistance the young woman began to shout at the approaching fiend.

"You miserable buzzard; you really think you can win? When I get out of this crap I'll kick your ass; your shitty feathers will fly in a dozen ..."

With one hand the devil grabbed her by the throat. When he did her moonstones flared to a brilliant blue-white light. Cringing away with a grunt of "Angelus trash!" the devil swept a backhand that broke the magic stones from the silver gorget, sending them flying off into the darkness.

Grinning he picked her up by the throat. As he pulled her face close she feared the handsome devil with red eyes and long curly hair would steal her first kiss. Instead, the devil glanced down. Selena realized the devil had noticed the holy protective enchantment on her armor breastplate.

The creature smiled and drew back his arm. With a glowing fist he struck her chest with a blow so powerful it took her breath away and shattered her breastplate. As the fragments fell away, the devil laughed. After a few moments intense pain exploded in her midriff as the fiend punched her vulnerable belly.

"That the best you got?" Selena choked out; normally she'd have doubled over from such a blow but the strong devil was holding her up off the ground by her throat. With the miasma tendrils' wrapping her from below, it was as if she were strapped into a rack; she couldn't bend.

After a third punch caused a terrible tearing pain, she saw stars and blood sprayed from between her teeth. Selena realized she was about to suffer a very painful death and with little hope of rescue, she began to pray.

When the devil realized what she was mumbling, he gave an evil laugh and leaned in to lick some of the blood from her lips; as its tongue slithered into her mouth the helpless priestess couldn't help but groan at the disgusting sensation of being violated like this.

Before the devil could strike again both were blinded by a red flash as the surrounding miasma burst into a brilliant cloud of flames. The devil seemed confused; and looked up at the sky.

Remembering this from Laris, Selena looked about desperately after the red glare passed. She laughed as she saw the Dragon Lord striding towards them across the courtyard.

"Yu in fo' it now, shi' fa brains! Ee, ee finks ahm pretty!" The lady stammered through bloodied lips.

The devil followed her gaze; when he saw a tall man walking towards them he laughed. Tossing the beaten woman to the cobblestones the villain turned to face the approaching idiot.

Maia Gravis had been so focused on recovering her strength and agonizing over her sister's plight she hadn't even noticed Drachus' slow approach. When the miasma flashed into flame she realized he was there.

Recognizing the embroidered dragons and the slouch hat fluttering away from the descriptions she's heard, her mind raced. "Whose side is he on?" she wondered.

Approaching the miasma its tendrils had reached for him. Drachus swatted them away like he had in Laris and just as it did back then the miasma exploded into bright red flames. His big hat flew away from the hot flash of wind caused by the burning stuff but Drachus decided not to retrieve it; scurrying back for it would certainly diminish the impact of his approach.

That approach was slow mainly because he wasn't sure of what to do next. Without heavy weapons Drachus had few other options right now. Feather-freak had no forehead gem; that was out and this guy looked too smart to fall for the prank with a boomer. Besides with the red-head so close it might kill her too; all that left was intimidation.

That doesn't work so well when the target is a foot taller than you are. The Dragon Lord was desperately trying to think of something that might prove to be effective.

"What is that bizarre aura that surrounds you? What sort of devil do I see here?" the winged freak asked.

When he reached the dark angel Drachus smiled. Ignoring the question he quietly said "Nice dress you're wearing there pretty boy! Did you come all this way just for a dance with me?"

When Bird-man didn't respond to the dress insult – and rather confused as to why it called him a 'devil' – the Dragon Lord realized he would have to use obvious things to keep it off balance; insults didn't seem to have an effect on demons from this world. Instead of intimidation or insults he would just baffle it with confusing references.

Big black-wing hadn't noticed him until he was only a few steps away so Drachus didn't have time to be all that creative. To buy some time to come up with a few good ones he ignored the devil as if it wasn't a threat. Looking down at Selena, he spoke as if he were scolding a child.

"Little girl, you are such a mess. Honestly, why are you always crawling around on the ground like this? I told you before; a lovely young lady like you should take better care of yourself. Brawling with ruffians in the streets might scar that sweet face of yours; a man might have to think twice about marrying you. I mean, really, when are you going to learn; you are a beautiful young lady - you should act more like one!"

Curled up on the cobblestones and bent over double in agony from her injuries Selena Rose had been trying to spit out the disgusting sensation the devil's tongue had left in her mouth. At the

Dragon Lord's words she coughed out a painful laugh saying "I'm Shorry!"

Drachus looked back at the confused bad guy and grimaced. "Damn! Are you some sort of rotting undead thing or did you just shit yourself?" he called out.

Then he broke into a grinning laugh as he drew his pistol and fired where its heart should be; the dark-angel-thing was not much bigger than a man and the bullet was made of silver - it might work. Feather-face staggered back a step in surprise at the flash and noise of the gunshot.

Drachus was startled by the sudden whine of a ricochet and the flash of dark light emanating from the devil's chest as the silver bullet was deflected! 'Verdamnt; some sort of magic protection' he thought to himself.

"Well, that didn't work" the mercenary called out loudly as he holstered the gun "so let's try these instead." With another laugh he snatched his gloves from his belt and waved them in the dark-thing's face. He made a big show of slowly pulling them on while grinning at the devil's confusion. Once they were on Drachus wiggled the fingers of his left hand and laughed again to attract its attention.

When the bad guy looked at the wiggling left hand Drachus stepped forward and hit it on the nose with a roundhouse right. The dark-thing was taken by surprise; he seemed quite distracted by Drachus' odd actions.

Though the Dragon Lord didn't know it, the devil he faced was confused; the mercenary was nearly as tall as a devil, was speaking in heavily accented but fluent Demonic but had no wings or demonic aura. It also assumed Drachus had 'breathed flames' like a dragon to clear away the miasma. The baffled villain didn't know how to react to Drachus - because it didn't know what it was fighting here!

As it staggered from the force of the blow the devil stumbled on Lady Legs' staff lying on the ground; it sparked when he stepped on it. Hoping it was still charged with whatever spells she had used, Drachus reached down to pick it up.

As he did the devil recovered from confusion and the now furious creature pointed his clawed hand down at Drachus' face and a let loose a huge blast of dark magical energy. While it didn't cause any damage, it was bright.

After closing his eyes the Dragon Lord grasped the staff, stood and smiled. The devil was now even more confused; his most powerful magic attacks had no effect on this strange creature! Opening his eyes Drachus called out in English with his voice distorted to sound twangy, like a radio sports caster he'd once heard in Texas.

"With a 458 battin' average, 261 homers and 976 RBI's ... steppin' to the plate is last year's MVP, Dragon Lord Drachus his-self. Batter's up!" he shouted.

The devil assumed these strange words were a magic incantation; it stepped back to see what spell was coming. Drachus swung the staff and hit the bad guy like it was a baseball bat. The strike brought lightning from the sparkling center of the staff's cast iron headpiece - and grunts of pain from the bad-guy.

Now it was even angrier than before. The devil blasted Drachus with shot after shot of bright but ineffective magic. It was the same as when Sora had shot her magic lights at him – it tingled but he suffered no injuries!

After several exchanges it was obvious the devil was losing this fight. After stumbling on Selena's dropped poleaxe, Feather-face flew into the air out of reach; from its groans it was apparent he was weak and hurting.

"What's this: can't handle a fight with a grown man? Is big bad demon boy flying way high in the sky because he can only win in fights against little girls?" the Dragon Lord taunted to goad it back into staff range.

At the mention of little girls, the bad-guy glanced to his left. Following his gaze Drachus noticed a helpless woman with long black hair leaning on the railing of an upper balcony on the cathedral. With an evil laugh and a huge smile the devil quickly flew towards her.

As the devil approached Maia Gravis knew what it planned; it would skewer her heart to drain away her life energy to replace its own power to continue fighting with the Dragon Lord. For once she wished she'd followed Selena's oft-repeated advice to wear armor; even a decorative piece would give her some protection from the lethal mauling she was about to suffer. With little chance of survival, the priestess began to pray.

Atop the colonnade the little blonde had recovered from the beat-down. Hope grew with every burst of sparks as she watched the tall man beat the devil so badly he had to fly away to save itself. Seeing this strange warrior might be able to destroy the devil and end her servitude to the cult she felt real hope for the first time in her young life.

As it flew toward the helpless priestess she knew the devil would drain the life from the helpless woman to keep fighting the tall hero. Without thinking she picked up the empty silver coffer; any silver would hurt devils. She flew up behind the evil creature as she raised the heavy box high above her head.

Drachus looked about for some sort of projectile he could throw to distract the devil from the helpless woman but all he saw was Selena's heavy poleaxe. Reaching for his pistol in desperation he saw a flash of golden light appear in the darkness to dart up behind the devil.

It was a small girl with a fluttering cloud of long blonde hair so bright it glowed. She lifted a silver coffer, the kind the cultists used to hold miasma and brought it down on the devil's head. The tiny girl probably wasn't all that strong but the impact seemed to hurt the devil a lot.

With a roar of rage it twisted in midair and grabbed the little flying blonde by the throat. Drachus watched in horror as the devil stabbed her through the heart with his clawed fingers! As she dropped the coffer it was obvious she was in agony but couldn't scream; it had her by the throat.

Drachus looked around for several seconds for something to throw before seeing the lower end of the electric staff had a sharp silver point. As he flipped it around the little girl's limp body landed nearby; with a shout he hurled the staff at the hovering devil. After a long second it hit its left wing.

Dark-thing-dipstick hadn't even seen it coming; it became stuck in the wing. As fingers of lightning flew from the headpiece to envelope the devil, feather-face screamed like a girl and fell to the ground.

Drachus ran to the little blonde. He wasn't sure which side she was on - she might have dropped the miasma in the first place but she had also tried to stop the demon. It didn't matter - he couldn't just let the little kid die; sometimes being an overprotective big brother could be a real pain in the ass.

Through a gaping wound in her chest Drachus could see her rapidly-beating heart squirting blood like a broken garden sprinkler! Tossing his gloves aside he poured out a golden healing berry from the glass vial.

After mashing it between his fingers he smeared it over her tongue and then held her mouth shut; that had worked with Raledon's big sister. Closing his eyes for a moment he prayed.

"Dammit, you've got to work!" he muttered.

Glancing back at black wing Drachus saw he was still squealing like a stuck pig as he struggled to shake out the sparking staff. Checking out the two ladies he saw that Selena had managed to get to her hands and knees but was still spitting blood; the busty one wasn't conscious but he saw blood trickling from her mouth as she gasped for air.

Both were alive but likely had serious internal injuries; they wouldn't be able to fight any time soon. His eyes darted back to the girl; with a sigh of relief he saw the wound in her chest had started to close.

Up on the balcony Maia Gravis was amazed; this Dragon Lord had fought the Devil Prince to a standstill. She saw Selena was moving but was obviously not able to fight yet; Trina Aries was still unconscious. Looking back at the Dragon Lord as he ministered to the fallen girl she prayed for her to recover.

As the villain neared the Priestess had seen the little devil-ling fly up behind him to slam the silver coffer down on its head. Seeing the girl's face in twist in agony had torn at the priestess' own heart - she could do nothing to help the child. 'Please let him save her' she prayed.

After a few more moments Drachus heard a gasp from the girl and saw her bright blue eyes flutter open. Through the torn dress he could see the smooth dusky skin between her breasts was now unblemished.

He smiled down at her, stood her up and handed her the berry vial. "Take these over to those ladies. Make each of them eat one; tell them it's an order from the Dragon Lord."

She seemed a bit dazed but took the vial. He turned her around and gently pushed on her back to start her to the injured women. Setting his face back to intimidation as he stood, Drachus turned to the Dark-sider. He'd finally shaken the staff loose and stood there holding his injured wing. The devil's face was twisted with rage.

"Dragon Lord? Dragon or Lizard, it matters not to me; you shall suffer a thousand years in screaming agony for what you've done here this night. Prince Adeya-khan will *not* fall to the likes of one such as you; I will feast upon your putrid soul before that can happen!" he shrieked.

Using plain old intimidation at this point Drachus gave the weakened bad guy a snide grin. "You don't have fangs tough enough to bite into me, you clipped-wing reject from Hell" he snickered.

With a furious growl the devil thrust his arms out. "Come Death!" he screamed and began changing into a big, dark ... something else.

Drachus glanced back at the ladies. Selena was sitting up and no longer spitting blood; the little blonde girl was bent over the buxom one. He knew even with healing berries they would not be able to help with this in time. As it let out a deafening roar Drachus turned to get a good look at the new bad thing.

He saw it was now a black winged lizard the size of a locomotive with horns, huge claws, a spiked tail ... and a glowing red forehead gem! Smiling in relief as it charged, he drew his pistol, aimed and opened fire; it was only one big step away when the gem shattered after his very last shot.

Like the ones before, it let loose a loud scream and fell. After a huge red glow appeared it disappeared in a massive burst of swirling red flames. Catching his breath he reloaded and put his gun away.

Walking over, Drachus could see the buxom babe was still dazed. As he helped to her feet he noticed broken parts of her heavily lacquered breastplate fall away; that devil had kicked her really hard. When her 'skirt' swayed to the side the lingerie connoisseur noticed she wore lacy panties; the leather leggings she wore under her armored boots even had lace tops!

'Lace undies are real common here; even women warriors on this world certainly seem to like them' he thought.

"Are you all right?" he asked as he pulled a handkerchief from his pocket and began wiping the blood from her lips. Before she could answer, something warm, soft and squishy glommed onto his back. Over his shoulder he saw a huge mane of bright red hair – the sobbing Selena was clinging to him.

"It destimee; we all meneet for are other! Twice; You; Me!" she babbled hysterically. Drachus couldn't blame her; he had saved the cocky and powerful young woman from certain death – again! After he handed her to the buxom one, Selena began rambling to her. "Trini! Did You; He see! Us; We! It Twice!"

'Trini' wasn't fully recovered yet and just got more confused at Selena's babbling. To buy her time to come to her senses, Drachus handed the handkerchief to 'Big Sister'.

"You are a mess sweetheart; clean your pretty face with this" he told her. Giggling hysterically Selena Rose took it and began wiping away the blood, sweat and tears she had shed during the fight.

With that under control he walked over to pick up his slouch hat. Fortunately, it had been outside of the swirl of flames and was undamaged. Drachus looked around and saw the little flying blonde girl standing by the wall crying; She was holding the torn top of her dress closed. As Drachus headed over to check on her there were shouts and hoof beats on the cobblestones.

He saw a force of at least 20 mounted knights enter the courtyard at a gallop and, stomping through the field of a hundred robe-clad skeletons, head over towards them. Since he wasn't certain if they would see him as friend or foe, the mercenary thought it a good time for him to leave.

The little blonde girl had probably been on the other side until just a few minutes ago so he wasn't certain how she would fare. After he turned to warn her - he saw she was already gone.

"Smart kid" he said heading out to avoid the troops.

It was a long hike back to the restaurant. On the bright side, there were no more cultists. Drachus arrived just after dawn. As he walked up city guards moved to stop him but when the doorman welcomed him back like he was a long lost rich uncle, the guards decided to let him in.

As the Dragon Lord walked into the dining room upstairs he had only just realized they were serving breakfast - and he was starving - when Sora, Chia and Yuma jumped all over him to welcome him back.

As he sat to eat the girls filled him in on last night's restaurant action. They were so proud of big sister Yuma they couldn't stop smiling. Drachus also gave her his thanks, commended her bravery and cleverness. Then he gave her a rather sharp stare.

"But if you ever take on a professional assassin with a table knife and a cooking spell again I'll spank your tight little butt so hard you won't be able to sit down for at least a week!" he scolded her.

Yuma seemed almost happy hearing that. When the other two laughed she joined in but none of them knew him quite well enough yet; they couldn't really be sure he was just kidding.

During the night Lady Eva and several other important nobles had been extracted by a force of Royal Army Knights to protect them from the large panicked crowds and occasional surviving homicidal cultist. Now that the sun was up and the city was calmer, the other well-fed nobles had begun heading home protected by only on their own bodyguards.

Drachus suggested that he and the ladies do the same. He picked up the throwing scythe the assassin had used and took it along. He was always curious about strange new weapons – it was an occupational hazard.

As he examined the well-crafted and finely-balanced weapon Drachus saw that Sora was lucky to have survived. The dull outer edge was what shattered her wrist. If the razor-sharp inner edge had struck it would have likely severed her hand from the wrist! She would have certainly bled to death before she could cast a healing spell.

Back at the hotel they all had a nice bath - Drachus was last as he seemed to shut off the magic that heated and cleaned the water in these things. By the time he was done the others were already in bed, so he decided to get some sleep himself.

They slept through lunch, had a nice early dinner then back to bed.

Chapter 12

And now the Demon Slayer is a bookworm.
and a babysitter?

Shortly after breakfast two days after the battle in the capitol Drachus sought out a fine arts store. The concierge was happy to direct him to one a few blocks away where he sold three more paper money souvenirs.

When he had asked Tofferd about a 'discrete' dealer he knew the tailor would spread rumors quickly. Stories of these unique works of art had come from Laris as hoped; he got 30 Gold Crowns for these.

Shortly before dinner that same day a hotel maid came to the door to say that Laika, High Priestess Maia Gravis' personal maid wished to visit their suite.

Drachus thought her outfit was similar to the maid uniforms worn by staff in many high-class households and European royal family estates.

The lady was not what he would call beautiful but carried herself with a self-assured air. Her eyes were a blue so light they could almost pass for silver; they sparkled with barely contained mischief as she spoke.

"My Lady, the High Priestess Maia Gravis wishes to invite the Dragon Lord to join her tomorrow for morning tea. She wishes to express her personal gratitude for his defending of the capitol" she said formally.

"You may tell your mistress I would be honored to accept" Drachus replied just as formally. Laika curtsied and left; though she'd glanced at her, the maid hadn't spoken to Sora. 'Well,' Drachus thought 'it's their issue. I hope it won't cause problems.'

The priestesses had exchanged notes confirming their safety after the incident but nothing more. Even real sisters sometimes had conflicts; the priestesses weren't related by blood, only by their positions. Drachus was certain there must be some serious bad blood between them.

Early next morning Drachus had his clothes laundered, hair trimmed and a proper shave; it was a special occasion. The others would stay at the hotel; Chia was demon-touched, Yuma was a disguised dark elf and for some reason Sora seemed reluctant to visit her elder sister in person - plus the invitation had only mentioned him.

At the Holy Cathedral the maid Laika greeted him at the gate with a polite, warm smile and seemed at ease; but he was certain he saw her fingers trembling several times as she opened doors for him. He was guided to a fancy parlor designed for small tete-a-tetes. As he entered he saw the walls and door were extraordinarily thick – they were probably sound-proof!

Waiting inside was a stunningly beautiful young woman with an incredible figure in a fancy dress. He hadn't had a real good look at her during the fight but he recognized her as the exhausted woman with the fancy staff up on the balcony that the devil was trying to kill.

As she rose from a padded chair next to the well-set table and curtseyed he saw her dress had a long flowing skirt (that was probably hard to walk in) but the bodice was close-fitted and rather low cut; the lady had a magnificent pair of breasts.

As she politely invited him to sit he knew that, between her stunning looks and those mammaries, he'd have to make an effort not to stare. Focusing on her eyes he saw she had violet eyes as well – and those twin orbs actually seemed to sparkle!

'That makes four sets I've seen here now' he thought; Drachus realized he really liked eyes that color. Violet eyes must be common on this world. Mion and Surra had them, so had Lady Legs, Selena's buxom battle buddy. Now Maia Gravis showed up with them. On his old world they were rare; in all of his travels the Dragon Lord had never seen even *one* set of eyes that color – though he'd heard of them.

Though it might seem a bit rude, but with no choice, he shifted his attention to a spot on the wall just past her, not on her eyes, her lovely face or those distracting breasts that threatened to pop out with every breath.

If she noticed his efforts to remain polite, she didn't mention it. The lady couldn't notice; she was busy dealing with her own issues. Though he couldn't see it Maia Gravis' heart was racing; she was sure it wasn't from fear but couldn't tell what was causing it. Even though she seemed at ease there was strong tension in the room.

Dragons are more powerful and destructive than demons; there are rumors that they ate people. There was also the fact that this ... man? ... had destroyed the Devil Prince Adeya-khan – the most powerful devil ever seen in this world; even with the kingdom's greatest holy relic, she couldn't drive it away! Then there was his amazing aura. For different reasons, this tea-time meeting was going to be quite stressful - for the both of them.

In a polite and very sensual voice the lady spoke first. "My most important concern is this – are you our enemy, sir?" Her words were blunt but not rude so Drachus had to think carefully before replying. He wasn't a diplomat and this meeting had to be very diplomatic.

"My enemies are villains, those trying to hurt me, my friends or those who depend on me. Otherwise I harbor ill will to none" he said. She seemed satisfied with that.

"Why have you come to the capitol; was your arrival and the cultists' simultaneous attack a coincidence or part of some sinister agenda?" she asked. That was an easy one.

"It was pure coincidence; I came only to purchase supplies and tools to improve the lives of the bunny-folk of Karrat Kommons - who I am now responsible for." His reply seemed to satisfy her and she smiled.

"But," he added "in all honesty, some here may suffer adverse impacts as I improve the bunny-folk's lives."

"What sort of impacts?" she asked curiously.

"I can't predict exact details" he replied. "But most likely they will be related to commerce."

"You will go into business?" she asked in surprise.

"Not exactly but my actions will have effects on some businesses. Other than that I am uncertain at this point, so I regret that I cannot be more precise" Drachus said.

Everything he'd just said was absolutely true. He had to be absolutely truthful here. Before leaving for tea Sora warned him that Maia Gravis had spells to tell her if someone was lying to her. He wasn't sure if he was safe from it; if the spell affected her, would his weird magic immunity even come into play?

Besides, while he was no Boy Scout lying wasn't a thing with him; he'd learned years ago he was really bad at it! He knew the improvements he planned would certainly impact a medieval economy; it was inevitable. Some fields would see improvement while others might disappear. He really couldn't tell which ones.

From history classes he knew that a seemingly unrelated advance could have impacts elsewhere; petroleum refining virtually eliminated the whaling industry. Within a single generation, port towns and their ship-building enterprises that had been around for centuries had ceased to exist as whale oil went from a daily use necessity to a rarely seen oddity. There was no way to tell what long term effects his improvements would have on this world.

"Well, my official concerns have all been addressed, thank you." Maia Gravis continued. "On a personal level, though it is still somewhat official I must add, I have another inquiry." she said.

"Ask away" Drachus responded.

"What have you done to my dear sister Little Sora; why does she dress so strangely now and what are your future intentions towards her?" she inquired with some emotion - and quite a stern expression on her face.

Drachus almost choked on his tea cake. He was curious as to why Maia Gravis' tone of voice was almost maternal as she asked about 'Little Sora.' "That sounds like something her parents should be asking, not a church official" he remarked before replying.

"Sora was being bullied by one of your church toadies" he said bluntly. "I helped her acquire a bit of freedom. With her cooperation I am working to improve the lives of her vassals, the bunny-folk, whom I am now responsible for. As this will further my own plans I see it as a cooperative effort to our mutual benefit. There is nothing more than that between us."

His answer made her uncomfortable at first but by the end she was quite satisfied with it. Maia Gravis assumed the 'toady' he spoke of with such scorn was the former overseer at Karrat Kommons; she was told he had been dismissed by Sora at the Dragon Lord's urging.

She'd heard nothing but bad rumors about that man; stories of how the bunny-girls suffered under his 'management' were well-known. The priestess had met him only once but felt he was no good to begin with. The lady was quite pleased to know that horrid man would have no further impact on Sora's life.

"Well, I see nothing else for us to discuss. I would like to express my gratitude for what you did to help this city and for all the lives you saved during the cultists' attack. I think it possible the city and even the kingdom could have fallen if it were not for you. I also wish to thank you for saving Selena and Sora in the Laris incident" Maia Gravis said rather formally.

"Is there any sort of reward you wish in return? If it is within my power I would see that you receive it" she added in a friendlier tone.

"I fought the cultists because they were being rude to my friends and for no other reason" Drachus said. But, seeing a chance to do some valuable research he continued.

"However, I am unfamiliar with this world I now call home; that ignorance might cause an unnecessary tragedy. Study could prevent such incidents. I saw a large library as your maid escorted me in to tea. If I could be allowed time to peruse it, I would consider any debts paid in full."

This surprised Maia Gravis. 'The Dragon Lord only recently came to our world?' she thought to herself. She suddenly remembered reports that cultists may have recently released the Demon Warlord Kreeger from the Shrine of Hope – but that it may have been destroyed there as well. Had this Dragon Lord really come here to deal with that evil creature? Recovering quickly, she spoke.

"I shall make arrangements this afternoon. You will be able to begin your studies in the morning and may read for as long as you wish" she said with a lovely smile.

Drachus stood to make his exit and she to say goodbye. He took her hand, bowing slightly while she curtsied. He didn't kiss her hand as that might be considered too forward and the two parted ways.

Maia Gravis remained in the tea room for some time. She had seen with her own eyes just how powerful and dangerous this Dragon Lord was. She assumed that her racing heart, shortness of breath and the thin sheen of perspiration under her dress was due only to that concern. Despite how powerful and destructive she knew he could be - for some reason she found she wasn't afraid of him.

She certainly hoped she wasn't becoming as addled as her love-struck sister Selena. The master healers were baffled as to how she had completely recovered so quickly from the massive injuries she suffered while fighting with the Devil Prince Adeya-khan. She spent her days giggling as she wandered her palace oblivious to anything around her.

After leaving the cathedral Drachus rinsed his head with a dipper of cold water; talking with a woman like Maia Gravis could be – stressful for a womanizer like him!

After lunch, he gathered the others to purchase the supplies. It soon became obvious he wasn't going to get any work done. His trip to the art dealer had been short; these efforts took more time and covered a lot of territory. Stories of the Dragon Lord killing cultists, a demon and a devil had spread like wildfire getting wilder with each retelling.

Wherever he went crowds formed thanking him for saving their lives, their children's lives, their cousin's lives and so on; he'd been seen saving so many the entire city seemed related to one of them. Only a few minutes after starting, they headed back to their hotel.

"I'll have to give the shopping lists to you" he told Yuma as they walked. "You can take care of them and make arrangements to move the goods back to Karrat Kommons."

"Do you think I can do all of that by myself?" she asked nervously.

"If we can find Virian, I'm sure you can; he does owe us. We'll go over things each night to make adjustments. Once Maia Gravis sets things up for me to use the library I'll be there most of each day" Drachus said.

As they walked back he had noticed a figure moving from rooftop to rooftop; it appeared to be following them.

"You all go back ahead of me" he told the ladies. "There's something I need to look into first."

"Let's get more of those sweet cakes!" Chia cried.

"Oh, yes, lets" Sora added.

"Not too many; we just had breakfast" Yuma said.

Sora and Chia were acting more childish every day while the former nun was sounding more and more like their mother!

Drachus needed to find out who the figure was after, so he headed back by another direction; it soon became obvious he was the target. Finding an empty alley the Dragon Lord stopped to shout "I don't know who you are or what you're after but I don't have time for this. Come tell me what you want so we can get this over with!"

A few seconds later a tiny girl with long shining hair flew out of an adjacent alley. He recognized the girl from the battle, the one who nearly had her heart ripped out. He didn't get a good look that night; she'd disappeared so quickly all he remembered was shiny golden hair and bright blue eyes. In daylight he could see she had pretty features, though her eyes seemed sad.

As she landed he saw it wasn't her hair glowing; she had short, glowing translucent wings extending from her back; her hair was just reflecting it. They didn't flap as she flew down; upon landing they seemed to collapse, pivoting down her back like a folding paper fan as they stopped glowing. Her wings slid under her hair until they were completely covered. Without the glow, both were the same bright gold color. The wings blended in perfectly, hidden under her long blonde hair.

"Look" he said sternly. "You can't follow people in daylight by flying around on the rooftops, especially with those things glowing like ..."

He was interrupted when she leapt up, wrapped her arms around his neck and kissed him!

"Cut that out" he snapped. "Let me go; if anyone sees they'll think I'm some child molesting pervert." That was a real danger; this girl was almost as tiny as Chia. With tears in her eyes she just kept kissing until he grasped her by the shoulders and firmly sat her on a nearby barrel.

That's when he saw she had draped her long blonde hair over her front to cover the torn dress. Seeing it up close in daylight Drachus realized her dirty, tattered dress was sheer - mostly see-through; it was an old negligée. And like bunny girls – this natural blonde didn't wear underwear!

"Who are you, what do you want?" Drachus asked.

"My name is Twerle; I belong to you now" she said.

"Twerle?" he repeated. He recalled that was the name of the thief who'd helped rescue the girls back on his old world so long ago. As he looked closer he saw that she did resemble the beautiful French-Algerian girl quite a lot.

Between Selena, Coramak and now Twerle he wondered if any others from his old world would show up here. Momentarily thinking this might be a weird dream, he shook it off; he had to deal with this issue first.

"Look, you don't belong to anybody but yourself. I don't do the slave thing" he told her.

"You saved me" she said. "I would be dead if not for whatever you did to heal me. Then you killed the devil that tried to kill me. It's only right that I belong to you now." Her logic was solid by medieval standards but it could be problematic, especially as young as she seemed.

"Go home, you're free, I release you; go do whatever you want" he said. Drachus hoped that was enough but she then looked sadder than before.

"I have no home. My father was a devil who took my mother as a slave so he could molest her. Mother died when my devil father was destroyed years ago. I've only ever been a slave; I have no family, no home" she whispered.

Drachus was quiet for a bit; now he couldn't send her away. "Look, you belong to you, but you can stay with me. I do owe you for helping me in that fight" he said to try and get this under control.

"That means I am yours then" she said with a smile.

Drachus knew it would be impossible to have a rational argument on such a serious subject with a little kid. As she jumped off the barrel to leave he noticed she had rather large breasts for a girl her size; like Sora, short as the little flying girl was - she wasn't actually a kid!

He also saw she wore a slave collar; the long golden hair draped over her shoulders had hidden it until now. "Before *we* go, *this* has to go" he said with a snarl. When he grasped the lock on the collar he felt a tingle in his fingers - it was some sort of magical thing.

"So long as the one who put that on me lives, it won't come off" she said with an even sadder face than before.

Seeing it was only a miniature lock like you'd find on a ladies' jewelry box, he wasn't too concerned. He carefully twisted it so when it broke her throat wouldn't be injured. With some effort it broke with a metallic 'Crack', a small flash of light and an electrical 'Snap'.

With the lock gone he removed the collar. As the girl touched her throat in surprise her pretty face broke into the widest smile yet. Drachus could see the skin under the collar was deeply creased; the poor girl must have been wearing that verdamnt thing for years!

Seeing tears well up he guessed what was next and grasped her shoulders to stop her jumping on him again. "Don't hang all over me in public, OK? That just doesn't look right; especially with you in that see-through dress. We'll get you some proper clothes later – and underwear" he said sternly.

"Yes, Master" she said.

"And don't call me master" he snapped.

"Yes, Milord" she said.

"That neither" he retorted.

"As you wish, Dragon Lord" she almost sang.

"And not that either!" This back and forth banter continued throughout what seemed like a very long walk back to the hotel.

Drachus suddenly realized he now had *four* to take care of; he really needed to get these women safely moved to Karrat Kommons as soon as he could.

Once back at the hotel introductions did not go smoothly. The moment Sora saw her she became furious. "That girl is evil; she's a devil-ling! Why on earth is she here?" she shouted.

In the face of Sora's verbal assault Twerle clutched Drachus' coat sleeve hiding her face behind his arm. She'd recognized the High Priestess and knew this could cause a lot of trouble. Drachus remembered hearing something about 'devil-lings' a while back but couldn't recall details.

"She helped me in the fight with that devil. You don't have to like her, just don't fight with her. She'll be traveling with us - because she has nowhere else to go" he said.

After a moment a quieter Sora replied "Of course she doesn't have anywhere to go; it's a death sentence for a devil-ling to even *be* in the city."

Drachus glanced at Twerle; the girl looked up and nodded. 'No wonder she's clinging to me, I'm the only one who would protect her and probably the only one who could' he thought. "How did you know what she was" Drachus asked. "Except for the dress, she doesn't look much different than any other girl right now."

"Devil-lings have dark, evil magic in their aura. Spell casters can see it easily" Sora explained politely; she was calming down quite a bit as the conversation progressed. His saying that Twerle had helped in the fight with the devil seemed to have improved the priestesses' opinion of her.

Drawn by the earlier shouting Chia entered from the bath where she'd been brushing her hair. "Oh; she's so pretty; look how her hair shines - just like Big sister Sora's" Chia said as she embraced Twerle.

"Hi, I'm Chia. "Who is she? Her dress is torn up; and you can see through it! Can she wear one of my new ones; I have a lot of them?" Chia asked Drachus.

"This is Twerle; she'll be traveling with ..." he began.

"Over my dead body" Sora screamed at the top of her lungs. Drachus and the others were shocked at her outburst. She'd seemed to have calmed down about the new girl but after watching Chia hug her she was madder than before.

"Don't be like that Big sister. Your name is Twerle? That's a sweet name; I'm Chia. Let's see which dress looks best on you. I've got so many now I'll never be able to wear all of them." Glancing down she saw Twerle wasn't wearing any underwear. "I think some of the panties should fit you but I don't really think any of my bras will" she said as she led Twerle by the hand to the bedroom the girls shared.

"No!" shouted Sora as she stormed out of the room. Drachus and Yuma shared glances.

"What just happened?" he asked.

"I have no idea" the baffled Yuma said.

For the rest of the afternoon Drachus and Yuma carefully went over the list of supplies they'd need, where she was likely to find them and how they'd need to be transported. Virian could help with the details; Drachus felt he would since they helped him get to the capitol.

They were often interrupted by fits of temper from Sora. She wouldn't even be in the same room as Twerle and it was hurting Chia; she kept shuttled back and forth trying to make peace between the two blondes.

Drachus had lunch and dinner sent up; it would be a disaster to take this domestic dispute to the hotel dining room or worse, to the Silver Table. Yuma wasn't much help; like the Dragon Lord she was also inexperienced with young girls. They were at a loss as to how to fix this.

After learning about the little bunny-girl who resembled Chia so much and what had transpired when she had died years before, they both realized that old trauma in the priestesses' heart had reopened. Sora had begun clinging to the little demon-touched to try and heal it.

With all the improvements in her life Chia was now such an open and trusting child that she immediately accepted Twerle as a dear new friend. That much the former nun and Dragon Lord had figured out.

Insecure and worried that her new relationship with Chia might be fragile, Sora saw Twerle as a threat to it. She was resisting, using the girl's devil-ling nature as an excuse to fight with her to try and drive her away. Unfortunately neither Drachus nor Yuma had enough experience with young girls to have figured that last part out just yet.

Everything blew up at bath time. Sora insisted on joining Chia as always but Chia said Twerle should be there too. The argument finally degraded into a shouting and shoving match between Sora and Twerle that left Chia in tears. She ran into the servant's bedroom alone and held the door closed while the two blondes glared at one another.

Yuma had been surprised at how fast the fight broke out and hadn't been able to stop it. Afterwards, she went downstairs to find Drachus. He'd gone to speak with the concierge. After she quietly explained the situation he stormed back upstairs.

"Enough is enough; this ends right now" he muttered. Up in the suite they heard noises from the girls' shared bedroom. When he opened the door, ready for a full-blown shouting match – and a spanking if needed - he found the girls sitting on the floor next to the bed. All three were quite disheveled but seemed to be uninjured as they held one another, crying, hugging and apologizing.

"I guess it's settled" Yuma said after a bit. Shaking his head Drachus went back down to finish his inquiries.

When he returned later it was nice and quiet. Yuma waved him over to the door of the girls shared bedroom. When she opened it, he saw all three girls were sound asleep in each other's arms, with Chia in the middle.

"I can't believe this" he said. "Now I'm a Dragon Lord, a Demon Slayer ... and a Babysitter!" That comment made Yuma giggle. In fact, she spent much of the night giggling about it.

The three girls woke early the next morning as the best of friends. They bathed together quite happily; Twerle was a bit embarrassed that both Chia and Sora made a fuss over her pretty wings and large breasts - which were apparently even bigger than Drachus had first thought.

Comments comparing Twerle's breasts to Yuma's notable set made her blush; Drachus was uncomfortable with those remarks as well. He often found himself appreciating those remarkable assets whenever he was alone with the former nun. Like he'd done with Maia Gravis, he often had to look past her to some point on the wall when they were discussing business.

The last thing he needed right now was to complicate things by involving his self with the lady; the womanizer was looking forward to getting back to Mion and Surra!

After the three girls had finished playing in the bath they stood quietly and repentantly in a line while Yuma scolded them like a mother for all of the fuss they'd made yesterday. After a token slap on the wrists, they all went down to breakfast with them behaving like good little girls.

Drachus never did ask what suddenly made them best friends; so long as it was worked out, he was happy.

The next week passed by quickly. With Virian's help Yuma was successful with the purchasing of tools and supplies as well as making transport arrangements; Drachus rarely had to step in. The two of them also arranged with several companies to have coal and other supplies delivered from their mines in the nearby mountains directly to Karrat Kommons; it was not only more discrete, it was cheaper.

Yuma would go out with either Sora or Chia. Since it was dangerous for Twerle to be in public, she always stayed back in the hotel. Whichever of her new 'sisters' wasn't with Yuma would keep her company. They spent the time playing dress-up or doing their hair, just like sisters.

Chia had lots of clothes and accessories for them to play dress-up with; when Sora went out with Yuma she'd sometimes order another dress ... or three; Twerle needed special clothes. Her wings didn't flap but they did need to be extended for her to fly; it was some sort of magic power she had inherited from her devil daddy, not normal winged flight. The back of her dress had to be open, wide open, below her waist, nearly to the top of her butt cheeks. They also had to buy her special halter-style bras. Despite how short the young lady was, her breasts were quite large!

The ladies handled these purchases on their own; Drachus didn't need to be involved with any of that. It seemed almost too convenient that all three were nearly the same size – though their breast sizes were quite varied.

For some reason they liked dressing the same too. With a bit of extra cost, they were able to have a schoolgirl outfit, pajamas, ankle-strap pumps and other matching clothes made for Twerle. There was no problem with money; Drachus had been paid a ridiculous amount for art he'd sold and he never objected when *Chia* asked for more.

He knew that Sora was deliberately sending her to ask for the coin but he was OK with that; trading a bit of money for a chance for Chia to become closer friends with the other girls was well worth the investment in his mind. The smiles of the girls who reminded him so much of his adorable younger sisters – who he would likely never see again - were worth much more to him than gold coins!

Drachus did try to get the girls to wear normal skirts. "Romis' style wasn't exactly normal; I'm sure you've seen how most of the ladies in the city dress..." he tried to explain. He stopped suddenly when Sora reached down and pulled her skirt up, exposing *everything* she wore below!

"So, you don't think this is pretty?" she asked coyly. Drachus had a face that was quite easy to read; the cunning girl easily saw his womanizing tendency collide with his overprotective big brother attitude. Before he could do more than stammer in response, Yuma, Chia and Twerle returned from the bath where they'd been dressing.

"Miss Sora" Yuma shouted as she flipped the girls' skirt down. "That is inappropriate! Master Drachus, go downstairs … have the concierge send up lunch" she added.

When he got back from that errand the girls were dressed in much more appropriate skirts. After that they did wear the longer skirts when out and about; you couldn't see the tops of their stockings anymore.

However, in the hotel suite the shorter skirts were all they wanted to wear. Though she often scowled at the exposed stocking tops, Yuma didn't raise objections so long as the panties and garters were covered. However, those were often visible whenever Yuma was absent.

Drachus didn't take the girls' teasing seriously. Once their figures had started to develop his younger sisters had also taken to pushing the limits of their wardrobe choices. Since they reminded him of his sisters, Drachus didn't get too flustered about Chia, Sora and Twerle's fashion shows.

However, after a while he began to think that Yuma's bust was growing! That or the décolletage of her blouse was shrinking. He kept reminding himself she had been a nun; she wouldn't get involved in these sorts of childish, girly behaviors – would she?

During the days Drachus did research in the Holy Cathedral's library. Maia Gravis' maid Laika would greet him each morning at the west gate and escort him to the library to be certain there were no issues with the other staff.

She'd bring mid-morning tea, arrive at noon with a fine lunch, in the mid-afternoon with another lovely tea and at sundown she would escort him out as well.

Even though the High Priestess had made the arrangements, the librarians were nervous at first; they were dealing with the Dragon Lord who had killed a Devil Prince! 'Big Brother' Drachus was always very polite since the librarians here were all young women. These daughters of noble families were highly educated but unlikely to marry well for reasons he discovered much later.

They often had trouble finding the books he wanted to see; he could tell them what *subjects* he wanted to read about but not in which of the ancient *books* they were in. They didn't have an organized filing system that he could see; a single volume might have as many as 12 different subjects hand-scribed within.

He never got upset, patiently waiting as they tried one after the other among the thousands of tomes in this, the largest library in the kingdom; they'd eventually find the right one. Later he introduced them to the concept of a card catalog and numbering the volumes on their shelves.

Some of the texts he read were in tomes so ancient they hadn't been opened in centuries. Both he and the librarians were amazed to find he could read the Common language, Elven, Dwarven, Orcish and Dark Elf as well!

According to everything he could find, this world was no more advanced than the 10th century. They had paper but books were rare – usually hand-scribed; there were only three printing presses in the kingdom - and they belonged to the church.

He also had issues with their oil lamps; they looked like something straight out of the Arabian Nights. Drachus mused that he could probably summon a genie if he rubbed one – though he didn't try; he was dealing with too much magic stuff as it was. With open flames (and not a lot of usable light) they were clearly inappropriate in a library; he did most of his reading in the main hall, well-lit by windows in the ceiling above.

He was surprised by how small the 'world' was - a near-rectangular island some 600 miles long. After seeing census records of the larger cities and finding that most of the interior was virtually abandoned he realized this whole 'world' couldn't have more than 3 or 4 million people.

Some of the old census records hadn't been read by the authorities in decades; he soon realized this world's population was in a slow decline. Given what the angel who summoned him had said, he wasn't surprised. He was more than a little dismayed when he realized she had expected him to fix it; how the hell was he going to manage that?

There are currently only three 'kingdoms'; Stihlheim to the north, Cromwell in the south and Durakkon, the largest, in the center of the world.

The King of Stihlheim is a ceremonial post. The Wyvern Knights – strong orc warriors who ride flying wyverns – are the real power. The 16 major and 21 minor clans rule their sections of the kingdom; clan warfare is common. Most of the population there is at least partly of Orcish blood.

The Border Mountains to the north kept the wyvern-riders from raiding south. Drachus theorized thin air at high altitudes forced wyverns to fly through low valleys making them vulnerable to ground fire. The orcs who raided in Durakkon had to travel on foot – horses didn't like orcs!

The Cromwell Kingdom is ruled by a strong royal house. They are the main sea-borne power here. Their ships are built of wood bought from the heavily forested Elven Realms far to the south; Human merchants commonly operate these and recruit orc rowers from Stihlheim.

Durakkon is a kingdom in name only; the royal line perished during Plague Years a century before. The nobles who should have chosen a new king instead formed a council to rule the land themselves. The 'kingdom' is an amalgamation of the original Durakkon, the former Ancien Principality to the north and the

Strolls Duchy to the south. Ancien and Strolls lost their ruling houses during the Demon Wars and were absorbed by Durakkon.

The plagues also caused the non-human peoples to suffer intense suppression, so Durakkon is almost exclusively human.

The Fae lands have no government, just clans of brownies, pixies, faeries and similar creatures. They have four towns; two are small ports where Cromwell ships trade with the Fae. Stym to the north handles commerce with Stihlheim; Clym to the south deals with Whitewater Clefts. Adventurers travel around in the Fae Lands exploring the many ruined cities found there.

The Demon Realms also has no central government; it consists of independent city-states. There weren't many demons there anymore; most perished during the Demon Wars but the name stuck. Almost all the other races are common in this region.

Devil-lings do not come from the Demon Realms. These girls (always girls!) are the results of demons molesting human or elven women. The women rarely survive being attacked by the big, rough creatures but some do manage to live through the ordeal. These children usually have demon-like deformities (like claws or horns) and some sort of magic powers.

Demon-touched are far more common. After studying the records for a while Drachus realized they had no relation to demons – poor diet and rampant in-breeding among the isolated villages in the desolate interior were responsible for the typically minor physical deformities that often marked these children.

There was little in the way of concrete information on demons and devils. Most of what was written was either contradictory or utter fantasy. Drachus did discover several bits of data that he could personally confirm.

Only the most powerful had wings, however at least half of them could use magic. They were known to be vulnerable to silver weapons. There were some reports of a glowing red crystal in their head but this was also mentioned as being on their chest sometimes.

However, 'instant death' from having it hit by silver wasn't mentioned. Given how tall the demons usually were, hitting the red spot with a silvered sword or halberd was likely to be almost impossible; fortunately his silver bullets made it fairly easy.

There were reports about devils stabbing victims through the heart with their claws. Apparently as the victim died, the devils could absorb their life force to replenish their power and repair any damage they had suffered.

The weather along the costs was remarkably warm; snow was a rare thing. The Elven Realms and Lizardman Marshes almost never see snow due to the extremely warm coastal ocean currents. However the mountains inland are cold in winter; snow was common 4 to 5 months a year.

Trade between cities had pretty much died out during the Plague Years. It had only recently resumed to any significant degree. 'That's why banditry is such an issue' Drachus thought. That was why a kingdom with only a million citizens had a standing army of 30,000 – almost 3% under arms! That was quite a large percentage without a war to deal with.

If you included the City Guard, the merchants' and nobles' private forces they probably had 3 or 4 times that but they weren't very mobile; that and the declining population is why they didn't have many military campaigns.

There was another 'world' to the north but they had no maps for it; this was simply known as The Dark Lands. Those adventurous souls who sailed there rarely ever returned. Those who did were usually deranged, rambling about monsters or in a daze with little memory of what they'd seen.

The only accurate information said it was a warmer land mass nearly the same size as this 'world' covered by thick forests. It was reported to be occupied by huge hungry monsters and violent ape-like creatures.

A large island-like promontory to the south was covered in scrub forests but attempts to build settlements ended quickly – all of the colonists who moved there perished within weeks!

There was no 'blue-water' sailing; the only ships here were small galleys. Like Viking longships, galleys sail/row along the coast by landmarks; they could even row up some of the larger rivers. Ships would pull onto shore at night; they only travel after dark in an emergency. Some had elven pilots; they could travel on moonlit nights - elves had exceptional night vision.

There were trade winds and sea currents on both coasts running from south to north. No one who sailed to the open sea had ever returned.

Drachus made notes on useful and unusual information in small ledgers he kept in his duster pockets.

At night he had meetings outside the cathedral with glassblowers, black-smiths, stonemasons, alchemists, perfumers and papermakers arranged by the concierge. He wanted to speak on sensitive matters and it needed to be at night to avoid the throngs of grateful townsfolk which often still gathered around him.

Some of the things he wanted made had to be described by shape, size and material – nothing like them had ever been made here before. The blacksmiths made iron items he called 'form tools' but no one could figure out what they were supposed to be used for.

Using stone so hard that it would not crack even under extreme heat (like in a glass furnace) he had stone masons chisel out several shallow flat pans. He had potters make tall, ceramic cones that he called concentrators.

He bought some tin from casting shops; they mix it with copper to make bronze but he only wanted the tin.

While meeting armorers to get details on the weapons and armor used here, Drachus learned more about the 'knights' of this world. He'd noted little 'chivalry' among them; the ones he'd seen behaved more like ordinary soldiers than a Sir Galahad.

He eventually learned a 'knight' on this world was just a heavily armed and well-trained soldier. They didn't have lands, keeps or other domains; the only criterion to become a knight here was a family member or patron to buy the expensive equipment and hire a good trainer.

Other than occasional lance charges they rarely fought from horseback; without stirrups swinging a sword would be tough to manage. Drachus realized their big advantage was wearing heavy armor; infantry couldn't march very far or fast carrying all that weight but sitting on horseback they could not only wear heavier armor they could move much farther and a lot faster.

Though they were called knights, on this world they were little more than mounted heavy infantry. They were more akin to the Dragoons of old European armies, the kind that Ernst von Mansfeld had used so effectively.

There were four types of knights; Holy Knights, Army Knights, Nobles' Knights and Merchant Knights.

Holy Knights of the church were typically the first-born sons of important noble families. They were generally arrogant, expecting to be treated with respect. These were often generational; sons would follow fathers into service.

The knights employed by noble families tended to be relatives of the head of household. Their behavior was more varied; abusive households employed abusive knights while beneficent ones had much nicer men.

Merchant knights were professional fighters loyal only to their employers.

The Army Knights were probably the best behaved of all. While many were from prominent families more than a few were promoted through the ranks – earning knighthoods by personal actions both combat and social. Knights could also earn noble ranks, though Baron was usually the highest. A very skilled knight might even receive a commission; Knight Captains commanded outposts.

Knights were exclusively men in the three kingdoms. The Elven Realms to the south did have some female knights but in the lands of humans 'knight' meant 'man'. Women with combat skills became adventurers; some armorers made armor for women, but not many.

Walking back to the hotel one evening Drachus spotted a man lighting a pipe with what looked like a match; since he didn't smoke, he hadn't noticed before. At Karrat Kommons there was always a lit candle in the kitchen and the bunnies brought one to his room as needed. At the hotel the maids did the same.

Asking around Drachus eventually found the toothpick-sized wooden sticks were called 'Scrubbers' here; they were quite common. They were stained dark grey at one end. The thin wooden box they were usually carried in had a smooth ceramic plate; you 'scrubbed' the stained end on this until friction heated it enough to ignite the stain. Nobles and wealthy merchants carried Scrubber Cases made of tooled silver.

From the smell Drachus could tell the stain was made with mixture of sulfur, charcoal and a nitrate – the components of gunpowder! He looked into it to reload his cartridges – he was running low – but the nitrates were expensive and difficult to obtain in enough quantity for gunpowder. It would have to wait.

After a week Yuma had gathered the materials on his lists and Drachus had more than enough information to start his efforts to improve the lives of the bunny-folk.

With his research done he asked Laika to arrange another meeting with Maia Gravis to express his thanks for her assistance and to take his leave, so another mid-morning tea was scheduled.

The next morning Drachus saw the High Priestess was even tenser now than she had been at the first tea.

"Has your research gone well?" she asked politely.

"Yes, it has though I do have questions I was unable to answer with books. I hoped you might be able to help with these" Drachus asked.

"Certainly," she replied cautiously. "I'll tell you anything I can if it will help" she said, thinking to herself 'Anything to get this man and his distracting aura away quickly can only help me sleep better at night!'

"Agriculture in the cursed lands today is difficult though 500 years ago it had been rich farmland. Exactly what happened?" he asked.

"The demon warlord cursed those lands before he was sealed away. That is all anyone knows" she said.

After considering that for a bit he asked his next question. "About the Midland River - did it dry up at exactly the same time?"

"No, that is not true" she began. "Most legends claim so but historical records exist that state in fact the drying of the river preceded the curse by decades. There are some that imply it may have started *even before* the Demon Wars – a few say it could have been as early as the Great Catastrophe itself" she finished.

As a smile tugged at the corners of Drachus' mouth it seemed to her that information pleased the Dragon Lord, though Maia Gravis couldn't understand why it would.

"Then there is the Crystal Crypt" he said.

With that remark the lady almost dropped her teacup. It took her a few moments to regain her composure before she answered. "That is merely a legend, believed by some to be the final resting place of the three Angelus Sisters" she finally said.

"Even though the public is taught they returned to the heavens to protect the kingdom from further demon invasions?" Drachus asked. Looking uncomfortable Maia Gravis hesitated before replying.

"Yes, that story circulated after the war when conditions were very difficult. The knowledge one was known to have perished and the other two had vanished without a trace was deemed too likely to demoralize the people. Public confidence had to be restored so the lie was told. Unfortunately that lie has become so believed that it is now an unshakeable truth; even some within the church accept it!" she finished.

'When legend becomes the truth, you teach the legend' Drachus once heard a literature professor say about Robin Hood. He decided to press on this one.

"But the church does have records of the location, yes? I found one reference that said the Crypt was under an ancient castle ruin in the Demon Realms where Lunai fell in battle. Another said it was in the west of Durakkon. A third said it was deep below the Shrine of Hope itself."

Maia Gravis' brow glistened with beads of perspiration. Even if the room was soundproof, the two of them were openly discussed one of the church's most closely guarded secrets. She desperately needed to end this conversation as soon as she could.

"I'm sorry but I don't know more than the rumors you've already mentioned" she said as she set her teacup down with trembling fingers. Drachus felt he might be pushing too hard here and moved on.

"Let's leave that alone" he said - to the ladies' relief.

"My last question will be a bit different" he told her.

Maia Gravis cringed at that but replied "Ask away."

"I'm curious about the status of your 'sister', the High Priestess of the Moon Selena Rose, and that buxom lady 'Trini'; the one she partnered with in the fight" Drachus began. "I haven't seen either all week and I'm concerned; they were both badly injured by that verdamnt devil."

Drachus knew they had suffered serious internal injuries and wasn't sure if the berries had been able to help them enough for them to survive. The lady allowed herself a nervous laugh, relieved that this was going to be an easy one to answer.

"Both are fine, physically" she began. "Selena wanders around in a daze gripping a dark handkerchief like a love-struck tween. She'll occasionally bury her face in it as if it held the scent of wonderful cologne." Now it was Drachus' turn to choke on his tea as he realized that was likely the handkerchief he'd given her after the battle.

"Trini, the 'buxom one' as you called her is Katarina Aries, though most call her Trina – she doesn't like the long form of her name. They are childhood friends; in fact Trina's mother was the personal maid of Selena's mother. After she passed away the maid became Selena's wet nurse; the two of them grew up as close as sisters" she said.

After a sly grin, Maia Gravis continued. "Trina is a famous adventuring priestess. The lady is so powerful that had she been born male she'd be a Bishop in the church one day, maybe even a Cardinal! The day after the battle she went to a shrine near here. She has been pestering the nuns to teach her all they can about cooking, sewing, - even child-rearing; all manner of common domestic tasks."

Hearing the name Drachus got that deja-vu feeling again. Señor Arevalo's kidnapped daughter was named Katarina; her brother Diego had called her 'Trina'. Hearing names from his old world was getting a bit creepy. Shaking it off, the Dragon Lord resumed listening as Maia Gravis explained about the ladies.

"Miss Trina believes she will marry soon. Her partner Malen Trill is worried about her emotional state; she's asked for her to be watched closely until she recovers from this 'latest bout of fantasy'. You see, Trina Aries is famous for wild predictions; oddly, her more outrageous predictions often come true" the priestess was saying with a sly smile.

Drachus realized it was best he was leaving in the morning; from what he recalled of the pretty brunette, she would likely be ... distracting! He noticed a rather serious expression appear on Maia Gravis' face.

"Was there more you wanted to talk about?" he said.

After a few moments hesitation Maia Gravis decided to ask. "It has been reported that cultists freed the Demon Warlord Kreeger from the Shrine of Hope; the creature threatened a nearby village some weeks ago. However, it hasn't been seen since. When the Grand Marshal and a column of Army Knights visited the shrine they found many cultists' remains and a large scorch mark, typical of those left behind by destroyed demons. Did you ... could you tell me ..." she stammered.

Drachus thought for a bit and decided to come clean on this issue – at least partly. "The first thing I did upon arrival was destroy that foul creature. It poses no threat to any on this world" he said quietly. With a wide smile Maia Gravis tugged gently on a small silver ring that likely rang a bell outside the soundproof room to summon her maid.

"I am concerned about one last thing" Drachus said as he rose; "have you been unwell?" Surprised at the sudden change in topic, Maia Gravis hesitated a bit.

"Unwell? Have you heard rumors?" she asked.

"No," he said. "I noticed all during our meeting that you seem flushed, your breathing is a bit fast and you are perspiring as if you have a slight fever. Am I mistaken?"

The Dragon Lord had learned she rarely left the cathedral so her pale complexion was common knowledge. In contrast to her long, black hair it was always noticeable but it made today's flush even more obvious.

"Yes, I assure you I am in fine health; I am grateful for your concern though, good sir" she said quite properly.

"You should get out more. A daily walk in the sun can improve a lady's complexion" he said as Laika came in.

"My duties are many; they do not often permit me such indulgences" she said a bit tartly.

"You should convince your mistress to at least have tea outside on the balcony more often. I expect the fresh air and sunlight will greatly improve her color" he told Laika in a loud whisper as he left the room.

"I shall endeavor to overcome her ... reluctance to do so sir" Laika said with a smile as she closed the door.

"You jerk!" Maia Gravis shouted once the thick door was closed. As she stormed to the window she realized it was obvious she was perspiring. She saw her flushed face (and bosom) reflected in the smooth window glass.

Whether it was from the Dragon Lord's concern over her health, his effort to appeal to her maid directly or something else she couldn't say. It wasn't a response to the wonderful news of the demon's destruction. Though her heart had fluttered when he admitted to the deed, it was just as he had mentioned; she had been afflicted all throughout the meeting.

Maia Gravis remained in the tea room for several minutes after the Dragon Lord had departed; it took some time for her to calm herself enough to resume her official duties that afternoon.

Before that she did need to take a bath and change clothes. To Maia Gravis' annoyance Laika had arranged fresh attire and a bath *before* she escorted the Dragon Lord away; the maid had known she'd need it!

Afterwards the priestess was further irritated when she saw Laika had set up tea *outside* on a garden balcony. Though perturbed the lady did not complain. With some effort she ignored the faces of the men in the windows above as they leered down at her. It was obvious what they were looking at; the tight-bodiced gowns she preferred made her breasts evident when viewed from above.

Despite that, from then on Maia Gravis had tea out on the balcony every day, weather permitting; she was disappointed when she couldn't. Laika procured a large parasol – to protect the ladies delicate skin from sunburn.

Of course, it also blocked the men from leering at her from above. After a few days many in the Cathedral noted how much both her complexion and mood had improved.

Far from the Holy Cathedral was a small circular cavern with walls lined by amethyst gems. At the center there stood three tall columns of pure, clear crystal. Floating within were the images of three beautiful angels.

Two of the images frowned at the third as the center spoke. "Sister, I know you were a skilled matchmaker but should you really be influencing these young women so much? He finds their company ... desirable but they shouldn't be so strongly ... swayed in that direction ..."

"I am doing nothing of the sort" the one on the right interrupted. At their surprised looks she added even more.

"He has always had an air about him that women find desirable; they feel he can be trusted to treat them kindly – and he does! In this world if a man goes to great lengths to save her from mortal danger it makes him seem even more attractive to her. These last few ... rescues seem to be more susceptible to those feelings; they can be ... excessive with their gratitude."

When their faces showed her 'sisters' were dubious she decided to add a bit more to her explanation.

"I did enhance his ... aura where women are concerned; he is alone in a new world. Finding comfort in their embrace should motivate him to acclimate quickly so he can provide all the people of this poor world with much better lives. I assure you - my blessing was not powerful enough to *unduly* influence them into his arms; they find themselves attracted to him quite naturally" she finished with a giggle.

Her sisters moans made it clear they weren't certain her motives were so totally pure.

Early the next morning Drachus and the ladies packed up in Sora's coach and left the hotel. Just outside the city waiting for them in a livestock holding yard they met with seven wagons and a dozen mounted guards. Virian headed the caravan, his man Coramak commanded the guards.

Four of the huge wagons held the supplies for the new craft shops that the ladies knew about but the others held craftsmen, tools and their personal belongings. Drachus had convinced them to move to Karrat Kommons to help him set up the new shops.

Chapter 13

Just how much can I do for these people?
I'm no damn genius!

During the long boring morning ride back to Karrat Kommons Drachus spent his time reviewing. He had made many notes in small ledgers as he researched information in the library of the Holy Cathedral and needed to decide which projects to get the craftsmen working on first.

Yuma spent much of the time reading one of the many books she had acquired during the shopping. Apparently the lady liked to read novels but had never had much of a chance to back at her old shrine; recreational reading wasn't very high on the nun's list of daily priorities.

Normally these were quite expensive but once word got around that she was working for the Dragon Lord (and she liked reading) many of the merchants began giving books to her as gifts when she arranged for purchases. In a medieval economy, giving gifts to the minions of important persons was considered a legitimate business expense!

During one of the numerous rest stops along the way Drachus took a look at one. At first her books seemed to be romance stories; a quick scan of the pages of one described scenes that were a bit graphic. There was a ripped bodice, uncontrolled moans of passion and lots of heaving bosoms glistening with perspiration being grasped by rough hands!

He was a bit surprised that the serious former nun would find that particular subject entertaining. It reminded him of a book that he'd read while working in France. It was a copy of one banned in England, about a Lady Chatterley.

Sora, Chia and Twerle spent most of the first few hours sleeping on the front seat. Their departure had been rather early and the girls tended to chat for hours before falling to sleep at night; they were still a bit tired.

Once awake they seemed rather bored, until Chia mentioned a pretty stained glass window she had seen. Sora was familiar with it because she grew up in the capitol but Twerle had never seen it – it was in a church and a devil-ling would never go near one of those if she valued her life!

Using her golden scepter Sora twisted and colored bits of light until it became a fairly detailed glowing image of the stained glass window. Both Twerle and Chia were amazed; Drachus was rather impressed too.

"You really are quite skilled with that" Yuma commented. For some time Sora would craft images of cute animals and famous statues to entertain her little sisters.

"You should be careful; using that much mana can be exhausting" a worried Yuma cautioned.

"It's not a problem; when I channel the light through my scepter the mana cost is practically nonexistent!" Sora said shaking her head. However, after an hour it became obvious she was getting tired. When she noticed strain on Sora's face Chia took the scepter away.

"Enough; don't overdo it to keep us from getting bored" she said. Sora pouted for 10 minutes before falling asleep on Chia's shoulder; she really had been overdoing it.

Sora's coach was much faster than the ox-drawn cargo wagons and made it back to the village just before dinner.

That night Mion came to Drachus' room for a sponge bath. After having to deal the beautiful (but untouchable) Yuma every day plus the frequent encounters with the absolutely fabulous (but forbidden) Maia Gravis he was quite happy to be able to cuddle with a lovely lady without worrying about serious consequences.

Just before midnight Surra came to his room to welcome him back herself. As he watched the two ladies kiss one another's' cheeks as they passed in the doorway it occurred to him this was a bit strange.

"Isn't it odd for the two of you to be ... OK with all of this?" he asked her as they cuddled later. From the slightly confused look on Surra's face he saw it took a bit for her to understand what he was referring to.

"Oh, you mean ... sharing? It is unusual; we rarely form a steady relationship with a male. In spring we pair up for a week but otherwise there are no permanent couples. Besides, Mion and I are both happy with this; it is rare we are treated so ... gently by a man" she said with a smile.

After a bit more cuddling she began to show him just how happy she was with the circumstances; he didn't get a lot of sleep that night but the man wasn't going to complain!

Late the next day the cargo wagons arrived. As the drivers, apprentices and bunny-folk unloaded them Drachus met with the craftsmen about projects he wanted them to start immediately. Within a few weeks parts of Karrat Kommons that were cleared of crops was to become a Medieval Manufacturing Center.

The stonemasons started on a glass furnace; along with the hatch for accessing molten glass near the bottom there were two heat concentrators on the top. These would collect and concentrate the heat allowing them to make glass panes faster. Seeing the obvious resemblance to the locals, the stonemasons christened it a Bunny furnace.

Drachus showed the bunny potters how to make 'S-shaped' ceramic shingles. He'd seen these in his old world and knew they would be sturdier and more weather-resistant than the split wooden shingles and straw thatch they used here now.

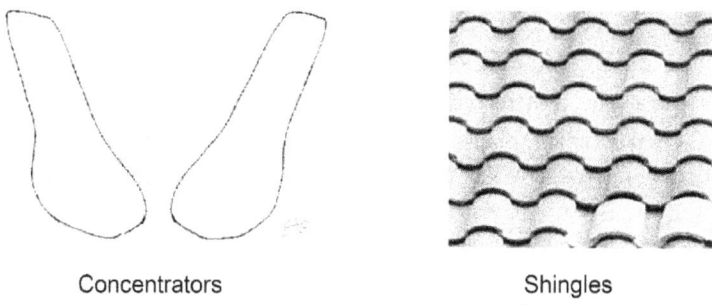

Concentrators   Shingles

Before installing these, the carpenters covered the wood planks below them with canvas treated with linseed oil. Though not waterproof, this would eliminate many of the leaks that plagued the village during the rainy season.

While that was going on Drachus showed the blacksmiths how to make stirrups. The bunny-folk leather workers modified the saddles for these and added taller heels to the men's boots so they could use them properly. Romis was sensitive about her short height; she'd already worn boots with a high heel so she didn't have any issues with the makeshift stirrups Drachus had made for her.

Initially using the stirrups to mount caused the saddles to dislodge and the men to fall to the ground. After he spent a few hours studying them, Drachus realized the saddles didn't have proper underpinnings to keep them in place during mounting. Once these were installed, the stirrups worked fine.

With a few hours of training the guards realized the stir-ups would let them fight effectively from horseback, a skill some knights never mastered even after years of practice. They were crafted to be detachable; Drachus had the men drape a long narrow blanket over the stirrups when they were attached to the saddles. He still hoped to keep them a secret until he was ready to sell them to the army.

After several days the craftsmen finished the Bunny furnace and the new blacksmith's forge, then began to work on the bunny-folk's homes. Once the Bunny furnace was up the glass blowers made several 3-minute hour-glasses – so the bunny-medics wouldn't have to recite that nursery rhyme to time boiling water for medical treatments!

After that they made clear glass jars and glass panes for windows. Drachus' new form tools made this easy.

In a shallow rectangular stone pan they placed tin and the powder mix of silica sand, soda and lime for clear glass. Once set on top of the heat concentrators these would melt and the lighter liquid glass would float atop the heavier liquid tin to cast flat, glass panes with remarkably smooth sides – perfect for windows.

Once the panes became available, he worked with the bunny-folk carpenters to craft double-glazed single-hung sash windows with muntins to replace the shutters now used to cover the windows in all of their buildings.

The bunnies saw how much warmer this would keep their homes in the winter. It would let in enough light to reduce their dependence on candles during the winter days. They'd also improve ventilation in warmer weather.

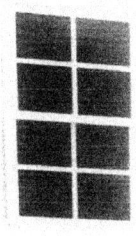 

Muntins   Canning Jars

Before the Spain fiasco Drachus had worked to set up security at a small laboratory in England; a guy named Bickerstaff was experimenting with this floating process to make plate glass.

Drachus showed the glass crafters how to use rectangular iron form tools to make glass canning jars. After a bit of practice, they learned how much molten glass to blow into the polished inner cavity to make glass jars. After cutting them off while they were still warm and soft they would press in a hot cast iron plug mounted on a wooden handle into the open tops to form a near-perfect mouth.

Once the jars were ready Drachus showed the cooks how to 'can' fruits and vegetables. This practice was common in farm communities where factory canned goods were expensive.

Waxed string wrapped around a formed glass lid would melt when placed on the still-warm jars after boiling. This would form an airtight seal as the jars cooled. The string could be pulled to break it open.

Covering the top with cloth would let them write the date the foods were canned. When he told the bunny-folk this process could keep the foods safe to eat for months they were stunned. Since the glass was clear, they could also tell if the foods had spoiled before they even opened the jar.

Once they began canning in earnest he tried to show them a labeling system to make it easier to tell which were the oldest. Unfortunately, he didn't understand the local calendar;

embarrassing as it was, the powerful Dragon Lord had to learn along with the rest of the kitchen staff.

After a class taught by the snickering Sora and the embarrassed Yuma, he learned it was late summer in the Year 1216 on the Calendar of the First Royal Conclave, typically just abbreviated as the Royal Year 1216.

Drachus found they worked from a Lunar Calendar here; months and weeks from his old world didn't exist. A new month started on the new moon and lasted about 30 days. They used the lunar phases for interim time-keeping; first quarter, half, third quarter etc. Over time most of those who talked with the Dragon Lord came to realize when he spoke of 'weeks' it meant a lunar phase; they began using that simpler term instead.

Since there were three months for each season the months were easily identified as early spring, mid-summer, late fall, etc. Solstice and equinox festivals were used to time semi-annual intervals. The years here were 355 days long - shorter than on his old world. In Leap Years the church would decree a spring festival would be two days long.

Working from drawings the blacksmiths made small stand-alone iron stoves. These were far more efficient than a fireplace; they burned only a fraction of the wood or coal to produce the same amount of cooking and heating. They had carried the supplies for these in the wagons; future shipments of iron and coal would come directly from nearby mines.

As time passed many of the men paired up with bunny-girls. The bunny-folk had rarely experienced consensual intimacy outside their mating season and found they really liked it. Given the lack of privacy in dormitories these areas were partitioned into smaller rooms; even then privacy was rare. It became common to find a passionate couple in odd places most any time of the night; sometimes even in the daytime!

There was no competition for girlfriends; the male to female ratio among the bunny-folk was not 50:50. After a careful count Drachus found there were 98 males and 286 females. He asked Mion and Surra about the disparity.

"When we have a child" – "we can't have another for three years" – "that's how it's always been" the bunny-ladies tandemed.

Drachus figured the odd ratio seemed appropriate, though it did seem too convenient to be random.

Permanent bunny-folk couples hadn't been allowed before; during spring eligible women took temporary partners for mating season. Once a mother-to-be was so heavy with child she couldn't safely work the fields, she was moved to indoor work.

Once the children were walking the moms would return to field work; older children and the dispensary ladies took over child care during the day.

Once it was known permanent relationships were now permitted, dozens of the bunny-folk coupled up. With no priest to perform weddings, they were just boyfriend/girlfriend couples but they took themselves seriously; seriously enough that the carpenters put up a whole new building for couples!

Once glazing and canning were underway, Drachus spent several days working with the blacksmiths and carpenters building a thing he called a 'crossed bow'. It looked like the child-like short bows the cultists' used but it was much stronger and mounted sideways on a narrow sculpted wooden post.

Ordinarily a bow that strong couldn't be drawn with one hand. By stepping on an iron handle mounted at its front the men could use both. There was an iron latching mechanism to hold it cocked until a bolt was placed; then it could be fired whenever.

The bolts were difficult to describe. The craftsmen knew about arrows but short, stubby bolts with big fins were something new. At first they made 'toy' arrows like the cultists had used.

When the craftsmen asked Drachus where to get the poison to make them deadly he was surprised to learn the cultists coated the points of their arrows with a poison derived from snake venom. 'That's why those little toy bows were considered so dangerous' Drachus thought.

To resolve the issue he pulled the thinner bolts from his vest to show the craftsmen what they were supposed to look like. After that, they were able to craft them properly.

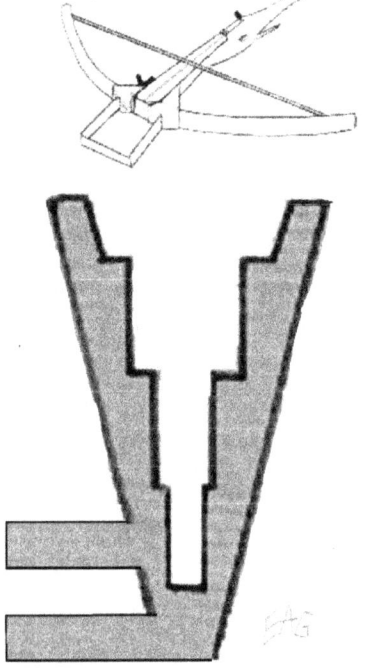

Making the crossed bows wasn't hard but a task he called 'fixing the sights' took time and needed several test firings. A thick V-shaped brass piece was firmly mounted near the front on one side. This brass 'sight' was smooth on the outside but had stepped openings on the inside. These were 'fixed' to match the space between a man's shoulders at 20, 40, 80 and 150 paces.

Once he'd spent time showing the guards how to line these up with a short post at the middle of the crossbow they were accurately hitting targets, punching through old wooden shingles to duplicate light armor up to a 150 paces away. These were feats that often took traditional archers years to learn to do easily.

As he was going through the process Drachus used his own bolts to demonstrate. He knew these were higher quality – better balanced and properly fin-stabilized for best accuracy. This would give the bolt-makers a good example and an incentive to improve theirs to be just as accurate. He didn't use the boomers for training; unnecessary explosions would disturb the bunny-folk and their livestock – a lot!

One day shortly after crossed bow training, Yuma spoke to Drachus in the dining hall. "Tonight is the first night of the full moon" she started.

"Yes, I'm surprised time has passed so quickly" he said. It seemed she wanted to say more but didn't quite know how to put it into words when he realized "You need to make berries!"

"Yes, that's right. I'll need a private place where I can be exposed to the moon. I'll need honey and someone to ... to take care of me after ... when I can't ..." Yuma said with an embarrassed smile.

"I'll speak with Mion and Surra" Drachus told the blushing lady. The bunny-girls were confused but happy to help. Yuma asked them to find a place where no one could see the process but where she would be exposed to the light of the moon. She said it was ... rather noisy ... so it needed to be a bit remote.

They decided to use a small walled pasture away from the dormitory usually reserved to hold sheep and goats ready to have lambs and kids. You can't schedule deliveries and hungry newborns could be noisy at all hours of the day and night making it difficult to sleep nearby.

Meeting there at midnight the bunny-ladies spread a blanket then watched as Yuma undressed, the sensations overcame her and she collapsed. Mion placed the golden healing berries in the honey-filled glass vial as instructed while Surra wrapped the trembling dark elf in a blanket.

"That was so wonderful" – "you sound so satisfied" – "and it lasted so long" – "you are so lucky!" the duo hit her with comments from both sides; they had misconstrued the nature of her overstimulated responses!

"What do you mean?" asked Yuma. That's when the confused bunny-girls innocently spilled the beans about what those sensations *seemed* to be. As they gave her the details (including all of the mechanics) of sexual gratification the former nun blushed from head to toe. Then she screamed as she wrapped herself up in the blanket.

After failing to console her after several minutes, Mion ran to get Drachus. He'd stayed up just in case something unusual happened. The Dragon Lord was soon sitting next to the still sniffling Yuma.

"Look, Mion and Surra are just a bit confused" he began. "The Mother Superior explained it all to me back at the shrine; those sensations are just the result of the ... intense energy your body is being exposed to. Despite appearances, they are *not* ... that. You do seem to be exceptionally ... sensitive to this sort of thing but that's not a real ... problem." His explanation only brought a few more sniffles from the huddled young woman.

"Your berries save lives; they are very important" he added. Even after that there was still nothing from her; Drachus realized it was going to take a while for this very shy woman to get over this. Recognizing his inexperience in counseling embarrassed women, he picked her up blanket and all to carry Yuma back to her room.

Once there he left it to Mion and Surra to get her into bed as he took the berries to the kitchen to be honey-pickled. After they exited, he tried to explain all of this, to make certain they didn't feel responsible for it.

"Please understand - this is not your fault! I should have told you what was going to happen with this ... earlier" Drachus told the bunny-ladies.

"What's wrong?" – "She enjoyed it so!" the very distressed duo said in tandem.

"That's the problem" he said "She was raised as a nun." The bunny-girls didn't understand – they didn't know what a nun was! He tried to explain again but with no luck.

"She was taught it was bad for her to have those feelings, even if they really aren't ... *those* feelings" he finally just told them. Repeating it was not their fault, he made them promise not to tell anyone what they'd seen and sent them to bed.

As he headed back to his room Drachus recalled a conversation he'd had with a lady athlete he'd met in England as he was leaving for Spain. The lady didn't like to travel by boat so she had fortified herself with several brandies before their ferry left for France; she was in quite a talkative mood.

She told him she was a competitive runner. Sometimes, after an intense run, she'd find herself aroused; overstimulation was caused quite often during those runs - but they dissipated after a cold shower she admitted.

Drachus had heard about a 'runner's high', a euphoric condition some athletes reported having after an intense run. Maybe, channeling the moonlight caused a similar reaction in Yuma; it did seem to be quite intense.

Mion and Surra had only seen her reactions; maybe they didn't know about the 'traces'. The bunny-girls had only wrapped Yuma in a blanket afterwards; the Mother Superior had examined the girl for injuries. Maybe the stimulation really was just coincidentally similar to ... *that*.

Yuma refused to come out of her room all the next day. Mion and Surra took breakfast and lunch in to her but told Drachus she didn't eat any of it. That evening when *he* took dinner in he found her on the bed wrapped in the same grass-stained blanket from last night. The dried tear stains on the pillow said she'd been crying quite a lot.

He was about to haul her out for some tough-love counseling when she spoke up in a very quiet voice. "I'm so embarrassed" she practically whispered.

Sitting on the bed he started to explain. "Look, those sensations are not what you think ..."

"That's not it" she interrupted peeking out at him.

After a few moments she admitted "I know it's not ... *that*; the Reverend Mother did explain it all to me ... twice in fact. But I like it; I always have but ... it's embarrassing. Being naked, the heavy breathing, sweating and the sounds I make when it ... comes over me; I couldn't bear to be seen like that!" she cried.

'I guess she's a lights-off girl' Drachus thought.

"And tonight will be worse" she whined. Drachus was relieved; he'd worried she might never make them again. After a bit she jumped up with a frantic expression.

"Chia, Twerle, Sora, the children, they can NEVER see me like that; EVER!" she pleaded. Drachus didn't hear her at first; he was distracted because she was naked after the blanket had fallen away. This was the first time he'd seen her naked in daylight. The lady was a knockout; her body was fantastic!

He remembered reading about legends that said women lose magic powers if they lose their virginity; right now that was a possibility. Summoning some willpower the habitual womanizer gently pushed the naked beauty away, wrapped her in the blanket and got up off the bed.

"Mion and Surra will take care of you when ... when you're out there. They've seen it all already so they won't be surprised; OK?" he asked.

She smiled and nodded but then asked "You won't be there?" He couldn't tell if that was what she wanted or not so he decided to go with the safe bet.

"I think it best. Otherwise we might have ... complications" he said.

She was confused until his eyes darted down; then Yuma realized she was very exposed. Blushing, she wrapped the blanket tighter around herself.

"Now you eat" he said pointing to her dinner. "The girls will escort you to the pasture and I'll carry you back after ... just like last night." As she was about to reply her tummy growled rather loudly; she blushed again as Drachus smiled and left.

Outside her door there was quite the crowd waiting. "She's fine now. It was just a case of nerves" he told them. A wave of relief spread among them; rumors had been running wild that the popular lady healer was ill or injured. Starting from the right, he began to issue instructions.

"Mion, you and Surra - take her to the enclosure just like last night. Afterwards, one of you fetches me and I carry her back here. Pass the word that no one else goes near there until she's finished. Later, I'll tell you a lot more of the details about this – it's not what it seems. Oh, and bring her a second dinner plate; I'm pretty sure she's rather hungry."

"She's not hurt or ill, just very nervous" he said to the medics. Then he looked at Chia, Sora and Twerle.

"You three come with me. I have something I should have explained to you before about ... all of this."

In the privacy of the manager's old office, he told them how Yuma made berries. He didn't detail the aftereffects; just that she found them embarrassing and was uncomfortable with people seeing the process.

They knew how important the berries were, how shy Yuma was and that only she could make them. Though worried about their dear big sister they politely agreed to give her privacy for this important task. Drachus didn't believe them for a minute.

Despite orphanage life and her serious schooling as a High Priestess (or maybe because of it) Sora had begun behaving more like a little kid every day. Chia and Twerle had been overworked and abused as slaves all their lives; they'd never been allowed to be little kids while growing up. Since those times were now behind them, the girls had somewhat reverted to the childhood they had never been permitted to have before.

Drachus saw nothing wrong with it so long as they realized they did have to be mature when necessary – which so far they had managed just fine. For the foreseeable future, he had no issues with them getting a second chance to experience the childhood they'd been denied. In fact, he rather liked the idea of them playing like little kids. But there was the occasional issue with that, like right now.

Late that night, just before Yuma, Mion and Surra were to leave for the enclosure, the three young girls snuck out through a side door in their pajamas. Before they got three steps they stopped as they heard his voice.

"And where are you going, as if I didn't know" Drachus said. Looking they saw him leaning against the wall by the door. "You think I was born yesterday ... all three of you, come here" he said. Growing up with young sisters he knew how childish girls could be.

They went to the classroom where each girl wrote 'Big Sister Yuma deserves privacy' 100 times. Once done with the complaining, the whining and finally the writing, it was over; he may be indulgent but if they were misbehaving like little kids, he'd punish them like little kids.

By then Surra had arrived to take him out to pick up Yuma and carry her back to her room after the strenuous process of making ruby red berries.

The next morning, Drachus had one of those two red berries used on a bunny-girl who still had disabilities from previous serious injuries. After several hours she was completely healed just like Chia's leg.

The other red berry was placed in a silver-stopped honey-filled glass vial so it could be easily differentiated from the golden ones and only used when appropriate.

As Sora, Chia and Twerle tried to sneak out again the third night to see how Yuma made the berries Drachus caught them in the hallway this time. He marched them to the classroom again where they wrote *200* apologies each.

Just before lunch the next day Drachus saw Yuma staring out the window, watching Chia, Sora and Twerle playing with bunny-kids. Due to her strenuous three nights she'd been told to sleep in; she wasn't allowed to do any sort of work before lunch.

Other than berry making, she worked during the day and slept at night like everyone else now. At the shrine she'd been their main night shift nun since she was so vulnerable to sunburn. She'd always been lonely because of that; when she joined with Drachus and the girls she shifted her wake-sleep cycle to be awake with all the rest of them.

Yuma used to avoid sunburn in a dress covering her from neck to ankles and a big bonnet. Now she wore her pirate outfit and a big floppy hat; that worked just as well and it seemed to make her happier – at least whenever Drachus saw her wearing it she was always smiling.

Yuma seemed wistful watching the children at play waiting for the lunch bell. Even kids had to work on a farm but Drachus insisted their load be lighter than the former overseer had demanded; they were happier now.

"You didn't play much as a child" Drachus noted.

"No" she said. "There was always work to do; my first memories are of helping in the kitchen. Besides, there were no other children at the shrine to play with anyway."

As they watched, one of the kids found a fledgling bird that had fallen from its nest. Twerle unfurled her wings and carried the baby bird back to its nest to the applause of the girls – the boys just stared up at her.

Sora grabbed Twerle by the ankles, pulling her down to the ground while scolding her. After a bit, the two embraced and went back to playing with wide smiles. Drachus shook his head; Sora had been upset by the boys looking up Twerle's short skirt as she flew overhead.

No matter what world you were on, some things don't change; boys everywhere were fascinated by feminine mysteries!

"I never did find out what made those two stop fighting with each other and become best friends" he said.

"Didn't they tell you?" Yuma asked in surprise.

"No, did you ever find out?" he asked.

"Yes" she began. "During that last fight, it seemed to be getting out of hand and might get worse. That's when I ran downstairs to tell you about it. After I left their shouting match did get worse; it turned into shoving, slapping and hair-pulling match. It sometimes happens with girls; even nuns!" Yuma added quickly as she saw Drachus frown.

'I guess that's why they were so disheveled' he thought. "And then?" he asked after a moment.

"While I was downstairs the fight moved out on the balcony. After Twerle shoved her, Sora stumbled and fell over the rail! Before she could even scream, Twerle flew out and grabbed her. She can't fly with that much extra weight but she did help Sora hold onto the railing so she didn't fall. Thankfully it didn't cause a scene; they were so high up that no one saw them hanging there even if her wings were glowing" Yuma said.

After a pause for a wide yawn the dark elf continued. "Chia heard them calling and helped Sora back up. Once she was safe, Twerle flew back in. After such a dreadful scare, they hugged, cried and apologized over and over until they fell asleep together" Yuma finished.

"It's amazing what it sometimes takes to get through to little kids!" Drachus said shaking his head. Looking back outside, he suggested "You should have some fun too. Why don't you join in?"

"What? I'm too old to play like that" she scoffed.

"Come on, you can't be more than 16, maybe 17 – you're already like their big sister; I'm sure they'd love for you to play around with them" Drachus retorted.

"If you please, sir" she responded hotly. "I happen to be much too mature for that sort of thing; I am 29 years old!"

"You can't be that old" he said. Then he recalled the raid that resulted in her birth was 30 years ago. "Right, some of the books I read at the cathedral library said elves do live a lot longer than humans" he muttered.

"So do half-bloods and therefore we both mature slower than humans" Yuma pointed out. She was quiet and thoughtful for a bit after that. "Do I really look that young?" the half-blood dark elf eventually asked timidly.

"Yes" Drachus said. "If you were human you'd be just out of jailbait status, not much older than Sora."

Lost in thought, he walked away as she continued to watch the children play. She was so deep in thought herself - trying to figure out what 'jailbait' was - she didn't even notice he'd left. After what seemed a long time Yuma started toying with the open collar of her white blouse before turning back to where Drachus had been.

"Do you think ... could you like a dark elf ... who looks ..." stopping in mid-sentence when she saw he was no longer there. Amid a bright red blush she muttered "You can be such a jerk, even if you are the Dragon Lord!"

Chapter 14

I've Settled In – and Now I'm Moving?

"Just how old are all of you girls?" Drachus asked several he had gathered in the classroom after lunch. "I found records that said Sora is probably 18 and I just found out Yuma is 29. What about you?" he asked looking at Chia.

"Some people in the village said I was born between the Great Eclipses; that was another reason they thought I was so badly cursed" she answered as she touched her face near her different-colored eyes.

The Great Eclipses were a total solar eclipse followed 15 days later by a total lunar eclipse – quite the unusual sequence of astronomical events. With surprise obvious on his face Drachus shook his head.

"I read the Great Eclipses were 17 years ago! You can't be 17; you look like you're 9, 10 at the most" he said.

"Remember, she had a hard life in that hellish village she grew up in" Sora reminded him as she hugged Chia.

'True', Drachus mused. 'Nutrition in a poor region was never good. It was worse if you were a slave. She likely hadn't been fed properly and was worked half to death from the time she could walk; that really would stunt her growth'. Besides, he had already noticed that everyone on this world seemed to be short to begin with.

"What about you Twerle?" he asked.

"My mother was taken captive at the big demon raid that wiped out the Salkas trading village; I was born a year later" Twerle responded.

"Oh, I just read about that in the history class yesterday" Mion said, her hand up like an eager student.

Along with all the crafting supplies Drachus had bought several expensive books for teaching reading, writing, arithmetic, geography and history. Each morning Sora taught classes for the adult bunny-folk. In the afternoon, the adults would teach the children. He wanted to give the bunny-folk an education; other than basic arithmetic most of them were illiterate!

Though the Angelus decreed the church would take care of them, that didn't rate even a minimal education. Demi-humans in this kingdom really were considered little more than animals.

"Salkas was the last of the big demon raids. It was the year before I was born; I'm 19 so Twerle is 20!" Mion said.

"Impossible" Drachus called out in shock. "Even if everyone here is tiny, she's a munchkin; she can't be 20!"

"Actually, she's 19" said Chia counting on her fingers. She'd been helping Sora with the classes and was proud she could do arithmetic now.

"Yes" Sora added "since devil-lings take a full year to be born after they are ... conceived" she finished with a frown as she recalled devil-ling conception was the result of a human girl being molested by a demon. Drachus' felt a tug at his sleeve and found a frowning Chia there.

"Is 'mon-chi-kin' a bad thing?" she asked. With a glance he saw that Twerle wasn't happy; in fact, it looked as if she were about to cry. 'Maybe she thinks I called her a bad name' he thought. "Twerle" Drachus called out "*Munch-kin* means you are very tiny and very cute; it's not bad at all! I also read that devil-lings tend to be even shorter than average anyway, so that was my mistake. Besides, girls from my old world would love to be called Munchkin!" he lied.

Chia ran back, they hugged and all was well again. Drachus was re-learning how to prevent tears when dealing with young girls; it had been years since he'd needed to do more than negotiate with grown working ladies – or whip raw recruits into shape!

"Twerle, I've seen that you seem to fly more than walk..." he said to change the subject.

"Walking is slow and makes me tired; when flying I'm faster, I can keep up with people without having to run. It's so much easier that way. Is it wrong?" she responded with a frown.

"Around here, it is not a problem at all. But if you ever go back to a city, just walk. Oh, and even here, don't fly so high unless you have to. Just try to stay about this low if you can" indicating about 2' high with his hand. "It will make things ... easier all around" he said.

"Why?" she asked with a confused expression.

As Drachus hesitated Sora blurted out "Because stupid boys and big perverts will look up your skirt to see what color panties you're wearing!"

Twerle blushed as he nodded. Suddenly he recalled she hadn't worn anything under her see-through negligée when they first met. "You do wear them, right?" he asked.

Before the blushing girl could answer Sora shouted "Of course she does; now!" Since she wore short skirts her panties were often seen anyway.

Once moved to Karrat Kommons Drachus had tried to get the girls to be more conservative with their skirts. When the bunny-girls started wearing lace underwear Sora had led quite a counter-campaign.

After pointing out that he hadn't had a problem with Romis wearing a skirt that short Drachus couldn't fight back very effectively. As a result all three girls – and a remarkable number of the bunny-girls – now wore skirts that often left their panties exposed. As much as he wished they wouldn't, he couldn't stop them; his give-it-all-away face made it clear he liked the view!

Yuma's skirts were still of a more proper length plus she wore tights to keep her legs from getting sunburnt so there were no garters or panties to show but Drachus was sure her décolletages were now even deeper than before!

As he looked at Surra she looked a bit surprised as she raised her hands saying "I'm 18; really!"

"On that subject" Sora began, "why do you find it so hard to accept how old we are? I know you've said people here seem to be short; is everyone where you're from built like a giant?" After she asked that Sora saw both Mion and Surra were blushing.

She suddenly recalled that those two and Drachus were lovers; the two bunny-girls had seen more of him than she had. From the reactions they considered him *tall* in many ways. When that settled in she joined the others in blushing as they all realized what she had just inadvertently asked.

"Where I'm from, I am considered bigger than average" Drachus replied innocently. After that, he realized why the ladies were blushing. Several camp followers had noted he was much better 'equipped' than many of their other clients. He decided to change the subject.

"Where I'm from you can usually tell how old a girl is by how ... tall *she* is. This varies from place to place but nowhere would you find a 19 year old as tiny as Twerle or a 17 year old as small as Chia or, for that matter, a 29-year old that looks as young as Yuma" Drachus said.

"Continuing with that line of inquiry" Yuma began quietly "how old do girls from there have to be before they are seen as ... grown up?" Before he could answer Mion raised her hand.

"More importantly, how do *you* decide if *you* think a girl is ... 'grown up' ... enough." They all seemed to be very interested in that answer.

He hadn't slept with Mion or Surra since that first night back from the capitol; they might think he'd lost interest because they seemed too young. He'd learned bunny-girls mature faster than humans; they are adults at 16. That wasn't it - he was just tired from all of the work of setting up the shops.

The six ladies leaned forward like hungry diners when the food is being delivered, staring as he tried to formulate age (and gender) appropriate answers to these delicate questions. Just then there came a knock at the door.

"Come in, please!" Drachus called out desperately.

Virian opened the door and began "Master Drachus the ..." his voice trailed off when he saw all six girls silently glaring at him like he had committed some flagrant offense.

After a bit the merchant continued. "The craftsmen are curious about the plans of that bath house you drew; they want you to explain some things?" he asked hesitantly.

"I will be right there!" Drachus shouted gratefully and practically ran from the room. As he closed the door he heard at least two of the girls muttering "You Coward!"

After their conference with the Dragon Lord the stonemasons started working on the bath house. He'd laid it out like ones from the Orient with changing rooms, showers and tubs of hot water where one could soak.

"This design will need lots of coal, to keep the water hot" Virian warned. "Don't worry; we'll have plenty delivered directly from the mines" Drachus said. "I doubt we'll have any issues" he finished confidently.

As if to make up for lost time, Mion and Surra began coming to his room rather often after this. Even though he was losing a lot of sleep Drachus wasn't about to complain. He didn't think he needed to worry about 'complications' either; bunny-girls are only fertile in spring so he didn't expect there would be any problems of that nature.

As she came into his room one night Surra tripped and her wrist was burned by wax that splashed from the candle she was carrying. As Drachus was about to run to the dispensary for a golden berry she smiled.

"Don't be foolish; it's not bad and I have Rosen Salve" she said to calm him down. As he carefully spread the salve Drachus recalled Yuma saying that this happened a lot; she had to treat wax burns almost daily.

Later, he lay there thinking about the candle issues. Cast pillar candles had to be thick if they were to be moved when lit, otherwise the flame might go out or splash hot wax on the hand of the person holding it. This made them heavy and they consumed a lot of expensive wax.

Also, after a while the flame would burn down forming a hole inside with the side walls blocking the light. Those walls would have to be trimmed away which meant all that wax was nothing more that excess weight anyway. Plus the newly-trimmed candles were more prone to splashing hot wax when moved.

The next day he looked for Virian to see if the two of them could come up with a way to fix the issues.

"They use chambersticks in homes of the wealthy for moving around at night" the old merchant said. When he saw the Dragon Lord was confused he explained.

"A chamberstick is a candle holder with a small pan and a handle; it's easier to move the lit candle around but they tend to be expensive – forging metal that thin costs extra. Besides, even if it doesn't splash hot wax the flame flickers too much for really good light to move around by."

Drachus almost gave up but then he recalled they used glass globes and chimneys on lamps in his world. These stopped flickering and made the light brighter. They already had chambersticks but adding glass globes to the current designs might be profitable.

After he had described them to glass-crafter Terrell he agreed. "That would stop the flickering and keep wax from splashing onto the holder. With a proper form tool they would be easy to turn out quickly."

After a few tries they got one to fit. However, the candle dimmed and went out. Realizing it needed airflow Drachus had the blacksmiths forge a new post to hold the candle a bit higher - so they could poke ventilation holes in the post below the candle.

Now it burned brighter but melted a hole faster; it needed trimming more often. On a hunch, Drachus replaced the cast candle with a thin taper and they had a winner!

Not only did the globe keep the flame from flickering, the hot air rising up the chimney drew in fresh air through the

Chamberstick

Old Oil Lamp

holes below and let it burn brighter than the cast candle. It also burned hotter; more of the wax vaporized rather than dripping down making the thinner candles last near as long as the thick ones.

As they celebrated Drachus remembered the issues he'd had with the local 'oil lamps' that seemed to have come straight out of the Arabian Nights. Glass chimneys would eliminate the flame but would be tough to fit on that particular design.

Alcohol Lamp

He discussed the issue with Terrell; he said "Apothecaries use alcohol lamps for their work. If we filled one with lamp oil and added a glass chimney, it might work better."

It turned out that the density of the lamp oil made it impractical to use the basic alcohol lamp design. They had to redo the mechanism completely to allow the wick to pull the thicker oil up to be burned. But after a few adjustments they had practical oil lamps.

Master Terrell had a cousin who sold chambersticks in the capitol. He sent him the new designs and several glass globes on the condition his cousin would send a pound of glass compound - sand, soda and lime - for each Sovereign of profits from selling them.

Oil Lamp

That would help; they hadn't made arrangements for these to be delivered. There was plenty here but harvesting was time consuming; everybody was too busy.

Three weeks later a wagon load of compound arrived with an order for a hundred globes and promises for lots more compound.

"These are selling so fast my cousin had to hire two new blacksmiths full-time to do the metal-work!" Terrell said after reading the accompanying letter.

A few days later Drachus was cleaning his pistol when he did a count of how much ammunition he still had; 22 silver rounds and only 12 lead ones. He did have 42 empty brass cases but no reloading tools or supplies. As he pondered the problem he remembered the militiaman's rifle ammunition; he had 32 of those large caliber black powder cartridges.

Working with the blacksmiths he made a kinetic bullet puller and a small hand press. With these he could disassemble the rifle rounds into their components to provide some supplies that he could use to reload his empty pistol cartridges.

Using their tools he managed to dismount the barrel and cylinder of the revolver with the cracked frame.

With a red hot chisel he carefully shaved the flat base of the big 43 caliber rifle bullets down to the correct weight for pistol rounds. After salvaging the primers and redistributing the black powder he seated these with lubricated cloth patches into the 45 caliber pistol cases. The thick patches let the slightly-smaller diameter bullets engage the pistol's rifling. Testing with two of them he found they were not quite as accurate as the factory rounds but were fine to about 30 yards.

Using the makeshift reloading tools he managed to create 30 reloaded cartridges for his pistol. Now he had full Prideaux loaders for his gun belt pouches; he kept two loaded with silver bullets in his vest pockets.

A week after the 'how old are you' meeting, Sora went to speak with Yuma in the dispensary. With everyone working hard minor injuries had become common. The healer spent most of her time there lately; Sora would take care of most of the injuries outside where Yuma might be burnt by the sun. More serious injuries were taken to her in the dispensary. The dark elf had just bandaged a broken finger when Sora arrived.

"You've been busy" the little priestess remarked.

"Yes, our Dragon Lord keeps all of his ladies working quite hard" Yuma laughed. The ladies close to him had started calling Drachus 'our Dragon Lord' for some reason.

"Speaking of that butt-petting pervert," Sora began "do you know what he's been up to lately?"

"You mean the bath house?" Yuma asked.

"No. He's been working with Coramak and some of the other guards" Sora shook her head as she replied.

"Ah, the crossed bow training?" Yuma asked absentmindedly as she made notes in her treatment ledger. Drachus had asked her to keep track of injuries to see if the work of any crew or shop was more hazardous than usual. That way they could make changes as needed to prevent future injuries.

She had also told him about several contagious illnesses common among the locals. With names like 'sweat-head', 'blue-tongue' and 'lumpy-neck' he had no idea of what the equivalent maladies were on his old world. But she had told him that once someone had some of these, they never got it again.

Recalling the Spanish Flu Pandemic, Drachus asked her to find out who had already had what. With a list of these folks, they could have them nurse the ill without worrying about the caregivers getting sick as well.

"No, it's not about the crossed bow stuff. They're mostly talking. And it's not about cute bunny-girl butts - despite how many they've been sampling" she snapped shaking her head.

"I haven't heard any complaints from the girls, so I guess they are being polite with their ... sampling" Yuma said with a bit of a blush. Sora pointed out the window.

"Look, there's the four of them now. I just know something's up" she whined.

"That's Parco and Tarff isn't it? Didn't they tie in that silly horse race he set up yesterday?" Yuma asked.

"See what I mean; they also did well in that crossed-bow thing the other day. I know that butt-petting pervert and those cottontail-chasing creeps are up to something sketchy!" she said.

A few days later Drachus stood up at dinner. "If you'll all excuse me I have an announcement to make."

"See?" Sora hissed. Yuma nodded and shushed her.

"The roofs have been shingled with ceramic tiles and water-proofed with the linseed oiled cloth; rainy season should be nice and dry this year. The glassworks are turning out jars as fast as the crops are harvested and panes as fast as the glaziers can mount them" Drachus said. The craftsmen smiled, happy that their work was being noticed.

"The blacksmiths say the first of the improved iron stove will be ready to be installed and fired up by the end of the month" he added.

"Earlier; things will be nice and hot by the end of the week!" cried Gannet the head blacksmith to a round of laughter. The first ones had cracked under heat; the blacksmiths tried a change in the composition of the iron to correct the problem.

"This winter should be comfortable, especially for those in the couples' dormitory" Drachus said. There were giggles at that.

"In fact things are going so well I've decided to start a new project." At the groans from the craftsmen he added "Don't worry fellows; you won't be involved in this one." There was a lot of chatter after he said that. "In fact, this won't even take place here" Drachus said with a grin.

"See, I told you" hissed Sora. Yuma's lovely face was now twisted with a concerned look; she could be just as easy to read as Drachus.

"Coramak, Parco and Tarff will be leaving with me very early in the morning to take care of it. We might be gone for a while, maybe two months." Many cries of disagreement sounded at that.

"Don't fret! Work here is going well. I have total confidence the ladies and Virian can handle any issues that come up. This project is important and we'll return as soon as it's done. Now enjoy dessert and have a good evening" he finished and waved as he left the dining hall.

His ladies descended on him right away. He gathered them in the classroom, the only place with enough chairs. "Now class, who has questions" he asked flippantly.

Sora jumped to her feet shouting "What the hell do you mean you're leaving you pervy jack ass?"

Before she could lash out again Drachus waved at her. "Calm down, sit down, please; I'll explain. While researching at the cathedral I learned a lot about the cursed lands and the problems they are still having out here. I think I can dispel the 'curse'" he said quite seriously. That was followed by gasps from all the ladies.

"There are still settlements all throughout here; many are in much worse shape than Karrat Kommons. If I can lift the demon's curse, tens of thousands of people will be able to live much happier lives and the land will once again provide good harvests; those may alleviate hunger throughout the kingdom. I think that is at least worth trying" he said with a wide grin.

"The key is getting the Midland River flowing again. The only places that can grow food out here now are those with deep wells, like Karrat Kommons. Clean water is what they need and a lot of it." Drachus waited for that to sink in before continuing.

"With what I've learned, I believe I can get the river flowing again which will eliminate the curse. I can try; I have to at least try. I delayed until Karrat Kommons was secured before taking care of this. I want to be certain everyone here is going to be all right before I leave."

Drachus knew fixing the river would help. In Argentina a landslide had diverted a mountain river causing the farms downstream to go fallow. To feed their workers the company had dispatched a team of engineers (and a few guards) to dynamite the blockage. Once it was flowing again, the farms went back to producing food for their biggest customer – the mining company.

Drachus expected a lot of questions. However, the ladies formed a circle at the back of the room whispering among themselves. With a simultaneous cry of "Right!" from all they stood up. Yuma and Surra walked up to him.

"How long will it really take?" Yuma finally asked.

"Two weeks to get there, maybe a week to get it done and another two weeks back, I think. If we hit bad weather or rough terrain it may take a week longer. Now is the best time; travel will be easier with long daylight hours and warm nights. If I get the river flowing soon, they can plant bigger crops in spring so they'll have plenty for next winter!" he said.

Surra then asked "Will the four of you be enough to fix the river? Won't you need more help?"

"No, if it will take what I think it should, we can gather all of the materials that we'll need for the job between the four of us" he said. Then Sora came forward by herself.

"Can you really trust us not to screw things up here, running it all by ourselves?" she asked bashfully. Cupping her blushing cheeks in his hands, he looked into her eyes.

"You have matured quite a bit of late; you've become very reliable, when you're not goofing off with Chia and Twerle" he said with a grin. As she scowled at his teasing Drachus looked at the others.

"The same for the rest of you; Yuma, you don't jump every time someone yells; you can actually give orders when needed. Mion and Surra have become comfortable coordinating between bunny-folk workers and the human craftsmen. Chia and Twerle, you two are having a blast running around with messages, finding people, helping out in the dispensary and babysitting the younger kids. Yes, I believe I can rely on all of you" he said smiling slyly at their beaming and blushing faces.

"Besides, I'll only be gone a few weeks. Just how badly could you ladies screw things up here in that little bit of time?" he said with a laugh. Their smiles turned into scowls of outrage at his teasing.

He spent a lot of time in tearful goodbyes with Chia and Twerle before they'd go to bed; he was leaving before they'd wake in the morning.

Back at his room, Mion was waiting. After a bit of cottontail cuddling a soft knock at the door announced that Surra was here to say goodbye. Drachus didn't get a lot of sleep but he wasn't complaining.

An hour before sunrise, a sleepy but very relaxed Drachus met with Coramak, Parco and Tarff at the stables. Five horses, four with saddlebags of supplies and a pack horse with even more, were waiting for them.

"OK fellows; we have a long ride. Let's get started" he said.

When they reached the gate he stopped them so they could all turn around and wave to the 200 or so very worried faces in the candle-lit windows watching their departure. Then the four of them headed out.

Tough and smart as he is, can the Dragon Lord actually fix a river? Can he even get there? He does have to cross half of the known world on horseback through territory infested with bandits, marauding orcs and the occasional hungry dragon. Find out in Volume 2 – Rise of the Dragon Lord: The Keep!

Appendix – Pronunciation Guide

Some of the names of the characters who play recurring or major roles in this tale may be rather hard to pronounce properly – many are from foreign lands or non-human languages. The following guide may help the reader to understand them a bit better; the **Bold-face** portion in the dominant syllable.

Arianne	Ah-**re**-ann	Nova Elize	**No**-va e-**Leez**
Beal	**Bay**-al	Orrendo	Oh-**ren**-dough
Brynn	**Brin**	Parco	**Par**-ko
Chia	**Key**-ah	Raledon	**Rally**-don
Chloe	**Klow**-we	Romis	**Roh**-miss
Chorale	**Ko**-rail	Renne	Ren-**nay**
Daulle	**Doll**	Rille	**Re**-lay
Delia	**Dee**-lee-ah	Sepet Vee	Se-**pet** Veee
Doriel	**Do**-ree-el	Shirakiin	She-rah-**keen**
Drachus	**Dray**-kus	Sora Glarus	**Soar**-rah **Glah**-rus
Drelled	**Dre**-led	Solai	**Sew**-lie
Fayla	**Fay**-la	Solven	**Sol**-ven
Fulya	**Fool**-ya	Surra	**Sue**-rah
Funta	**Foon**-ta	Tarff	**Tar**-fuh

Jakob	**Yay**-cub	Tion	**Tea**-yon
Jayla	**Yay**-lah	Tolai	**Toe**-lie
Kaede	Kai –**Ay**-day	Trazet	**Tray**-zett
Kieran	**Key**-ran	Trina	**Tree**-nah
Krallen	**Crawl**-len	Twerle	**Twirl**
Kryton	**Cry**-tun	Vania	**Va**-knee-yah
Lareel	**Lah**-reel	Vellist	**Veh**-list
Liigo	**Lie**-go	Vennit	**Veh**-knit
Maia Gravis	**My**-ah **Gra**-vis	Ylia	**E**-lia
Milan	**Me**-lan	Yuma	**You**-mah
Mion	**Me**-yon	Zange	**Zan**-gay

Don't worry if you didn't recognize all of them; some of these characters don't appear until later, in Volume 2 or 3.

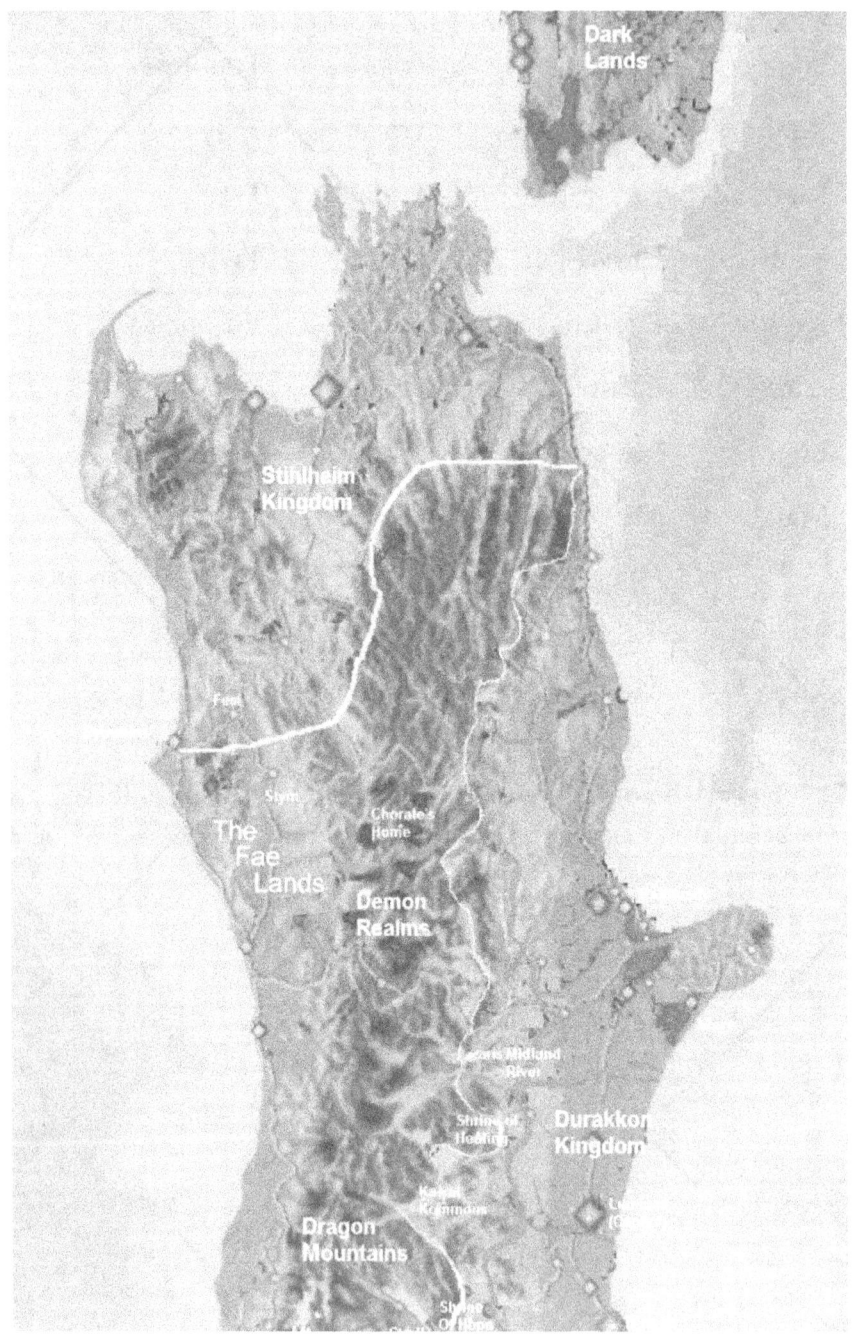

RISE OF THE DRAGON LORD - VOLUME 1

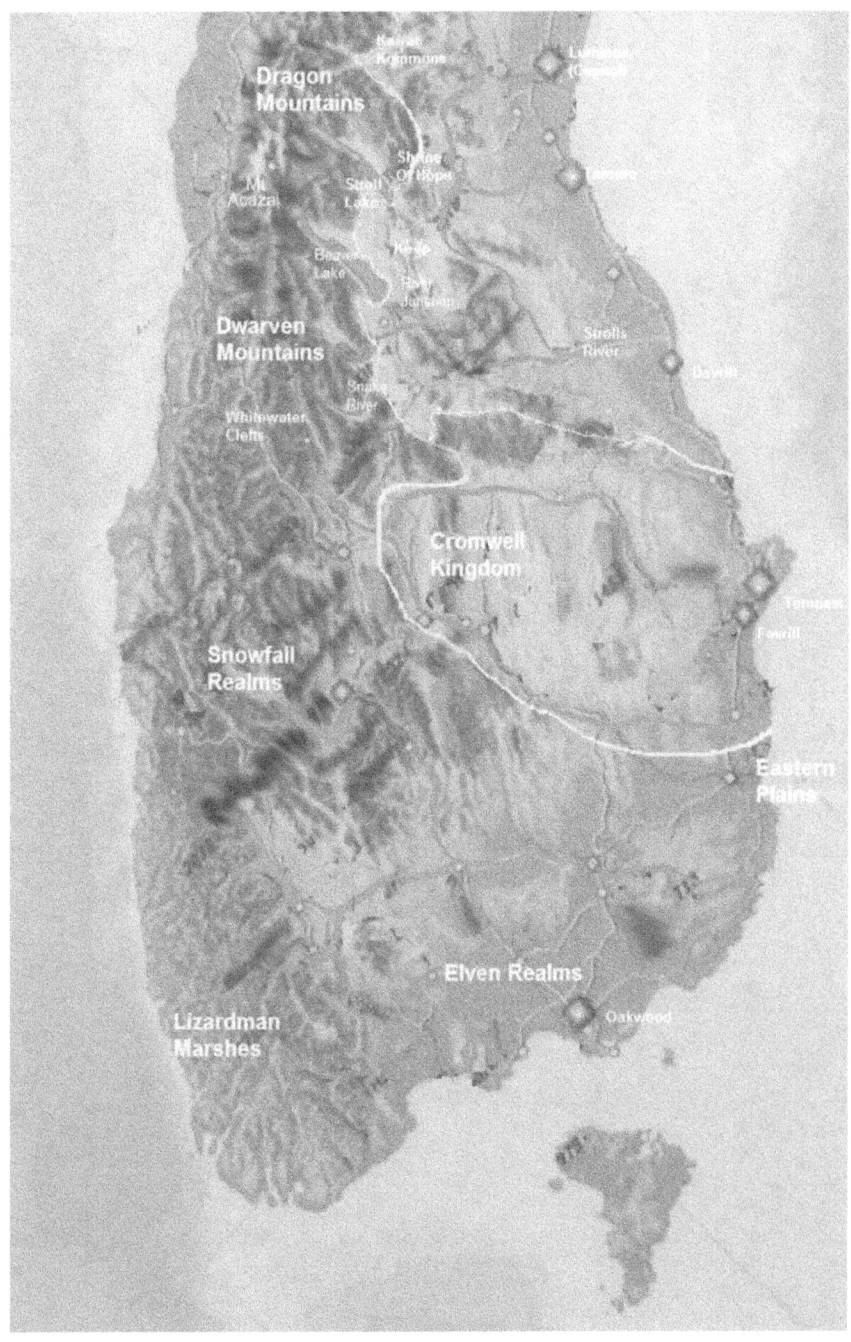

www.ingramcontent.com/pod-product-compliance
Lightning Source LLC
LaVergne TN
LVHW021756060526
838201LV00058B/3122